FIRE IN THE SKY

The radar diamond was superimposed over the *Tomcat* to the left side and slightly behind the F-4 *Phantom*. The aircraft was large in his windscreen, and the tone in his helmet earcups was crisp and clear—the heat-seeking weapons he carried could see the target as well.

He squeezed the stick-mounted trigger. An infrared-guided Matra Magic missile jumped off its launcher rail beneath his port wing and tracked the two hot engines in front of it. A rope of white smoke followed the missile.

The fighter bunted forward with the impact. Its right motor turbine section came apart, spinning blades of metal through its engine casing. Three of the *Tomcat*'s four aft fuselage fuel cells were burning.

The Iranian Revolutionary Guard had his seventh kill.

SIDEWINDER

Mike Dunn

AVON BOOKS NEW YORK

SIDEWINDER is an original publication of Avon Books. This work has never before appeared in book form. This is a work of fiction. Details of weaponry and military combat technology, as well as the people and events herein, are the products of the author's imagination. The opinions or assertions here are those of the author alone and are not construed as official or reflecting the views of the Department of the Navy.

AVON BOOKS
A division of
The Hearst Corporation
1350 Avenue of the Americas
New York, New York 10019

Published by arrangement with the author
Library of Congress Catalog Card Number: 91-92103
ISBN: 0-380-76371-0

First Avon Books Printing: August 1991

Printed in the U.S.A.

RA 10 9 8 7 6 5 4 3 2 1

For Linda,
a rare woman, a beautiful mother, and my best friend

ACKNOWLEDGMENTS

I owe special thanks to Navy Lieutenants Mike Good and Mark Wralstad and to Commander Don Bringle for their invaluable assistance and technical advice. To the real Fighting Aardvarks, 1985–88, for their unbelievable inspiration. To the United States Navy, specifically naval aviation, for the opportunity to become a fighter pilot. To authors Jeffrey L. Ethell and Barret Tillman for their honesty and recommendations. To Julie Castiglia of Waterside Productions, Inc. for her encouragement, patience, sense of humor—and especially for the chance. To Tom Colgan at Avon Books for his commitment. And finally, to Lyle and Jacqueline Dunn, for just about everything else.

All of them made this book better.

"The fighter pilots have to rove in the area allotted to them in any way they like, and when they spot an enemy they attack and shoot him down; anything else is rubbish."

BARON MANFRED VON RICHTOFEN
World War I Ace

"Why let rank lead, when ability can do it better?"

RANDY "DUKE" CUNNINGHAM
Vietnam Ace

"Often . . . I find it best to do what must be done without going through the usual channels."

LOUIS L'AMOUR
The Warrior's Path

"In difficult ground, press on;
in encircled ground, devise strategems;
in death ground, fight."

SUN TZU,
Chinese military general and philosopher,
China 400–500 B.C.,
from his essays on *The Art of War*

PROLOGUE

Ali Abdul Rajani twisted the wheel of his red Cadillac convertible as the paved roadway ended and a narrow rutted dirt trail began. He broke hard in the turn, and the Cadillac's front wheels locked, then slid toward the center of the trail. He stomped on the accelerator, swerving in the direction of the aircraft hangars just south of the airstrip at Bandar 'Abbās. A six-wheeled Iranian half-track was negotiating the dirt trail from the opposite direction. The gray and olive-drab military vehicle was transporting fourteen troops and several crates of sensitive electronic equipment, but moved off the rough trail—into the stubble and rocks—and allowed the bright red blur to pass. Rajani did not seem to notice the truck.

A militia sentry in fatigues stood beside a tiny wooden guard shack at the perimeter gate leading to the hangars. He lowered a Soviet-built AK-47 assault rifle and snapped a salute toward the approaching Cadillac. Ali Rajani did not return the salute. Instead, he jerked the steering wheel until the convertible's circular silver hood ornament was superimposed over the Iranian at the gate. Rajani stared through the ornament as if it were a gun sight, and grinned. The Cadillac accelerated. It bounced toward the sentry at more than seventy-five miles per hour. There was little time for the man in the camouflaged fatigues to react. He dropped the AK-47 carbine and dove toward the shack just inside the gate. Rajani swerved again toward his target. The large convertible grazed the perimeter gate, missing the sentry by a few inches.

Past the gate, Rajani broke and again locked the wheels. The convertible, all four of its tires and brakes scorched and smoking, slid to a stop beside the tallest hangar at the airfield. Personal vehicles were not allowed inside the gate, and no vehicles, even those with military markings, were allowed onto the tarmac beside the hangar. But no one prevented Ali Rajani from parking his red Cadillac there. He jumped from it and ran into the hangar.

At least thirty Iranian Revolutionary Guard officers jammed the makeshift ready room inside the tall hangar. The doors at either end of the room had been pushed shut, and thick cigarette smoke hung over the men. Each of them wore dull green jackets over unbuttoned shirts of the same color. And each of the men wore a bright red ascot around his neck. Stripes of the same red color ran down the sides of their trousers. Their laughing and coughing ceased when Ali Abdul Rajani opened one of the doors and stepped into the room. He wore shorts and a European-style polo shirt.

The smoke wafted out of the room, past Rajani's head as he stood there. He peered at the men—the pilots and Radar Intercept officers he had not seen for more than one full year. They stared back, each of them with awe and some fear of this man. He was taller than any of them. He seemed somehow even taller as he stood there. They stared up and into his eyes. They were hateful eyes, deep-set and black. A dark beard rode up his face, nearly all the way to those eyes. None of the others wore beards. They were not allowed among aviators—beards interfered with the fit and function of an oxygen mask. Rajani didn't wear an oxygen mask when he flew. It was not his style. He enjoyed the beard, however, and would not shave it.

There were F-14 Tomcat and F-4 Phantom pilots in the room. There were backseat Radar Intercept officers there, too. Ali Rajani was a Tomcat fighter pilot. And he was a fighter pilot known throughout Iran. He was especially well known among these men of the Iranian Revolutionary Guard.

Ali Rajani was also an ace. He had, in fact, been credited with downing more than the requisite five aircraft that would make him an ace. He had destroyed six—all of them Iraqi Mirage F-1 fighters. He had destroyed two of them in a single dogfight nearly two years earlier. And it had been that single dogfight that began Ali Abdul Rajani's reputation as a legend among the IRG. He accepted their awe of him. In fact, he reveled in it. Rajani was not the most senior officer among the men in the room, either. But he showed no respect to those who were senior to him. None of them were aces, after all, and only he had been rewarded with a red convertible Cadillac.

But Rajani was also an impatient man, and the year without flying had been a long year indeed. He wanted to fly. He *needed* to fly again. In fact, none of the Iranian Revolutionary Guard aviators gathered in the room had flown in more than a year. There had been political reasons for disbanding the IRG, of course. But Rajani was apolitical in these matters. He was a fighter pilot and nothing more. And he did not fly for Iran or for Allah. He never had. He did not fly for these men of the Iranian Revolutionary Guard, either.

He flew for himself alone. He flew to hunt and annihilate aircraft and the men who flew them. He flew to fight and to win. When he won, he did so for the greater glory of winning, and not because it pleased government officials in Teheran.

Ali Abdul Rajani stood there until the smoke had cleared behind him. He stood there, confidently and with arrogance. He was not impressed by the men who stood before him in the ready room. And it seemed none of them would speak until he did.

"Cowards," he said to himself as he looked down on them. But he had not flown for a great while, and this was to be a meeting about flying—the Guard would be flying again. He would accept the awe of these men. And he would lead them if it was required—if it served his purposes. He pushed at the door behind him until it slammed, then walked slowly to the center of the room.

"On this day I am reborn," he announced. "On this day the Iranian Revolutionary Guard is reborn. All around this great nation, others in the Guard are also meeting on this day. They will join us in this campaign. It is time to prepare for battle."

The men in the makeshift ready room encircled Rajani as he stood there. Some of them reached out to touch him. They cheered loudly and lit their cigarettes.

DAY ONE

JANUARY 5

The *Khasaab*
0750

Shail Bakhash turned his small wooden cargo dhow toward the north. The boat moved away from the Omani peninsula, entering the Strait of Hormuz. Bakhash tugged at the bottom of his torn goat-hair sweater, tucking its loose ends into a pair of stained oversized trousers. It was rarely cold in the straits. This winter day was colder than any he could remember.

Bakhash turned his back to the wind, rubbing his old hands against each other for warmth. His son and the son of his dead brother crouched together against the *Khasaab*'s stern—down and out of the wind near the dhow's warm and groaning diesel engine. For a moment, as the breeze whipped at his white hair, Bakhash considered raising the two canvas sails. But the boys were unfamiliar with dhows and with the rigging of sails. And even with their help, the process would take nearly an hour. It was too cold for that, the old man decided, and the diesel was pushing his boat at an acceptable five knots.

Shail Bakhash had never enjoyed sailing alone. Still, he had never before allowed the boys to accompany him to Didamar. Sailing was the work of grown men, he had always said. For nearly thirty years he had sailed with his older brother—his only brother—in the *Khasaab* and in dhows like the *Khasaab*. During their many years together, the brothers had always carried the same cargo in the dhows—rice, cotton or tobacco, tea, and sugar beets. The brothers had earned a reputation for delivering a good product, and had always fetched fair prices from the merchants at Didamar. Together, he and his older brother had traveled this route countless times—from Bukha to Didamar, then back again to Bukha.

Bakhash had always lived in Bukha. It was the northernmost coastal village in Oman. From Bukha, a string of stony island outcroppings pushed further north, into the center of the Strait of Hormuz. The last and smallest of the stony islands was Didamar. Many large container ships put in to the anchorage at Didamar, where they on- and off-loaded cargo. The anchorage marked the edge of Omani territory and the halfway point between Bukha and the southern coastline of Iran. In the past twelve months, since his brother had lost his long battle with pneumonia, Shail Bakhash had sailed this route alone. Finally, he had decided to allow his son and nephew to travel with him into the strait.

"If your father were alive this day, he would be proud to see you in his place on the *Khasaab*," the old man stated above the sound of the wind and the diesel. The nephew stood proudly, striking a pose his father might have struck. The boy then raised his arm and pointed past Shail Bakhash.

"Uncle, there is a boat," the boy said. "It is coming at us."

Bakhash turned and peered over the bow of his small boat, squinting through the haze to the north. Giant container ships were common in the Strait of Hormuz, and he had learned long ago to avoid their large wakes on his journeys to Didamar. Smaller craft were less common, unless they too had goods to sell to the merchants at the anchorage.

"It is not a dhow," he stated. "It is very fast."

The old man twisted the wheel a full turn to the right, and the *Khasaab* slowly steadied on a northeasterly heading. He would resume his course to Didamar after the small vessel passed. It did not pass. Instead, it shifted quickly to counter his turn, moving left to right on a course to collision. Bakhash pulled back on the engine throttle control, and the *Khasaab*'s diesel idled weakly.

"What do they want? Who are they?"

The old man turned to his son, who had crawled over two dozen bales of rice and now stood beside him near the wheel.

"I do not know. That boat is not Omani."

Shail Bakhash had seen Boghammer boats only once before. Three winters earlier, he and his brother had watched three of the fast-moving cigarette-type boats encircle a Japanese merchant vessel anchored off Bukha. After harassing the vessel and cutting her anchor chain, the Boghammers had sped away.

The flag that flew over this particular Boghammer seemed as large as the craft itself. The flag was colored with three horizontal bands of green, white, and red. In its center was an emblem encircled by words that Shail Bakhash could read only after the two boats were less than fifty meters apart. The words were Arabic—*Allah Akbar,* it read—"God is Great." The Boghammer boat slowed quickly and aligned hulls with the dhow. Its flag drooped with the sudden deceleration, and fell across the shoulders of a short man in military fatigues poised behind a deck-mounted recoilless rifle. Four other soldiers raised automatic weapons to their shoulders as the Boghammer went dead in the water less than five boat-lengths from Bakhash and his dhow. Each of the men wore cocked red berets on his head.

"They are Iranian," he whispered without looking toward his son. "I will talk with them."

A thinner soldier—a man whose beret was trimmed in white—stepped onto the bow of the Boghammer. He pushed long locks of jet-black hair under the edges of the cap, then pulled a silver pistol from his belt. Bakhash wished no confrontation with the Iranians.

The old Omani drew a deep breath, then cupped his hands and yelled toward the soldier on the bow of the Boghammer.

"Praise God, and greetings to our Iranian brothers!" The thinner Iranian lowered his weapon and began to laugh aloud. When he turned toward the four soldiers farther aft, they were laughing absurdly among themselves. Only the short Iranian behind the recoilless did not join in.

As the Iranian raised his pistol a second time, the laughter subsided.

"You are the commander?" The Iranian asked the question while focusing his aim at the old man.

"It is my dhow, but I am no commander. This is my boy and his cousin." Bakhash turned and gestured toward his nephew, taking a half step in front of his son. "And you are in charge of that vessel?"

"I am." The Iranian took a half turn toward his men and bowed like an actor receiving an ovation. The soldiers laughed loudly again.

"You and your boat have violated Iranian waters, Commander. You will follow me and my men to Hengām. The island is not far. After questioning, you and your family will be allowed to return home. Your boat and her cargo are to be confiscated."

Shail Bakhash steadied himself on the deck of his dhow, twisting aft, looking past his nephew and toward the village less than ten miles behind them. He knew of Hengām Island. He wished very much to avoid going there.

"In the name of Allah . . . we are sellers from Bukha! We sail for Didamar, and these waters are Omani. I have navigated them for—"

The recoilless rifle bolted an instant after the thinner Iranian had nodded in the direction of his gunner. The single round caught the nephew of Shail Bakhash in the chest and shoulder, throwing him down and into the idling dhow engine. The old man threw his arms out in terror, pulling himself past his son and then over the bales that separated him from the boy. His nephew stared up at him in pained terror. His small eyes were shocked and wide—he tried to cry. Only blood and part of what once was a lung exited his mouth. The Omani boy then gurgled some kind of sound through the remains of his insides, twisting his upper body and left arm in panic. His right arm, severed above the elbow, lay weirdly between his feet.

Shail Bakhash crouched beside the convulsing body of his brother's son, looking with horror toward the Boghammer. The old man attempted to speak, but his words mixed instead with the vomit in his throat.

"Commander, you and your dhow are suspected of supplying weaponry to enemies of the Iranian Revolutionary Guard. My men will board your boat now to examine your cargo. You and the other young one will please hold your hands in the air. We will attend to the wounded one."

The son of Shail Bakhash lost his balance when the two boats bounced together. When the old man had helped the boy to his feet, three Iranian soldiers, all three still clutching their automatics, had jumped into the dhow. One of the men climbed clumsily aft to the wounded Omani. The boy's battered upper body now quivered more slowly. His jacket and trousers, as well as the burlap bags around him near the diesel engine, were soaked red with blood. The soldier poked with his weapon at the pale head of the old man's nephew, then drew away. He turned and looked up at the thin Iranian, who still aimed his pistol from the bow of the Boghammer.

"Captain, this one is dead soon. He will greet Allah long before the rest of us." The Iranian on the bow glanced toward the gunner, now standing casually against his recoilless. Both grinned.

"You are a great Satan, *Captain*." Shail Bakhash screamed the Iranian officer's rank as he would a vulgar word. He seemed unconcerned with the pistol still directed at his head. "You have murdered the only son of my dead brother. Allah will surely deny you and your cutthroats!"

The Iranian drew a breath to respond, but was

interrupted by a report from one of his men in the dhow.

"No weapons, Captain. Only these bags." The soldier returned a seven-inch knife to the scabbard clipped to his web belt. The captain leaned over the edge of the Boghammer's bow, surveying the cargo. Most of the burlap containers had been ripped open and emptied, their contents littering the deck. The spent bags had been tossed to the stern of the *Khasaab,* where they now covered the still body of the old man's nephew. Shail Bakhash lowered his hands to his face. His weeping grew louder as the Iranian soldiers stepped out of his dhow.

"You are blessed, Commander. I have decided you shall not accompany me and my men to Hengam. You and your boat are free to go. Such is the mercy of the Iranian Revolutionary Guard."

The old Omani opened his hands and eyes, staring at the Boghammer captain through heavy tears. The Iranian continued to aim his weapon even as the cigarette boat motored slowly away. When the Iranians had moved to ten meters' distance, the son of Shail Bakhash dropped his arms and walked slowly toward the pile of burlap that marked the body of his cousin. As he walked, the boy did not notice that the Iranian captain followed him with his silver gun. The gun reported twice before the boy began falling to the deck near a large pile of rice mixed with beets. The third shot caught the wooden mast between the Iranian and his target. The old Omani opened his mouth to scream again, but no sound emerged. He tried to run to his son but remained frozen by the wheel. Instead, Shail Bakhash could only watch as the Iranian, still on the bow of the Boghammer, steadied his aim from more than twenty meters. The final pistol report was weak in the wind and in its distance from the dhow. What Bakhash did hear clearly was the snap of a final bullet entering the skull of his son.

DAY TWO

JANUARY 6

Seeb International Airport
Musat, Oman
1430

British envoy Terrance Hill sighed loudly, then eased into an aisle seat nearly all the way aft in the cramped Omani 727 airliner. It had been the only seat remaining on Flight 118. He adjusted the briefcase on his lap, twisting as he sat to scan the cabin. He searched the faces of the passengers around him. He had hoped to find another conservatively attired Brit among the colorful native costumes there. He saw none. Saudis in flowing cotton thobes bantered near the center of the plane, while two tall Arabs—Hill guessed they were Bedouins—sat quietly across the aisle. Occasionally their white and crimson headdresses brushed against the jetliner's overhead. Mostly, the jet was filled with Omanis. To him, their traditional robes of saffron, green, blue, and black seemed a more comfortable fashion for travel than his three-piece tweed suit.

He snapped open the briefcase and checked his itinerary while a handsome Omani stewardess recited the mandatory aircraft emergency instructions. She spoke in Arabic, Persian, and then in a Turkish dialect Hill did not recognize. Although Terrance Hill had been assigned to the British embassy in Musat for nearly nineteen months, he was making his first official trip outside Oman. According to his schedule, the 727 would first land in Ankara, Turkey. Then, after a two-hour layover, he would switch air carriers and depart Turkey in the early evening for a morning arrival at Heathrow International. He hoped someone at the embassy office in London had arranged for his ground transportation there—he'd had no opportunity to make any phone calls before the flight. He reread the teletyped message that had prompted his return to England. It was vague.

> HILL, OMANI OFFICE
>
> URGENT YOU ATTEND MEET. TOMORROW 7 AM LONDON.
> REPORT MILITARY AFFAIRS OFFICE, FOREIGN STAFF BUREAU.
> REGRET SHORT NOTICE.
>
> REPEAT. URGENT YOU ATTEND.
>
> LUCK, LONDON

Hill's duties in Musat were exclusively administrative in nature—he had always been very good at such things. He managed the staffing of embassy civilian and government employees, and was the senior ranking ministry official in the region. But he had nothing to do with the direction of day-to-day military operations in the Omani region. He knew such operations existed only because he had read about them in the *London Times*. As it always had, his office acted only as a conduit for salary payment to a squadron of British pilots and support personnel located in Thumrait, Oman. Such officers and men were known to be Royal Air Force mercenary volunteers who flew and maintained thirty-one Hawker Hunter fighter-bombers for the Sultan of Oman Air Force. Hill had often wondered why a man would volunteer to fly with the RAF in Oman. He had heard that Thumrait was an incredibly desolate place.

Hill hoped the Foreign Staff Bureau people in London would not question him about the mercenaries. He did not consider himself equipped to speak credibly about them—he knew absolutely nothing of their mission. He refolded the teletyped message. Someone in the home office would know why he had been summoned, Hill decided finally. He settled back in his seat, closed the briefcase, and contemplated the damp winter weather he knew would greet him when he had touched down at Heathrow.

"You are American?"

Terrance Hill turned. Over his right shoulder, standing near the row of seats across the 727 from him, was a black-haired man in a dark blue suit.

"British, actually. But I didn't expect anyone aboard this aircraft to speak English. Name's Terry Hill." The envoy extended his arm, assuming that since the man was dressed in Western fashion, he would understood a handshake. He did.

"My name is Kalil, and I'm afraid my English is not so good, Mr. Hill."

"On the contrary. Your English is excellent. Much better than my Farsi, I'm afraid. You are Iranian, aren't you?"

"Yes. From the north, in the mountain region."

Kalil was sweating, and seemed uncertain how to continue the conversation. "I am surprised to see a British person on this flight," he said after pausing. "I did not observe your name on the manifest, Mr. Hill."

Hill pursed his lips in a smile. The envoy wondered how an Iranian would have access to the list of passengers aboard an Omani airliner.

"Yes, I consider myself fortunate. Seems there was a last-minute cancellation." Hill was also beginning to sweat.

"The airplane is about to move away from the terminal, Mr. Hill. There is a business I would like to discuss with you before that occurs. I apologize for the request, sir, but I am not a passenger on this flight, and I must go before the doors are closed."

Terrance Hill's stomach sank. *What possible business does an Iranian have to discuss with me? Does he know I represent the embassy? Did he read that message over my shoulder? Damn!* Everything he remembered from his foreign service briefings told him he should not stand up and follow the Iranian in the blue suit to the rear of the jet. But he did. Kalil turned and quickly stated his business.

"Mr. Hill, I would ask that you leave the jetliner." The Iranian stated his words without offering an explanation.

"What? Why? And why me? Who are you, Kalil?"

"There is a flight later, Mr. Hill. You would still arrive in Ankara before your connection to London, England."

"How do you know of my connection to England?" Hill's voice squeaked an octave higher in nervous chatter. He turned, searching the 727's center aisle for the handsome Omani stewardess. As he turned, his knees buckled beneath him. His backside stung with poker-hot pain. He rolled from his stomach to his back, between the aft-most row of seats. He peered up at Kalil, who was wiping blood from the shaft of a silver switchblade. None of the brightly dressed passengers seemed to notice.

"Again I am sorry, Mr. Hill. But it now appears that you will be unable to travel to Ankara today," Kalil said. "You are in need of medical attention." The Iranian smirked, then turned and ran out the cabin door and into the airport concourse.

The British Embassy
Musat, Oman
1620

"It's deep, sir, but it isn't a serious wound. Nothing much but fat and a little muscle in that part of the body, you know. The pain should subside quickly with the painkiller."

Terrance Hill rolled onto his side, nearly tipping over the portable medical gurney set up in his office. Behind him, a British corpsman applied tape to the dressing on his buttocks. One of the embassy secretaries, a young man named Malcolm Jennings, walked through the wide double doors and into the room.

"If you don't mind, Jennings, this is rather embarrassing."

"Dreadfully sorry, sir. I thought you might be interested in the news."

Still facedown on the gurney, Hill pulled at the bloodstained suit pants around his ankles, working to cover his exposed rear.

"What news, *dammit*!"

"Flight 118—your flight, or at least the one you were supposed to have taken, sir. Apparently there was an explosion. The plane went down in the Strait of Hormuz. All aboard are feared dead."

DAY THREE

JANUARY 7

USS *Enterprise*
Subic Bay, the Philippines
1020

Lieutenant Dirk Buzzell and six other VF-141 Aardvark junior officers were "riding the rails" aboard the *Enterprise*. Each officer stood two paces behind the line of sailors assigned to him—part of an unbroken line of sailors that defined the perimeter of the 1100-foot-long aircraft carrier. Officers and men from the Black Eagles of VF-231—the Aardvark's F-14 sister squadron—were also on deck. There were officers and enlisted men from each of the seven other Air Wing squadrons as well.

The *Enterprise* navigated slowly between bobbing red channel markers until jungle-covered cliffs finally appeared through the white haze. Off the bow to the right, Grande Island marked the entrance to the narrow inlet. Beyond the inlet was the harbor. Above and past the harbor were lush green hills. The sailors—gleaming in their white crackerjack uniforms—stood elbow to elbow at parade rest. From the island beaches and from pier-side at Subic

Bay, locals waved at the nuclear-powered behemoth and its 500-man picket fence. Against direct orders from the air boss in the ship's tower, some of the enlisted men waved back. Their conduct was completely appropriate preliberty behavior, Buzzell thought, and he pretended not to notice.

The air boss barked another order across the 5-MC flight deck loudspeaker, and the picket fence snapped to attention. The carrier rendered honors to a ship anchored at the mouth of the inlet—the USS *Bluegill*. The narrow gray vessel was home to the Commander, Battle Group Juliet, and served as the *Enterprise* battle group flagship. Above the *Bluegill*, rolling in a weak Philippine breeze, Buzzell saw the flag—a single white star on a field of blue. The admiral was embarked. The carrier saluted the flagship with blasts of her huge whistle, then continued to steam toward the harbor.

The air boss broadcast a final order, and Buzzell returned to parade rest—it was a more comfortable way to pass the time. From his position forward of the square *Enterprise* island, he could make out Pier 16, the largest slip in the Subic anchorage. It lay ahead, just port of the bow, and less than two miles away. But as the *Enterprise* crawled into the harbor opening, it would be more than two hours before the ship was tied to the pier and her huge crew permitted to go ashore.

Through the wet haze, the sky was more gray-blue now, and a few cotton-ball clouds touched the highest peaks of Luzon Island. Buzzell shifted his position behind the men assigned to him. They were formed and talking quietly among themselves. A few of them adjusted their Dixie cup hats, wiping sweat from their foreheads.

The P.I. couldn't happen at a better time for Dirk

Buzzell. He was certain he would find the same diversions there—the cheap beer and liquor, the deafeningly loud and crowded nightclubs that jammed both sides of Magsaysay Boulevard in Olongapo City—the same diversions he had found in the Philippines during his first cruise with the Aardvarks. The Philippines were nothing if not consistent.

Each of the nightclubs would be lined with countless numbers of very young and very persistent Filipino girls. The girls seemed to know precisely when the fleet was in town—they were always anxious to meet rich American sailors. They had been especially eager to meet naval officers, Buzzell remembered. They clung to his arm as he stepped into the clubs—jumping up and down, giggling in some bizarre combination of English and their native Tagalog, winking at him with dark tiny eyes—all competing with one another for his attention. He remembered how one of them, or sometimes two of them, would jump on his lap while he ordered rounds of fifty-cent San Miaguel beers, and how they would listen intently to his endless stories of carrier aviation and his love of flying the F-14 Tomcat. The girls would understand nothing he and other squadron pilots said to each other around the crowded tables, but would smile as if they did.

Evenings at the clubs would always end in the same way. A Filipino girl would beg him to pay her "bar fine"—a pittance in Philippine pesos that would allow him to escort her to a hotel for the night. It had been a very long month since the *Enterprise* had left the coastal waters off San Diego. To Dirk Buzzell, it seemed an unlikely time to think about Marti.

In the six years he'd known her, he'd fought

valiantly to avoid a serious relationship. Avoiding relationships was something Buzzell had always excelled in—being single was a badge he wore proudly. But since returning from his first deployment to the Western Pacific—during the long twelve-month turnaround leading up to this, his second cruise—he felt he had been losing the fight. And he felt he had been losing the fight willingly. That fact troubled him most. Yes, she was beautiful. But he'd known many beautiful Utah women.

A year after meeting her, he left Salt Lake City for Pensacola, Florida—for Aviation Officer Candidate School. She stayed behind, of course. He had decided that AOCS would take his mind from her. He'd chosen to make a living flying jet-powered aircraft on and off the decks of aircraft carriers. The relationship with Marti would simply end.

It did not end during his two years of flight training. They were exciting and difficult years, and Buzzell earned the flight grades necessary to fly Navy fighters. He didn't have the time to chase women then. And Marti was more convenient. She traveled seven times in six months to see him in Texas. They lived together while he trained and flew in Meridian, Mississippi. And on the day he had earned his wings of gold, she was there to pin them to his uniform. They moved to San Diego together.

Dirk Buzzell had, despite his best efforts, already committed himself to a woman. And just as it had during his first port visit to the P.I., that commitment would not allow him to pay a bar fine in any of the Olongapo nightclubs. He owed her that much, at least. He stared down at the black flight deck, thinking of Marti.

A ski boat approached the aircraft carrier from the harbor and sped around it. The officers and men dressed in white became increasingly restless as the *Enterprise* inched its way toward the pier still 2,000 yards away. No one was looking in Buzzell's direction. He slid a letter out his top white pants pocket and tore open the envelope.

He had found the letter in his mailbox early that morning—it was dated December 26—eleven days earlier. First-class mail was excruciatingly slow in reaching the Philippines from the United States. It was a short letter, and Marti admitted to having been hung over when she wrote it. He read that she had bought a plane ticket to Manila and planned to meet him in Subic Bay. She apologized for the short notice, but wrote that it was very important she see him there.

Buzzell refolded the envelope and slid it into his back pocket. He was not disappointed with the news. He was smiling when he noticed one of the Aardvark enlisted men had turned out of ranks. The sailor was looking at the officer, and was grinning knowingly.

"What's so funny, Airman Michaels?" Buzzell tried to sound stern. "You're supposed to be facing front, and dreaming about liberty in the Philippine Islands."

"I know, Lieutenant . . . and I was thinking about going into town tonight. But I never been to the P.I. before, and I was kinda thinkin' you might know a good place to go, sir," the airman said, then turned and rejoined the other squadron sailors.

Buzzell smiled again, recalling again his first cruise with the Aardvarks and his first night on the boulevard in Olongapo City. He stepped forward, then bent down until he could whisper into the airman's ear.

"Try the *Sierra Club*, Michaels. It's about two

blocks past the gate into town . . . on the left side of the street. Take a rubber.''

The officer stepped back, scanning the formation of uniforms that ringed the flight deck. Now, as the Subic tugboats rushed to meet *Enterprise* and push the carrier pier-side, it seemed like much more than one month since he'd left Southern California, and Marti. He stared into the milky skies over the bay, remembering everything about her. He took a deep breath of the hot wet Philippine air, and realized for the first time that his white uniform was soaked with sweat. It clung to his back and to his legs. He could not imagine being any farther from home.

Lieutenant Greg Bright, another VF-141 junior officer, stepped quickly away from the group of enlisted men clustered together near the ship's bow. He walked aft, toward the *Enterprise* island, and tapped Buzzell on the shoulder.

''Buzz, you *dog,*'' Bright said coyly. ''Why didn't you tell me about your P.I. welcoming committee?''

Dirk Buzzell stepped to the edge of the flight deck, searching the pier sixty feet below him. Marti had already found him in the sea of white uniforms, and was waving a large cardboard sign.

HI SAILOR. NEW IN TOWN?

Iranian Revolutionary Guard
Military Aerodrome
Bandar 'Abbās International Airport
Bandar 'Abbās, Iran
1120 (local time)

A single runway accommodated both military and commercial air traffic in and out of Bandar 'Abbās

International. The runway ran east and west for a little more than 8,000 feet. A single passenger terminal serviced commercial airliners at the north perimeter of the airfield. Four hangars paralleled the runway on its south side, and were restricted to military use. The largest hangar, nearest the tall Bandar 'Abbās control tower, was utilized by the Iranian Revolutionary Guard alone.

Five air-traffic-control personnel manned the tower. But none of them was monitoring the takeoff of a DC-9 passenger jet on the runway. Instead, they focused their binoculars on the figure emerging from the IRG hangar. The figure was strutting toward one of the two Iranian F-14 Tomcats parked between the tower and the tallest hangar. The controllers whispered among themselves as they watched. One of them observed that the figure wore no anti-G suit under his torso harness as was normal aircrew procedure when manning a high-performance tactical fighter.

"That pilot does not require a G-suit," one of the others responded.

Ali Abdul Rajani did not preflight his aircraft, either. Instead, he approached the swing-wing fighter, kicked its large port tire, then climbed immediately into the front cockpit.

"I do not conduct preflight inspections," Rajani had bragged to other IRG aircrew inside the hangar. He had ordered his backseater, a young radar intercept officer named Nori, to prepare the jet for him.

Nori was already strapped into the Tomcat. As he waited patiently for Rajani to do the same, an IRG F-4 Phantom taxied from the parking area and took the duty runway. The F-4 became airborne at the same moment external electrical power was applied to Rajani's jet.

"ICS check," Nori said through the intercom system to his pilot. A check of the Tomcat's ICS was considered standard operating procedure for the IRG.

"Since this is our first flight together, I will tell you exactly what I tell all my rear-seat baggage," Ali said calmly to the RIO. "If I wish to hear your voice, I will ask you a question. Adjust your knobs and flip your useless switches. Do not talk to me."

Checker 201 and 212
A section of VF-221 Tomcats
The Gulf of Oman
1125

Lieutenant Commander Bud Sturgis glanced over his right shoulder, through his front cockpit canopy and toward his wingman. The wing pilot, Lieutenant Danny Travis, had maneuvered his Tomcat to within 100 feet of his lead. Travis was waving hand signals to Sturgis and Sturgis's RIO, Lieutenant junior-grade Bill Milkeen.

"Milk, see if you can figure out what Travis's problem is. I got to keep my eye on this AWACS." Milkeen snapped his ICS twice to acknowledge the pilot, then turned his attention toward the wingman's aircraft.

Sturgis was the F-14 flight lead for a *Burning Sand* escort mission. He and his wingman had launched from the USS *Carl Vinson* less than one hour earlier. They had rendezvoused with a Saudi Arabian E-3 AWACS just south of the southern entrance to the Strait of Hormuz. They were to escort the multiengine AWACS through the strait at 27,000 feet. In less than twenty minutes, when the E-3 had transited the center of the strait and was steady on a course that would return it home to Saudi Arabia, he and his wingman would hand over escort duty to a division of four Saudi F-15 Eagles.

Sturgis had escorted the *Burning Sand* AWACS twice before. Both flights had been uneventful, even boring. He checked his heading. It was due north, a course that paralleled the Omani peninsula as it pointed into the center of the strait. The three aircraft would turn left to west in less than two minutes. Just north of the turn point was the crooked southern coastline of Iran.

The E-3 was flying abeam Travis's left side a little more than one mile away. It was a large aircraft. At an indicated airspeed of only 270 knots, it seemed to hang in the air as it flew. The AWACS was an airborne early warning and reconnaissance platform. Her crew monitored electronic emissions as they flew above the strait.

"Yo, Milk. What's wrong with our wingee?" Sturgis said to his RIO across the ICS.

"Not sure. I don't think he's got a radio transmitter. But I'm pretty sure he can receive." Bud Sturgis keyed the mic switch to his number-two UHF radio. It was set to a frequency only he and his wingman were monitoring.

"Trav, this is Sturg. How do you hear me?" Danny Travis flashed his lead a thumbs-up, and Sturgis returned his attention to the AWACS. "He can't talk, but he can listen," the pilot said to Milkeen over his ICS. "That's good enough. Let's press on."

Sturgis led the E-3 and his wingman in a lazy port turn around the top of Oman at the island of Didamar. Already, he could see where the narrow strait was beginning to widen into the eastern Persian Gulf.

Iranian Revolutionary Guard
Military Aerodrome
Bandar 'Abbās, Iran
1130

Ali Abdul Rajani's assigned wingman, a senior IRG pilot named Omid, had already started both of his Tomcat's engines and completed his poststart checklists. Still, Omid and his RIO waited patiently for the ace before taxiing to the runway—their jet was ready to fly. Rajani's jet was not. A large party of technicians scurried underneath Ali Rajani's fighter. One of them moved out from under the F-14 until the pilot could see him through the closed canopy. His coveralls were soaked red with fluid, and he held a broken silver hydraulic line in one hand. The mechanic then shrugged his shoulders and walked slowly beneath the jet. The Tomcat would not be repaired quickly.

Rajani beat angrily against the side of the Plexiglas canopy as he raised it. Before he climbed down, he made a loud and short ICS transmission to Nori, his RIO.

"*We are going flying!*"

Ali Rajani did not bother to secure the aircraft's turning engines as he jumped onto the boarding ladder. Someone else could do that, he decided. Surprisingly, he waited for Nori to descend the ladder behind him. While he waited, he spit onto the side of the F-14.

"Piece of shit airplane," he announced to the RIO.

Omid signaled that he was ready to taxi, and IRG

personnel hurried to remove rubber chocks from in front of and behind the Tomcat's large tires. He had planned to be Rajani's wingman during this mission, but he was also prepared to fly as a single.

Rajani strutted toward Omid's jet. He grabbed one of the ground personnel by the collar of his coveralls, then ordered the man to rechock the jet.

"*No!*" Rajani said flatly. "Do not remove these until you see *me* give you the signal."

Ali Abdul Rajani then turned and walked a few paces, out from beneath the wing to a spot on the tarmac where Omid could see him clearly.

Slowly, Rajani mouthed the Farsi words for "get out." He made a similar gesture with his hands. Omid understood Rajani's meaning immediately, but looked away from the bearded pilot toward one of the ground crewmen—no one was going to take *his* airplane. Omid signaled again that his chocks be removed. He was ready to taxi.

"*NO!*" Rajani's voice could be heard clearly above the scream of the jet engines. He shook his head slowly as he reached into the breast pocket of his flight suit. He pulled a silver .45 caliber pistol from the pocket and raised it toward Omid. Again, Rajani formed the words slowly with his lips: "Get out."

Checker 201 and 212
1145

Lieutenant junior-grade Bill Milkeen could see the division of Saudi F-15 Eagles. Their aircraft appeared as four distinct smudges on the radar display in the backseat of Checker 201. The distance of the smudges was 80 nautical miles.

When the range between the VF-221 Tomcats

and the F-15s had closed to 70 nautical miles, Milkeen made an advisory radio call to the USS *Carl Vinson* Strike Operations controller on the number-one UHF set—on the KY-58 secure-voice frequency being monitored by the E-3 AWACS crew.

"Strike, this is 201. Ops normal here. We're ten minutes to escort turnover."

The ship's Strike controller rogered the call. At nearly the same time, Sturgis and Milkeen heard another voice over their "protected" UHF communications network. It was the voice of a different controller—an airborne controller in a *Vinson* E-2C Hawkeye more than 150 nautical miles to the south. The voice reported another radar contact. The contact was 32 miles behind the Checker Tomcats and their AWACS. The contact was also flying at the same altitude as the *Burning Sand* escort, and at the same airspeed. The controller was not certain of the type of aircraft it was tracking. The voice guessed the contact was military, but not necessarily Iranian or even hostile.

"Then he is *not* closing on us?" Milkeen asked the E-2C controller.

"Negative, 201. He's still in trail of your flight at 32 nautical miles," the airborne controller reported. Finally, Bud Sturgis broke into the conversation.

"If he *isn't* getting any closer to us and if he's *not* necessarily hostile, what would you like us to do, Strike? We're *seven* minutes from AWACS handoff." The pilot's voice was impatient across the radio.

There was more than 90 seconds of buzzing radio comm between the Hawkeye and the *Vinson* Strike controller before a decision was reached. The separation between the Saudi AWACS and the F-15s was now less than 50 miles.

"Checker 201. You are to *investigate* the contact." It was the voice from inside the E-2C Hawkeye. "And 201, Strike directs," the voice was more deliberate. "Weapons Red and Tight. Repeat . . . Red and *Tight* on that contact. Join and identify it only. Do not release your weapons unless fired upon."

Sturgis knew the rules of engagement only too well—this was his third *Burning Sand* escort in as many weeks, and his fourth month in the Indian Ocean. He had memorized the complicated matrix of events and conditions that made up the ROE. He was insulted by the radio call.

Condition White, Weapons Tight began the weapons release matrix and described a scenario where either no threat existed or none was expected to exist on a particular mission. Weapons were never authorized for use in a White and Tight scenario. Yellow and Tight was similarly restrictive to the Tomcats. A yellow condition existed whenever a carrier battle group operated near a potentially hostile threat or threats. The threats could be airborne fighters or Surface-to-Air Missile shooters. SAM threats were defined by a separate matrix with its own complicated conditions and variables.

The most difficult scenarios existed when the fighters flew under circumstances further modified as Red and Tight. A threat was airborne during Red and Tight conditions. That threat might or might not have the capability of launching air-to-air missiles of its own. How that hostile aircraft maneuvered—if it maneuvered at all—was integral to the matrix. Most important, of course, was a determination of the weaponry carried by the airborne threat.

That determination could come in only two ways—by joining and escorting the threat to visually determine its missile load-out, or—and this is where Sturgis had his major complaint with the rules of engagement—by being attacked by the airborne threat. If Sturgis and his wingman were fired upon by the airborne radar contact behind them at 32 nautical miles, the ROE for weapons release would be satisfied. Assuming he and his wingman were able to survive such an attack, they would then be able to return fire. Under the matrix, conditions that allowed the release of missiles from American F-14s were described as Red and Free.

"Did you copy, Checker 201?" It was the voice from the E-2C again. "Weapons *Red and Tight*." The reminder further angered Sturgis.

"Tell that *asshole* that we understand the *ROE*," Sturgis directed to Milkeen across the ICS. "That contact is probably an airliner, anyway."

Cactus Zero One, an Iranian F-14
1155

Ali Abdul Rajani rarely followed orders. As a rule, he despised the men who gave them. Four of his six Iraqi Mirage kills were the direct result of such contempt. He preferred to think for himself in the air.

"Those who direct us are *not* fighter pilots and are *not* aces," he had announced once to a group of Iranian Revolutionary Guard aviators. The men had gathered around him as he spoke. They always gathered around him. "I am the ace. Listen to them and you will be killed. Listen to me and you will do the killing."

It was advantageous to Rajani to listen and to follow orders on this mission, however. If he did so, he might enjoy the opportunity to down yet another aircraft. Rajani and his RIO orbited over Bandar 'Abbās airfield at 2,000 feet as directed. Nori selected a prebriefed UHF channel on his backseat radio, and the two of them listened in on a conversation across the frequency.

"Cactus Zero Seven . . . Site Two. Maintain your course, altitude, and airspeed precisely. The American fighters have been ordered to intercept you. Do not be alarmed, Zero Seven. The Americans have also been ordered *not* to employ their weaponry against your aircraft."

There were two Ground Controlled Intercept sites on Qeshm Island. The island sat off Iran's southern coast not far from Bandar 'Abbās. Site One, at Qeshm's northeastern edge, was nearest Rajani and Nori as they orbited the airfield. Site Two was nearly thirty nautical miles to the south and west, where Qeshm Island nosed into the Strait of Hormuz. The radar facility at Site Two was better equipped to monitor the *Burning Sand* escort. From there, the GCI controller could best direct the Iranian Revolutionary Guard Phantom, Cactus 07. The pilots and RIOs in the IRG Phantom and Tomcat could only guess at how Site Two was able to know so much about the airborne American fighters.

"Cactus Zero One, Site Two. Are you also monitoring this frequency?"

Nori sat uncomfortably in the backseat of Ali Rajani's airplane. He had already been instructed not to speak. He assumed his pilot would respond to the call. Instead, Rajani keyed the Tomcat's intercom system.

"Answer him, *idiot*."

"Yes. Cactus Zero One is monitoring," Nori said over the UHF.

"Excellent, Zero One. Your vector is two-two-five degrees. Two American F-14 Tomcats at 51 miles on that bearing. *Remain at* your present altitude. Your aircraft will avoid detection if it remains at low altitude."

Nori repeated the instructions over the UHF to Site Two, and Ali Rajani pushed at his throttles until both engines were stabilized in full afterburner. When the IRG Tomcat was steady on a southwesterly heading, it accelerated to 550 knots, and began to climb away from 2,000 feet. Rajani was already disobeying orders. But a climb to higher altitudes would increase his jet's Indicated Mach Number. Fifty-one miles was a considerable distance to travel. He would arrive at his destination more quickly if he flew at 35,000 or 40,000 feet. And to Rajani, getting there quickly was far more critical than being detected. The pilot ignored the controller's repeated instructions to descend. Nori dared say nothing to either of them.

But the ace in Cactus Zero One was not detected as he closed on the IRG Phantom and the two American fighters. The fighters were not looking for him, and the *Vinson* E-2C Hawkeye did not see him. As he and Nori closed the distance at Mach 1.4—at nearly 15 miles per minute—the GCI controller at Site Two fed them more information.

The AWACS was heading home to Saudi Arabia. Four Saudi F-15s were escorting her there. The F-15s would be no threat to either IRG aircraft, the controller added. The two U.S. Tomcats had already rendezvoused with Cactus 07—the Iranian F-4 Phantom. The two American jets were abeam the Phantom on both sides and slightly in trail of it.

According to Site Two, one of the Tomcats was talking to a controller aboard the USS *Carl Vinson*. It seemed the other F-14 was unable to operate its radio. Cactus Zero One, with Ali Abdul Rajani and Nori, was less than 15 nautical miles behind the F-4 and its two American fighter escorts when the GCI controller relayed a vital piece of data.

"One of the Americans has just suffered a complete electrical failure." The Site Two GCI controller was somehow monitoring the protected UHF frequency.

"Which one?" Rajani interjected the question quickly across the UHF frequency. He despised GCI controllers. He found them worse even than RIOs, and more useless. He had never listened to them, or been able to trust them. He had never before required their assistance, either, and was not a man given easily to change—he had destroyed six aircraft without the help of a ground controller. And this one—this one in particular—had a voice that grated on him. But Rajani had never before engaged an American aircrew flying an F-14 Tomcat, either. He nosed over his jet until his altitude was the same as the Americans—27,000 feet.

"Which one?" he said again. "Which one has the failure?"

"The same as had the radio problem," Site Two confirmed. "The one to the north side of Cactus Zero Seven."

Ali Abdul Rajani was headed west and behind the Tomcats at six nautical miles. He was closing rapidly—his jet was still supersonic—and he could see smoke trails in the haze just below the horizon.

The one to the north would be the right-hand Tomcat, he decided. Rajani knew the Tomcat well—its electrical system and its weapons system. He was flying the same aircraft as the *Carl Vinson* pilots. With an electrical failure, the right-hand fighter would be unable to fire its missiles. He screamed across the ICS to Nori, who jumped in his seat at the sound in his headset.

"Lock up the other man. *Lock the American to the left!*" he ordered.

Ali Rajani was proud of his six kills. He was proud to be the only living ace among the Iranian Revolutionary Guard. He was not so proud that he would not accept an easy shot for his seventh kill, or his eighth. And these were Americans. His fame was guaranteed now. "A kill is a kill," he had said many times before to the other IRG pilots. "No matter how easily it comes to you, the kill is all that matters."

The radar diamond in Rajani's Heads Up Display was superimposed over the Tomcat to the left side and slightly behind the F-4 Phantom. The ace was now directly behind the Tomcat. The aircraft was large in his windscreen, and the tone in his helmet earcups was crisp and clear—the heat-seeking weapons he carried could see the target as well. Still, to eliminate all doubt, he demanded the range from his RIO.

"*How far!*"

"Less than one mile. Point-eight miles," Nori answered obediently.

Ali Rajani squeezed the stick-mounted trigger. An infrared-guided Matra Magic missile jumped off its launcher rail beneath his port wing, and tracked the two hot engines in front of it. A rope of white smoke followed the missile. LCDR Bud Sturgis and his backseater, LTJG Bill Milkeen, could not see the Magic as it accelerated toward the exhaust plume of their fighter's starboard engine. The fighter bunted forward with the impact and the right engine stall warning tone blared into their headsets. Checker 201's right motor turbine section came apart, spinning blades of metal through its engine casing. Three of the Tomcat's four aft fuselage fuel cells were burning.

Rajani had already pulled the nose of his fighter to the Tomcat on the other side of the Phantom. The second Tomcat was huge in his HUD. He squeezed the trigger before verifying the range with Nori, but not before the U.S. fighter had already begun to maneuver.

The heat-seeker tore right from the missile rail beneath Rajani's starboard wing. It guided farther right, torquing and twisting in flight.

Lieutenant Danny Travis banked left. The missile veered right again, and Ali Abdul Rajani knew instantly that his second Matra Magic had failed.

Rajani banked hard, and followed the missile in its right-hand turn as the American continued to the left. The heat-seeker's rocket motor was burning. But it saw no target—it was unguided and wasted. It dove down, toward the waters of the Strait of Hormuz. Rajani leveled his wings when Qeshm Island, and Site Two, were on his nose at a little more than twenty miles. The Iranian Revolutionary Guard ace was out of missiles—he had launched with only two of them. He had one kill. That was enough. There was no reason for him to remain. LT Danny Travis and his RIO followed impotently behind the IRG fighter as it flew to the north. The American fighter pilot pulled repeatedly at his trigger, but nothing came off his jet.

The Hotel Continental
Baguio City, the Philippines
2340

Dirk Buzzell bounced from the small bed and ran naked to the room door. Marti pulled at the sheets until they were tucked under her chin, watching Dirk take the wooden room service tray from the hotel waiter.

"Stay right there," he directed to the Filipino boy, who stared past Buzzell's bare backside to the female American waving from the bed.

"There you go," Buzzell said, folding a wad of multicolored pesos and shoving them into the waiter's shirt pocket. He slammed the door in the boy's puzzled face.

"The poor kid's probably never seen the aftermath of world-class lovemaking before," he bragged, looking around the room for an available spot to place the tray. His white Navy uniform trousers, shoes, and hat were scattered about the small room. Marti's red dress hung from the lone light fixture above the bed. He could only locate one of her black high-heeled pumps. The other was probably somewhere in the frantic pile of luggage near the door.

"You're nuts," she said, smiling with her pale blue eyes from under the covers.

"Yeah, what about them?" he asked. They giggled like teenagers as he placed the tray on a pillow near the headboard.

"Room service, too. I am impressed, Lieutenant."

"Not easy to come by in these parts, ma'am," he responded in a bad John Wayne imitation. "Got some rice here, some lumpia with sweet and sour sauce, and, by the looks of it, the cheapest bottle of champagne in their cellar. At least it's cold. May I pour?''

''You've lost weight,'' Marti said as Dirk walked to the far side of the room, covering his short black hair with the white uniform hat. He was otherwise unclothed.

''Navy cooking, babe. Absolutely the worst in the world. One can only eat so much *fried* fish and *fried* beef and *fried* pork and French *fries*. Had to cut down on the beer too. You know, after two cruises, I still haven't been able to locate the *Enterprise* bar.'' The two laughed again as the plastic cork flew out of the wine bottle, ricocheting off the hotel room dresser mirror.

Dirk walked to the bed, pushing down on the brim of his hat until Marti could no longer see his eyes—only his slightly oversized nose and the bushy black mustache under it.

''What are you up to, Dirk? I don't see any wineglasses.''

''Don't need any. Please expose your breasts, young lady.''

''What? No way, not on . . .''

Buzzell had already grabbed at the bedding, pulling it down to Marti's waist. While she fought with the sheets, he emptied a quarter of the bottle onto her upper body. She sat straight up, staring at him—failing in her attempt to look angry. She flicked with her tongue at the few drops of champagne on her chin.

''My, my, what a mess,'' he said sternly. ''I better clean that up right away.''

''It's a good thing I arrived when I did, babe,'' she laughed as she kicked back the wet sheets.

"You're acting like you haven't seen a woman in more than a month."

Dirk settled beside her on the narrow bed, kissing her gently on the lips, easing her head onto the pillow, then sliding his caresses down her neck. Marti's chestnut hair was streaked with white champagne bubbles and lay across her breasts. He had always thought they were breasts too large for the slender body that supported them. He pushed the hair aside, and began tonguing at the wine.

"Dirk . . . ?" Marti was suddenly in the mood to talk. "If we had a kid . . . what do you think he or she would look like?" The question caught Dirk Buzzell off guard, and he pretended not to hear it.

They both ignored the first knock at the door, but were distracted by the second and then the third. Finally, Marti again pulled the bed sheets up and around her chin as Dirk slid into his white trousers and ran across the room.

"I am sorry to interrupt a second time, sir." The same young Filipino waiter was standing in the doorway. "There is a call from Subic for you in the manager's office." Dirk Buzzell did not feel like getting dressed again.

"Why can't you transfer the call up . . ."

Buzzell looked around the room, scanning the nightstands and dresser top until he found what was left of the telephone—he had nearly forgotten about ripping the phone cord out of the wall after placing his order with room service. He found his tropical white uniform shirt under the luggage. It was crumpled and still reeked of sweat.

"Marti, I'm sorry, but I had no choice. I had to tell the squadron duty officer where we were going. That's SOP when the ship's in port," he said, tucking his shirttail into the pants. "I'm sure it's nothing. Nobody's gonna screw up our weekend together.'' He slammed the door behind him, and followed the young Filipino to the stairway.

Marti lay there alone in the room. She slid her hands beneath the sheets and felt at her stomach. It was swollen slightly, she thought. But Dirk had not seemed to notice.

DAY FOUR

JANUARY 8

USS *Enterprise*
Stateroom 03-93-2L
0640 (local time)

Even two wool Navy blankets did not keep Dirk Buzzell warm. A series of tiny vents allowed an abundance of cool air into the small stateroom he shared with two other Aardvark pilots. Air-conditioning was a scarce luxury aboard the USS *Enterprise*—it made the stateroom an exception to normal living conditions on the 0-3 level, where most of the air-wing staterooms were located. Other rooms relied on portable electric fans for ventilation. On this particular morning, however, Buzzell didn't appreciate the efficient air-conditioning system. And he didn't feel like climbing down from his top rack to secure its flow, either. Instead, he lay there, awake and cold.

Two blasts from the *Enterprise* whistle filtered through the inch-thick steel flight deck over his bunk, and rang through the blankets covering his head.

"Sounds like we're steaming past the *Bluegill*

again, and leaving paradise behind." One of his stateroom-mates, "Spanky" Pfister, rolled out of the narrow lower rack and clicked on the fluorescent tube overhead the stainless-steel sink.

"Yep," Buzzell answered solemnly. He held the blankets over his head, shielding his eyes from the light, and holding in the moist warmth of his breath.

"This has *got* to be a bad dream," he said aloud, squeezing his eyelids tighter together. "Maybe I'm not really back aboard this ship. Maybe I'm *really* asleep in that same little hotel room up in Baguio." Buzzell enjoyed the way the dream was taking shape inside his mind. "In a minute or so, I'll *really* wake up, walk over to that hotel-room picture window, and look out over the waterfront. There'll be a few sailboats on the bay, and I'll see people walking the streets in front of the hotel." Buzzell's roommates ignored him as he rambled on from under the blankets.

"I'll turn around and find Marti curled up with her pillow. She'll wake up slowly, then stare at me with those *gorgeous* blue eyes of hers."

The ship heaved, then rolled underneath him as it steamed against the current out to sea. Buzzell decided he wasn't dreaming. He pulled the covers from his face, squinting across the room at the mirror. He watched Spanky Pfister shave around a scrawny blond mustache.

"Nope. This is *definitely* a nightmare, Spanky. You don't look anything like Marti." Pfister turned toward Buzzell, then curtsied with a wide grin on his face.

"Any idea what's going on?" Buzzell asked.

Mark Caine, sliding out of the center bunk, stumbled to the stateroom door and switched on the remainder of the lights. "Yeah, haven't you heard? We're gonna go shoot some Iranian towel-heads."

Bandar 'Abbās, Iran

Motorcades were a decadent Western tradition, and were something very foreign to the Islam population of Iran. But as Ali Abdul Rajani led a procession of eleven vehicles past the mosques that filled the center of Bandar 'Abbās, even he was surprised by the throngs of Iranians there to cheer him. Tens of thousands of Persians and Azeri Turks and Kurds and Arabs lined the narrow streets. The people waved giant Iranian flags and large posters with the likeness of the long-dead Ayatollah Ruholla Khomeini. American flags burned on the streets. Teheran radio and television representatives followed the motorcade. Reporters and photographers from the Islamic Republic News Agency rode in the long military vehicle directly behind the ace.

Ali Rajani had insisted on driving the lead vehicle himself. He refused to be chauffeured in one of the IRG sedans designed to carry religious leaders and other such VIPs. He drove his new Cadillac convertible with flair and arrogance. It was red, like the previous model. But this convertible was newer, longer, and its interior was finished in white leather. Rajani did not find it ironic that he was driving an American-made vehicle. It was a fine automobile, and he had become accustomed to finer things. He pounded at its horn as he drove. And he luxuriated in the attention. Nori, his RIO, sat quietly in the backseat.

Rajani led the procession off the roadway that paralleled the coastline south of Bandar 'Abbās and onto the dirt and stone trail that led to the military aerodrome and the tall Iranian Revolutionary Guard hangar. A sentry at the gate there stepped back as the Cadillac approached. The convertible was new, so Ali Rajani did not swerve at the man. Instead, he slowed the auto. He drove it carefully through the gate and underneath the port wing of an F-14 Tomcat positioned beside the hangar. Ali climbed quickly out of the red convertible. The radio and television and newspaper people swarmed around him as he leaned against the Tomcat at its boarding ladder. He fluffed up the red ascot beneath the collar of his flight suit. He stroked at his dark beard.

"This is the aircraft I was flying when I achieved my *seventh* and *eighth* kills," he sneered. Nori remained in the Cadillac as Rajani had ordered. The RIO said nothing to the reporters who occasionally poked microphones into his face—the ace had directed the backseater's silence as well.

Rajani continued. "And with this aircraft, I have beaten the best of the American aircraft carrier pilots." The photographers could not seem to take enough pictures of the pilot and his Tomcat.

The makeshift press conference had been well planned and completely contrived, of course. The Iranian propaganda machine was operating in overdrive. There had been few opportunities for such a media event in recent months. And it was only logical that the propaganda surrounding Ali Abdul Rajani would include news of *two* U.S. Tomcats going down in flames over the Strait of Hormuz instead of one.

The lie would serve many purposes, not the least of which was its effect on the populace. A military victory of such magnitude would double the Iranian loyalists' resolve against the United States—the

Great Satan. And Rajani did not resist the lie. He had been promised by certain officials that his face would be seen on the cover of magazines and newspapers around the world. The promise had a predictable effect on his ego. He felt he deserved such notoriety. And he was now the proud owner of two convertible Cadillacs. All that was asked of him was his cooperation with the media. One of the state journalists there, one of many who had written of the ace's exploits on other occasions, pushed his way through the mob until he stood beside Rajani and the huge swing-wing fighter.

"The people would like to hear you give thanks to Allah for your successes," the reporter suggested.

Government officials had directed Ali Abdul Rajani to make such a statement, too. But the ace was neither diplomatic nor a religious man. And he was not willing to share the credit for his kills. He looked away from the reporter and toward the aircraft behind them. There was little compromise in him.

"Allah provided for me the finest flying machine in the world. But I alone supplied the skill necessary to defeat the United States Navy fighters." The photographers took more pictures.

Omid and a small group of Iranian Revolutionary Guard aircrew stood together, across the tarmac from the ace, near a doorway leading into the tall hangar. They watched the crowd grow around Rajani and the F-14.

"You should not have allowed Ali to remove you from that aircraft yesterday," one of the other IRG aircrew stated to Omid.

USS *Enterprise*
Ready Room Six
0700

Buzzell and Caine stepped through the VF-141 Maintenance Control spaces and into Ready Six. The Aardvark CO had already cornered Rich Collins, the squadron intelligence officer—the spy—near the front of the ready room. Collins shook his head, pleading ignorance to most of the commanding officer's repeated questions. At the same time, the spy thumbed through piles of charts and transparencies, trying to prepare his brief. Buzzell joined a group of JO's huddled together at the back of the space, stopping along the way to pull a warm Diet Coke from the inoperative refrigerator there.

Except for Buzzell, the officers wore black T-shirts under bright orange flight suits. Black and orange were the VF-141 squadron colors. Adorned on the shoulder of each flight suit were patches bearing the likeness of the Aardvark, the animal of "B.C." cartoon fame. The animal resembled a bizarre cross between a dog and an anteater. Buzzell wore khaki pants and a white jersey. Although he had been ordered back aboard *Enterprise* after only half a night with Marti, he had not been scheduled to fly. Instead, as the Aardvark's senior landing signal officer, he would spend the day recovering air-wing aircraft from the flight deck LSO platform.

"First . . . let me apologize for the emergency recall last night." The squadron CO paused as the last few Aardvark officers found their chairs. Collins inserted a final slide into his projector tray, then signaled a thumbs-up to the CO. The spy was ready with his brief, but the skipper continued. He was staring at Dirk Buzzell.

"I know *some* of you had girlfriends or wives in port for the long liberty weekend. I can appreciate how both of you must have felt after receiving that midnight phone call. Hell, when we finally got hold of the ole XO here, he was barricaded up in the Manila Hilton. He'd already rented a suite and refused to believe anyone over the telephone. He figured this recall had to be some sort of commie plot. I had to rent a car, drive two hours through the mountains, and *personally* persuade him that what's going on here is legit."

The CO shifted his gaze to the executive officer, who sunk in a tall chair in the front of the ready room. The XO was embarrassed, and was suffering from an acute hangover. Buzzell wasn't laughing, but most of the officers sitting around him were. Instead, he was suddenly enraged with the United States Navy and with the man standing at the front of the room.

Marti had been furious, too, the night before—it had been easy to see it in her face. She had said very little during their long taxi ride down the mountain from Baguio City. But it had been difficult for either of them to be furious or enraged as they stood together on Pier 16 beside the *Enterprise*. He had tried to convince her he didn't know the reason for the recall—and he hadn't. But she refused to understand, and she hadn't cared to hear an explanation. She didn't want him to leave.

"It's probably got something to do with the Persian Gulf—the Iranians or the Iraqis. They've been blasting the crap out of each other for a long time,

Marti. I don't *know* what's going on,'' he remembered telling her.

Eventually, she had tried to change the subject. She tried to joke, and suggested the two of them run off together—to one of those small and remote Philippine islands, somewhere the Navy would never think to look—and allow the fighting in the Persian Gulf to go on without the man she loved. Dirk Buzzell wasn't lying when he told her he liked the idea.

Collins flashed the first slide onto the screen at the front of the room. The word *SECRET* was upside down and backwards. Normally, the Aardvark officers would have screamed and laughed at the obvious briefing faux pas. On this occasion, however, they did not. The spy clicked to the next slide, and a public-affairs photo of the nuclear-powered aircraft carrier USS *Carl Vinson* came into focus.

''Yesterday, at approximately 0400 Zulu time—that's about noon for us in the Philippine Op area—the *Vinson* battle group was located here.'' Collins grabbed an orange-and-black-striped pointer, stabbing at the third slide on the screen, a God's-eye view of the North Arabian Sea. At the top of the slide, halfway between the coast of Pakistan and Oman, a tiny blue dot indicated the *Carl Vinson*'s position.

''Three hundred miles northwest of the carrier, two F-14s from VF-221, one of the two Tomcat squadrons aboard the *Vinson*, and four Saudi Arabian F-15s were coordinating an escort of a Saudi E-3 AWACS radar surveillance aircraft. The Saudis utilize the AWACS as a reconnaissance platform from which they monitor operations in the Gulf region—specifically the military operations of the navies and air forces of Iran and Iraq.

"The Saudi's consider the E-3 a very-high-value unit, and since Uncle Sam sold the AWACS to Saudi Arabia and shares in the intelligence it gathers, the Navy has been directed to offer its F-14s as air cover while the E-3 flies through the Strait of Hormuz on its final leg home to Ryadh. The AWACS escort mission is code-named *Operation Burning Sand.*"

Buzzell grew increasingly impatient. He leaned closer to Greg Bright, who sat beside him three rows back among the ready room chairs. Bright was pinching a large piece of snuff into his mouth. "Why does it always take so long for these intel geeks to get to the point?"

Bright shrugged his shoulders, and turned to whisper an answer to Buzzell's question.

"No idea," he whispered back. "They're probably getting paid by the word."

"The escort was westbound," the spy continued, "more than halfway through the strait when sources picked up the launch of an Iranian F-4 Phantom from an airfield near Bandar 'Abbās. The F-15s assumed escort of the E-3, and the two F-14s vectored to intercept the Phantom. From here on out, the message is rather vague," Collins added. "Apparently the F-4 Phantom was trailing the AWACS by more than 30 miles, well outside air-to-air missile range.

"The Tomcats joined on the Phantom, then radioed back to the *Vinson* that the F-4 bore markings of the Iranian Revolutionary Guard. They also reported that the Phantom was unarmed. The two Tomcats had just received word to detach from the F-4 and return to the *Vinson* when one of them was struck rear-quarter by an air-to-air missile. The targeted F-14, according to the message, was destroyed." Bright sat straight back in his chair, turning to Buzzell, who was leaning forward in his, and playing with his mustache while he listened.

"The remaining *Vinson* Tomcat reportedly chased a *second* bandit—not the Phantom it had joined on, but *another* bandit—back toward Bandar 'Abbās. The message continues, and states that the VF-221 aircraft was unable to return fire on the Iranian fighter. That same Tomcat had experienced an electrical malfunction a few minutes earlier. The *Vinson* aircraft broke off its pursuit after following the bandit into Iranian airspace."

Buzzell didn't realize he had stopped breathing. He began again in the black silence of the ready room. He slid back in his high-backed chair as the VF-141 commanding officer stood and walked to the light switch. "*Jesus Christ!*"

The skipper looked to the rear of the room, uncertain how to continue. Collins interrupted before he could.

"Unfortunately, the *Vinson* aircrew taken under attack were unable to eject from their jet. The message says they're searching for remains. But so far they haven't even been able to find any pieces of the downed fighter."

"*Shit!* This is gonna piss off everybody at the Pentagon," the CO added.

"Yes, sir. We think so."

"So what was it that ass-holed the Tomcat?"

"Well, Skipper, we believe it was a heat-seeking missile . . . most likely a Sidewinder or a Matra Magic. The Iranians have purchased hundreds of Magics from the French in the last couple of years."

The commanding officer looked toward the spy.

"Those frogs are *whores*. They'll sell anything to anybody."

Greg Bright raised his hand. Intel briefs were always informal, and the CO glared at him.

"*What!*"

"Le'me see if I've got the whole picture here. The Iranians launch one Phantom as bait. He's got no missiles, right. The Tomcats join and get blind-sided by his unseen wingman. Why the hell didn't somebody know there were *two* Phantoms airborne out of Bandar 'Abbās?"

"We don't think the other bogey was an F-4," Collins interjected. "The pilot of the *Vinson* Tomcat ID'd that second Iranian aircraft as an *F-14*."

The ready room fell silent again. Rich Collins took the opportunity to walk across the ready room and click off the overhead lights.

"So." The commanding officer stood again and turned. "That's why we pulled out of Subic Bay early and some of you missed out on your liberty. That's unfortunate, and we deserved a little time off. But as you can see, the ragheads have just upped the ante in the Persian Gulf. I for one can hardly wait for an opportunity to return the favor."

Collins tapped at the remote controller in his hand, and continued through the slides.

"The *Enterprise* received a Flash Secret message straight from the Joint Chiefs of Staff last night. We are to proceed toward the *Vinson* anchorage at best speed. It seems the *Carl Vinson* has been ordered out of the Indian Ocean. As soon as we arrive, the *Vinson* is leaving. Originally, the *Enterprise* battle group wasn't due to be on station in the IO until the middle of February. Obviously, we'll be there a lot sooner than that. Our port visits to Singapore and Pattaya Beach, Thailand, have been canceled.

"So far, we've heard no mention of a retaliatory strike against Iran. That is still a possibility, of course, though I doubt seriously that the *Vinson* would be headed home if the JCS had a large strike in mind. We'll have to wait and see.

"Frankly, the intel community is *surprised* the Iranian Revolutionary Guard has taken this course of action now, especially in light of recent developments," Collins commented.

"They're *maniacs,*" the CO interjected. "I'm not surprised at all."

"Well, sir, other recent IRG activities do not point toward their aggravating the U.S. Navy. In fact, there is evidence they want us as far away from a conflict as possible—us and the British, that is.

"Since the end of our little war with Iraq, Iran has been building up its influence in the region. We feel that Iran has used Iraq's blunder as an opportunity to take stock in its dwindling military hardware, and to redirect its posture of terrorist aggression."

"Could you repeat any of that in English," Greg Bright asked from the middle of the ready room chairs. The comment elicited nervous laughter from the other squadron officers.

"Sure, Notso, and sorry. I'll use smaller words from now on." The retort drew even more response from the Aardvarks.

"Iraq and Iran were at each other's throats for years. During that time they bled each other dry in hopes of controlling the flow of oil out of the Gulf." Collins selected another slide, and a chart of the Arabian peninsula appeared on the screen.

"About six years ago, four years before his death, the Ayatollah Khomeini became convinced that he could not win a quick military action against Iraq. It was then that his people began dealing with Red China on the purchase of Silkworm surface-to-surface missiles. The Iranians originally purchased only a dozen of them. But in recent months, we've seen them constructing new launch sites on the islands of Qeshm, Larak, and Hengām in the northern strait. We have F-14 TARPS imagery of three new sites under construction.

"The missiles are designed for antishipping attacks—primarily against heavy oil freighters transiting out of the Strait of Hormuz. The Iranians had some early success with the Silkworms. And with a recent purchase of ninety more missiles, we feel they are putting more stock in them. Obviously, if they can close the strait with the threat of surface-to-surface missiles, they can control the flow of oil out of this region. It's not a bad plan for the Iranians, especially now that Iraq is in such turmoil.

"But the Silkworms are inaccurate beyond about twenty nautical miles—that's a little less than the distance between Iran and Oman. In the past, as large oilers moved into the center of the Strait of Hormuz, they were sitting ducks. Since 1981, thirty-nine oil tankers have been sunk or destroyed by Silkworms.

"About two years ago, not long after the Ayatollah died, Omani waters began opening up to commercial traffic. The Sultan of Oman simply stopped enforcing his country's twelve-mile coastal buffer zone. As a result, the shipping lanes have moved south, nearer the Omani peninsula, to avoid the missile attacks. Mership tonnage through the strait has been increasing. As a result, Oman's reputation among moderate Arab states is also on the rise. This is where the Iranian Revolutionary Guard comes in.''

''You're gonna tell me all this has something to do with that Omani jetliner that went down yesterday, aren't you, Rich,'' the CO speculated.

''Yes, sir, I am. Since the Omanis have begun allowing oil carriers to transit the strait inside the buffer zone, the Silkworm targeting problem has become next to impossible for the Iranians—big ships that far south in the strait are effectively out of Silkworm targeting range. The intelligence community believes these recent terrorist activities are Iran's way of forcing the Sultan to enforce his twelve-mile buffer. It's becoming obvious that the IRG wants to push the oil carriers out of Omani coastal waters and back into the middle of the Strait of Hormuz. That sweetens the Silkworm shots. For the Iranian Revolutionary Guard, it's a simple plan.

''There are also indications that the Ayatollah's son, a nifty fellow by the name of Ahmed, may emerge as the figure behind the plan. Even before his death, the Ayatollah had transferred considerable power to Ahmed. Ahmed, we believe, is the newest mastermind behind the IRG. And the IRG, of course, has complete control over the Silkworms. The Guard is a fanatic outfit, and better served by a younger, more aggressive leader. In fact, we believe these latest terrorist attacks would not have been committed if the Ayatollah were still alive.

''The single unknown variable in this scenario is the Sultan of Oman. Here's a guy who assumed power after a bloodless coup in 1970—Oman hasn't been at war with anyone for more than twenty years. From the very beginning, Oman has been completely neutral in every Persian Gulf conflict—the

Sultan has never shown any signs of desiring involvement. And, at the same time, he has worked hard and been successful in bringing Oman out of the Dark Ages. The nation is more literate, healthier, and wealthier than any of its neighbors.

"But the Sultan isn't spending all of his money on hospitals and playgrounds, either. Oman's defense budget last year was a little more than $1 billion—that's more than a third of its total budget. But the Sultan has a long way to go yet, and he is in no position to aggravate the Iranian Revolutionary Guard. We're not sure what he is trying to prove.

"And speaking of defense, also worthy of note is Oman's long-standing military ties with Britain. Oman's armed forces there are led mainly by British officers. And that's why it's important to mention that the only Britisher scheduled aboard the Omani airliner that blew up yesterday *did not* make the flight. The Iranian Revolutionary Guard terrorist who planted the bomb made sure of that. They took great pains not to kill him. Very unusual. They seem eager to provoke Oman, but not the Brits.

"An Iranian Boghammer, also manned by the IRG, opened fire on an Omani dhow early yesterday. The dhow was unarmed. They killed two kids but allowed the boat's captain to go free. That fact also goes against IRG standard operating procedures—witnesses usually don't survive. Apparently it was important to the Iranians that the Omani sailor be able to identify his attackers. That incident, along with the terrorist bombing of the airliner, may indicate a new twist in the Iranian Revolutionary Guard strategy. They might be moving in-country into Oman—a possible indication that they're not just lobbing Silkworms across the Strait of Hormuz anymore. We don't know, for instance, if the IRG plans to keep any of their people in Oman, or that they could succeed if they tried. Our guess is no.

"But they definitely had terrorists in position at the Musat International Airport before the bombing of that 727. And when they attacked that dhow, their Boghammer was well inside Omani waters. They killed those two kids only eight miles off the coast of Oman's northern peninsula—the Iranians were a long way from home. The IRG has become very brazen.

And it's all clearly premeditated—all except the attack on the *Vinson* F-14, that is. We don't think that was part of their plan. Yes, they've been interested in the *Burning Sand* escorts, and they've even launched a few F-4s before. The IRG probably thinks the Saudi AWACS can monitor their Silkworm attacks. But we've never seen their Tomcats launch against anything in the Strait of Hormuz. Yesterday's air-to-air attack was a first. And again, the intelligence community traces that decision to Ahmed. We weren't expecting it. Regrettably, it cost us the lives of two naval aviators and a $45 million fighter aircraft. And it is also unfortunate that the downing of a Navy fighter tends to galvanize many Arab states against U.S. forces operating in the Persian Gulf region. The IRG is getting a lot of press right now.

"The Iranians have always been very good at the game of terrorism. But personally . . . and with respect to the downing of the *Carl Vinson* F-14, we believe their Tomcat just happened to be in the right place at the right time yesterday. The IRG got lucky."

DAY FIVE

JANUARY 9

USS *Enterprise*
South China Sea
1110

Dirk Buzzell stepped up the half-ladder that joined the narrow starboard catwalk to the huge fantail of the *Enterprise*. All the way forward—more than 1000 feet away—A-6 Intruder and A-7 Corsair attack jets cluttered the bow in front of the island superstructure. Aft of the island, lining the perimeter of the flight deck, five F-14 Tomcats—three with the markings of the Aardvarks and two with those of the Black Eagles—were chained to steel pad-eyes in the deck. A single gray SH-3 Sea King helicopter filled the landing area just forward of the Landing Signal Officer platform. HS-61 maintenance personnel moved around the helo, while four enlisted men in purple flight deck jerseys tended to its refueling.

As her course steadied, the *Enterprise* cut a lime-green swath through the waters 165 nautical miles southwest of Subic Bay, the Philippines. The ship made 26 knots as it entered the narrowing straits north of Palawan Island. That, plus 11 knots of natural wind and a deck slick with salt spray, lengthened Buzzell's short walk to the LSO platform. He snapped together the buttons of his dirty flotation vest, then rolled two white sponge plugs into his ears—it would be noisy on the platform very soon. High and aft of the *Enterprise,* he sighted the contrails of jet aircraft approaching from the east.

He stepped off the landing area and onto the platform. Three LSOs were already huddled there. The men shouted in conversation above the shrill of the Sikorsky starting nearby. The helo engaged its rotors and lifted away, signaling the beginning of another air-wing recovery.

Hangar One
Sultan of Oman Air Force Base
Thumrait, Oman
1115 (local time)

Terrance Hill smiled politely at the British Royal Air Force lieutenant colonel standing beside him. The commanding officer had been rambling, nearly nonstop, for the better part of an hour. Mostly, he was boasting of the pilots and the machines of his Number 6 Squadron. But now, with the deafening whine of Hawker Hunter engines less than twenty meters away, Hill could hear nothing the officer was saying. It had seemed important to the lieutenant colonel that the British envoy stand beside him outside the hangar, near the tarmac where the aircraft were positioned.

Hill turned away from the RAF officer, motioned quickly to his secretary, then reentered the large pewter-colored hangar. The envoy had come to see the Hunters fly. He did not care to witness the starting of their engines. The RAF officer followed dutifully behind the two men.

"Dreadfully noisy beasts, those Hunters. I thought you might enjoy watching them crank up and taxi out," he said apologetically. "Their motors are manufactured by Rolls-Royce, you know."

"Couldn't hear a word you were saying out there, Colonel Thomas. How long before your pilots are airborne?"

"I expect them to taxi at any moment. All four should be 'wheels-in-the-well' in less than five minutes."

"As I mentioned earlier, Colonel, London dispatched me here only yesterday. Sorry about the bother and lack of proper notice. In all honesty, I've been meaning to visit this facility for several months."

"No bother. The Number 6 stands ready at a moment's notice." The lieutenant colonel clicked his heels together and drew himself to attention. "If you've never before seen the Hawker flown, sir, prepare yourself to see it flown expertly."

"I'm sure we will be impressed," Hill responded politely.

Terrance Hill folded his hands neatly behind his back. He felt foolish and out of place. *Someone from the London office should be standing here with this RAF lieutenant colonel . . . someone with experience in affairs of this nature—someone of military rank—someone unlike me,* he thought.

But Hill stood there, watching the last of the four Hawker Hunters taxi away from the hangar. And he stood tall, with his classic British chin square to his shoulders, as if he understood precisely why he had come to Thumrait. A light gust entered the hangar and blew at the hair that barely concealed his widening bald spot. He patted the hair back into place.

Jesus. This is no drill . . . this could be real—there could be . . . there might actually be some sort of military campaign right here in Oman. Hill dreaded his role in all of it. *This man standing next to me, this Royal Air Force officer—now here is a man perfectly at ease with such a prospect.*

Terrance Hill suddenly wished he were not standing there. He imagined himself instead in the thoroughly familiar surroundings of the Musat embassy. He'd rather be in his office—he was good at paperwork. He could not conceive of military action in Oman. He was neither trained nor prepared for it—he didn't understand any of it. And he hoped it would not happen. But he wished it was already over.

Hill glanced toward Malcolm Jennings, his secretary, who still held his fingers to his ears against the sound of the jet engines. He then returned his attention to the Number 6 Squadron commander.

"So tell me, Colonel . . . hypothetically, of course . . . how your aircrew and your Hawker Hunters might fare against . . . say, an F-4 Phantom or even an F-14?"

USS *Enterprise*

Dirk Buzzell took the LSO pickle switch assembly in his right hand. With it, he controlled aircraft landing aboard the ship. He slid his forefinger inside the trigger guard and rested it on the wave-off button, adjusting his grip. Pressing the button illuminated two rows of red lights on either side of the Mark–6, Mod 2 Fresnel Optical Landing System. He looked forward, up the angled carrier deck, and squeezed the button to test the OLS lights. The wave-off lights flared red, then went out. A Tomcat pilot and a landing signal officer, Buzzell had something the more senior air-wing LSOs liked to describe as "a good eye." He'd seen thousands of aircraft approaches to the *Enterprise* during day and night operations, and he'd seen thousands more back at Miramar during field carrier landing practice. He knew very well the difference between a good carrier landing and a bad one—between a safe approach and an unsafe one. Being an LSO was a dedication he took seriously. But mostly, Dirk Buzzell liked the job.

Lieutenant junior-grade Kurt Hansen also liked the job. Hansen was a landing signal officer under-training, a tall, thin, yellow-haired A-7 Corsair pilot from Knoxville, Tennessee. This was Kurt Hansen's first cruise, and Dirk Buzzell had sort of adopted the "nugget" aviator. Officially, Buzzell was Hansen's monitor. The two were members of the same LSO team. Whenever the young A-7 pilot worked the pickle switch and radios on the LSO platform, Buzzell was there to supervise and to back him up—to train him. Dirk Buzzell had already decided that Hansen would not only survive the difficult training regimen of a landing signal officer, but that he would breeze through it.

Hansen was a natural. In less than one week of work on the platform, he had already figured it out. He read the gauges and worked the controls on the flight deck LSO console—the point and line stabilization panel that displayed the *Enterprise* flight deck's degree of pitch, roll, and heave, the complex fresnel lens controls and rheostats, and even the subtleties of the Manually Operated Visual Landing Aid System, or MOVLAS—and he understood all of them instantly. Hansen seemed to comprehend, almost instinctively, the bizarre aerial ballet that is carrier aviation. He scanned the giant deck as aircraft launched from each of the four *Enterprise* catapults, he monitored the stacks of fighters and bombers and electronic jammers circling overhead, and he already seemed to comprehend each of the critical LSO techniques required to make it all happen efficiently and safely. He knew more than a new guy was supposed to know.

Hansen always seemed to be there, on the platform day and night—even when his LSO team wasn't scheduled—trying to get his hands on the pickle, to control the recovery—and marveling at the sight of aircraft flying into the arresting gear. If he wasn't airborne, he needed to be near flying aircraft. And there was no place in the world better for that than the LSO platform at the edge of a tiny landing strip aboard a nuclear-powered supercarrier.

And it didn't matter to Dirk Buzzell that Kurt Hansen's voice across the LSO radio was not exactly textbook. The Corsair pilot's drawl was thick as syrup. As he worked the radio handset, Hansen did not tell *Enterprise* aviators to "fly the ball" as they maneuvered aboard the boat. He told them to "flaw tha bawl." And it didn't matter to Buzzell that Hansen flew A-7s either.

"Fighter guys usually hang out with fighter guys," he had joked with Hansen. "And attack weenies usually hang out with attack weenies. But I might make an exception in your case, hayseed." Buzzell shortened "Hayseed" to "Seed," and Kurt Hansen immediately earned a new call sign.

The two of them stood together on the flight deck, a few feet from the LSO platform. They stared forward, up the flight deck, toward catapult number three. The last aircraft in this particular launch—an S-3 Viking—was flung into the air.

There would be very little flying between the South China Sea and the North Arabian Sea—too little flying for the pilots in the *Enterprise* air wing, Buzzell had decided. When the air wing did not fly, the carrier steamed at flank speed to the west—toward the Indian Ocean and ultimately toward Iran. And even when there were Tomcats and Hawkeyes and Intruders and Corsairs airborne, there were not many of them there. It took time to turn the ship into the wind to launch aircraft and to recover them—time that the ship's captain preferred to spend steaming west.

It had been decided that each air-wing pilot would fly only twice each week during the transit—once at night and once during the day. The missions they flew would be shorter than usual—to conserve precious jet fuel that might be needed at a later date—and primary sortie emphasis would be placed not on the quantity but the quality of their carrier landings. Even the CAG, the air-wing commander, agreed that two flights per week were not enough to maintain pilot proficiency in landing aboard the *Enterprise*. But two was all each aircrew would receive.

"If somebody looks really ugly out there behind this boat," the CAG had warned his LSOs, "I'll pull that son-of-a-bitch from the flight schedule so fast it'll make your head swim. I don't care how senior the pilot is or what kind of airplane he flies. We can't afford to break any airplanes now. We just may need to fight these jets *for real* in a week or two. I expect you boys to get everybody aboard in one piece." The CAG's threat was fresh in the minds of both Buzzell and Hansen as the two LSOs stepped back onto the LSO platform. The first two aircraft of this particular recovery had entered the ship's overhead landing pattern.

Dirk Buzzell squeezed the red pickle-switch button, and an F-14 fighter waved off. The jet roared by the platform less than ten feet above flight deck level.

"Too low for too long," Buzzell yelled over his shoulder toward the air-wing LSO standing behind him. Lieutenant Commander Phil Grokulsky, the senior man on the platform, simply nodded. Kurt Hansen stood beside Buzzell, and leaned even closer to hear the controlling LSO's voice over the scream of jet engines. Each and every attempt at landing aboard the *Enterprise* was graded. Buzzell dropped the UHF radio-phone to his side, turned, and yelled his comments to Hansen.

"Grade that one a wave-off," Buzzell began. "Not enough power on the start, settle-decel in the middle, low slow *underlined* in close to at the ramp." Hansen held a pencil and the grade book. He translated the comments into standard LSO shorthand: WO—NEP.X SDECIM LOSLOIC-AR. It was not a good grade.

The Tomcat banked left, soaring past the bow of the "Big E," climbing to 600 feet over the water and one mile abeam the ship. Dirk Buzzell keyed the UHF radio-telephone he held in his left hand.

"Two-oh-seven, get a better start this time," Buzzell said. He heard two mike clicks over the radio—an affirmative response from the airborne Tomcat pilot.

Buzzell and Hansen and Grokulsky stared at the F-14 as it flew around for its second approach. The LSOs monitored the jet's altitude around the racetrack pattern, and judged its engine power setting by the amount of exhaust that spewed from it. Buzzell looked away from the airplane to check the deck status indicators. A light on the LSO console in front of him indicated a "green" deck—a flight deck ready to "trap" the thirty-ton fighter, Black Eagle 207. Still, Buzzell turned to the third-class petty officer standing closest to the console. The enlisted man interpreted the glance, and responded to the officer's unspoken request.

"Arresting gear and lens set F-14 Tomcat, sir. Green deck," the petty officer reported after scanning a cluster of indicators and gauges in front of him. The third-class had received additional confirmation of flight deck and arresting gear status via his radio headset. The confirmation came from a variety of sources—from flight deck personnel stationed at the perimeters of the landing area foul lines, and from others monitoring and adjusting the arresting gear engines below flight-deck level. Dirk Buzzell rechecked the gauges and the green status light a final time.

"Two-oh-seven, Tomcat ball, four-point-six, auto." The transmission told Buzzell everything he needed to know. The fighter carried 4600 pounds of fuel, and the pilot had engaged the F-14's autothrottles. But more important, the radio call assured the LSO that the pilot had found the electro-optical landing aid somewhere near the center of the OLS fresnel lens—it was what Kurt Hansen kept referring to as "tha bawl." The ball glowed amber on the lens. It served as a visual indicator of the aircraft's position above or below optimum glide slope. The pilot would modulate his throttles and adjust his jet's airspeed in response to movement of the ball. The lens and its luminous ball hung awkwardly off the port catwalk amidships more than 400 feet behind the LSO console. Buzzell had his back turned to the ball. He couldn't see what it was telling the pilot in the front seat of Black Eagle 207. But he knew. Four years of LSO experience told him the aircraft was low.

"Roger ball . . . don't settle." The jet responded to Buzzell's call. The Tomcat's huge horizontal stabilizers shifted with each stick input. The fighter stopped its rate of descent for an instant—long enough for the jet to climb into the center of the glide slope, where it remained until touchdown. Its tailhook point spit sparks as it dropped to the flight deck 245 feet from the aft round-down at 129 knots, settling between the second and third arresting gear cables stretched perpendicular to the landing zone. The hook snagged the number-three wire, and the world's largest fighter was jerked to a complete standstill in less than 150 feet.

Twenty seconds later, the Black Eagle F-14 had cleared the landing area. Its wings were swept aft. An arresting gear engine somewhere beneath the landing area retracted the number-three wire. The wire moved aft. Buzzell watched it snap into place at the same moment an Aardvark fighter called the ball.

The LSO didn't have time to ask the petty officer beside him why the deck status light had not yet turned to green. Instead, it was red and flashing, and the Tomcat in the "groove" was less than five seconds from touchdown.

"Wave it off. Fouled deck," he said into the radio-telephone. At the same moment, he depressed the pickle switch that illuminated the red wave-off lights. The F-14 pilot responded.

Lieutenant Mark Caine was flying the Aardvark

fighter. Lieutenant Greg Bright sat in his backseat. The ball had been perfectly centered on the lens, and the red wave-off lights surprised both of them. Caine pushed his throttles full forward to 100 percent power, and eased back on the control stick between his knees. His craft roared away from the carrier and toward another start.

Buzzell turned to the enlisted man on his right, expecting to hear that a mechanical malfunction was responsible for the deck suddenly going foul. Instead, the petty officer pointed past the LSO to a tall man dressed in khakis. The man was running across the flight deck between the first and second arresting gear wires.

"The deck went red because of him, sir," the enlisted man stated. "He crossed the foul line when that Tomcat was about to land."

Buzzell shook his head in disbelief, then looked away from the carrier, out and over the edge of the ship then up toward the Aardvark jet approaching the abeam position. When he turned again and faced the LSO console, the tall man in khakis was grinning at him and Kurt Hansen from behind a pair of thick flight-deck goggles. Buzzell didn't recognize the man.

"What the *hell* do you think you're doing, pal? We almost landed an airplane on your narrow ass. Besides that, we don't allow spectators on our platform." Buzzell stared into the man's goggles, then turned toward Phil Grokulsky when the tall man did not immediately leave the flight deck. The senior air-wing LSO was chewing on his lip, his eyes fixed on Buzzell.

"Buzz," Grokulsky said in an unsteady voice, "I'd like you to meet Rear Admiral Jeremiah Curtiss, Commander, Battle Group Juliet."

Sultan of Oman Air Force Base
Thumrait, Oman

Terrance Hill poked at his secretary. Malcolm Jennings was dead asleep in his chair outside the hangar. The long drive from Musat to Thumrait on barely navigable roadways had tired him. The warm Omani sun had also taken its toll on the young Brit. Jennings awakened and slid up in his chair. Hill remained standing. His stab wound was well concealed by thick wool trousers—trousers far too heavy for the afternoon sun. He wanted to sit, but his buttocks wouldn't allow it.

The Number 6 Squadron lieutenant colonel continued his pace back and forth in front of the envoy. The officer strutted left and then right, checking his wristwatch in rhythm with each turn. He paused midstride, peering out at the approach end of the runway across the tarmac. The lieutenant colonel turned toward Hill and shrugged his shoulders. His pilots had launched a quarter hour earlier—they and their Hunters were late. Jennings slumped down in the chair and slept again.

USS *Enterprise*

Mark Caine strained against the tug of four longitudinal Gs as Aardvark 101 decelerated. Stopped in the arresting gear, he pulled up on the emergency wing-sweep handle just inboard of the throttle grips, and manually swept the Tomcat's wings aft. Greg Bright signaled a thumbs-up from the rear cockpit. A first-class Aardvark petty officer stood less than ten yards away—near the landing zone foul line. He returned the thumbs-up, then turned his back to the jet and the thunderous noise of its engines.

The petty officer screamed into a portable headset radio attached to his protective headgear. One deck below, in the maintenance control spaces of VF-141, a senior-chief petty officer copied the transmission.

"One-zero-one, on deck, up and up." Neither Caine nor Bright had discovered any major maintenance discrepancies while flying the airplane. It would taxi clear of the landing area, be refueled and readied to fly again.

Caine had added the usual amount of power to Aardvark 101. But instead of rolling out of the arresting gear as he expected, the jet's twin nose tires were cocked 90 degrees right—in a direction opposite to its usual parking spot aft of the island—and were wedged against the number-four wire. The pilot knew his aircraft was fouling the landing area, and that until the fighter was clear of the wires, no other aircraft could land. Others would be waved off by the LSOs as he had been.

"One-oh-one, get outta there! I got airplanes trying to land."

Caine recognized the voice of the air boss over the radio. The voice was loud and impatient. It always sounded that way. Caine added more power—too much power—to his jet. The Tomcat's twin Pratt and Whitney engines responded, lifting the nose tires up and over the arresting gear cable, and pushing the aircraft forward. When the nose tires touched down again, they remained cocked to the right. They bit into the flight deck nonskid covering and drove the fighter toward the petty officer wearing the headset radio. When the sailor turned, the cranial helmet and radio were immediately pulled from his head by the suction from Aardvark 101's starboard engine intake. Mark Caine had already chopped the throttles to idle, but the two turbo-fan engines spooled down slowly. The right engine spit sparks across the flight deck as its turbine section digested the metal and leather headpiece.

Caine thumbed at the nose-wheel steering control button on his stick and pounded at the rudder pedal brakes. Neither would respond to his inputs. The petty officer grabbed at the lower lip of the intake and pushed himself away from the churning jet. The black nonskid under his feet was slick with grease and sea spray, and his worn boots lost their grip. He fell to the deck as Aardvark 101 continued in a right turn. The 56,000-pound Tomcat failed to slow even as the fighter's starboard tire rolled across the enlisted man's legs at the ankles.

Dirk Buzzell jumped from the LSO platform, running up the angled deck against a thirty-knot headwind. At the time, running toward the crippled jet seemed like the right thing to do. Mark Caine—one of his roommates—was in the front seat of Aardvark 101. Caine's RIO, Greg Bright, was the best friend Buzzell had on this boat, or anywhere else for that matter. Buzzell could do nothing more than Caine or Bright could do to slow or stop the F-14. There was nothing anyone could do. Buzzell kept running. Kurt Hansen and Phil Grokulsky didn't move from their places on the platform. They didn't seem able to.

If anything, the Tomcat had gained momentum as it turned away from the *Enterprise* island and bounced toward the ship's port deck-edge. Buzzell could see the fighter's tailhook drop to the deck—a signal to flight deck personnel that Aardvark 101 had lost its brakes. Caine worked frantically to control the jet—he had panicked. Even with the engines at idle, the Tomcat rolled faster than a man could run. Through his cockpit windscreen, Caine no longer saw the black of the flight deck. Instead, he focused on the flimsy deck-edge catwalk and railing that rimmed it. Just beyond the railing, and sixty feet below flight deck level, occasional swells rose in the gray South China Sea.

"Boss, 101's got no brakes!" Greg Bright made the obvious radio call from the backseat. If there was a response from the air boss in the tower above and behind them, neither the pilot nor the RIO heard it.

Dirk Buzzell watched the Tomcat's long Plexiglas canopy shell rise in slow motion and twist above the aircraft in front of him—an ejection sequence in the F-14 always began in such a way.

Aardvark 101's nose gear tires bounced over the raised deck-edge scupper then down into the catwalk. Its nose dropped onto the catwalk railing, and the Tomcat's long radome snapped in half—revealing beneath it a surprisingly delicate radar assembly.

The RIO's ejection seat left the aircraft four-tenths of a second before Mark Caine's did, and less than a second before Aardvark 101 had broken entirely through the catwalk. Red and yellow flames propelled the two seats away from the Tomcat as it slid nosedown into the swells. Greg Bright swung once beneath his orange-and-white parachute canopy then fell into the waters abeam the LSO platform. Caine left the cockpit exactly parallel to the flight deck—just before the fighter splashed into the sea. The pilot remained strapped into the ejection seat as it skipped twice across the top of the swells. His parachute did not deploy.

Sultan of Oman Air Force Base
Thumrait, Oman

"They've arrived, Mr. Hill." The RAF lieutenant colonel turned to the envoy, exposing a severely gapped-tooth grin. Terrance Hill stepped forward, squinting against the sun. He looked high above the approach-end of Thumrait's main north–south runway. The sky was white with haze and blowing sand. He saw no Hawker Hunters.

"I don't see them, Colonel. How do you know they've arrived?" he asked.

"Do you see the cloud of dust off the approach end? I'm guessing about three miles." The envoy followed the officer's outstretched finger, but still found nothing—only a few rocks and scrub oak on the horizon.

"They're very low, Mr. Hill."

Terrance Hill watched as the few rocks grew into aircraft. He could not hear them, though it seemed to him they were close enough to be heard. Four Hunters flew a fingertip formation at just under 500 knots of airspeed. A Hunter leading the flight hugged the runway at an altitude far too low for formation flying. Two other jets slid back in an echelon to the left of the lead. The fourth aircraft was tucked into the right. Their wings overlapped as they flew.

"My God, Colonel. Isn't it rather dangerous to fly at such an altitude?" Hill turned to share the moment with his secretary. Malcolm Jennings remained slumped in the chair. He was snoring.

"Best you duck down a bit, Mr. Hill. My boys have begun their turn toward us. I would estimate the lead's altitude is less than twenty feet above ground level. Still just a tad high."

"*High?*" Hill was stunned. The four Hawker Hunters pivoted together in a right-hand bank. The British envoy squinted again against the momentary glint of sunlight off their canopies. He knew little of the details of flying, but had seen more than his share of air demonstrations. Such demonstrations were popular fare among the diplomatic corps. But he had never witnessed four aircraft in a formation as tight as the Hunters. And he'd never seen jet aircraft fly this low.

The Hunters hugged the dusty earth as they approached the lieutenant colonel and his guests. Only after they passed above the wide tarmac did the Hunters finally ascend. The four jets cleared the angled hangar top by what Hill estimated as only a few inches.

Malcolm Jennings dropped out of his chair and onto the sun-bleached asphalt as the blurs hurtled overhead. Terrance Hill and the RAF officer laughed out loud. Jennings looked up from the asphalt, shocked and embarrassed.

"Low-level flight is our stock in trade, sir. The Hunter is eminently qualified in such environs." The lieutenant colonel did nothing to curtail his pride.

"In fact, if I may be allowed to boast, sir . . . these pilots, and a dozen more like them under my command, are second to no air force in the world in a low-level ingress. I am convinced beyond any doubt that the aviator who is capable of navigating his weapons platform at treetop level will not only survive a conflict, but will enjoy the greatest degree of success in delivering his bombs on target. As you have witnessed, the enemy will be licking his wounds before he realizes we've dropped in for tea. Additionally, sir, the aircraft's air-to-ground ordnance payload is considerable. The Hunter is an absolute joy to fly."

The RAF officer again peered across the tarmac as the division of Hawker Hunters made a second low approach. Then, in order, the aircraft pitched nose high and away from the hangar. The jets decelerated as they climbed. Terrance Hill and his secretary heard the four Rolls-Royce turbojets wind down. When the four fighter-bombers had slowed to a position abeam their intended point of landing, their tricycle landing gear was lowered. Each, in turn, then swooped down at the runway.

"But in answer to your earlier question . . . yes, Mr. Hill. The Number 6 is qualified in the air-to-air arena as well—against F-4s and even the F-14, though our training to date has emphasized the utility of the Hawker Hunter in its ground-attack role." The officer paused, folding his hands carefully behind his back. "The Iranian Revolutionary Guard operates Phantoms and Tomcats, sir. May I deduce that your visit here today has something to do with the Iranians?"

"Yes, you may, Colonel. Unfortunately, London has not yet shared the details with me."

Hill watched the fourth Hunter flare to land and roll down the long runway. The first Omani jet had already turned off a taxiway parallel to the runway and maneuvered onto the tarmac. An RAF enlisted man directed the jet to its parking spot. Again, the envoy's secretary plugged his ears against the sound.

"But it is quite possible that you and your pilots will be tasked with countering a strike from Iran against the Sultanate here in Oman, Colonel

Thomas. We have reason to believe their targets will fall above 26 degrees latitude, north of Khor Fakkan . . . up the peninsula to Didamar into the Strait of Hormuz."

"Of course. It follows, Mr. Hill. The Omani 727 destroyed by the Revolutionary Guards could be a prelude to such a strike."

"The London office is apparently convinced of it, Colonel. They believe we will see more of such terrorism. But again, I am not yet privy to their reasoning. Personally, I cannot imagine why the Revolutionary Guard would provoke the Sultanate here, with Iran's forces already stretched so thinly against their numerous enemies. And why Oman's northern territories? I understand it's a desolate place . . . barely inhabited.

"Still, Colonel," Terrance Hill continued, "the bombing of that airliner was incredibly heinous. My blood boils each time I think of it. Although I must admit to a personal reason for those feelings." The envoy patted his backside, feeling at the bandages beneath his wool trousers while Thomas responded.

"The Iranians are raving madmen, sir. Trust me when I say I have studied their methods. The Guard is especially worrisome. Their missions are absolutely reprehensible, and are carried out with utmost zeal. And what's worse, they act without fear of consequences, and without fear of death. Dying in battle is, in fact, a great honor to the IRG—the ultimate sacrifice to their God. They are a difficult enemy, and they fly well."

Lieutenant Colonel Thomas looked away from the envoy, cursing under his breath.

"I apologize, Mr. Hill. It was not my intention to make a speech." Thomas searched for a way to quickly change the subject. "I understand the Yanks recently lost a fighter to the IRG."

"That is a fact, Colonel. And I am certain the Americans are sympathetic to our position. Unfortunately, it seems we cannot expect assistance from the United States."

"None is required, Mr. Hill. The Number 6 awaits its orders."

DAY SIX

JANUARY 10

Bandar 'Abbās, Iran
0625 (local time)

Ali Abdul Rajani had been awake for most of the night. He stared up at the ceiling fan twisting above his bed. The linen beneath him was soaked with sweat. It was already sticky-hot inside the room. He cursed loudly in the direction of the fan. The government officials who had provided him with the two-room apartment had also promised him an air conditioner.

"Such an apartment would normally accommodate fourteen or fifteen persons," one of the officials had told him only the day before. "You are fortunate to reside in these spacious rooms alone. But you are the *ace*—you are like the heroes we study in the Koran . . . some of the people say you *are* a prophet . . . like Muhammad. And the people willingly sacrifice for such a man as you. Please look," the official had said as he switched on the ceiling fan. "This apartment has electricity!" The official bored Rajani, though the ace allowed him to continue. The pilot surveyed the two rooms—he had never before lived so luxuriously.

"But the air-conditioning machines are another matter . . . and very rare here. I have been instructed to provide you with such a machine at the very instant one of them becomes available," the man had said.

Ali Rajani cursed again, then rolled off the sheets. He walked from the bed to the door of the apartment. The door was small. He pushed it open quickly, and it slammed loudly against its stops. It was early morning, and still more dark than light outside the room. But Iranians already filled the dusty street on the other side of the door—most of them were women. They were dressed in traditional Muslim attire, covered head-to-foot in robes of white and off-white. Most of the women carried clay and porcelain jugs filled with water. There was a well near Rajani's apartment.

Rajani stood naked in the doorway. He did not seem concerned by that fact. He concentrated instead on something else the official had said to him one day earlier—the man had stated that there would be no flying for the IRG today. Instead, there would be meetings in the Iranian Revolutionary Guard hangar.

"I am told the gathering will be ordinary and of no consequence. I am certain that the discussions there will not interest you. You are not expected to attend these meetings," the official had stated firmly—but without making the statement appear as a direct order. But it *had* been an order, and Ali Abdul Rajani was suddenly enraged by it.

A woman, her face concealed by layers of white, did not notice the naked figure standing motionless only a few feet away. She walked slowly and steadily. The pot she balanced on her shoulder was filled with water from the well. Rajani grabbed her roughly as she passed. He pulled her from beneath the pot, which shattered as it fell to the street. She squeaked a tiny scream as he dragged her through the door and threw her onto the bed.

"Do you know who I am?" he said very calmly over her. The woman, who was more of a girl, said nothing. She held the linen veil across her face from where it had loosened from the robe. "I am Ali. I am the ace. Are you one of those who think I am like Muhammad?" Again, the girl did not answer. But she allowed Ali Abdul Rajani to rape her repeatedly on the bed inside the spacious apartment.

USS *Enterprise*
Stateroom 03-93-2L
0645

"You know, there's only one thing worse than livin' on a Navy carrier at sea," Mark "Coke" Caine said while he sat at his tiny desk in the cramped stateroom. He massaged his fractured left forefinger through the splint on his hand. In the top rack, Dirk Buzzell was awake. Spanky Pfister snored in the narrow bottom rack.

"I can't imagine *anything* being worse than this," Buzzell stated.

"What's worse is livin' on this carrier and not being able to fly off of it."

You're right, Coke, Buzzell thought. It would serve no purpose to announce that fact aloud. Caine didn't need to hear him say it. So he lay there, hoping Mark Caine would change the subject, or wouldn't say anything at all.

There would be no flying for Caine or Buzzell or anyone else on the USS *Enterprise* on this day. Officially, they'd been told, this no-fly day had been scheduled for weeks—just another of the many no-fly days scheduled every month aboard the nuclear-powered aircraft carrier. Money was always the real reason behind no-fly days. It was incredibly expensive to operate an air wing at sea. And it seemed there would always be budget constraints.

The United States Navy preferred to label such days as "safety stand-downs." During this stand-down—like every other one—squadron aircrew would dedicate the day to studying aircraft emergency procedures—specifically, those procedures associated with operating jet aircraft on and off the ship. Studying took the form of day-long all-officer meetings. The subject of the marathon AOMs was always the same—safety. Dirk Buzzell detested no-fly days, regardless of what the Navy labeled them.

But safety stand-downs rarely followed a port call by only two days as this one would. Buzzell knew that fact and so did Caine. Both of them also knew that the stand-downs always followed the day an airplane was lost at sea. Mark Caine had been sitting in the front cockpit of a VF-141 F-14 the day before—just before that airplane had gone over the side and into the water. And Caine felt completely responsible—for the loss of the Tomcat, for the injury to the flight-deck petty officer, and therefore for the no-fly day itself. He continued to feel responsible, even after Dirk Buzzell, his roommate and friend, had spent most of the night before trying to convince him he wasn't. But now, before the AOM and the long no-fly day, Buzzell didn't want to talk to Caine about the accident or tell him again that it wasn't his fault. He only wanted a few more minutes of sleep.

"So, Buzz. Aren't you going to thank me for your day off?" Caine mumbled from his desk.

Dirk Buzzell had never been more thrilled to hear a phone ring. The sound interrupted his attempt to sleep, but it also interrupted Caine, who stood up and walked toward the telephone. The call was short, and Mark Caine did more listening than talking. He hung up the phone, then sat again at his desk. Buzzell had climbed down from his top bunk and was rinsing his face.

"They want to see me down in CAG's office, Buzz . . . in five minutes," Caine said wearily.

"Who wants to see you?" Buzzell asked.

"They've set up a mishap board for my accident already . . . the people on the board want to see me. I knew this would happen. They're gonna fry my ass, Buzz." Dirk Buzzell had turned toward Caine. Drops of water fell from his face into the sink. "And they want to see *you* at eight o'clock," Caine said as he opened the stateroom door and walked out.

Jetty One
Abu Dhabi, The United Arab Emirates
0750 (local time)

Sahil Al Damh stood patiently at the edge of the stone jetty. He held loosely to one of its rotted pilings, glancing over his shoulder, down the pier toward the Abu Dhabi waterfront. He checked the all-gold Rolex watch shining around his fat wrist. His transportation, as usual, was late. He crouched down and opened an eelskin attaché case. He unclipped the Rolex and replaced it with a cheaper, waterproof diving watch. His skill as a harbormaster earned him a very good living, but he did not want to risk exposing the Rolex to salt water. There was plenty of salt already in the air.

He tucked the gold wristwatch into the attaché, then checked the other contents of the case. Satisfied that his equipment and charts were there, he closed the eelskin and searched again for his transportation. A dinghy rose and fell through the swells several hundred meters off the jetty. It was pointed directly at him. Somewhere beyond the dinghy would be an oiler. The oiler would be anchored in deeper waters and filled with millions of barrels of rich Persian Gulf crude. According to his paperwork, this oiler was bound for Barcelona, Spain. It was of Liberian registry and had left the oil terminals in Kuwait one day earlier, on the ninth of January.

The ship would be long and deep—like most oil tankers—and difficult to navigate through the shallows of the Strait of Hormuz as its waters flowed eastward toward the Gulf of Oman. No oiler captain could risk Silkworm missile attacks by driving through the depths of the strait between Oman and Iran, and no oiler captain could risk running aground in the shallows hugging Oman's treacherous shoreline. In this region, a good harbormaster was well worth his fee.

Damh was very familiar with the waters that shaped the strait. He knew its channels and narrows and tides. He had been harbormaster at Didamar for eight years. But the threat of Iranian surface-to-surface missile attacks had pushed the oilers even farther south as they passed through the Strait of Hormuz. It had become necessary to guide the heavy oil tankers the entire distance around the Omani peninsula from west to east—not only through the hazardous waterways protecting Didamar itself. Silkworm missiles were bad for the oil business, but good for the business of harbormastering.

Damh would board the dinghy and then its mother ship. He would direct this tanker as he had other tankers a countless number of times. Afterwards, the same dinghy would then deliver him to Khor Fakkan on Oman's eastern shore. All told, he would ride the ship for approximately eleven hours during its seventy-three nautical-mile transit around the peninsula—some ships traveled more slowly than others. By early that evening, Damh would be 4,500 U.S. dollars richer.

The dinghy was larger than most he had ridden. It bounced lightly off the jetty as he stepped aboard. There were three other men in the boat. The man at its controls nodded politely at him, then turned the boat away from Abu Dhabi.

"My name is Sahil. What is the name of your ship?" Sahil Al Damh spoke English. That fact alone made him unique in the region, and even more desirable as a harbormaster. Most oiler captains and crews also spoke English.

"She is the *Majorca Azul*," one of the men answered. "This is her first journey to the Gulf."

Ready Room Six
1435

Even if there had been no safety stand-down—even if the *Enterprise* Strike Operations department had published a flight schedule—Dirk Buzzell would not have flown. He was a witness to a flight-deck mishap. The mishap boards had convened, and the officers on those boards were interviewing witnesses. Buzzell took little consolation in the fact that, because of the stand-down, none of his squadron-mates would fly either. When he walked into the ready room through the starboard passageway door, the Aardvark XO was walking out.

"How's it going, Buzz? Haven't seen much of you today."

Buzzell glanced at his watch for the first time since early that morning. He had been reluctant to do so during the long interviews. He'd spent most of the last four hours in the same uncomfortable chair, talking to people who outranked him. With them, he thought it might have been imprudent to check the time. It was best to act cordial, and cooperative, he figured.

"I've been sitting through a bunch of interviews, XO. They've put together three boards already. One for the accident itself, one for the legal stuff and the petty officer who was hurt, and one for Coke. They wanted to know everything I saw . . . every little thing. I guess I'm one of the only guys who saw it all. I told them as much as I could remember, and they kept taking notes. I hope I'm wrong, XO, but I get the feeling they're looking for someone to hang."

The executive officer nodded his head—it was a "no comment" kind of nod—then continued out the door. Greg Bright had walked from his chair in the middle of the ready room, and was staring at Buzzell. The backseater had an unusually large wad of snuff tucked under his lower lip.

"So . . . Notso. The board asked me a lot of questions about you this morning. I told them you're a great RIO. I lied through my teeth." Buzzell smiled. It felt good to be back in the ready room.

"Well, at least they *talked* to *you*. I've been sittin'

on my ass in here all day. And they haven't even asked to see me yet. You'd think the board would want to hear from the backseater who punched out of that goddamned airplane. Coke talked to the board for less than twenty minutes! They said they'd give us a call if they wanted any more details," Bright said angrily. "Why the hell were you in there so long?"

"Who knows? Maybe they hate LSOs. Maybe they're trying to find somebody to blame."

"Who are they blaming?" Bright's eyes were peering into Buzzell's.

"Well, they're not trying to blame you, Notso. You don't have a stick or throttles in the backseat."

"For Christ's sake, Buzz." Greg Bright paused. He didn't want anyone in the ready room to hear him yell. "The jet had no fuckin' brakes or nose-wheel steering. What was Coke supposed to do? If they try to pin this on him—" Greg Bright spit into a Styrofoam coffee cup. "Those guys are ass-holes," he said.

"You're preaching to the choir, Notso. I told the board that you two did everything you could. It was an accident. Your airplane broke. It's that simple. And I think it'll be okay." Buzzell scanned the ready room chairs, looking for Mark Caine. "How's Coke doing, anyway?"

"He's been moping around all day long. Go talk to him, Buzz. And tell him to relax. Maybe he'll listen to you." Bright motioned to the far side of the spaces. Caine was standing near the other end of Ready Six. The Aardvark CO was lecturing the junior officer.

"Excuse me, Mr. Buzzell. Look what I got in the mail from my folks today . . . our old high school paper." Yeoman Jordan Michaels looked up from his chair in front of the Ops department word processor in one corner of the ready room. He was holding a tattered copy of *The Cottonwood Colt*. The yeoman seemed even younger than most twenty-year-olds. He had a round and pimpled face. "Mom and Dad have sent me one every month since I graduated." He grinned. Buzzell and Michaels had both attended Cottonwood High School in Salt Lake City. The officer had graduated seven years before the enlisted man. The two enjoyed talking about the coincidence.

"Yeah. I've got a lot of family out there, too," Buzzell said.

The officer walked into the tiny cubicle at the far corner of the ready room, taking the paper from the yeoman.

"This paper looks a lot different. I worked on this thing when I was a senior there . . . when it was only four pages. We didn't have photographs back then," he remembered out loud. "Kind of makes you miss the good ole days, huh, Michaels?"

"Uh, yessir," Michaels said shyly, pausing while he shuffled in place. The enlisted man stared at the officer sitting in his chair, then looked away, down toward the white tile floor.

"Sir, I'd like to get off the ship and go home," the yeoman said. Buzzell looked up from the paper and laughed.

"Me too, Michaels. Me too."

"No, *really*, sir. I don't think I belong in the Navy . . . I don't want to be on this ship anymore. We never have any liberty and I don't want to go to that Iran place. I don't even know where it is." The young sailor wiped at his eyes as if to brush away the beginnings of a tear. "Would you talk to the CO for me?"

Buzzell folded the newspaper, stood out of the chair, and reseated himself on a stack of cardboard boxes behind the enlisted man's chair.

"Have a seat, Michaels. Let's chat."

Iranian Revolutionary Guard Aerodrome
Bandar 'Abbās, Iran
1450 (local time)

Ali Abdul Rajani didn't park his red convertible in its usual spot beside the IRG hangar. There were rows of military vehicles already there. He switched off the Cadillac's ignition, and climbed out. He had no intention of "not attending" the meeting inside the hangar. He walked past the row of vehicles, then stopped beside a drab-colored VIP sedan parked in what was *his* usual space. He spit onto the steering wheel, then watched the spittle drop from the wheel onto the floorboard.

He rounded the corner of the hangar and stepped quickly toward the long stairway leading to the second level of the structure, and to the Iranian Revolutionary Guard ready room there. He stopped abruptly when he heard the sound of jet engines. Rajani jumped from the foot of the stairs and ran toward the sound. On the other side of the hangar, the side nearest the runway at Bandar 'Abbās, he saw them.

Two F-4 Phantoms were preparing to taxi. Omid was sitting in the front cockpit of one of them—Rajani recognized his face behind the dark visor.

"*No flying today?*" he screamed above the engines and toward Omid. No one heard the ace yell. "You are all *filthy liars!*" He turned and ran to the stairway, climbing it four steps at a time.

He burst into the ready room, and again, smoke

wafted out of the door behind him. The officers sitting there turned quickly in their chairs—very few of the men were IRG aviators. Rajani recognized only one or two of the forty-odd faces in the room. One of the men—the one standing in front of the chairs—seemed to recognize him instead.

"Will you please take a seat, Ali?" the man said.

"*I was lied to!*" the ace screamed as he scanned the faces. "*By that PIG!*" He was pointing at the same official who had promised him the air-conditioning.

"You were lied to by *my* order," the man in front said. "I was given that order by Ahmed himself. My name is Reza. Please sit, Ali, and keep your tongue."

Ali knew of Reza, though he had never before seen the man. Even before the Ayatollah had died, when Ahmed, the Imam's son, had emerged as Iran's new military leader, he had heard Reza's name. Reza was Ahmed's henchman. If Ahmed was the guiding force behind the reemergence of the Iranian military structure, then Reza was the number-two man in that structure. Some said that Reza was politically motivated alone, and that he had in fact been responsible for the original decision to stand down the forces of the Iranian Revolutionary Guard. But it didn't matter. Reza was not a fighter pilot—and that was all that mattered to Ali Abdul Rajani. The ace would listen to this man, but he had already made up his mind to disbelieve what was said.

When Ali was finally seated, Reza continued at the front of the ready room. While he spoke, he walked between charts and models on the walls and on long tables in the room.

"Bandar 'Abbās will be *absolutely* pivotal to our mission," Reza started. "Our push to the south will emanate from here. It has, in fact, already begun—with surgical IRG operations in the Strait of Hormuz and across the strait into Oman."

Rajani listened as Reza recounted three recent IRG missions. He reiterated the circumstances by which an Omani cargo dhow had been successfully and precisely attacked, then gave credit for the attack to a tall man standing near the back of the ready room. The man wore a white-rimmed beret. The man was a Boghammer captain. There were other Boghammer captains in the room. There were Guard officers from every IRG community—from PTG patrol craft and the larger SAAM frigates, from select surface-to-air missile battery installations and Silkworm sites, militias, and even airborne patrol squadrons—they were all there.

A man named Kalil was asked to stand next. Reza described Kalil as a brave Guard operative who planted a plastic-explosives bomb aboard an Omani 727 airliner.

A third Iranian stood. He was balding, and what hair remained on his head was very white. He wore thick, black-framed eyeglasses. Reza said the man was an air-intercept controller from a radar site on the island of Qeshm. He was the man who had controlled Ali against the *Carl Vinson* F-14 Tomcats.

"But of course," Reza continued, "there is much credit to be given to our ace for that particular IRG success as well. Won't you stand, Ali?"

Ali did not stand. And he would not be won over by an ingratiating politician—even one as highly placed as Reza.

"If I am your ace, then why was I lied to?" Ali screamed, finally standing. "Why was I not expected to attend these proceedings? And please in-form me . . . why is *Omid* flying a Guard airplane at this precise moment and not your ace?''

''I expected such an outburst from you,'' Reza stated calmly. ''That was reason enough to exclude you from these discussions. You are difficult, Ali, and your love and loyalties to Allah are questionable. I know you.'' Reza was staring back at the ace. ''Your interests here are selfish. But you are a gifted pilot, and your talents are critical to the overall success of our mission. It is true that Omid is flying today. He and his RIO, and another crew, will fly two Phantoms to test a critical phase of Ahmed's plan. You do not fly the F-4 Phantom, do you, Ali?''

''No. I fly only the Tomcat.''

''Precisely. That is why you are not flying now, Ali. There was no requirement for a Tomcat today. You must trust me when I say that you will be flying again very soon.''

The *Majorca Azul*
1515 (local time)

Sahil Al Damh was impressed with the ship and her crew. He had his own chair and sextant table on the bridge. The table was enclosed by a myriad of sophisticated engine monitoring, sonar and navigation equipment. There was even a small CRT display labeled AIR SEARCH. Large oilers were sometimes tended to by helicopters. The *Majorca Azul* came complete with a helo pad. Damh guessed that the helos could be monitored on the air search display. He sat in awe of the precision satellite nav and communication gear in front of him. It seemed somehow criminal that a ship this complex required an old harbormaster to weave its way around Didamar.

The bridge was large—nearly thirty feet across and protected by high Plexiglas windows. The ship's captain had been on the bridge when Damh arrived. Both had remained there all day. Together, the two men continuously pored over the harbormaster's charts and notes, cross-checking them against the numbers flashing over the satellite nav panel on the *Majorca Azul*. Only three other merchant marines worked on the bridge. The men steered the ship, made endless notes on large white documents, and monitored the equipment. There had been very little conversation.

When Damh made a recommendation for a course change, the captain would check and recheck the charts. To Damh, the man appeared unnecessarily cautious.

"I haven't lost a ship yet, Raul." The harbormaster's comment brought an encouraging grin to Captain Raul Lizalde's face.

"I know you haven't. I checked on that before I asked for you, Señor Damh. But this is the *Majorca*'s first transit to and from the oil terminals, and only my second month as her captain. She's a beautiful ship. I'd like to keep her in one piece."

Through the tall Plexiglas on the bridge, Damh could finally make out the rocky outcroppings of Didamar. He estimated the tanker's position at four nautical miles southwest of the turn point. At six knots of speed, the turn point would come in about forty-five minutes, he calculated. The satellite system reported the distance at 3.79 miles and 44 minutes to the Didamar steer-point.

"Señor Damh," Lizalde began, scratching his big bald head. "Instead of going all the way around the top of Oman, I would prefer to turn the *Majorca* inside the anchorage slightly south of Didamar—between the island and the Omani mainland. That would save us a little time and lessen our exposure to, well . . . you understand, señor . . . any potential threats.'' The air-conditioning on the bridge was more than adequate. Still, sweat beaded on the captain's forehead. Sahil Al Damh reviewed his chart again. It was a cursory review. He had long ago memorized every coordinate on it.

''I would not recommend it, Raul. Given the tides, the rocks, and the draft of this ship . . . I would not recommend it at all. You're more likely to split your oiler wide open than you are to be found by a Silkworm. The currents also bring sand into the underwater valleys beside the rocks. Sand bars are not uncommon there. The time you would save is negligible. If you elect to cut short the turn around Didamar, I would insist on a log entry stating that I advised against it.''

''Very well.'' Captain Lizalde wiped his brow with an already-soaked handkerchief. ''You are correct, of course, Señor Damh. And after all, there have been no attacks for several weeks. And we are effectively out of their missile range, yes? Our odds are better if I accept your recommendations. We will remain on this course until the steer-point.'' The helmsman glanced over his shoulder at the captain and nodded.

1555

Dhows and smaller container ships were maneuvering in and around the anchorage at Didamar. On the bridge of the *Majorca Azul*, the helmsman studied the steering cursor on the digital display above his wheel. When it was centered, he turned the wheel. The anchorage moved to his three o'clock position at two miles. The oiler would turn slowly clockwise around Didamar until it was headed southeast toward the Gulf of Oman. The *Majorca Azul* was, by far, the largest vessel Sahil Al Damh had mastered through the Strait of Hormuz. Captain Lizalde mopped at his brow while Damh stared out the large windows to the north.

"Visibility is good, Captain—nearly twenty miles now. I am certain that is Hengām Island coming to the port beam."

Raul Lizalde said nothing. He stood directly behind the helmsman.

"We're nearly clear of the strait," the Captain said finally. "Give me eight knots."

Damh found a small speck just above the horizon through one of the bridge windows. The speck was paralleling the course of the *Majorca Azul* on a southeasterly heading, and trailing exhaust behind it. He walked to the CRT air search display, but found nothing on its screen.

"What is the range of your radar, Captain? I'm surprised it does not see the airplane off to port." Raul Lizalde stepped quickly to the bridge Plexiglas and found the speck. It had turned south and descended. As it turned, the single speck grew into two jet aircraft.

"Jesus Christe, no!" The captain's language had reverted to Spanish. "*Por favor, no!*"

The island and bridge of the *Majorca Azul* were situated to the stern of the ship. Through the windows directly in front of the helmsman, 1,400 feet beyond the bow, the two specks were driving toward the oiler. They grew larger as they approached and descended together. The two separated slightly, increased quickly in size, then flew down both sides of the tanker at bridge level. Damh did not recognize the aircraft type.

"Phantom jets," Raul Lizalde said in a terrified whisper. He ran across the bridge to its rear, tracking the two jets. "Helmsman, come port *hard!* Reverse your course. Do it *now!*"

"What? Why, Raul? Who are they?" Sahil Al Damh had seen aircraft overfly tankers before. It was not an uncommon sight. "Why are you reversing course? I *demand* a log entry. I will not be responsible for—"

"No chances, señor. I will take no chances. They are Iranian Phantoms. We will run toward the Gulf."

The big ship had turned less than 15 degrees when the two F-4 Phantoms had already circled the ship and descended for the second time. On their second approach, the pair were much higher—at least 5,000 feet higher—and in a steeper dive. Again, the Phantoms approached from above the bow of the *Majorca Azul*. The jet aircraft had also changed their flight formation. They trailed each other by a little less than one mile.

The lead F-4 flew directly at the bridge. It pulled up as it crossed the ship's bow. The second jet was higher, and seemed steeper still and faster than its lead. And it pulled up earlier, when it was still a half mile in front of the tanker. Captain Raul Lizalde watched its belly side disappear above and behind him. He felt, then heard, a thudding explosion. Just aft of the bow and just in front of the forward-most oil-holding tanks, flames and debris blew up and away from the *Majorca Azul*. The crude in its hold began burning instantly.

Sahil Al Damh fell forward as the blast lifted the

bridge, then rocked it back and forth. A fire alarm began wailing, and the forward third of the tanker disappeared in black smoke. There was a second explosion, and then three more—the final of which pushed the oiler sideways through the water just north of Didamar. The *Majorca Azul* stopped sliding, then began a slow list to starboard. It was too much of a list for the helmsman. He lost control of the wheel and fell against the Plexiglas windows on the right side of the bridge. The Plexiglas bounced the man back onto the ship's moving deck. As he pushed himself up to his knees, another explosion blasted out the windows behind the navigation equipment. The air-search radar display monitor was loosened by the blast and became airborne as the stern of the ship came down for the third time. The monitor tumbled queerly off the edge of the navigation table, then spun into the helmsman, embedding one of its metal corners into his skull just above the left ear.

Omid and his RIO were flying the lead Iranian Revolutionary Guard F-4. They had released their entire ordnance load of four 500-pound bombs. Only a single heat-seeking Matra Magic missile remained on the port outboard weapons rail. Omid's wingman had also emptied his bomb racks, but carried no missile. He was ordered to return to Bandar 'Abbās.

Omid stared down at the *Majorca Azul* as he flew his Phantom over her. The ship's bow was ablaze and billowed towers of dark smoke. Her stern had taken two direct hits, and a chunk of it had separated from the tanker altogether. The bridge was intact but settling toward the water as the stern slid into the strait. Omid selected the Magic, then pointed the Phantom's nose toward the burning hulk. The missile seeker-head growled to life in his headset. There were plenty of hot infrared sources emitting from the ship.

"Ali Rajani will not receive credit for *this* kill," Omid said to his radar intercept officer.

Captain Raul Lizalde had managed to strap himself into one of the tall bridge chairs. He sat there, coughing weakly as acrid fumes poured through the broken windows. Underneath his chair, wrapped awkwardly around its base, was Sahil Al Damh. Shards of Plexiglas erupted from the right side of his body and face. He was still bleeding, but Lizalde had not bothered to verify his vital signs. The contents of Damh's eelskin attaché, including the gold Rolex, were scattered about him. The two surviving merchant marines had left the bridge. Lizalde assumed they were among the other crew members in four life rafts floating beside a burning oil slick off the *Majorca Azul*'s starboard beam.

Lizalde had made no order to abandon ship. The thought had not occurred to him. Instead, he said nothing. He sat motionless in the chair. Raul Lizalde would not leave the bridge. He stared blankly through the windows and found a single F-4 Phantom diving again for his tanker. The black pillars of burning crude blew out momentarily, and the captain saw clearly a plume of white-gray smoke erupt from beneath the Phantom.

The smoke jerked right, then left, from about two miles. The Magic's heat-sensitive seeker saw the intense IR signature of the tanker's engine exhaust stack and occasionally even greater heat from the flames that burned on its bow. The Magic guided quickly to the *Majorca Azul*. Lizalde stared contentedly at the missile as it homed on the stack behind the bridge. He folded his hands on his lap as it flew.

Just before its impact with his ship, the missile was distracted by a tube of yellow-hot flame that grew suddenly from the superstructure just forward of the bridge. The missile began guiding for it.

But the Magic was already too fast and too close to the stack to negotiate a full turn forward to the hotter flames. The Magic's wing canards shifted—pulling it away from the exhaust stack. The missile hit the Plexiglas window just above Lizalde's chair on the bridge. The logic in the Magic's contact fuse was satisfied, and its warhead detonated violently. It was the last thing Captain Raul Lizalde saw.

USS *Enterprise*
Ready Room Six
1845

The first reel of *Call Girl Vampires* had broken for the fourth time in ten minutes. The ready room overhead lights blinked on while the squadron duty officer, Lieutenant Matt Hildebrand, scrambled to the projector. Occasionally, large wadded paper balls were directed at the SDO from the ready room chairs. Hildebrand, by virtue of his being the duty officer, was blamed for the delay. He worked to repair the 16-millimeter film while dodging the paper "stones."

The nightly "roll-em" was more than a tradition among the Aardvarks of VF-141—it was sacred. Every officer, unless he was airborne, was expected to remain in his seat throughout the roll-em. The ready room doors were locked during the movie. No business could be conducted. Two fluorescent signs hung outside the doors in both aft passageways. The signs read FIGHTER BRIEF IN PROGRESS. There was even a seven-page squadron *Military Instruction* detailing the outrageous decorum of Aardvark officers during a roll-em. The document, VF-141 notice #6969.4BJ, was very specific. The officers yelled, booed, or stomped their feet against the ready room floor in response to scenes in a movie, in accordance with the instruction. Aardvark roll-ems had become infamous aboard the USS *Enterprise*.

Dirk Buzzell slid down into his chair, taking the opportunity to sleep. Already, he had forgotten why he was tired—he'd forgotten about the long hours with the mishap boards. He had more trouble forgetting his long conversation with Jordan Michaels. The young yeoman had been unreasonable, almost desperate. The enlisted man had told Buzzell that he would do anything to get off the ship and back home to Utah. And the officer had promised to help, if he could.

Buzzell opened his eyes. Greg Bright sat next to him. Bright had stuffed his lip with more Skoal and was searching the floor for an empty Coke can to spit into. Neither of them noticed that the forward ready room door had been unlocked and was open.

"*Attention on deck!*" Both Buzzell and Bright were on their feet at the sound of the CO's voice.

Rear Admiral Jeremiah Curtiss stepped into the room, then turned and shook the Aardvark skipper's hand. Curtiss scanned the officers still standing in Ready Six. Dirk Buzzell moved slightly to hide his face behind the officer standing one row in front of him.

"Please be seated, gentlemen. This won't take long. I had originally planned on meeting with you tomorrow, but I heard so much commotion coming from this ready room a few minutes ago that I felt compelled to investigate."

The Aardvark commanding officer interrupted Curtiss, who was standing in front of the movie screen.

"Welcome to our ready room, Admiral. Could I interest you in some popcorn or a soft drink? Would you like a seat?" The CO peered sternly at Matt Hildebrand. The SDO, still standing beside the projector, responded by running to the refrigerator. Greg Bright and Dirk Buzzell were giggling in their seats.

". . . some popcorn or a soft drink?" Bright mimicked. "Gawd . . . what a brown-noser."

"No thanks, Skipper. Like I said, I won't be long," Curtiss said.

Buzzell slinked even lower in his chair as his eyes met those of the two-star admiral.

"First off, regarding yesterday's mishap . . . your second-class petty officer, the one who we Med-evac'd to the PI. I'm pleased to report that he's doing well. I received a message earlier tonight from the Subic Naval Hospital. They tell me he'll recover completely." Curtiss looked away from Buzzell and toward the VF-141 CO.

"And your young lieutenant, the pilot with the broken finger. How's he doing?"

"He's in excellent health, Admiral. And he's with us tonight," the CO continued. "Even a busted digit couldn't keep him away from the roll-em. He'll be out of that splint by tomorrow." Mark Caine raised his left hand, and waved his bandaged finger toward the front of the ready room.

"Too bad about the Tomcat, Lieutenant. But as I understand it, the loss was unavoidable," Curtiss stated sincerely. "We can always replace an airplane, but we can't replace those who fly them and those who work on them.

"But my main purpose in coming here is to give you some idea of what's been happening in the Persian Gulf. The recent escalation in Iranian Revolutionary Guard terrorism has the undivided attention of the President and the Joint Chiefs of Staff. We're watching developments there very closely. I just learned that those lunatics attacked another oil tanker off the coast of Oman this afternoon. And while I can't say whether or not there will be a measured response to the Iranians, I do know that all of you can look forward to a lot of flying once this ship is on-station.

"From a diplomatic standpoint, the situation is very volatile there. I can tell you that the United States has offered to assist the Omanis with Navy and Air Force assets. However, the powers-that-be in Oman are resisting that offer. And that fact places all of us in a very difficult position. If attacks are made against Oman, *we* cannot interfere—at least not in the present political climate. I won't bore you with the details, but you will all be thoroughly briefed on the rules of engagement in the Strait of Hormuz.

"Of course, we will assume the *Burning Sand* escort responsibility from the USS *Carl Vinson* air wing. The intelligence gathered from the Saudi A-3 AWACS is critical to our mission in the area. The Silkworm missile sites are a threat to the freedom of navigation in one of the most vital choke-points in this hemisphere. You and your Tomcats will work to guarantee that freedom. Unfortunately, as we have been ordered to steam into the Indian Ocean ASAP, it was also necessary to cut short your liberty in the Philippines. To be perfectly honest with you, gentlemen, I do not foresee another port visit in the near future."

"The 'Varks can pass on the liberty, Admiral. We're all looking forward to kicking some camel-jockey ass over there." The squadron CO finished his statement, then looked suddenly embarrassed for interrupting a second time.

"Glad to hear it, Skipper. And I look forward to getting to know your people better. I've already had the pleasure of talking with one of your pilots out on the LSO platform." Jeremiah Curtiss looked into the middle of the ready room chairs. The eyes of every other officer fell on Dirk Buzzell as well.

"Glad to see you again, Lieutenant," Curtiss said.

Stateroom 03-93-2L
2250

Dirk Buzzell had planned to write a letter. He had scribbled the date at the top of the yellow legal pad, but nothing else, not even the introductory *Dear Marti*. There were many things on his mind—most of which he hadn't been able to sort out. Writing Marti had always helped him do that. Writing her had become a kind of therapy for him—a method of focusing his thoughts.

He was always alone when he wrote her. It was a requirement. And if Mark Caine or Spanky Pfister had been in the stateroom, he would have collected his yellow legal pad and gone elsewhere to write, or he would not have written at all.

Mostly, he wanted to write her about Mark Caine. She would understand his frustrations about Coke—about the accident and the mishap boards. Maybe she could help Dirk help Caine get through it all.

But then again, maybe she wouldn't understand. Maybe she wouldn't want to read about an accident on the flight deck—an accident might be something she hated to think about. Nobody likes to hear about airplane accidents when the person who's writing flies the same kind of airplane. Writing about the accident would worry her, he decided.

But Caine was worth worrying about. He was a pilot fairly new to the Aardvarks, and he was good. Caine and Buzzell both adored flying Navy fighters, and the two of them had spent long hours talking about every aspect of it—about landing the Tomcat aboard the ship during day and night and in foul weather. They had spent even more time talking about fighting the F-14 in air combat maneuvering.

Caine was Buzzell's wingman. Together, they had fought a lot of ACM. Buzzell was also more senior and more experienced than Caine, and was therefore placed in the position of flight lead and instructor. Caine learned easily, and Dirk Buzzell had learned to respect and admire the way Coke handled the Tomcat. Their friendship had been forged from a relationship unique to wingmen. They took care of each other in the air—checking each other's six o'clock. It should be no different on the ground, Buzzell had also decided. But it was a relationship difficult to relate in a letter to Marti.

He knew she would understand the way yeoman Jordan Michaels was feeling—how the enlisted man detested living on an aircraft carrier and wanted a different kind of life. Buzzell understood those feelings very well. He had written Marti on more than one occasion with the same thoughts. But Michaels's problem was Buzzell's alone to solve. She didn't need to read about it in a letter.

Buzzell sat there, finally, drawing circles where

his letter should have begun. He tried to think of the best way to write about the Iranian Revolutionary Guard and the rest of the shit going on in the Persian Gulf. He wondered if she would understand the concept of the Rules of Engagement he'd been hearing so much about lately, and how those rules would affect his flying in the weeks to come. He wondered if *he* really understood the ROE. And he decided, again, that nothing good could come of a letter that talked about the IRG. He might have to deal with the IRG on this cruise, and "dealing" with them might include fighting them in the air. Fighting them sounded too much like combat—like war. He especially couldn't write Marti on that subject.

It would be safest, he thought, to write her about Baguio City in the Philippines, and how he wished the two of them were together there right now. He knew that subject was something they both understood. He could write about sex with her. But that wouldn't serve any purpose but to frustrate him.

Spanky Pfister unlocked the stateroom door and walked inside.

Buzzell tore the top sheet from his legal pad, wadded it into a tiny ball, and tossed it across the stateroom into a garbage bag beneath the sink.

DAY SEVEN

JANUARY 11

USS *Enterprise*
Aardvark 100
0545

The Tomcat was chained down just forward of the LSO platform on elevator number four. Its two Pratt and Whitney TF-30 engines turned at idle, but Dirk Buzzell didn't expect to go flying. He and Greg Bright disliked early alerts like this one. Still, as the sun broke the gray horizon, Buzzell decided it was good to be sitting in an airplane with his old RIO again.

Buzzell and Bright had been crewed together during most of the turnaround training—for the entire year that separated their first cruise from this, their second *Enterprise* deployment with the Aardvarks. During that time, they had flown more than 100 sorties together. They knew each other in the cockpit as few others have the opportunity to know each other. Greg Bright had learned to anticipate the way Dirk Buzzell flew the F-14—because every pilot flies it differently. He knew what to expect from the front-seater—how he fought and what he was thinking while he fought. As a result, Bright had always been there with the radar locks Buzzell needed.

When turnaround training took VF-141 to the skies over the desert near Yuma, Arizona, for the Fleet Fighter Air Combat Maneuvering Readiness Program, or FFARP, Buzzell made sure he was scheduled with Bright in his backseat. In the three weeks and twenty sorties of mock combat they fought while crewed together at FFARP, the two never "died." In a tight fight against even more than one adversary, Bright was the consummate backseater.

Buzzell had given all of the credit to his RIO. One night, after consuming more than his share of beer and kamikazes at the Marine Corps Officers Club there, Buzzell had publicly applauded Bright as "the best RIO in the world to have in your backseat when the air was full of bandits."

Still, the two had not flown together for more than two months—since before the cruise. Instead, Bright had been crewed with Mark Caine. But since Caine was Buzzell's wingman, the RIO was always close by—in the same section of airplanes—never more than one or two miles away. Even on this day, Bright would normally have been scheduled to stand the early alert with Mark Caine. But since the mishap boards had not yet determined Coke's role in the flight-deck mishap two days earlier, and since Dirk Buzzell's usual RIO was standing duty in the ready room as SDO, Bright and his old pilot sat in the Alert fighter together.

Didamar Island, Oman
0600 (local time)

It had been decided that the hulk of the *Majorca Azul* would be towed into the anchorage at Didamar.

But she could not be towed until her fires were extinguished. A slick of burning oil surrounded the aft portion of the tanker, and even more unburned crude followed the currents out of the Strait of Hormuz to the southeast. In all, 300,000 barrels of oil had drained from the ship or been burned away. Seven Didamar tugboats poured salt water onto her. The water seemed to have little effect on the rate at which the ship and her cargo burned.

Her stern was completely submerged now. Waves of oil and water lapped against the island structure in front of the fire. Her bow rose a little more than ten feet out of the shallows. The *Majorca Azul* was, however, somewhat grounded on an underwater outcropping, and would sink no farther. Only after the tugs and their salt water could extinguish the flames, or when the supply of oil was gone and the fire burned out, could the ship be searched for survivors and then towed free of the channel. From the piers and shoreline of Didamar less than two miles away, crew members of the *Majorca Azul* stared at their new ship. It had been a long night since the tanker had been attacked by the two Iranian F-4 Phantoms. The crew could only assume that the captain of their vessel, and the harbormaster who had boarded her at Abu Dhabi, were no longer alive. Thirty men, in all—more than half the ship's company—were either dead or missing.

Radio calls had gone out during the night. The facility at Didamar was too small to accommodate a disaster of these proportions. Any ship receiving the transmission was urged to help—to aid in extinguishing the huge fires, to help tow the *Majorca Azul* free of the rocks, or to assist in skimming the millions of gallons of crude that floated freely toward the Indian Ocean. Ships that could not help were anchored to the west and south of Didamar, closer to Abu Dhabi. None of their captains would be the first to navigate around the *Majorca Azul* now. That would mean steaming even closer to Iran—even closer to the F-4 Phantoms and the Silkworm surface-to-surface missiles. In all, forty-one supertankers were at anchor there. The vessels formed a monstrous flotilla that roadblocked a large portion of the eastern Persian Gulf.

USS *Enterprise*
Aardvark 100
0610

A thin yellow cable ran from the port catwalk, along the deck, then snaked up into the jet's nose wheel-well. *Enterprise* INS latitude and longitude data was fed to the Tomcat via the cable—aligning the aircraft navigation system computers, and giving the jet a stable weapons platform. Buzzell stared at his TID repeat. The small INS diamond jumped past a final tick mark in the buffer of his display. The alignment was complete. The airplane was "set" as the Alert-5 fighter, and could, if required, be restarted and airborne in less than five minutes.

Buzzell signaled his plane captain through the canopy, and the brown-shirted airman ran around the jet, securing the main-mounts and nose landing gear with long down-lock pins. The canopy was already open when the port engine spooled down. The pilot and RIO pulled off their helmets and settled into the two uncomfortable ejection seats. Buzzell checked his watch against the eight-day clock in the Tomcat. Their relief wasn't due for another two hours.

The *Enterprise* was behind PIM, or its point of

intended movement. As it transited south and west through the South China Sea, the ship navigated from PIM to PIM at a predetermined course and at a calculated speed through the water. The nuclear carrier rarely operated at its maximum speed, and were she alone, she could easily make up lost time and regain PIM. But most of her smaller battle-group escorts were not powered by nuclear reactors, and it was the speed of the escorts that slowed her progress toward the Indian Ocean.

In less than one hour, *Enterprise* would sail abeam the Spratly Islands, a bundle of tiny islands north of Malaysia. An hour after that, the aircraft carrier would reach its closest point of approach to the coastline of South Vietnam—102 nautical miles. There, out of Camranh Bay, the Soviets based a contingent of Badger and Bear bomber aircraft—and nearly two dozen MiG-23 Flogger fighter aircraft. It was not uncommon to see the Bears fly out and over the South China Sea when a U.S. combatant was near by. It was, in fact, very common. The Soviets routinely overflew American carriers, usually with one or two of their bombers modified as reconnaissance platforms.

But the Bears and Badgers also possessed the capability of carrying and employing air-to-surface missiles. An aircraft carrier is vulnerable to such missiles, and requires fighter protection. Buzzell and Bright sat in the Alert-5 Tomcat to provide such protection. If Soviet bombers became airborne out of Camranh Bay, the Aardvark pilot and RIO would launch to intercept and escort them.

The Aardvark spy, Ensign Rich Collins, had briefed the Camranh Bay air order of battle earlier that morning. He reported that the battle group intelligence people didn't expect air activity on this particular transit—not from the large bombers and especially not from the Soviet fighters. It seemed the Soviets had recently celebrated some kind of national holiday, and it was Wednesday.

"They're standing down from their alert posture, and we usually don't see them fly out of the mainland on Wednesdays," Collins had said. It was Wednesday, so Buzzell didn't expect to fly against a Soviet bomber.

Except for a single arrested landing the night before *Enterprise* had made its brief port call at Subic Bay, Buzzell hadn't flown in more than a week. The investigation into the F-14 mishap was winding down, and he was no longer required to remain off the schedule. Still, there had been little flying—only alerts like this one.

He reached down between the front cockpit starboard console and the rudder pedal on the same side, and pulled a pair of Navy-issue sunglasses from his G-suit pocket. The sun was higher and a bright yellow across the flight deck. Buzzell reached outside the cockpit, and pounded the side of the aircraft to get his RIO's attention.

"Hey, Notso. Do me a favor and call the bridge. Ask the captain if he wouldn't mind turning the ship a little. I can't get any sleep with the sun in my eyes."

Bright leaned out of his cockpit, and out of the shadow afforded by his pilot's ejection seat.

"Yeah, I'll get right on it, Buzz. And while I'm at it, could I run down to the wardroom and brew you a cup of tea?" Bright laughed to himself, then returned to his magazine. But the article didn't interest him, and he wasn't tired enough to sleep. He sat up in his ejection seat and yelled toward his pilot.

"So, Buzz . . . when are you and Marti gonna settle down, get married, and have some little Buzzes?" Dirk Buzzell had not expected the question.

"What? And give up this swingin' singles' lifestyle? Didn't I tell you, I'm married to the Navy—great food, great accommodations, and I get to visit exotic ports on this 'Love Boat.' Why give all that up? Besides, when did you become so nosy?"

"It's my nature. But I think you found a good one in Marti. I'd marry her."

"Okay, I'll line you two up when we get back to San Diego." Buzzell was laughing, too.

"Haven't you and Marti been, you know . . . haven't you two been living in sin?" Bright's tone was pure sarcasm. "I think that's disgusting."

"You sound like my mother. But since Marti's name is on the mortgage along with mine, I thought it was a good idea to let her move in. She's gonna look after the plants while I'm gone."

"What about when the cruise is over? You done any ring shopping? You gonna get married?"

"Who are you, Oprah Winfrey? I don't know. I haven't given it much thought." Buzzell had given it considerable thought, but he would never admit as much to Bright—or anyone else.

"Well, maybe you two don't know each other well enough yet. How long have you been seein' her . . . four or five years?"

"You're a dick, Notso. And for your information, it's been almost six years."

Still, Buzzell didn't mind talking about Marti to someone who knew her. In fact, he enjoyed it.

"She's an Idaho girl, you know. Fresh from the farm. I'm giving her the benefit of my worldly upbringing."

"Yeah, I hear they're pretty worldly up in Utah these days." Bright paused from his barbs to uncap a tin of Skoal.

"Are you kidding me? We met at the social event of the year in Salt Lake City. All the beautiful people were there."

"Really? I didn't know you attended rodeos."

"Rodeo? How gauche. It was a hockey game. We had a few Coors together. Very romantic."

Buzzell pulled off his sunglasses, squinting against the sun. Two small Malaysian dhows and a single bonka boat bounced through the wake behind the carrier.

"I don't know," Bright added. "Sounds like true love to me. But personally, I don't know what she sees in you."

The pilot laughed to himself, but didn't answer, and the conversation ended. Buzzell stared down at his knee-board. The card clipped to the top of it was entitled *Rules of Engagement*. He reviewed the ROE—its matrixes and caveats would govern his actions as a fighter pilot during potential encounters with Iranian Revolutionary Guard aircraft in the Persian Gulf region. He and every other air wing aviator were expected to memorize the card. There would be tests on the contents of the matrix.

Buzzell laughed to himself again. Some of the terms and descriptions on the card seemed to apply equally to the Iranians and to his relationship with Marti.

"During Red and Tight situations, maintain neutral stationing," he read from the card. "Distance yourself from the threat. Avoid engagements at all costs. If engagement is unavoidable, do not allow the threat to gain an offensive position."

The *Majorca Azul*
The Strait of Hormuz
0630 (local time)

Two Omani fishing trawlers joined the tugboats beside the burning tanker. They too directed their streams of salt water at the ship. A small civilian aircraft circled overhead—a single engine Cessna carrying journalists who captured the effort on film. The Cessna motored above the tanker for a few minutes, then departed to the southwest, where its cameramen would photograph the dozens of giant oilers huddled together inside the Persian Gulf. Except for the *Majorca Azul* and the small boats and trawlers working to extinguish the burning oil inside her, there was no shipping traffic entering or exiting the Strait of Hormuz.

The largest tongue of yellow-orange flame, the one just forward of the *Majorca Azul*'s island, suddenly died in the spray of salt water from the tugs. At nearly the same time, a smaller but more persistent wall of fire just aft of the island disappeared in the dark smoke. From the shores and piers at Didamar two miles to the south, crewmen from the huge tanker began hopeful cheers.

Two Omanis worked at the saltwater nozzles inside one of the larger trawlers. One of the men was the first to notice four more vessels approaching the smoldering tanker from the northwest. The boats were unlike any he had seen. All four were larger than his trawler, but were painted in the same white-gray scheme. They were not fishing vessels—there was no rigging or the usual assemblies of nets—although the men aboard the boats wore the kind of foul-weather coats common to fishermen.

"Their engines are large," one of the Omani men

said to the other inside the trawler. "They must be the harbor boats." The other man in the trawler looked up, giving the four craft a cursory glance.

"And no nozzles for fire fighting, either," he said. "Yes. They must be the boats that will tow this tanker to Didamar. Good. This fire is nearly out."

The first of the four large craft stopped just outside the ring of eleven trawlers and tugs encircling the *Majorca Azul*. The three other craft turned away from the first until the ring of the fire fighters was surrounded on two sides. A man in the first big-engined boat reached beneath his heavy fishing coat and removed a dark beret. At the moment he placed the beret onto his head, there was simultaneous movement on all four of the white-gray craft. In each of the vessels, heavy deck-mounted weapons appeared from beneath dull green tarps. The weapons were 50-caliber in size. The boats were outfitted with two such weapons each.

The four craft were not Boghammers, but were instead PTG patrol boats. The boats opened fire together. The 50-calibers were directed into the middle of the Omani fire fighters. After the guns had begun their report, one crewman in each of the patrol boats took the time to raise an Iranian flag.

The trawlers and tugboats were immediately pinned between their attackers and the *Majorca Azul*. The four Iranian Revolutionary Guard patrol boats continued to direct their fire toward the center of the ring. A trawler just outside the oil slick instantly burst into flames as a single 50-caliber round struck its running engine. The trawler lost power to the pumps that brought salt water to its huge fire-fighting nozzle. It was also unable to flee the barrage of gunfire. The nozzle was abandoned and slowed to a drip as the trawler crew dove overboard.

The remaining trawler and tugboats scattered. Some of their water pumps operated normally as the crews attempted to motor away from the patrol craft. The result was a queer and hideous water ballet. Two of the Guard PTG boats concentrated their four powerful guns on a lone tugboat near the stern of the *Majorca Azul*. The tug turned broadside to the guns as it drove slowly in the direction of Didamar. Three of the tug's five crew members waved their arms from the center of the boat in a vain appeal to the Iranians. As the gunfire ripped through the keel of the boat beneath them, the men tumbled down into the spray of lead projectiles. The tugboat split apart, drifted toward the burning slick aft of the *Majorca Azul*, then sank in two pieces.

A fifth Iranian Revolutionary Guard boat—a lone Boghammer—seemed to materialize out of the wave tops. It sped past the PTG boats, then into the center of the remaining tugs and trawlers. The Boghammer decelerated quickly, aligning itself with the raised nose of the tanker. It motored slowly, paralleling the oiler's thousand-foot port side. At each 100-foot interval, the Iranian Revolutionary Guard crewmen attached square magnetic devices to the huge hull. When the last device had been connected, the Boghammer sped away from the tanker. The four IRG patrol boats secured their deck-mounted weapons, then turned and followed the Boghammer toward the northwest.

The *Majorca Azul* would not be salvaged or towed away from the rocks north of Didamar. No search would be conducted for possible survivors aboard her, and none of the more than 500,000 barrels of oil still aboard the tanker would be salvaged. While the Boghammer and patrol boats sped back to Hengam Island in Iran, and the three remaining tugboats raced closer to Didamar, the *Majorca Azul* suffered ten separate explosions where the magnetic devices had been attached to her. The blasts split open her port holding tanks and lifted the huge oiler onto its starboard side. Even if the tugs had returned to the tanker, their tiny streams of salt water would have been ineffective in battling the new and larger blazes. The tugs did not return.

USS *Enterprise*
Aardvark 100
0730

Buzzell checked his watch, then studied the cockpit wet compass attached to the Tomcat's glareshield. He figured Camranh Bay was off to his right, and a little more than 100 miles away. He'd seen Soviet-built bombers before—five of the huge Bears with their odd counter-rotating propellers, and two of the older jet-powered Badgers. Joining on a Russian aircraft for the first time had been a thrill—the Soviet pilot and crew had waved at his Tomcat as it flew off their wingtip. On one occasion, Buzzell flew close enough to a Bear canopy to see an unfolded *Playboy* centerfold pressed against it for his entertainment. But after two or three more of the intercepts, the Bears and Badgers lost their thrill to him. The bombers were always unarmed, and had presented no threat to the carrier.

But the admiral and his staff were preoccupied with the bombers. If the Soviets were airborne, Rear Admiral Curtiss wanted a Tomcat joined in escort, even if that escort took place hundreds of miles from the battle group. Buzzell was convinced that if the battle group commander had evidence that a Soviet bomber pilot was taking a dump somewhere in Southeast Asia, the Alert-5 would be launched.

Dirk Buzzell preferred to think about the MiGs. He'd never seen a Flogger—he didn't know any Navy pilot who had. He wanted to see a Soviet fighter flown by a Soviet pilot. That's what he would see if he saw a fighter flying out of Vietnam. But it was Wednesday, and the warm morning sun made him drowsy. He drifted into a restless kind of sleep.

He awakened to the sound of voices. Lieutenant Commander Don McKelvey was already on top of Aardvark 100, casually preflighting the back of the jet, whose huge tail hung across the edge of the elevator, out and over the water sixty feet below. Bright was saying something about a rear cockpit circuit breaker, briefing the new Alert-5 RIO and unstrapping at the same time. J. T. Lester, Buzzell's relief, stood at the bottom of the boarding ladder. He was chatting with one of the VF-141 ordnance crewmen. It was nearly 0815. Lester and McKelvey were late. Buzzell unbuckled his leg restraints from the base of the ejection seat. He was already planning the breakfast he would order down in Ward Room One.

Greg Bright saw the yellow-shirted flight-deck petty officer running toward Aardvark 100 before Buzzell did. At first, the enlisted man's signals confused the RIO and pilot.

"It looks like he wants us to start up again," Bright thought out loud.

The RIO was straddling the canopy rail, half in and half out of the cockpit, while his backseat replacement, McKelvey, continued his stroll on top of the port wing.

"Now launch the Alert fighter!" The 5-MC speaker announcement sent deck personnel scatter-

ing in all directions. Buzzell reconnected his leg restraints while Bright jumped back inside the airplane. They were going flying. McKelvey walked toward the backseater, his hands on his hips. The pilot signaled his plane captain to connect starting air to the Tomcat, then yelled down to J. T. Lester as the canopy started down.

"Sorry about this, J. T., but thanks for *not* relieving us on time. Otherwise *you guys* would be launching instead of *us*."

McKelvey grabbed the ladder handhold, flipping Buzzell the finger as he descended to the flight deck.

Bright switched the backseat radio to button 8, and Buzzell heard the voice of Strike Ops controller. The port engine spooled up quickly, and the radio transmission died while the F-14's left engine-driven generator snapped on the line. The pilot followed the plane captain's hand motions, signaling a thumbs-up when he saw that his landing gear down-locks had been removed. Two RAMP lights illuminated on the caution/advisory panel—OBC was running. After another thumbs-up, Buzzell pushed forward on the throttles, then engaged the Tomcat's nose-wheel steering and followed his taxi director to catapult number three.

"Brakes." The RIO started down his list of take-off checks.

Buzzell answered, taxiing the jet forward and over the lowered jet blast deflector.

"Pumped firm and in the green."

"Fuel. I'm showing nineteen-point-six."

"Same up here . . . tanks and wings are full. Norm on the transfer, fuel dump is off. Tapes and feeds are even. Bingo set."

"Canopy's down and locked, handle forward."

"Roger that, my stripes aligned. Good seal, no light."

Bright followed the list from memory, and Buzzell verified each check. Their ejection seats were armed, and appropriate circuit breakers were verified either in or out. Past the JBD, the jet's nose came down as Buzzell kneeled Aardvark 100. A catapult crewman released the jet's launch bar. The pilot shoved the emergency wing-sweep handle forward, then lowered the flaps.

"Flaps and slats are down," Bright said over the intercom system.

"Yep. Trim's set."

Buzzell felt the slight tug of the hold-back fitting beneath the nose of his airplane. He taxied farther forward, then stopped. The catapult shuttle moved aft in the center of the cat track, sliding underneath the fighter's drooping launch bar, then forward until it clicked into place. The taxi director pointed toward an ordnanceman standing just forward of the Tomcat. Buzzell could see him clearly through the canopy's right quarter panel. When the ordie lifted his arms above his head, Buzzell and Bright did the same inside the cockpit, keeping their hands in plain sight—nowhere near a trigger or ordnance jettison button while the Tomcat's single Phoenix, two Sparrows, two Sidewinders, and Mark-61 20-millimeter cannon were armed.

Three red-shirts ran from beneath the aircraft. Each of them signaled thumbs-up again as they crossed the foul line, then disappeared behind a line of SH-3 helos parked near the island. Buzzell advanced both throttles to military power—100 percent—pushing the control stick left and right, full forward and aft, cycling his controls while Bright checked both sets of wing spoilers and the differential tail for freedom of movement. The pilot kicked at the rudder pedals, at the same time cross-checking engine turbine inlet temperature, fuel flow, and RPM gauges. The catapult officer was already signaling for afterburner when Buzzell found him, standing in line with Aardvark 100's left wingtip, less than twenty feet outside his canopy. He pushed both throttles past military power—past the 100 percent power detent—into afterburner. The Pratt and Whitneys churned behind him and Bright, spitting tubes of yellow-white flames against the upraised JBD. Buzzell saw the cockpit engine nozzle indicators slide clockwise to 5—full afterburner. He glanced over his right arm to the caution advisory panel. No lights. The Tomcat shuddered beneath him.

"Looking good up here, Notso. Ready to go flying?" Buzzell didn't wait for the RIO's answer. He saluted the catapult officer, then fit his right hand loosely around the stick grip. The Tomcat's nose dropped violently as the hold-back fitting broke free, throwing Buzzell's back against the ejection seat. Bright held his breath against the cat shot, grunting through the two seconds and 200 feet of catapult travel.

Aardvark 100 climbed off the deck at 160 knots. Buzzell slapped the landing gear handle to the up position and raised the flaps. He deselected afterburner, pushed the nose over, and leveled off at 200 feet above the water. He left the throttles at military power and pushed the external fuel-tank indicator rocker switch. Only six miles from *Enterprise*, Aardvark 100 had already burned 3100 pounds of jet fuel. The airspeed indicator read 480 knots when Buzzell rolled left and pulled the fighter away from the waves. He followed the voice of the Strike Ops controller to a radar contact eighty-seven miles to the north.

USS *Enterprise*
Stateroom 03-93-2L
2230

When Mark Caine pushed open the door into the stateroom, he saw Dirk Buzzell, Greg Bright, and Kurt "Seed" Hansen. Buzzell and Bright were both leaning back in their chairs—both had their feet propped up on Caine's desk. Hansen, the A-7 pilot and LSO, lived in the stateroom across the passageway, and had sort of crashed the impromptu party. All three of them held wardroom glasses filled with ice and liquor. Spanky Pfister's desk had become the bar. A mostly empty bottle of Jack Daniel's had been placed there. Pfister had been in his rack since before the party began. He was snoring.

"A little celebration toddy?" Caine asked. "Where'd you find the bottle?"

"Smuggled it aboard in the PI," Bright said. "Care for one, Coke?"

"Naw. I got the midnight Alert-5."

"Then you're back on the flight schedule? Shit hot," Buzzell said with a slur. Caine wore a wide grin as he nodded his head. Hansen chugged the last of his whiskey.

"Sure am. The mishap board said it wasn't my fault, Notso." Greg Bright added more Jack Daniel's to everybody's glass. Together, they toasted Mark Caine.

"I hope I'm not in that alert with you," Bright said. "I'm shit-faced."

"You're not. Skeds figured you and Buzz had

enough excitement for one day.'' Mark Caine climbed over the two sets of legs still propped up on his desk and sat in the fourth stateroom chair. ''So. You two were almost heroes out there today, huh?''

''Coke buddy . . . ya'll gonna love tha stary,'' Seed drawled.

Buzzell and Bright giggled together. Greg Bright decided he could tell the story one more time.

''So we launch out of the alert, right? We shoot off the 'Big E' and haul ass toward this contact. The ship's strike controller tells us it's a Bear or maybe a Badger. Then, even before we lock him up on radar . . . oh, I don't know . . . at twenty miles or so . . . the ship tells us our target is a Soviet fighter. Strike says it's a *probable* MiG-23 Flogger . . .''

''I've always wanted to see one of those things,'' Buzzell interrupted.

Mark Caine was enjoying the story. He especially enjoyed the way the three drunk aviators were telling it.

''Shuttup, Buzz. I tell it better than you do,'' Bright chided the pilot with a laugh. ''Anyway, we're fifteen miles from this guy and our Strike controller tells us the target is a confirmed Soviet fighter. It's heading for the ship, they say. And we're cleared to lock and load on 'im. They don't even want us to ID the airplane we're tracking. Just shoot it down.''

''Red and Free,'' Buzzell interrupted again, then allowed the RIO to continue.

''We even hear the admiral come up on our frequency. He tells us this fighter has demonstrated hostile intent. He's telling us to shoot the thing down! Okay, we say . . . who are we to pass up an easy kill? Buzz and I make sure the Master Arm switch is up . . . we even decide we'll shoot a Sparrow. But it just doesn't look right . . . we decide to take a closer look at this *Flogger* first,'' Bright said. ''This guy's at 35,000 feet and climbing—not exactly an attack profile. Anyway . . . it's a big target and it's *not* heading for the *Enterprise* at all.''

''It's a DC-9!'' Buzzell screamed hysterically.

''Dammit, Buzz. You *never* let *me* tell that part,'' Greg Bright said as he chugged the Jack Daniel's. By now, Buzzell, Bright, Hansen, and Caine were laughing out loud together. Spanky Pfister was suddenly awake and sitting up in his lower rack.

Bright finished the last of his whiskey and began unscrewing the top of a Skoal tin. The laughing subsided. The moment became almost solemn.

''It's really kinda scary,'' Dirk Buzzell said finally to the four other officers in the room. ''We were told to shoot down an airliner today. We were told to kill a couple hundred civilians.''

''An ya'll coulda dawn it, too,'' Kurt Hansen concluded. ''Shit, tha admiral gave ya the go head himself. Good thang ya'll din't listen to him.''

''Yep, sure is,'' Buzzell said finally. ''It's a good thing that Navy lieutenants never listen to anyone who outranks them.''

DAY TWELVE

JANUARY 16

USS *Enterprise*
Wardroom One
1140

Dirk Buzzell pushed the empty silver-plated coffeepot to the edge of a table in the corner of the wardroom. He flipped open its lid, a signal to the attendant messman that it needed refilling. A plump third-class petty officer grabbed at the pot, stepping over a knee-knocker into the forward-most cubicle of the spaces. When he returned, Buzzell and seven other VF-141 officers were listening lazily to a 1-MC announcement from the bridge.

"Good morning, this is the captain. Just wanted to give you all an update," his message began. "Right now we're a little less than seventy miles away from the southern tip of India. That means we're about to sail into the Indian Ocean. The ship is approximately nine-hundred miles from Iran. Since midnight last night, all eight of the *Enterprise* reactors have been on-line, and we're making good speed. I apologize if some of you had trouble sleeping last night, but we've encountered some rough seas down here at the equator.

"Just off the port side, we're sailing by the Maldives. They're not much to look at from this distance, but they may be the only land we see for the next couple of months. So come on up on the flight deck and take a look. Except for a little salt spray, it's beautiful out there." Buzzell poured another cup of coffee, then passed the silver pot down the table. The captain continued with his message, encouraging his crew of more than 6,000.

"But I have submitted a request for some liberty while the ship's in the IO, and there's a chance we'll have the opportunity to visit Karachi, Pakistan, or Mombasa, Kenya, later in the quarter. So . . . we have something to look forward to. Of course, I'll let you all know as soon as I hear any news. That's all for now. Have a nice day."

Buzzell sipped at his coffee. The announcement depressed him.

"Yeah, at least we have something to look forward to." Greg Bright's tone brought a slow smile to Dirk Buzzell's face.

"Hey, Buzz, remember Karachi? We had a nifty time there, huh?"

Every aviator at the table, except the two new RIOs sitting near Bright, remembered Karachi very well. The memories of Pakistan were not fond ones for the Aardvarks. The port visit had marked the halfway point of Buzzell's first deployment. He had drawn duty with the shore patrol, and was one of the first officers ashore. Buzzell had found himself standing on a rickety wooden pier, in company with five of the biggest sailors he could find. With them, he would try to ensure the off-load of liberty personnel was conducted in an orderly fashion.

The waters there had been very rough, and the small liberty boats moved slowly through the inlet to the pier more than three miles from the *Enterprise*. Some of those in the first liberty boats to reach the pier handled the pitching and rolling better than others. In a very short time, he remembered, the pier-side had stunk of vomit.

Everything in Karachi had seemed dark brown to Buzzell. The people, the shanty structures near the wharf—even the skies above the city—looked and smelled dark brown. The local poor had gathered behind the heavy gates leading out of Fleet Landing. Hundreds of them pleaded for U.S. dollars from the Navy sailors. Women in bright native dress—gold hoops through their noses—held still babies in their arms. The women had begged and cried loudly in their bizarre language. He vividly remembered the pathetic sight.

"If we get liberty up here," Bright said finally, "I vote for anywhere *but* Karachi. I think I got dysentery there last time."

Buzzell heard catapult one firing through the overhead above the Aardvark table. The noon launch had begun. He pulled a photocopy of the *Enterprise* air plan from the pocket of his khakis and unfolded it. An eleven-plane recovery would follow the launch. He grabbed the LSO float coat hanging on the back of his chair, slipping it on as he walked out of the wardroom.

Sultan of Oman Air Force Base
Thumrait, Oman
1200 (local time)

Lieutenant Colonel Reginald Sheffield Thomas pushed the Hawker Hunter's single throttle grip to 100 percent power and scanned the cockpit engine instruments. Momentarily, his engine oil pressure rose above its maximum allowable PSI, then settled into acceptable limits. The other gauges were normal. He then glanced through his right windscreen—toward the Hunter beside him on the runway. Major William Carlton, his wingman, signaled a thumbs-up. Both jets were hunched against their brakes at full power. Thomas had just begun his takeoff roll when he pulled back slightly on the throttle—to 96 percent RPM. Carlton, with the 4 percent of engine thrust advantage, would modulate his engine to remain abreast Thomas as the two aircraft accelerated together down the 12,000-foot runway.

At 136 knots, the lead Hunter's nose tire lifted off the concrete. Carlton's followed. The two fighter-bombers rose away from the hot desert airstrip in section. On a signal from Thomas, both pilots raised their landing-gear handles, and the two sets of retractable gear closed into their wheel wells simultaneously. Carlton loosened slightly his formation on the squadron commander's Hunter, then flipped a toggle switch just aft of his throttle grip on the port console. Fuel from each of the two external wing tanks began emptying into the Hunter's main fuselage cell. The major remained in a "loose cruise" position, 40 degrees aft of his lead's wingline, stepped up slightly, and exactly 100 meters to starboard. Lieutenant Colonel Thomas continued in his right turn past due north, then steadied on a heading of 50 degrees. Through his canopy's center windscreen panel, below and beyond the city of Musat, he could make out the ragged Omani coastline.

USS *Enterprise*

Stan Grokulsky, the senior air-wing landing signal officer, was already checking the UHF radio telephones as Buzzell walked onto the platform. He established communications with the air boss in the tower, then passed the phone to the enlisted phone talker standing in front of the LSO console. Overhead at 8,000 feet, an A-3 Skywarrior circled the *Enterprise*, awaiting its turn in the landing pattern. Affectionately dubbed "the Whale," the A-3 acted as an extra set of "eyes and ears" for the battle group. Its electronic suite belied the age of its airframe. Built originally in the 1950s, the Whale had been internally retrofitted with sensitive reconnaissance equipment. Its mission differed very little from the E-2C Hawkeye and it possessed some of the capabilities of the carrier-based EA-6B Prowler, but its speed and relatively long mission range outdistanced both the Hawkeye and the Prowler.

The Whale was not, on the other hand, equipped with ejection seats. That, combined with the fact that the airplane was woefully underpowered while "dirty"—with its landing gear and flaps down as it flew an approach to the ship—made the Whale especially difficult to bring aboard an aircraft carrier safely. Landing signal officers didn't enjoy watching an A-3 pilot try.

Its seventy-six-foot length and seventy-two-foot wingspan made it ungainly on the flight deck. Two F-14 Tomcats could easily occupy the deck space required to park one A-3 Skywarrior. Its engines and airframe were fragile. Spare parts were hard to come by—the Whale was a mechanic's nightmare when it required maintenance. And it *always* required maintenance. For each hour it flew, eighty maintenance man-hours were required to prepare it to fly again. As a result, the A-3 was rarely detached to a carrier under way, and then only when its capabilities were deemed a requirement by order of the Joint Chiefs of Staff. As the *Enterprise* moved around the southern tip of India and steamed north toward Iran, an A-3 Skywarrior had been directed to fly aboard her.

A section of Black Eagle F-14s trapped first. Two A-6s followed, while Buzzell stood at the rear of the platform. Grokulsky and an E-2C Hawkeye LSO trainee did most of the "waving." A section of A-7 Corsairs closed on the ship from astern. The first jet "broke" at the fantail—overhead the LSO platform, flying quickly to the abeam position—about a mile from the ship. His wingman extended upwind and ahead of the ship for fifteen seconds, then broke. Thus, their landing interval was established. The lead A-7 rolled into a steady angle of bank, floating to "the 90," a position perpendicular to the landing area at three-quarters of a mile. The jet was low, and Buzzell walked forward to the platform console, expecting to hear the senior LSO say something over the UHF radio telephone. The pilot of the Corsair said something first.

"At tha NINETY I gut no power . . ." The transmission was weak, but Dirk Buzzell recognized the voice instantly. Phil Grokulsky was in charge of this particular recovery. He stared at the A-7 from the LSO platform, then raised the radio-telephone and asked for more information.

"Corsair, say again your problem."

Lieutenant junior-grade Kurt "Seed" Hansen heard Grokulsky's voice over the radio. He ignored it—not because he didn't care to further share his problems with the air-wing LSO, but because he could not afford to take the time to do so. At the moment, aviating his aircraft was far more critical than communicating from it. Kurt Hansen had a little less than 350 flight hours in the A-7E Corsair, and had been, until now, enjoying his first cruise on the *Enterprise*. He was also a U.S. Naval Academy graduate and the youngest squadron pilot among the "Blue Blasters" of VA-49.

Serious in-flight emergencies were not common in the Corsair. The Vought Corporation had put a lot of thought into the subsonic light-attack bomber—and the A-7 had served the Navy well for twenty-five years. But since the A-7 was also a single-engine attack jet, most of its critical airborne emergencies invariably involved that engine. Hansen had developed a healthy respect for the airplane. And until this moment, the Corsair had always taken him where he wanted to go.

He had pulled back on the throttle and extended his speed brakes in the break overhead the LSO platform—it was the only way he could bleed off airspeed before lowering his landing gear—and he'd done it in exactly the same way a hundred times before. But as he had floated to the 180 position abeam the *Enterprise* landing area—at the position he had always chosen to look inside the cockpit to verify his airspeed and altitude—his stomach sank at what he saw there.

A generator warning light stared him in the face. Since the main generator in the Corsair was an engine-driven generator, Hansen immediately scanned his engine performance instruments. The generator had quit because the engine had quit. The lone Pratt and Whitney's RPM was rolling down through 30 percent when it should have been much higher—

closer to 65 or 70 percent. Other lights blinked on inside the cockpit—the kinds of lights that verified an engine failure. Seed Hansen swore into his oxygen mask.

He lowered the jet's nose in response to the warning lights—the Corsair's motor was windmilling as it descended, rotating just enough to sustain the pumping of vital hydraulic fluid to its flight controls. In the descent, Hansen was faster and lower than normal at the abeam position. He thumbed-in his speed brakes and delayed dropping his landing gear—both would only serve to increase drag and further tax the hydraulics. Instinctively, he pulled at the emergency generator handle attached to the base of his canopy console, and a small ram-air turbine fell into the windstream above his starboard wing. The RAT spun to life quickly, and a few of his cockpit warning lights went out. He had already gone through his engine restart procedures—he'd cycled his throttle and worked at the fuel control switches while his jet descended through 300 feet at the 90. He'd made only one radio call—the one the LSOs had heard weakly—and was already working through a second restart attempt. The engine RPM continued to wind down. It was suddenly very quiet inside the A-7.

The airplane leveled its wings, driving from right to left and descending.

"Get out of that thing, Seed," Buzzell whispered, hoping Kurt Hansen could somehow hear him from the back of the platform. "Get the hell out."

"You're *low*!" the CAG LSO warned, not sure exactly what to say. Buzzell heard no transmission in response from the jet, only Grokulsky's repeated power calls.

A section of Hawker Hunters
The Gulf of Oman

RAF Lieutenant Colonel Thomas rolled his jet left, then right, at an altitude of 20,000 feet. Major Carlton remained in formation through the turns. Thomas scanned the waters ten miles off the coast of Musat, searching for the low-flying aircraft he knew were nearby. A division of Hawker Hunter "bogies" had launched from Thumrait thirty minutes earlier than he and Carlton. By now, the lieutenant colonel figured, the four aircraft had rendezvoused and begun their simulated strike into mainland Oman—just as a raid of Iranian F-4 Phantoms might begin the same kind of attack. The target of their attack exercise was the abandoned airfield at Rostak, seven miles into Omani territory. The Number 6 Squadron commander and his wingman were tasked with defending Rostak, and to that end, with the "destruction" of the simulated invaders. Technically, their mission was BARCAP, or Barrier Combat Air Patrol.

But Thomas and Carlton could not attack the invaders unless they could first locate their squadronmates over the gray Omani coastal waters. The radar in the nose of the Hunters was optimized for ground mapping, terrain avoidance, and target identification—not for an air-to-air search mission like this one. Thomas had to trust his eyes to locate "the enemy."

"Carlton, do you see anything?"

"Negative, Colonel. Are these the correct coordinates?'' The major's question infuriated Thomas. Not only was the Number 6 commander unable to locate the four Hawker Hunters where he was certain they should be, but his wingman doubted his navigation skills as well.

"These *are* the proper coordinates, Major. I do not apprecia—" Lieutenant Colonel Thomas broke off his radio transmission in midsentence, rolling his Hunter nearly inverted and pulling down toward the water in a split-S maneuver.

"Tallyho. Four bandits directly below us at the wave tops. I believe my navigation has been accurate after all . . . *Major!*"

Carlton followed, dumping his nose and accelerating in his turn through 18,000 feet, then 15,000 feet, until he found the division of raiders below and in front of his lead. Four Hawker Hunters flew in a trail formation—each only one airplane length behind the other. The leader of the four-plane was crossing over the dark lowlands just north of Musat as Thomas and his BARCAP wingman descended through 4,000 feet. The two diving fighter-bombers were indicating 580 knots of ground speed and overtaking the attackers, who were too low to accelerate further.

"Approaching weapons parameters, Major. I'll have a shot in 20 seconds. Do you have a tally?"

"I see them, Colonel . . . I'm a quarter kilometer behind you."

Thomas was unaccustomed to carrying air-to-air missiles, and he delayed taking the shot. He was an attack pilot with nearly 9,000 hours in the cockpits of attack aircraft. He knew very well how to fly low, and he understood ground targets. Thomas had destroyed more than his share of them. Targets that flew were another matter. The Firestreak missile he carried sensed the hot engine exhaust of the low-flying aircraft in his sights. The tone in his headset indicated the missile seekerhead had locked onto its target. The missile on his Hunter was live—its fuse and warhead were live—and the lieutenant colonel delayed further, double-checking that his master-arm switch was not engaged.

"There's a simulated heat-seeker on the trail bandit. That bandit is dead. Trail Hawker, pull off." The words rolled off his tongue like some foreign language.

The fourth fighter-bomber, monitoring the same frequency, rose away from the water to the right, performing an aileron roll—acknowledging the "kill."

USS *Enterprise*

The A-7 dipped its left wing, aligning its flight path with that of the ship. Its only engine had failed, and the Corsair was a poor glider.

Kurt Hansen pulled back cautiously on his control stick. The attack jet's nose rose sluggishly toward the horizon. The cockpit barometric altimeter needle was momentarily superimposed over 80 feet on the gauge. In his mind, he had already ejected and was swimming alongside the *Enterprise*. He was already answering questions that he knew his commanding officer would ask: *Did you try an engine restart? Were you out of fuel? Did you accidentally shut the engine down, Seed?*

Hansen felt the airframe of the jet shudder around him. His A-7 was approaching stall airspeed. And there was no time to attempt another engine relight. He took a final second to look toward the water beneath him. He wondered if it might be easier to ride the A-7 into the waves than to jump out of it. He imagined what his jet must look like from the vantage point of an observer on the flight deck. He decided he'd rather be on the flight deck, with Dirk Buzzell and Phil Grokulsky—on the LSO platform. Time had expanded for him, and his A-7 descended in long five-foot increments. It seemed, for a while, that it would take all day for his altimeter to wind below 70. He thought again about an engine relight, then immediately decided to get out.

"Time to geeve ya back to tha taxpayers, ole friend," he explained to the Corsair.

Hansen grabbed the yellow and black handle between his knees and pushed his head against the upper portion of his ejection seat. He pulled up and out on the handle with both hands.

Abeam and now starboard of the *Enterprise*, the jet had sunk below flight deck level, to less than forty feet off the water, and had begun a gentle roll to the left. Its port wing pointed toward the wave tops. Staring from the LSO platform, Grokulsky concluded the A-7 pilot could no longer hear his calls. He lowered the radio phone to his side. The ejection sequence began at the same instant. The Corsair's canopy blew away from its fuselage first. The tiny Plexiglas and metal shell twisted toward the sea, then skipped across the top of its waters.

It seemed an eternity before the ejection seat—with Kurt Hansen strapped to it—finally exited the jet. During that tiny eternity, the jet continued its roll to the left. The A-7 could not have been more perfectly inverted than during the final portion of Seed Hansen's ejection sequence. The pilot fell, more than was blasted, out of the cockpit. The seat's rocket motors formed a grayish white steam as the seat itself burrowed into the Indian Ocean, driving its occupant seventy feet underwater. Now pilotless, the Corsair rolled further to the left, pitched nose high, then stalled completely. It splashed tail first into the sea less than 100 yards from the ship. There was no orange and white parachute canopy in the water, nor any sign of the ejection seat, or of Kurt Hansen.

Deck crews ran into the landing area, some of them throwing spare life vests over the side—marking the spot where the aviator had entered the dark waters. But the SH-3 helo was already overhead. Its rotor-wash spread the smoke and steam in every direction. The ship heeled port, then starboard, in a 90 degree, then a 270 degree Williamsen turn, sluggishly reversing its course. Buzzell watched a search-and-rescue swimmer drop from the hovering Sikorsky. The swimmer paddled toward a piece of the A-7 still afloat, and then toward a raft—or something that looked like a raft bobbing in the water near the steam.

The A-3 Whale climbed out of low holding over the ship and joined a KA-6 tanker at 10,000 feet. The Skywarrior plugged into the tanker and took 2,000 pounds of gas, then descended again, while the helo landed on the *Enterprise* bow. Two SAR crewmen scrambled out of the Sikorsky on either end of a stretcher, with Seed Hansen.

Thirty minutes later, following two more sections of A-6 Intruders and one EA-6B, the Whale trapped aboard. Buzzell and Grokulsky, satisfied that Hansen had survived his ejection, joked about the landing grade for his aborted carrier approach. The two LSOs walked off the flight deck, then down the ladder to the 0-3 level hatch.

"What should we give him, an *OK*, a *Fair*, a *No Grade*, or a *Wave-off*?" Buzzell asked sarcastically, listing the possible landing grades in descending order of point value.

East of Musat, Oman

Lieutenant Colonel Thomas and his wingman had dispatched all four of the Hawker Hunter bandits with their Firestreak missiles, and as the two BARCAP jets turned toward Thumrait ninety nautical miles further inland, the division of four joined the two-plane formation from behind.

"Like shooting ducks on the proverbial pond," the lieutenant colonel radioed to his flight. "Bring on the Iranians, eh, gentlemen?" There was no response from the Hunters around him, and Thomas quickly regretted having made the transmission. The scenario had been "canned"—too easy, and the other Hunter pilots knew that fact as well as he did. Thomas and Carlton had known exactly where to find the flight of attacking jets, and the attackers had not tried to defend themselves. They had, in fact, been briefed not to try. It had been the Number 6's first attempt at air-to-air warfare training. And while the day's mission had been successful, no one in the flight—most especially the squadron's commanding officer—believed an Iranian fighter would die so easily.

"Loosen up, chaps. Let's return to home plate." Thomas pushed forward on his control stick and descended from 500 feet to less than 50 feet above the Omani desert floor. As he did after every mission he led, the lieutenant colonel would return to the airfield at low level. The five wingmen dove behind their flight lead, each airplane descending in turn until a column of six fighter-bombers streaked one behind the other over the sand and sparse vegetation east of Thumrait.

Lieutenant Colonel Reginald Sheffield Thomas was not easily followed as he turned and jinked and dove his Hunter at twenty-five feet above ground level at 510 knots. As he rose over small sandy knolls, then dropped into the dry and narrow rivulets on the other side, the squadron commander's Hunter often disappeared in the storms of dust in his wake. Major Carlton, still second in the six-plane column, climbed to fly free of the storm and to keep sight of his zigzagging lead. Behind Carlton, each airplane flew even higher for the same reason.

For Thomas, flying at low altitude was more than a training objective or a requirement for survival against an enemy—it was an obsession. On more than one occasion, Number 6 squadron pilots had found Lieutenant Colonel Thomas on the tarmac after a landing, walking around his Hunter and picking small scrub-oak branches from the pylons that hung under its wings. He enjoyed flying *very* low.

"Coming north, gents." Thomas made the transmission, and the five Hunters behind him banked right to follow. The lieutenant colonel always came north before entering the airfield boundaries. North of Thumrait was the only paved roadway leading there. Very rarely, because it was a poor excuse for a thoroughfare, there were vehicles on the roadway. But if a vehicle of any kind were discovered there, it was always subject to an unannounced attack from the Oman-based RAF. Thomas, more than any other RAF aviator, loved to surprise the occupants of automobiles or trucks driving toward the airfield.

When the distance measuring equipment on his VORTAC indicated he and his flight were fourteen miles from Thumrait, Thomas pitched his nose up in a climb. He leveled his Hunter at 3,500 feet, surveying the roadway as it snaked through a shallow valley—searching. His wingmen ascended behind him, still in column.

"We're in luck, gentlemen," he radioed. "A yellow sedan at our 1130 position. Looks like a foreign make . . . German, I believe."

He banked right again, driving his flight farther behind the sedan moving from his right to left, then climbed another thousand feet.

"You've got the lead, Mr. Carlton. I'll slide into trail. Let's give our guests an appropriate reception, shall we?"

Major William Carlton was surprised by the lead change. The lieutenant colonel had never before made such an offer.

"Understood, Colonel. I have the lead," he answered.

Carlton rolled his Hunter back to the left, sliding underneath Thomas's jet. He dove toward the blacktop below, and rolled out less than two miles behind the yellow sedan. His altitude was forty feet. He lifted his left hand off the throttle and adjusted his radar altimeter warning system for seven meters—a little more than twenty feet. He told himself he would fly no lower than that over the roadway and over the automobile. His airspeed was 475 knots, and he was closing on his target from behind at nearly 500 miles per hour.

The major pulled up as he saw the sedan disappear under his nose. The four wingmen behind him did the same, each performing aileron rolls in front and just above the vehicle. Thomas had not yet begun his run. Instead, he had orbited his Hunter above the flight, laughing into his oxygen mask as the yellow sedan swerved out of its lane under the five aircraft.

"Well done, Major!" he broadcast. "Proceed to home plate for debrief. See you on deck."

Lieutenant Colonel Thomas watched the five-plane join together, then turn for the primary north–south runway at Thumrait. The sedan steadied on the blacktop and continued toward the same destination. Thomas was certain the occupants of the sedan would not expect a sixth assault. He jammed the throttle to 100 percent and nosed his Hunter down. Passing through seventy-five feet, the aircraft stopped accelerating at 565 knots. It would fly no faster.

He switched his radar altimeter off. He did not want to be bothered by its warning tone. One mile behind the sedan, Thomas bumped his nose down even farther, thumbing at his elevator trim and lowering the jet below ten feet of altitude above ground level.

"Look in your rearview mirror, my good man. You've a Hawker Hunter on your tail," he laughed.

Time began to expand for the Number 6 Squadron commander. The sedan grew slowly in his windscreen, and he considered copying down the vehicle's license plate numbers as he approached it. He could make out two figures in the front seat, and he could have sworn he saw them carrying on a conversation. The pilot was in his element. Flying didn't get any better than this.

Thomas had planned to remain at ten feet of altitude as he crossed over and then in front of the sedan, but as the yellow blur disappeared under the Hunter's nose assembly, a dull thud rocked his airplane. He decided it was prudent to climb. He pointed the Hawker Hunter toward the airfield at Thumrait.

Thomas chopped his engine from idle to off and the Rolls Royce wound down. He was already unstrapped inside the cockpit. He pulled open the canopy and jumped quickly onto the boarding ladder. Two RAF enlisted men were standing beside the jet when he reached the ground. One of them was trying to stifle a laugh, but was unsuccessful in doing so.

"Good flight, Colonel?" the enlisted man asked.

Thomas did not answer. Instead, he hurried beneath the Hunter to its starboard side, then swore out loud. His right external fuel tank was gone. Instead, only a short cannon plug and two shredded electrical wire bundles hung from the wing station. He turned toward the two men and cursed a second time. Behind the men, Major Carlton and the four other Hunter pilots were running toward the CO and his airplane. Farther behind them, the yellow sedan had pulled up beside the Number 6 hangar and stopped. The vehicle's roof came to two points at each side window. Its top was smashed and its rear window shattered. The lieutenant colonel felt his stomach sink.

"*Damn*," he yelled, looking toward the hangar. "Whoever they are, they obviously know who is responsible. Damn, damn! Surely I could not have been *that* low."

Thomas politely accepted a handshake from Carlton and slaps on the back from the other RAF pilots. They seemed proud of him. But in his mind, Thomas was already considering the price of repairs to the automobile parked beside the hangar.

"This will cost me four months' salary at least,"

he admitted to Carlton. "It may, in fact, cost me much more."

He strode briskly away from the jet and toward the yellow sedan. Its occupants were apparently unhurt, but were unable to push open the vehicle doors from the inside. Thomas pulled at the passenger side handle, and the door swung open. He recognized Terrance Hill immediately.

USS *Enterprise*

Debriefing had gone slowly. The final night recovery had been over for two hours before most of the air-wing pilots had been read their landing grades. Each pilot had seemed less interested in his landing grades than in the A-7 Corsair ejection. And each had wanted a detailed description of what Buzzell had seen. Having witnessed two ejection sequences in less than a week he had become something of an expert. Their curiosity and their questions had delayed the LSO's rounds to the ready rooms. The final space, those belonging to the Red Dragons of VA-59—the only A-6 Intruder squadron aboard *Enterprise*—adjoined the officer wardroom two levels below the hangar bay on the second deck. Buzzell leaned against the ice machine there, nursing a glass of iced tea. The tea was awful. It tasted of jet fuel. But it was wet and cold, and he refilled the glass.

Lieutenant Dan "Wrongway" Harrington walked into the wardroom as Buzzell turned to leave. The two glanced at each other, then stared. They walked toward each other, and shook hands fiercely. Harrington seemed relieved to recognize a familiar face on the *Enterprise*.

"Guess they'll let just about anybody be an LSO

these days,'' he joked. Large dimples formed on his freckled cheeks as he tugged at Buzzell's dirty float coat. Harrington hadn't changed. He had always enjoyed making insults.

"And I guess they'll let just about anybody fly Whales these days, too,'' Buzzell shot back. "But you and that deathtrap are perfect for each other. You're *both* too old to be flying around the boat.'' Buzzell, in return, had always dwelled on Dan Harrington's age—less than two months more than his own, but always worthy of note.

Harrington was tall and wide, a red-haired, bushy-browed aviator of pure Irish descent. He and Buzzell had first met in Florida, where the two attended Aviation Officer Candidate School together. As newly commissioned ensigns, the two had flown their first Navy aircraft while students in the same South Texas training command squadron. Harrington and Buzzell had finished advanced jet training in Mississippi, and both had received their wings on the same day. Buzzell had known Harrington as long as he had known anyone in the U.S. Navy.

"So were you on the platform when I brought that beautiful A-3 aboard this tub?''

"I was,'' Buzzell snickered. "And to be quite honest with you, Danny boy, that was the single lousiest piece of ball flying I've ever witnessed.'' Harrington drew back and struck a boxer's pose. He made small fake jabs at the LSO, like a man challenged to a sparring match. By now, they were both laughing.

Buzzell read Harrington the landing grade comments from his LSO book—he had graded the approach an *OK*—then changed the subject again to flight school. Harrington talked about A-3s and Buzzell about F-14s. Dan Harrington flew Whales out of Diego Garcia, a tiny dot of land dead center in the Indian Ocean. Except for very rare detachments aboard carriers, Harrington had been living on the island since Buzzell had seen him last. They both decided it had been a long three years.

"So, are you and that airplane gonna be able to help us out up north in the Gulf?" Buzzell asked, again refilling his glass.

"Hope so. That's why we're here. But to be real honest, Buzz, I don't know what they expect us to do. The Iranians used to be fairly predictable. Now those sandy little ragheads are getting wily," he added.

"Then you guys heard about the *Carl Vinson* thing, and that they nailed a Tomcat up there." Buzzell paused, searching for a better choice of words. "If you and your jet had been airborne that day, would you have known the Revolutionary Guard had launched an F-4 or an F-14—even if our fighters or the E-2 couldn't see it on their radar first?"

Harrington pretended to ignore the question, scanning the wardroom, counting the other officers standing and sitting there. Instead, he leaned toward Buzzell, winking.

"If you got something better than this tea to share with your thirsty old pal here, I might be able to shed a little light on that particular subject. Know what I mean?" Harrington wrinkled his furry red brows.

Dirk Buzzell led the A-3 pilot out of the second deck wardroom, up three ladderwells, and forward toward his stateroom. On the way, Buzzell gave Harrington an informal tour of the *Enterprise* 0-3 level. Harrington followed him inside CAG's outer office, where Buzzell's final official act of the evening was to deliver the LSO grade book to Phil Grokulsky. Grokulsky was sitting at his desk there. The old LSO was staring into the blank screen of a word processing computer.

"Kinda late for you to be working, isn't it, Ski?" Buzzell mentioned while scanning the rest of the tiny spaces. A half dozen yeomen, two of them chief petty officers, were also at work. Across the room, CAG's inner-office door was closed, and there was a hand-written DO NOT DISTURB sign taped to it.

"What's goin' on in there?" he asked Grokulsky.

"Kurt Hansen didn't make it," the senior airwing LSO stated slowly. He turned in his desk chair and squinted toward Dirk Buzzell. "We just got the word from Medical."

"What the he—" Buzzell started.

"If you'll excuse me, Buzz, I got a bunch of messages to write. Sorry."

The Officers Club
Sultan of Oman Air Force Base
Thumrait, Oman

Malcolm Jennings, secretary to British envoy Terrance Hill, nursed a tall pilsner of Guinness Stout Ale at the Officers Club wooden bar. Lieutenant Colonel Thomas stood beside Jennings, waiting there while the Omani bartender fetched him two more tins of the dark brew. When the tins arrived, the officer placed a few coins on the bar and grabbed at the ale. Behind him, at a poorly lighted table, Terrance Hill rubbed at his forehead.

"I don't know what to say, sir. I have no excuse," the lieutenant colonel apologized. "I might have killed you this afternoon."

"It's just a scratch, Colonel. I believe I'll live." Hill took the ale and sipped at it.

"I will, of course, submit a complete report of the incident, Mr. Hill. I am prepared for any and all consequences of my actions. My second-in-command is very capable. He and the Number 6 will continue nicely in my absence." The RAF officer raised his ale tin and drank half of it in three large gulps.

"Nonsense, Colonel. I don't plan on filing any report, and I don't expect to see one from you either. There are many reasons why my vehicle could have been damaged. As you know, the roads in this vicinity are very treacherous, and my secretary is notorious for falling asleep at the wheel. We will keep this incident between you and me. Your services as commanding officer here are far more critical to the Sultanate of Oman than is the roof of my Mercedes. The embassy will cover the damages, I assure you. Is that understood?"

Lieutenant Colonel Thomas stared across the table in disbelief. His thin lips parted in a wide smile.

"Of course, Mr. Hill. If you insist."

"I do."

The officer signaled toward the bar, and two more ales were rushed to the table.

"Before I am unable to speak without slurring my words, Colonel, let me tell you what I've learned from our people in London." Hill placed the large tin on the table and opened the briefcase beside it. Except for Hill, the lieutenant colonel, Hill's secretary, and the bartender, the Thumrait Officers Club was deserted. It was late. Still, the envoy spoke in a whisper.

"I'll be damned if I know the source of London's intel, Colonel, but they have provided us with a timetable. You and your pilots are to continue with your training exercises through the middle of next week. I urge you to make good use of the short time allotted you. Then, beginning on the twenty-second of the month, your people and your Hawker Hunters will begin standing runway strip-alerts beginning one hour before sunrise and ending one hour after sunset. The Number 6 will man two aircraft during those times and be prepared to fly north at a moment's notice to intercept Iranian Revolutionary Guard Phantoms or F-14 Tomcats. London doesn't expect F-14s, by the way. It seems their F-14s are not capable of delivering air-to-ground ordnance."

"Alerts only during daylight hours, sir? The Iranians could just as easily attack at night. They have done so in the past against the Iraqis. It is my recommendation that the Hunters be manned around the clock, Mr. Hill."

"No, Colonel. London leads me to believe the raid will occur only during daylight hours, if it occurs at all. The alerts will be stood only during the times I specified. The remainder of your squadron personnel and aircraft will fly normal sorties while the alerts are manned. Operations at Thumrait must appear completely normal. It is important that the IRG not suspect we are on to them."

"Yes, of course, Mr. Hill. I understand completely."

DAY SEVENTEEN

JANUARY 21

USS *Enterprise*
Aardvark 107
1200

Dirk Buzzell pushed against both throttle grips with the heel of his left hand. Aardvark 107 seemed ready to fly. Only a thin catapult holdback fitting held the Tomcat to the carrier flight deck. Twin flaming afterburners bit into the jet blast deflector raised behind the aircraft. But the fighter would not fly until the catapult was fired, and the catapult would not fire until the catapult officer was satisfied that 107's pilot was ready to fly. Buzzell should have saluted by now—it was the signal the cat officer was expecting from him. Buzzell was not ready. More to the point, his aircraft was not ready. He announced that fact over the land/launch radio frequency.

"Suspend cat three. Suspend catapult number three!" At the same time, he shook his head from side to side. The catapult officer saw Buzzell's head move inside the cockpit. The air boss in the *Enterprise* tower heard the radio call and responded to it.

"You're suspended, one-oh-seven. You're *not*

going anywhere.'' The boss, perched high in the carrier's island superstructure, looked down upon the flight deck and the dozens of aircraft that crowded it. Judging from the tone of his voice, the boss wasn't in a sympathetic mood. ''What the hell's your problem, one-oh-seven?''

Buzzell snapped the fighter's engines out of afterburner, then further back to idle. He swore over the ICS to Lieutenant Junior-grade Kyle ''Bird'' Herrin, his RIO, before answering the radio call.

''I need a few seconds, boss. My wings are AFU.'' He stated the nature of his malfunction matter-of-factly. The boss did not attempt to understand what Buzzell meant by AFU, nor did the pilot elaborate over the UHF frequency.

''Roger that,'Vark zero-seven. You've got *one minute* to fix your jet. Otherwise, I'm gonna pull you off the cat and shut you down! Clock's running.''

Behind his dark visor and under his oxygen mask, Buzzell repeated the boss's call sarcastically. ''You've got one minute to fix it . . . Jeez.''

''What's up, Buzz?'' Everything in the backseat of Aardvark 107 looked good to Bird Herrin.

''I got a bright red warning light staring me in the face up here . . . looks like our wings are out of detent. Don't want those things to accidentally sweep aft during the cat stroke, now do we? I don't feel much like swimmin' this afternoon, Bird. Lemme try something.''

Buzzell pulled up on the flap handle and swept his wings from 20 to 68 degrees, then farther aft until they slid into oversweep. Fifty circuit breakers were paneled beside his left and right knees against the cockpit bulkheads. He pulled the first two in the fifth row on the left side, depressed the master reset push-button above his landing gear handle, then returned the wing-sweep handle to its full forward position. He snapped the breakers back into place then lowered the flaps. He felt, then heard a mechanical *thunk* as the wings dropped into their detent at 20 degrees. The warning light went out.

"Yea!" he said to Herrin, happy in his little victory. "Now we can go flying. Sometimes you have to *will* these big bitches into the air."

Buzzell overbanked Aardvark 107, extending his speed brakes and pulling power on the two Pratt and Whitney's. He slid into position abeam a KA-7 tanker at 11,000 feet above the *Enterprise*. His wingman, Mark Caine, had launched first and was already plugged into the tanker's fifty-foot refueling drogue. It was good to see Coke back in the air again. Buzzell extended his Tomcat's inflight refueling probe and slid into the tanker's basket when Caine had moved off the KA-7. Both fighters took 2,000 pounds of JP-5. Both were topped off. He pulled out of the basket, retracted the refueling probe, then led Caine away from the tanker circle overhead the ship.

Fifty miles farther north and a little deeper into the middle of the Indian Ocean, a section of A-7s awaited the two Tomcats. On this sortie, the Corsairs would simulate Iranian F-4 Phantoms. Buzzell and Caine would fight them as if they were Phantoms. It was good training, and it was great flying.

A Beech King-Air
Near Musat, Oman
1300

Prince Khamed-al-Far wore the title of Minister for Defense. The title was entirely ceremonial. As a first cousin to the Sultan of Oman, he had no experience with defense matters or with fighting war—or with the management of those who might fight it. He hadn't even been involved in the coup that had brought the Sultan to power. The prince understood completely his role as figurehead, and as a member of the Omani royal family. He had, by bloodlines alone, earned the position and its considerable yearly stipend. Should war be declared or fought—if any decisions regarding the defense of Oman were to be made—Khamed was certain that his cousin would know what to do.

The prince had been vacationing in Monaco when the *Majorca Azul* was first bombed then mined by members of the Iranian Revolutionary Guard. And he would have preferred to remain on the French Riviera. But it seemed that the sinking of a tanker off the coastal waters of Oman was a matter for the Minister of Defense. As a result, Khamed had been summoned to Musat. He was not certain how he should perform his duties in this case, but he had already been told he would be flying north to Didamar.

Prince Khamed loved to fly. He sat in the right seat of the Beech King-Air VIP transport, directly beside the pilot. Each of the six cabin seats behind the prince and his pilot were unoccupied. Since launching out of Seeb International Airport in Musat—more than an hour earlier—the pilot in the left seat had not touched the controls. Instead, Khamed worked at the yoke. The prince peeked above the King-Air's instrument panel glareshield and through the windscreen. He was a tiny man, the shortest and plumpest of the Sultan's cousins. And his enthusiasm for flying was far greater than his skill.

He refused to employ the aircraft's autopilot. The

King-Air rose and fell above and below its assigned altitude of 8,000 feet. He pushed at the two turboprop throttles constantly. He was not satisfied with a cruise speed of 220 knots, and he was curious why his cousin, the Sultan, had not purchased a faster aircraft. Occasionally, he would jump on the left or right rudder pedals. The aircraft would slide through the air in something less than controlled flight. The pilot would offer encouragement, or recommend an updated heading to their destination. For the most part, however, Prince Khamed ignored him.

The pilot pulled back on the twin throttles as the King-Air flew over the village of Bukha, and the aircraft began a slow descent.

"The oil tanker is directly ahead at twenty kilometers, Excellency," the pilot said. "It will be best to survey the ship from a lower altitude." Prince Khamed nodded, then returned his full attention to the control yoke. The King-Air continued to twist and yaw as it descended toward the Omani coastline.

Bukha, on the northern coast of Oman

The wife of Shail Bakhash shuffled around her market stand, arranging large baskets of nuts and dried dates. The lifting and placement of the larger burlap bags—the heavier ones filled with tobacco and beets—she left for her husband. The market was already bustling with buyers from the village, and the tobacco and beets were not yet in their proper position beside her stand. She could see her husband across the dusty square. He was standing near a fountain in the square. His back was to her.

The fountain contained no water, but Bakhash stared into it as if it did.

When he finally joined her at the market stand, Shail Bakhash's wife was quibbling with another merchant about the price of sugar beets. He noticed that his wife had already managed to drag the large burlap bags into their proper place.

Aardvark 107
1340

Dirk Buzzell pushed both throttles past the military power detent into afterburner. He bunted the nose forward and the Tomcat accelerated. Zero G floated him from the front cockpit ejection seat cushion—maybe an inch or two, until both lap restraints took up the slack. He leveled his wings, sliding to the outside of his wingman flying in Aardvark 111.

"Coke, Buzz. You've got the lead," Buzzell said over the radio.

Mark Caine pulled the section of F-14s toward a single radar contact left of his nose and slightly high at eight miles.

"They're coming downhill. I'm tally one," Caine radioed.

Buzzell brought his eyes back inside the cockpit of 107, scanning again the dark green TID just in front of his stick. The screen was blank, and as useless now as the radar that normally fed it information. A TM acronym flashed in the lower left corner of the display. The fighter's AWG-9 radar transmitter was suddenly lifeless.

He and his RIO no longer had the big picture—neither of them had any picture at all. Even the RIO's DDD, his digital data display, which normally fed Herrin raw video and operated independently of the TID, was black. Buzzell cursed at the displays in the front cockpit as if they could hear his reprimand of them.

Coke could lead the section, Buzzell decided. And someone had to. Judging from the UHF radio calls he'd heard early in the intercept, Coke's radar was solid, and Greg Bright was in his backseat.

The fighters and the Corsair attack jets were closing on each other at 970 knots—the four aircraft were merging at thirteen miles per minute. Caine accepted the lead, and was content to get himself to the merge with the one bogey he saw—the one locked by 111's radar—and with the one he didn't. Buzzell held on, one mile abeam and 3,000 feet below Mark Caine's jet. He drew an invisible line from the nose of his wingman's airplane to a point in skies where he hoped to see Coke's contact. He saw nothing—no jet, no trail, and no black speck in those skies that would give Buzzell a direction to turn his Tomcat.

"No joy on your bogey," he said across the UHF radio.

"Tally two now." Caine seemed to be yelling, his voice a falsetto of excitement.

Notso Bright, sitting in Caine's backseat, knew that Buzzell and Herrin could see nothing from inside Aardvark 107. He stared into his DDD, describing the information it displayed.

"The leader's level . . . the trailer is low. They're lined out left. Four miles. Good lock . . . there's a simulated Fox-one on the leader."

The low A-7 Corsair pulled hard right on the call, as he might if he were an Iranian F-4 Phantom and had seen a real missile erupt off the F-14. The Corsair exposed his belly to the Tomcats in his turn, showing enough fuselage silhouette for Buzzell to gain sight.

"Buzz's tally one now, Coke. I'm visual on you."

A Beech King-Air

The river of black crude was visible from beyond fifteen nautical miles. It snaked with the current southeast from the Didamar anchorage. The oil seemed to dissipate and lighten in color where the Strait of Hormuz emptied into the Gulf of Oman. Prince Khamed released the control yoke and climbed onto his seat cushion to take a better look at the spill. The King-Air pilot in the left seat took advantage of the opportunity to steady the airplane.

"Much wasted oil," the prince commented. "Many millions of gallons."

"And many people killed, Excellency. Twenty or thirty at least," the pilot echoed while peering through his windscreen.

"I am well aware of that fact," Khamed said sternly, hoping to convince the pilot of his compassion for those killed in the attack.

The King-Air slowed to 150 knots and orbited overhead the *Majorca Azul* at 500 feet. The ship no longer resembled an oil tanker. But though blasted and torn, most of the oil remained stubbornly above the surface of the Strait of Hormuz. She was held there still by the rocky reef beneath her twisted frame. The flames that had engulfed her more than ten days earlier had burned out, but oil continued to pour from her sides. A single Didamar tug patrolled the wreck—it drug a makeshift barrier designed to trap the leaking fluid. But to Khamed, still standing on his seat cushion, the barrier seemed ineffective. The exposed keel of the *Majorca Azul* reflected brightly the high Omani sun.

"A tragedy," the prince pronounced solemnly. "I understand it was a new ship."

"Will this bring war to Oman, Excellency?" the pilot asked.

"You will have to ask my cousin that question, but I believe not. Tankers have been attacked before . . . there will be others in the future," the prince said as he grabbed the control yoke and pushed forward on the two throttles.

Bukha, Oman

Shail Bakhash was content to watch his wife conduct business at the market stand. He preferred to continue mourning the death of his son and nephew. Occasionally, his neighbors and friends would pass by the fountain. They would grab at his goat-hair sweater and hug him and console him in his loss. Sometimes, one or two of them would purchase handfuls of tobacco or nuts or beets from his wife.

"Will you go to the *Khasaab* and return to the sea?" one of them asked finally. The old man did not answer. Instead, large tears welled in his eyes.

"You must return to the dhow, husband," his wife had told him. "There is too little money to be made here at the market, and Allah will not return our son to us."

Bakhash turned and walked away from his wife, and toward the waterless fountain. He would be alone with his grief while she sold from the stand. She grabbed a cup filled with dark brown tobacco and held it up in front of passersby at the market.

Four men approached her stand from the square. Each of them carried heavy burlap bags—each of the bags seemed to contain boxes of identical size. One of the men stopped where she held out the cup. She did not recognize him, though he was dressed like most men in the square. He took a tobacco leaf from the cup, then smelled it and put it in his mouth. As he nibbled on the leaf, he reached into his robe and took out money enough to buy a small sack of it. The wife of Shail Bakhash did not notice that when the man walked away from her stand, he left behind one of the heavy bags.

Aardvark 107

Buzzell's airplane was "lead-nosed"—sort of a half-neutered Tomcat. Without the AWG-9 radar, his constructive load-out of radar-guided Sparrow missiles was useless. The 107's radar had always been suspect. Buzzell had read nearly a dozen maintenance "gripes" on the AWG-9 system before signing for the jet. He and Bird Herrin didn't expect it would work for them during this sortie either. Ironically, the radar had operated flawlessly for thirty-five minutes. It had chosen to die at the most critical point in the intercept.

He and Herrin's cockpit ICS was up "hot mike," and Buzzell could hear himself breathe through his oxygen mask. He was without the use of radar missiles, but his load-out also included two heat-seeking AIM-9 Sidewinders.

"At least we still got a couple of 'Heaters,' " he said to his RIO, who, without a radar to read, was quiet and temporarily out of work.

"Buzz . . . Coke's comin' right."

Right? Buzzell saw Caine roll Aardvark 111 into a steep angle of bank, then pull. The fighter flew across the top of his cockpit—less than 1,500 feet separated the Tomcats. Caine pulled hard, and humid Indian Ocean air condensed into visible moisture as it moved over his swept wingtips. *But right?*

The A-7 Corsair—the only Corsair Buzzell saw—had peeled from right to left at the merge, and was lower now, moving farther left across his windscreen, then into his port canopy quarter panel. Given the A-7's size as it moved down out of the blue-gray, then into the white horizon line between the sky and the ocean below it, Buzzell estimated his range to the attack jet at a little less than two miles. It moved quickly from his 1130 to his 10 o'clock position. Mark Caine had turned tail to the only bogey Buzzell saw. He stated his deduction to Bird Herrin.

"Coke must be on the other Corsair. I see one of 'em, going to nine o'clock now," he told Herrin. "Find the guy Coke's on."

Buzzell pushed his nose over, and followed the lower bogey.

Aardvark 107 chased its target, digging low and left under the A-7, erasing range at 365 knots and at 20 degrees per second of turn rate. Herrin, fighting the pull of 6½ Gs, found Coke and the second Corsair through the thick Plexiglas canopy over his left shoulder, just outside his Tomcat's twin tails.

"Tally the second bogey, Buzz. Left seven-thirty. He's no threat to us." Buzzell followed the call, picking up his lead and the A-7. Both of the jets flew across the circle from his turn and slightly high—two tiny arrows slicing through the light blue air.

"Fox-two on the high A-7." Coke's voice was easier now, relaxed.

"Half a mile, Buzz." Herrin sounded surprised. His pilot had seen the radar diamond appear in his

HUD only a fraction of a second before his RIO's range call on the low bogey. His target was inside the diamond. Somehow, their radar system was alive again.

"Roger that," Buzzell said, "but we're min range."

He thumbed at his stick weapons-select switch and watched the symbology on his HUD switch from Sidewinder to Gun. The gunsight pipper danced across Buzzell's windscreen as Herrin counted down the shrinking distance between 107 and the second Corsair.

At just inside three-tenths of a mile—roughly 2,000 feet—Buzzell and Herrin were moving into lethal range of the Tomcat's Mark-61 six-barrel cannon. But the angles were all wrong. Now, the Instantaneous Lead Computing Optical Gun Sight pipper was pegged high and right in Buzzell's HUD. He needed more lead. And his options were simple. He could accept the angles he'd already made on the Corsair, then pull hard to free the pipper and rake the bullets across the back of the A-7. The snapshot offered him a nominal percentage of kill. In the real world, against a real bogey, he might even get lucky with a gunshot like this one. But a kill was unlikely.

After the snapshot, he could then roll his F-14 high and right, outside the A-7's flight path, and preserve his offensive position. More important, he could maintain his energy and airspeed advantage over the bogey. The A-7 was slow—at least 150 knots slower than his Tomcat. Buzzell figured, as he studied the way it was turning, that the Corsair was down around 170 or 180 knots. That airspeed gave the A-7 no vertical move. The F-14 had an altitude sanctuary, if it wanted one. Buzzell could perch high above his prey, then finish the fight at his leisure. It was perfect: a quick shot, an offensive position, and the opportunity for reattack. Buzzell seemed pleased with himself. He had considered the smarter of his two options, but had already begun another move.

Kyle Herrin kept a verbal cadence with each decreasing tenth of a nautical mile between the two jets.

"Point-two," he called over the ICS. Quickly, the RIO felt himself roll farther left, from 30 or 40, to nearly 90 degrees angle of bank. He found himself looking left, over the canopy bow beside his pilot's ejection seat and straight down into the glassy waters three miles below. Buzzell then relaxed the backstick pressure a little, floating to a point farther aft of the A-7's wing-line and toward the bogey's extended six o'clock position. The Tomcat accelerated from 320 to 360 knots. But the A-7 had too little airspeed and G available of its own to force the F-14 into an overshoot. And since the bogey couldn't run, it would try to hide from the fighter's gunsight pipper. The A-7 had no other game plan but to hold its best turn. Its best turn might defeat the Tomcat's first gun attack—maybe even the second. The fight would end when the Corsair ran out of altitude and was forced to climb away from the water, or when the Aardvark F-14 ran out of bullets.

Herrin saw the closure and was leaning forward to call "point-one" when he felt the airplane abruptly squat beneath him. He blinked to focus his eyes as his G-suit squeezed at his legs and stomach muscles, forcing blood through his upper body and into his heavy head.

Buzzell didn't notice the G-meter, but he felt what it must have registered. Both engines had been pulled out of afterburner. He'd taken his left hand from the throttles and placed it with his right hand on the control stick. Dirk Buzzell had decided he wouldn't overshoot the A-7, wouldn't climb high and outside the bogey's turn, and wouldn't wait for a later opportunity for the kill. Where the gunsight pipper had lagged the Corsair, it suddenly led it. In millimeters of movement of his HUD, the pipper jumped more than 200. In degrees of turn, about 70—all in less than three seconds. The pipper retical fell to the bottom of his windscreen, then slid to the middle of the HUD, and laid in line with the A-7's tail pipe.

"Airspeed," Buzzell demanded from his backseater. He was too occupied outside his aircraft to check the gauge for himself.

"One-eighty," Herrin replied in a grunt, still feeling the effects of G. The pull had cost Aardvark 107 nearly 200 knots. "Still point-one on the range. No closure."

"Roger that. We're saddled in there now . . . cospeed," Buzzell said. "He's got nowhere to go. Pipper's on."

A Beech King-Air

The pilot monitored the King-Air's altitude closely as the prince turned the aircraft toward the south. He encouraged Khamed to climb away from the waters near Didamar, and was surprised when the aircraft altimeter read exactly 3,000 feet in mostly level flight.

"I shall report my findings to the Sultan upon our return to Musat. That ship and her cargo are a complete loss. The incident is an embarrassment to the entire region. Something *must* be done."

"I recommend we climb to a more fuel-efficient altitude, Excellency. Only two and one-half hours of fuel are remaining. The shortest route to Musat is across the Gulf to the southeast," the pilot directed.

"We are in no hurry and I prefer lower altitudes," the prince answered, then paused. "The Revolutionary Guard is an unholy vermin. May Allah curse those terrorist thugs." The prince tried to sit straighter in the right seat of the King-Air. When he did, he was unable to reach its throttle controls or rudders. He slumped forward again, and grabbed tightly at the yoke with his small hands.

"If I was a younger man, I would fight the Iranian Revolutionary Guard myself."

Bukha, Oman

The wife of Shail Bakhash had been productive. All of the tobacco and most of the beets and nuts had been sold. The deck of the *Khasaab* was brimming with more of it—along with bales of cotton and some potatoes that her husband would normally have delivered to Didamar two weeks earlier. She might be able to sell more tobacco if it was retrieved from the dhow. It had to be sold before it rotted on the boat. She found her husband near the fountain again. They talked for a moment, and he began walking the half kilometer distance to the pier. She returned to the market stand to wait for him.

The *Khasaab* was tied to its regular spot beside Bukha's lone wooden pier. Shail Bakhash hesitated at the foot of it. Four men stood beside his boat—he recognized none of them. One of the men seemed anxious about the time. None of the four seemed to notice the old man.

Bakhash stooped down behind the pilings at the base of the pier as a long boat emerged from one of the rocky inlets northeast of the village. He clutched at his chest with both hands—holding his heart. He recognized the boat immediately as a Boghammer. The long boat accelerated quickly, and when it was beside the pier, the four men jumped into it. They were greeted with laughter and hugs by the driver of the Boghammer boat. The Boghammer backed away from the pier and began running north into the Strait of Hormuz. There was no large flag hanging above the Boghammer, but Shail Bakhash was certain it was Iranian—other markings on the boat were Iranian—and the men on the pier had spoken Farsi. The old man stood there for a moment, wondering what he might have done to the Iranians had he been armed. Shail Bakhash had never before thought such things.

Bakhash stood slowly from behind the pilings. He felt his heart still thumping wildly in his chest. He stepped cautiously up the rotting pier as the IRG boat bounced into the strait, then disappeared. Bakhash was preparing to board his dhow when he heard the first explosion. It crackled from behind him. He was certain it came from the market square. He turned and ran down the pier.

The wife of Shail Bakhash had been negotiating the sale of sugar beets when something inside the large burlap bag beneath her stand detonated. The blast had torn through the stone and wood in front of her. Stone and splinters of wood from the stand and fragments from the bomb itself ripped through her. Her small body was tossed up and onto the dusty roadway twenty feet behind the square—it had fallen in a queer heap of twisted limbs. Shail Bakhash fell to his knees beside her. He did not notice the bodies of two other Bukha women beside his wife in the dust.

A Beech King-Air

Prince Khamed did not see the first blast as he flew the twin engine King-Air over the village of Bukha. But he witnessed the second and finally the third and fourth, which occurred almost simultaneously. From an altitude of 3,000 feet, the detonations were not spectacular—mostly there was dust and debris in the center of the square. Only after the prince had handed over the King-Air's controls to his pilot, and after the pilot was able to descend to roughly 500 feet above the stands in the market, did the total result of four separate bomb blasts become obvious.

Khamed stood on his seat cushion and peered down through the sloped windshield and over the nose of the Beech. In the village streets just below him, men and women scattered from where the bombs had exploded. It seemed that every living thing in and near the market was running—there were a few dogs and chickens running, too. Only Shail Bakhash and the body of his wife, the two bodies beside her in the dirt, and nine others scattered around the market stands did not move.

"*Good God!*" Prince Khamed yelled while he stood on the seat. "Will this Iranian cowardice never end!"

Aardvark 107

To Buzzell—to any fighter pilot—a gun kill was the ultimate kill. Strangely, it was a hard thing to come by in the F-14. The Tomcat's high-speed capability and bristling weapons load-out was greater than any fighter in the world. Long-range and medium-range and short-range missiles virtually guaranteed the F-14 a victory long before it approached the Mark-61's effective firing envelope. Against a small target, like the A-7, an F-14 pilot was not expected to kill with his shortest-range weapon system—it simply shouldn't be necessary to employ the cannon. But Buzzell had passed up several missile shots for the gun kill.

And it had felt so good getting there—getting saddled in there—that Buzzell reveled briefly in his victory. The Corsair pilot pulled and rolled his aircraft, working to somehow elude the fighter behind him. The Tomcat remained there, and followed the A-7 through each escape attempt.

"We're like a booger on his finger," Buzzell commented to his RIO over the ICS. "He can't shake us."

The attack jet had been beaten. And Buzzell knew better than most the reason why. He was not vain enough to credit himself entirely. Anyone with even the tiniest appreciation for thrust-to-weight ratios or fighter energy maneuvering diagrams could have predicted the winner of this engagement. Airplane to airplane, the Corsair had been outclassed. An F-14 should be able to beat an A-7. Still, dissimilar ACM was good training.

But the A-7's next move surprised and confused Buzzell. He'd never seen it before and hadn't expected it. The jet suddenly tore away from Buzzell's pipper, and was moving left to right, out of his HUD and under his wing. The pilot at the controls of the A-7 pulled hard. Given the airspeed of his jet at the time, he pulled far *too* hard. In the jargon of naval aviators, his pull was categorized as "a last-ditch guns defense" maneuver, a final attempt to break free of the fighter tracking him from behind. But in terms of his speed through the air, in terms of aerodynamics, and in terms of pure physics, the A-7 pilot had asked his airplane to do something it was simply not capable of doing.

The A-7 rolled left before slicing back to the right. As it left Buzzell's windscreen, it had rolled onto its back and began yawing in a strange way. It was no longer flying. Its wings no longer created the lift required for controlled flight. It was spinning out of control.

Buzzell tried to follow the Corsair as it fell away from him, but could not. The A-7 was no longer moving forward through the air, only downward toward the Indian Ocean water 14,000 feet underneath it. The jet flopped and spun from its back to its belly, upright but twisting as it descended. It floated like a queer Frisbee, and pirouetted around itself. Buzzell could see the A-7's tiny horizontal stabilizers shifting as its pilot worked at the control stick. But the stick inputs were ineffective. The Corsair was still spinning as it entered a thin layer of clouds 2,000 feet above the water.

A Beech King-Air

Prince Khamed had ordered his pilot into one final orbit over the village of Bukha. At the point in that orbit when the King-Air was headed due north, he instructed the pilot to level the aircraft's wings.

"But why, Excellency? There is barely enough fuel aboard to reach Musat . . . we must turn around now. We cannot continue farther on this heading."

"It is my wish to continue," the prince stated flatly. "Your only concern is to fulfill that wish. Continue."

The King-Air motored at 500 feet. Oman's coastline fell behind the aircraft's wing line and Bukha disappeared. Ahead, Khamed saw only the wide waters of the Strait of Hormuz. Beyond the strait was Iran—Hengām and Qeshm and Larak Islands, and eventually Bandar 'Abbās. He stared at the fuel gauges. He did not understand how to read them, but would not admit as much to his pilot.

The prince sat back in his seat. He rubbed his face with his fat little hands. It would be necessary for Khamed to report his findings to the Sultan.

"Dear cousin," he practiced aloud to himself. "After viewing the tanker wreckage at Didamar, I was then witness to further terrorist activity in Bukha on the northern peninsula. Omani villagers were killed savagely by bomb explosions there. I am certain this activity is further evidence of Iranian Revolutionary Guard aggression. The Sultanate must begin diplomatic dialog with government officials in Iran at once. As your Minister of Defense, and as a witness to these atrocities, it was my decision to fly to Teheran to begin such deliberations."

The King-Air pilot stared at Prince Khamed as he spoke—the expression on his face needed little interpretation.

"I too am terrified by the prospect," the prince admitted. "What chance do we have of reaching Teheran safely?"

"None, Excellency. *None!* There is not enough fuel, and Iran's air defenses will not allow it. It is suicide." The pilot wiped beads of sweat from his forehead, then adjusted the cockpit's air conditioner to a cooler setting.

"Then we are not cowards ourselves if we return to Musat. That would be the prudent thing to do," Khamed said finally. The pilot interpreted the prince's statement and immediately reversed his course toward the mainland of Oman.

Prince Khamed took the controls and flew clumsily. He sat too low in the cockpit to notice the Iranian Boghammer boat approaching the twin-engine aircraft from the south. The boat skimmed quickly over the waves eight nautical miles north of Bukha. The men inside the Boghammer had first seen the King-Air as it orbited the market square—each of the men assumed their boat had been spotted by its pilot as the aircraft then began to fly north into the Strait of Hormuz. When the King-Air had reversed its course and flew directly toward the Boghammer boat, the five men inside it prepared their weapons. One of the five, the Iranian at the wheel and throttle, idled the boat until it was steady in the water.

A pair of Soviet-built SA-7 Grail surface-to-air missile launchers were the longest-range weapons systems aboard the Boghammer. The Grails were shoulder-launched and required IR energy to satisfy their seeker-head logic. The two turboprop engines that drove the King-Air through the air at 500 feet produced less IR energy than jet engines. As the aircraft closed to within two miles, the SA-7 could not yet "see" it. Instead, the Boghammer's deck-mounted recoilless rifle fired first.

The recoilless erupted continuously. Its rounds

formed a deadly rainbow of lead that flew toward the King-Air. The IRG gunmen had expended most of the 50-caliber rounds before their target was within range. At three-quarters of a mile, a single 50-caliber round hit the aircraft's horizontal tail just forward of the port elevator surface. The 50-cal's high-incendiary explosive fuse did not function. The round simply punched a six-inch hole through the King-Air's aluminum skin. The pilot felt and heard it—a sharp thud and metallic snap he did not recognize. He decided immediately that what he had felt and what he had heard were due to Prince Khamed's rough control yoke inputs, and nothing else.

Then the Beech pilot saw a lone tracer round—the first of many large and fiery tracers that flew above and then past the aircraft. He and Prince Khamed were still at 500 feet of altitude, and less than one-half mile from the Boghammer. The tracer rounds grew in number and circled around the outside of the cockpit. Price Khamed did not notice them. The pilot followed the tracers to their source, simultaneously pulling back on his yoke in a climb. Prince Khamed looked puzzled as his pilot began screaming incoherently. A round skimmed across the belly of the aircraft as it ascended. There was the sound of a tiny rippling detonation, but the King-Air continued to fly normally.

Three or four seconds later, a pair of 50-caliber rounds entered the cabin. They had easily pierced the landing gear doors beneath the nose of the twin-engine VIP transport. The rounds fused together beneath the cockpit instrument panel, then blew through the panel just forward of the pilot's throttle controls. The prince watched the pilot's right hand disappear in an orange and white blaze atop the throttles. The pilot grabbed at the bloody stub where only his forearm remained. Red control panel warning lights illuminated in front of the prince. One of the lights read FUEL and a second read HYD. Prince Khamed was not sure what they meant. The lights flickered dimly, went out, then reilluminated.

Khamed held tightly to his control yoke. He twisted it quickly—first left, then right, then left again. The nose of the King-Air sliced, then fell toward the strait from the apex of its climb—1,100 feet. When it did, Prince Khamed found the Boghammer. Smokey tracers flew up at him, then past the cockpit on either side. A large flare of white erupted from the boat, and an SA-7 began guiding on the heat generated from the King-Air's left engine. The prince screamed above the sound of the missile hitting the engine. The pilot in the left seat was either already dead or could not scream.

The Beech King-Air corkscrewed farther left around the torn wing and the prince tried to counter with his yoke. The nose of the aircraft came down and Khamed aimed it at the center of the Boghammer from an altitude of 400 feet. But the King-Air no longer responded to the yoke, and Prince Khamed-al-Far knew that he would die as the airplane dove into the Strait of Hormuz more than three boat-lengths behind the Boghammer.

USS *Enterprise*
2240

Dirk Buzzell unlocked his stateroom door and stepped quietly inside. His two roommates were in their racks. He assumed that both were asleep. Amazingly, Spanky Pfister was not snoring. Buzzell clicked on the tiny fluorescent light above his desk and laid an armload of paperwork beneath it—the paperwork had been jammed into his mailbox in the Aardvark ready room. He rarely did anything about his work until it jammed his mailbox.

He shuffled through the myriad of U.S. Navy instructions, messages, and memos, then stacked them neatly across the desk in descending order of priority. A great wave of weariness washed over him. Ever since Seed Hansen's death Buzzell had had little patience with all of life's small daily annoyances. Suddenly it was too late for work, Buzzell decided, and none of the paperwork couldn't wait another day. He hadn't written Marti in nearly a week. And though he wasn't alone in the stateroom, he was convinced that his roommates were asleep and would not distract him while he wrote her. He covered the stacks with a yellow legal pad, and smiled as he wrote her name across the top of it.

He began by apologizing: *I should be writing you more often* . . . The remainder of the letter dealt with the subject of flying. It was a subject he enjoyed describing to her in endless detail. Marti used to tell him that she wanted more romance and less "hardware" in his letters from the ship. It had never occurred to him that he wrote more intimately about the F-14 Tomcat than about her. But it was easier for Dirk Buzzell to write about flying.

"Kyle Herrin was riding with me today. Notso was flying in Mark Caine's backseat. We were fighting a couple of A-7 Corsairs," he wrote. He described the entire sortie to her—from catapult launch to recovery. He wrote as if she would completely understand the Navy terminology he scribbled across the pages.

He downplayed his engagement with the A-7 before it had spun, saying only that he had been lucky, and had found himself behind the Corsair. He decided not to tell her how terrified he had been when the aircraft he had been chasing fell through a layer of clouds only a couple thousand feet over the water. He didn't write her that he had expected the attack airplane to tumble into the sea.

We flew under the clouds, looking for the A-7, he wrote. *Somehow, the Corsair pilot isn't spinning anymore. He's flying again and shows up behind us! He's trying to shoot* us! *It was a great fight.*

Buzzell folded the letter and began searching for an envelope beneath the piles of unfinished paperwork. Beside the stack of work that had earned his lowest priority for completion, he noticed for the first time a torn piece of memo pad. He was intrigued by the way it was addressed: *For Lt. Buzel.* He opened the note and immediately recognized the handwriting.

21 jan.

sir,

Thank you for talking to the skipper for me. But I already foun out that he wont let me off the boat like I asked. Its not fair, sir. I dont belong on this boat. He does not understand. When he told me that, I went back to berthing and got some drugs from a guy I know. If I took the drugs, then the skipper would let me go because I know they dont let sailors do drugs in the navy. I did not do the drugs, but I almost did. Because I could get out off of the boat if I did. I wanted to tell you this because I want off of this boat very much. I would do almost anything to get off of the boat. I wanted to tell you all of this.

Thank you,
YNSN Jordan Michaels.

Dirk Buzzell walked across the mostly dark stateroom and dialed the Aardvark ready room phone number. The squadron duty officer answered the phone and gave him Jordan Michaels's berthing compartment number. Buzzell walked out of the stateroom quickly and turned down the port 0-3 level passageway toward the aft end of the ship.

DAY TWENTY

JANUARY 24

Iranian Revolutionary Guard Hangar
Bandar 'Abbās, Iran
1600 (local time)

Omid and his RIO had been seated in the hangar ready room for more than one hour. Ali Abdul Rajani's RIO, Nori, was there as well. All three were staring at Reza, who in turn stared at the clock hanging on the ready room wall.

"Where *is* he?" Reza said finally.

"Was *the ace* ordered here for a 1500 meeting?" Omid asked sarcastically.

"He was. By *me*!" Reza had become infuriated as he waited.

Omid glanced at his RIO and then at Nori. None of the IRG aviators were surprised. The pilot was smirking.

"Then *that* is why he is late. Ali is never prompt. If you had ordered an earlier meeting time, he might have arrived by now," Omid stated.

There was the sound of a door slamming shut, and then footsteps. Ali Abdul Rajani had arrived, finally. He walked through the open ready room door. He held a newspaper in one hand and a cigarette lighter in the other. Ahmed did not have the opportunity to reprimand Rajani before the ace began a loud tirade. The vehement outburst was directed toward Omid.

"And you have the pride to call yourself a fighter pilot? Haaa!" Rajani turned the newspaper toward Reza. Omid's picture was there, under the main headline. The pilot had been photographed standing between two F-4 Phantoms—the two Phantoms Omid and his wingman had flown in their attack against the Spanish oil tanker, the *Majorca Azul*.

"You see, Reza. Your ace is a jealous man," Omid observed. "He is not willing to share the spotlight with me. And he does not fly for the greater glory of Allah as do I." Again, Rajani did not allow Reza to respond.

"Greater *glory!* Yours was a bombing mission . . . how dare you call yourself an Iranian Revolutionary Guard fighter pilot! You sank an oil barge. A barge that could not shoot back. There is *no* glory in what you have done. You have always been a coward, Omid." The ace began walking slowly toward the front of the ready room.

"The sinking of that vessel was a great victory for Islam. Again, you are jealous of my accomplishments and of my notoriety. You must learn to share the headlines with your fellow Guard pilots, Ali."

"Here is what all real fighter pilots think of your 'victory' over the oil tanker, Omid!" Rajani held the newspaper by one corner and clicked on the lighter. "Congratulations on your *very* dangerous mission."

"Ali, if you desire ever to fly an IRG Tomcat again, you will put away the lighter and *sit* down."

Reza was convincingly restrained. "It is within my power to ground you forever. Do not test me further, Ali."

Ali Abdul Rajani would not test Reza. He held the paper and the flickering lighter, but did not bring them together.

"In two days time, you and Omid will fly on the same mission," Reza stated matter-of-factly. "That mission is precisely what we are here to discuss. As is the usual case, Omid will pilot the Phantom. You will fly the F-14, Ali. Each will be in the aircraft he knows best. It is imperative to the success of the mission that the two of you work *together*." Reza was coming across more like a coach than a military commander. "And when you launch together the day after tomorrow, it is my hope that you will redirect your hatred for each other toward the Omanis."

USS *Enterprise*
Wardroom One
1620

Dirk Buzzell walked forward, up the port side of the *Enterprise* 0-3 level, and past the ready room of the VF-231 Black Eagles. He stopped behind the line of Aardvark officers already formed outside the wardroom. He leaned against the bulkhead, removed his sunglasses, and rubbed his eyes. They stung from exposure to JP-5 jet fuel. JP-5 burned in the engines of most *Enterprise* aircraft. As those aircraft turned and taxied across the carrier's flight deck, their engine exhausts carried mostly burned JP-5 into the air and across the LSO platform. Usually, the exhaust fumes did not bother him.

Buzzell didn't mind spending his LSO days on

the platform, or even walking across the ship and up and down its ladder wells to debrief air-wing pilots. And he wasn't tired, but his feet ached, so he leaned against the bulkhead, watching the messman inside the wardroom scullery spray high-pressure water against dirty plates and silverware. The spray shot through the scullery doorway, into the passageway, then onto his khaki pants and white LSO jersey. He didn't move. He looked up the line of VF-141 aviators that stood in line ahead of him.

"So, what's this evening's *specialty* of the house?" Buzzell asked the question in a poor French accent. Lieutenant Commander Ron "Cheez" Kraft heard the question first, then stepped back against the passageway bulkhead opposite the scullery. He read from the plastic menu board that hung above the line of Aardvarks.

"Oh, you're in luck, Messier Buzzell." Cheez's French was only slightly better than Dirk Buzzell's. "We have *zee* savory Salisbury steak, *zee* steamed baby carrots and, of course, an exquisite Idaho baked potato."

Kraft's comic rendering of the menu broke Buzzell and the rest of the officers into laughter.

"Salisbury steak, huh?" Buzzell repeated. "You know what that means, don't you?"

Kraft quickly answered the question. "Yep . . . '*Nairobi Trail Markers*!' And they're oh-so-good for you, Buzz."

Meals were served buffet-style in Wardroom One—the "dirty-shirt" wardroom. Most of the pilots and naval flight officers ate there. On the second deck, aft and three decks below, was Wardroom Two. Ship's company officers and other nonflyers preferred to dine there. The food was always better down on the second deck. And officers were better attended to there, as long as they wore a crisp pair of khakis and minded their manners. Wearing a flight suit to breakfast, lunch, and dinner was usually worth the trouble of eating in the topside wardroom.

Buzzell pushed a meal tray across the metal slide in front of the kitchen. He pointed to a softball-size ball of fried beef.

"I'll try one of the trail markers," he said, smiling weakly. An enlisted man, his face dripping with sweat, scooped Buzzell's dinner onto a plate, then pointed with a large spoon down the line toward the carrots. The carrots were not orange, but yellow-orange and overcooked. He stared at his entrée. It was dotted with white and red seasonings. Onions and peppers, Buzzell hoped. They would suffice as his vegetable dish.

"Just a few of those Idaho baked potatoes, if you please." The potatoes weren't baked, and they most likely weren't from Idaho, he decided. The messman grinned, then filled the remainder of the plate with French fries. Buzzell continued down the line, grabbing two slices of bread. A petty officer watched him pour a glass of powdered chocolate water, then announced to the officer that Ward Room Two still had a supply of real white milk. Buzzell thanked him, then took his tray and walked toward the group of Aardvarks seated in the far corner of the room. He would not have time before the next recovery to make the trip downstairs.

Sultan of Oman Air Force Base
Thumrait, Oman
1650

Major William Carlton unbuckled his torso harness and shifted his weight from one side of his butt to the other. At over six feet and more than 220 pounds, there was little extra room in the cramped cockpit of his Hawker Hunter. An RAF captain by the name of Steadman was strapped into the second Hunter. The captain looked out of his aircraft toward the west. The sun was settling into a bronze Omani horizon, and he no longer had the light necessary to read his magazine. Both aircraft were positioned between the main taxiway and the approach end of Thumrait's duty runway, a little more than 300 meters from the Number 6 Squadron hangar.

Neither of the two aircraft engines was turning. Instead, gas-powered generators rattled beside the fighter-bombers, providing them with electrical power. Carlton readjusted the volume control on his UHF radio. It was the only piece of electrical equipment he had switched on. A steady side-tone in his helmet earcups told him the radio was operating normally. Another radio in the Number 6 Squadron spaces was being manned. If it was necessary for him and Steadman to start and launch their Hunters, that order would come over the radio. But until the two RAF aviators heard that order, they would only sit in their parked jets.

The major checked his watch. It was nearly 1700. He had climbed into the Hawker Hunter three hours earlier. In one hour, when there was no longer a sunset and the skies over Thumrait had darkened completely, he would climb out of the Hunter, and complete his second strip alert in as many days. The two alert aircraft had been manned continuously by Number 6 Squadron pilots—from one hour before sunrise to one hour after sunset—for three days. None of the fighter-bombers had launched. No Iranian fighters had attacked mainland Oman. Major Carlton shifted again in his ejection seat. He was very uncomfortable, and his right leg had fallen asleep. He was beginning to believe there would be no attack.

Aardvark 104
1740

Greg Bright switched his UHF radio to button 17 and checked in on the Marshal frequency. He and his pilot were established in their holding pattern twenty-two miles behind the USS *Enterprise* at 7,000 feet.

"One-zero-four, Marshal. Expected approach time is five-two." Bright rogered the call, tapping the rear cockpit clock. Its second hand was frozen in place. He keyed the Tomcat's ICS.

"Hey, Coke. What time do you show? My clock is tits up—it's dead."

Bright felt the F-14's autopilot kick on as Mark Caine steadied the jet and reached for the oxygen mask dangling to the side of his helmet.

"Seventeen forty-one, straight up. I show eleven minutes to push." The RIO responded with two quick snaps of the ICS, acknowledging the time hack. He again adjusted the clock. Neither the minute nor hour hands responded to his commands.

"Forty-five million bucks a copy for a state-of-the-art fighter, and the damned clock doesn't work," he added across the ICS. Bright rolled up the left sleeve of his flight suit. His wristwatch read the same as his pilot's cockpit chronometer. "Well, Coke. At least my ten-dollar Timex is still ticking."

Greg Bright contemplated his recent designation as a "category two" RIO. With one WestPac cruise under his belt, he had begun his second deployment flying with new squadron pilots, like Mark Caine.

It felt somehow odd to be back in the air with Caine. The mishap on the *Enterprise* flight deck had shaken the pilot's confidence. Bright felt certain of it. And although Caine had been cleared of all wrongdoing in the loss of a squadron aircraft and the injuries to the Aardvark petty officer, Bright was not convinced that Mark Caine had forgiven himself.

During his first cruise, Greg Bright had flown almost exclusively with the then-commanding officer of VF-141. The former CO had flown F-4s before transitioning to Tomcats. Between the two fighter aircraft, he'd had nearly 4,000 hours of experience. Bright never had to tell the old CO how to conduct business around the ship. But with Caine or with any new pilot—especially with Caine—the RIO had suddenly learned to pay closer attention. The RIO placed a red plastic filter over the brilliant green radar DDD staring him in the face. It was getting dark outside Aardvark 104.

The sortie had originally been advertised as a "good deal" hop—a little air-to-water strafing of a six-foot metal spar towed behind the ship. Twenty-millimeter practice rounds were scarce, and aircrew rarely had the opportunity to fire the Tomcat's Mark-61 cannon. Caine and Bright flew 30- and 45-degree dive patterns at 2,000 yards behind the ship. Twice during the firing runs, Caine had claimed to see sparks fly from the tiny spar as it occasionally bounced out of the huge *Enterprise* wake. Bright didn't believe Caine could hit the small moving target—more senior pilots rarely made the same claim. Maybe Mark Caine was regaining some of that confidence. Still, the RIO loved the way the Tomcat growled and shuddered with each burst of the gun, and he encouraged his pilot.

But that had been more than an hour ago, when

the sun was still bright in the skies over the Indian Ocean. Now, outside the canopy, he caught the starboard wingtip as it flashed green. Caine had already switched on the F-14's external lights. Past the wingtip, the sun turned orange then red. The RIO found a few stars already showing through the pink sky over his canopy. He returned to the cockpit and made final adjustments to his instrument lighting. It would be even darker when they pushed from the Marshal stack.

The jet nosed over when Caine's Tacan DME read twenty-two nautical miles. He and Bright were fifteen seconds late commencing their approach. The Marshal controller didn't seem to notice.

When Caine read 5,000 feet on his barometric altimeter, he pulled back on the stick slightly. The jet slowed its rate of descent from 4,000 to 2,000 feet-per-minute. He would level off at 1,200 feet and maintain 250 knots until ten miles from the back of the ship, where procedures called for him to dirty up—to drop his landing gear, flaps, and tailhook.

Bright knew Mark Caine was intimately familiar with the numbers required to find his way to the back end of the boat—every student naval aviator who survived flight training was. He worried more about the last mile of this particular carrier approach. For the first time since being crewed together, Caine had to get them aboard *Enterprise* at night.

The RIO glanced at the rear cockpit fuel totalizer.

"Showin' six-point-nine on the gas back here, Coke. Check your hook."

"Hook's down, Notso. And six-nine up here, too. My favorite number, sixty-nine."

The RIO laughed politely over the ICS. *Good.*

Maybe Coke wasn't all that concerned about this particular night arrested landing.

He sure as hell should be, Bright said to himself in the backseat.

"Get me aboard the first time, funny man, and I'll buy you a soda down in the ready room," the RIO said.

"Can do, pal. Just sit back and enjoy the ride."

At three-quarters of a mile from the fantail of the USS *Enterprise*, Aardvark 104 was on course and on glide slope, Bright checked the fuel total again, then stomped his right foot on the deck-mounted UHF mike switch.

"One-oh-four, Tomcat ball, six-point-two." The RIO heard Dirk Buzzell's voice at the other end of his call.

"Roger ball, Tomcat. Twenty-six knots."

"Perfect," Caine said aloud. F-14s seemed to like about 25 knots of wind across the angled flight deck.

"Three fast . . . one fast . . . on-speed." The RIO called Caine's airspeed deviations as the pilot flew the ball. Bright had computed, given the fighter's fuel load, that on-speed was 128 knots. "Little decel, two slow . . . on speed." Bright was impressed. The old CO had always been at least 5 knots away from on-speed.

The backseater thought it an awkward time to feel at ease. The jet felt right. The LSOs hadn't said a word since the ball call. That was good, too. Bright's eyes left the rear cockpit airspeed indicator and jumped through the forward port-side canopy windscreen to the carrier deck now less than 200 yards away. He found the fresnel lens at the same moment the wave-off lights flashed on.

"Wave it off. Fouled deck." As usual, the landing signal officers backed up the red lights with a radio call.

"Shit! We were in there." Mark Caine pushed both throttles to the military power detent—to 100 percent. The Tomcat flew up the *Enterprise* angled deck and climbed toward 1,200 feet. Passing 900 feet the jet banked port, and was swallowed by low-lying clouds.

"This is great, Coke. I didn't feel like landing anyway." Bright felt suddenly sardonic. Caine didn't answer. He was too busy cursing at the ship, and at anything or anyone else who might have contributed to the landing area going foul.

"So I guess you owe *me* that soda now, eh, Coke?" Bright rubbed it in. He knew full well that Caine had no control over the wave-off, but decided to blame him just the same. The RIO deselected his ICS, smiling. His thoughts shifted to the upcoming turn towards "final," where he and Coke would try again to trap aboard the ship.

One-zero-four was two miles abeam the ship, at 150 knots and dirty—flying straight and level—and still in the clouds. Caine had lost the horizon. A few seconds earlier, it had been easy to see where the edge of the black ocean met the bottom of the not-yet-black sky. The pilot stared at his instruments, but preferred to see them agree with what he saw outside the cockpit. Now, he saw nothing but his Tomcat's flickering wingtip lights bouncing off dark gray air.

Caine remembered entering the cloud layer. He'd made a climbing left-hand turn—he guessed about 25 degrees angle of bank. Now, his VDI—his artificial horizon—told him he was level—steady on a heading reciprocal to that of the ship's. Everything in the airplane told him that. He believed none of it. He pushed the control stick right until his middle ear was satisfied. The Tomcat's heading moved 15 degrees before the pilot recorrected to the assigned downwind heading. Caine swore he was turning circles in the sky. Wings level again, he pushed himself away from the canopy rail. He felt heavy against it. His mind, and the weather, had conspired against him.

Bright felt the aircraft rolling through the sky. "Hey, Coke. I paid for a smooth ride back here."

"Yeah, listen, Notso, I got 'the leans' real bad. Do me a favor and back me up on your gyro, will ya?"

"No problem. We'll break out of this 'goo' any minute now." The RIO tried to encourage his pilot. There was not much else he could do.

On final, but still two-and-a-half miles from the ship, Aardvark 104 flew out of the clouds. Mark Caine broke away from his instrument scan and searched for the bottoms of the cloud deck. Nothing.

"Dark as shit out here tonight," he admitted finally to his backseater.

With no control stick or throttles in the rear cockpit, Bright stared into his radar display. He had taken a radar lock on the ship. He could determine the aircraft's drift in relation to the huge blip on his scope. He compared the lock with his Tacan DME. Given the jet's range from *Enterprise*—two nautical miles—and assuming the optimum glide slope for a precision carrier approach—3½ degrees—the RIO could determine the Tomcat's lineup altitude deviations. He decided Caine could use the help.

"Check left ten, Coke. I got us right of course a little and slightly high . . . about twenty feet."

"Roger that." Again, Caine had rolled right to appease his mind. At a little less than two miles, he could make out the running lights of the aircraft carrier. They shimmered like the stars he'd seen above the clouds. They might as well have been stars. Seeing them didn't help. He knew he should fly down to them, but he was not convinced of his own position relative to the ship. He needed more help.

"One-oh-four's a Tomcat ball, five-point-one. *Vertigo*." Bright made the call. It was time the LSO's were let in on Mark Caine's problem, he decided. Buzzell answered the transmission without hesitation—as if he was not surprised by it.

"Roger ball, 22 knots. Level your wings." The big fighter weaved down the glide slope, first left, then right of centerline. With each wing rock, the new pilot pushed forward on the throttles. The jet gradually slowed its rate of descent. Caine was ready to fly down to the flight deck.

"You're overpowered. Start it back to the left." The LSO shifted quickly from descriptive to directive call to the Tomcat pilot. He could hear 104's engines spool up. He could see the fighters soaring above glide slope. "Don't climb. Come left."

Caine had driven his jet high and was lined up well right of centerline. Phil Grokulsky, the senior air-wing LSO, stood inches behind Buzzell. He had been a casual observer until now.

"Get rid of him," he ordered.

Mark Caine was almost relieved to see the flashing red wave-off lights.

"No way we can get there from here," he mumbled through the ICS.

Greg Bright had seen a few other black nights like this one. No moon and no horizon. And vertigo wasn't uncommon either, even among cruise veterans. Still, he couldn't remember any pilot suffering this badly from its effects. He wasn't certain of what he should be saying to his pilot. For some reason, his mind was instantly filled with the vivid memory of his ejection with Caine. He hoped the same memory was not filling his front-seater's mind. Greg Bright wanted to be somewhere else.

At full power, it took only seconds for the Tomcat to climb back to 1,200 feet.

"So . . . how's things?" The RIO feigned his lack of concern about Aardvark 104's declining fuel state.

"About the same. But no problem, Notso. We'll get aboard this next time." Caine's confidence was not reassuring enough to the RIO.

The pilot clicked on the Tomcat's autopilot to hold his altitude and the auto-throttles to maintain his airspeed. The fighter flew toward another approach. With strained concentration, the pilot stared into the VDI, telling himself he believed what he saw there. Bright flipped quickly through his knee-board cards until he found one marked with bold lettering. **Indian Ocean Divert Facilities**. The nearest suitable landing strip was 430 nautical miles from *Enterprise*—the ship was working in "Blue Water" ops. Even with twice the fuel now registering on his gauge—more than even the airborne tankers could give—Aardvark 104 could not fly 430 miles before its engines flamed out.

With or without vertigo, Caine had only one landing strip available to him—the same landing strip he had been unable to fly aboard in two attempts. Bright shoved the divert information deep into the pile of cards on his knee-board—he wouldn't bring up the subject to his pilot. The approach controller again asked Caine and Bright to relay their fuel status. Bright reported 4500 pounds—not much gas for an F-14 at night—barely enough fuel, in fact, for the fighter to remain airborne another thirty minutes.

USS *Enterprise*
Carrier Air Traffic Control Center

Lieutenant Commander Michael Dexter was the VF-141 representative in CATCC. The Air Operation Officer, a full commander named Shumway, leaned back in his chair, searching the row of squadron reps seated behind him until spotting Dexter.

"So how's this Caine guy been doing around the boat, Mike?"

"Real good, sir," Dexter shot back instinctively. It was the standard answer. "Just a new pilot having one of those nights," he added. The lieutenant commander slid back in his chair, trying to look unconcerned.

"Isn't he the same guy who jumped out of that jet on the flight deck the other day?" the commander asked while peering at Dexter.

"Yes, sir. But that was an aircraft problem . . . not his fault." Dexter didn't want to sound defensive. "Caine's a good stick, sir."

"Good. That's what I'll tell the captain when he calls down here."

Dexter looked up to the television monitor strapped to the bulkhead above the Air Ops officer's chair. The PLAT featured cross hairs for glide slope and lineup centered on the screen. A deck-mounted camera looked high and aft of the *Enterprise*, focusing on the lights of approaching aircraft. There were monitors like it hanging on the bulkheads of every ready room. PLAT monitors were the center of attention during night recoveries. Dexter hoped, and began to pray a little, that the new Aardvark pilot would fly his jet into the center of the TV cross hairs on his third approach.

Two A-7 Corsair light-attack jets trapped aboard before Dexter saw the lights of a Tomcat appear on the screen at three miles. A transparent plastic board next to the monitor listed the aircraft still airborne. On the other side of the board, an airman updated fuel states, writing neatly with a grease pencil, and in reverse, so Shumway could read the numbers. The Aardvark jet now carried less than 4,000 pounds of fuel. The Air Ops commander reached up and adjusted the volume on the PLAT. Dexter heard the LSOs already talking to Caine.

"Now level your wings and start it down." Buzzell's voice was easily recognizable through the monitor loudspeaker. "You're just a little high. That's a good rate of descent right there. Come left. Call the ball when you've got it." The lights of the F-14 were about an inch above the center of the cross hairs when Dexter heard Greg Bright call the ball for his pilot.

"Looking good," the VF-141 lieutenant commander said, hoping to be overheard by Shumway. At half a mile, the Tomcat's wingtip lights were clearly visible on the screen. They swayed unsteadily in response to the LSO calls. Caine continued to fight vertigo inside the jet. With less than five seconds of flight between the airplane and the flight deck, Dexter saw the lights fall below the PLAT cross hairs. He heard a power call from Buzzell. The fighter settled farther below glide slope.

"Power! You're *low*." Buzzell's tone was impatient. He wasn't getting any response from the pilot. The airplane descended farther. "*Wave it off*."

From the edge of his chair in CATCC, Dexter could see a small wo flashing in the upper right-hand corner of the screen. The wave-off lights were on. Still, the F-14 was low and going lower. "*WAVE OFF. POWER . . . WAVE IT OFF*!"

Even on the old black-and-white PLAT monitor hanging over Shumway's head, it was easy for Dexter to see Aardvark 104's starboard landing strut collapse as it struck the *Enterprise* ramp at the ship's aft-most round-down. The wheel assembly, now free of the Tomcat, tumbled past the PLAT deck camera and off the angle deck into the sea. The screen was bright white with showers of sparking metal as the F-14—with its stubbed main strut and twisted right wingtip—slid toward the carrier's island.

DAY TWENTY-TWO

JANUARY 26

USS *Enterprise*
Ready Room Six
1245

Mark Caine was off the Aardvark flight schedule. He sat at the front of the ready room at the desk near the PLAT monitor and the telephone—he was wearing a khaki uniform. The other officers there wore their orange flight suits. Caine watched Greg Bright enter Ready Six, grab a briefing card from the pile of cards on top of the duty desk, then hurry to a high-backed chair next to the one Dirk Buzzell occupied. For the second day in a row, Caine was the squadron duty officer. His usual RIO, Greg Bright, would be flying with Buzzell instead.

Dirk Buzzell made a few notes on his knee-board card. He was waiting for the ship's TV weather brief to begin. Bright pretended to make the same kind of notes—the two of them were very aware of Caine's stares. And it was very obvious to them both that Mark Caine was being punished.

The Aardvark commanding officer hadn't called it punishment, per se, when he had ordered Caine off the flight schedule, or even when he had ordered Caine to wear his khakis in the ready room instead of the usual flight suit. But the punishment was blatantly obvious to every Aardvark junior officer. Mark Caine would stand the duty as SDO—every day—until the findings of his most recent mishap investigation were made public. And that could take weeks. JOs detested standing shipboard duty even once a month. It seemed the Aardvark CO had already judged Mark Caine—Coke had already ejected from one Tomcat. That Tomcat had been lost as it rolled over the side of the flight deck three weeks earlier. Now, the CO was convinced, Caine was guilty of nearly destroying *another* of his costly fighters. Mark Caine was a two-time loser—the Aardvark skipper was determined to keep him out of the cockpit.

Buzzell drew circles on his briefing card as he waited for the weather brief. From his seat in the middle of the room, he returned Caine's stare.

Dirk Buzzell had decided that Caine and Bright were indeed lucky to be alive—lucky to have survived their landing attempt two nights earlier. They were even luckier that their tailhook had snagged the number-two arresting gear cable as the jet slid across the flight deck toward the *Enterprise* island. Dirk Buzzell had seen it all from the LSO platform and still couldn't believe it. The Tomcat could be repaired, of course. But Buzzell wasn't certain the same could be said for Caine's career—he wasn't sure his wingman could survive a second mishap investigation. And he could guess how the investigation and mishap boards would decide this time.

"Vertigo notwithstanding," they would say, "Navy fighter pilots must be able to land aboard the ship at night."

The CO walked into Ready Six as the brief began. The Aardvark's Operation Department chief petty officer, a tall and thin man named Perkins, had followed the skipper through the door. The chief worked for Buzzell. He was holding a manila folder in his hands.

"Dirk. *Get up here*!" The commanding officer barked the order above the sound of the television weather report. Buzzell glanced quickly toward Greg Bright, then stood out of his chair.

"I thought you and Michaels had worked things out, Lieutenant," the CO said sternly. "What the hell did you say to him?"

Chief Perkins handed Buzzell the envelope, and began to explain its contents.

"It's the medical report, sir. Yeoman Jordan Michaels apparently tried to commit suicide about an hour ago. They found him in one of the shower stalls with a belt around his neck," Chief Perkins announced. "They've got him down in Medical now. He'll be okay."

Dirk Buzzell heard the chief petty officer, and he could see the same thing written in the report. But none of it made any sense to him.

"I can't believe he did this, we talked just the other—" The CO did not allow Buzzell to finish.

"Believe it, Lieutenant. Your boy Michaels is gonna regret pulling this little stunt."

"Sir, I'd like to take care of it myself. I'd like to see him. I'll find someone else to take my hop. Michaels has been through—"

"Bullshit! You're going flying. You obviously have no influence over him, anyway. His ass is *mine*, now. That's all, Lieutenant Buzzell," the commanding officer said finally.

Sultan of Oman Air Force Base
Thumrait, Oman
1255

Major Carlton approached his Hawker Hunter. He strolled casually around the fighter-bomber. He bent over and picked up a strand of silver safety wire and then a small stone from the asphalt under the aircraft's nose. Should he be required to start the Hunter's Rolls-Royce engine, the small pieces of "FOD" might be sucked into the engine and damage it. He was in no hurry to man the jet. His back side still ached from his last strip alert.

Lieutenant Colonel Thomas was already strapping into the second Hunter. An RAF plane captain assisted the Number 6 Squadron commander in the process.

"Whenever you're quite ready, Major," the lieutenant colonel yelled to Carlton. "This could very well be our day!"

The major reluctantly snapped together his torso harness and climbed the Hawker Hunter's boarding ladder. *At least it's only midday,* he thought to himself. January nights on the tarmac were becoming unbearably cold. This strip-alert would be over well before sunset. He slid across the side of the cockpit and into the uncomfortable ejection seat. A plane captain followed him up the ladder.

The two pilots connected their oxygen masks and helmet communication cords. The radios in both aircraft were already switched on. The previous strip-alert aircrews had left them that way. Thomas and Carlton radioed each other to verify the UHF systems, then settled into the seats.

Iranian Revolutionary Guard Hangar
Bandar 'Abbās, Iran
1345

Cactus Zero One and Zero Two, a single F-14 and a single F-4 Phantom, were positioned together between the hangar and the runway at Bandar 'Abbās. Ali Abdul Rajani was late. Nori had already preflighted the Tomcat and was strapped into the rear cockpit. He sat there, waiting with his hands folded neatly across his lap. Omid and his RIO, another young IRG aviator by the name of Mottahadeh, completed their poststart checklists. Even at idle, the Phantom's two General Electric power plants screamed.

Omid watched Ali Abdul Rajani as the ace strolled out of the large hangar. Ali walked toward the F-14, but stopped as he passed Omid's port wingtip. He held his helmet in one hand, and did not seem to be bothered by the Phantom's engine noise. Ali held his nose as he looked over the F-4—as if there were an unbearable stench emanating from the jet. Omid glared at him from the front cockpit—he hated the bearded pilot standing beside his aircraft.

Rajani bent down, concentrating his attention on a pylon of four 500-pound bombs that hung under the wing. Both of the F-4's wings were equally configured. The ace stood up, took two steps back, then ran at the rack of 500-pounders. He kicked up at one of the bombs. From the cockpit, Omid and Mottahadeh felt the kick. Ali walked out from underneath the Phantom. He was smiling. Satisfied that the bombs would not detonate prematurely, he flashed a thumbs-up toward Omid, then continued toward his F-14.

Aardvark 101
1435

Dirk Buzzell was getting used to flying with Greg Bright again. His style was unlike Kyle Herrin's. Bird was a "nugget"—a new guy—a RIO filled with more enthusiasm than experience. But in a bizarre sort of way, Buzzell enjoyed flying fighters with someone who had not seen it all before—someone still overwhelmed with the experience of catapulting from and landing aboard a tiny floating airstrip in the middle of some body of water.

It was that relative inexperience, Buzzell guessed, that prevented him and Herrin from flying together on this particular mission. Bright, on the other hand, knew the airplane better than most backseaters—better even than some of the more senior naval flight officers in VF-141.

Bright was, in fact, the kind of RIO that would have made a good carrier pilot. But his eyes were bad, and he was relegated to riding in the backseat of F-14 Tomcats. Buzzell adjusted his front cockpit mirrors, finding Bright in the reflection. The RIO was working busily at the radar. His wire-rimmed Navy spectacles flashed briefly in the afternoon sun. Buzzell looked away, down into the milky green waters twenty nautical miles southwest of Jask, a small coastal airstrip facility in Iran—already his mind was wandering. He was suddenly very angry with Jordan Michaels—he tried to picture the yeoman hanging from some *Enterprise* shower stall with a belt around his neck.

"That stupid little shit," the pilot said aloud in

the front cockpit. "I ought to strangle him myself." Dirk Buzzell couldn't afford to let his mind wander, and decided he would worry about Jordan Michaels later.

The Iranian Revolutionary Guard sometimes flew Phantoms from the airstrip at Jask. *Enterprise* intel had briefed there were four or possibly five operational F-4s positioned there. But nothing had been reported airborne at Jask in several days. Numbers of latitude and longitude ran across the top of Dirk Buzzell's TID repeat. The destination steering pointer on his VDI told him his Tomcat was 2.7 miles south of its assigned CAP station.

An E-2C Hawkeye, Wallbanger 603, monitored the Aardvark fighter from a slow orbit more than 120 nautical miles to the southeast.

"Aardvark 101, Banger. I show you on-station. Your signal is max conserve." Greg Bright answered the radio call.

Buzzell rolled the airplane into 20 degrees angle of bank and flipped two autopilot goggles just aft of the throttle quadrant on his left console. The airplane hung in the air at 23,000 feet and 220 knots of indicated airspeed, making lazy circles around its station. At 10 units angle of attack, his F-14 flew at "maximum endurance," burning a little less than 4500 pounds of fuel per hour—just enough fuel flow to keep the Tomcat airborne. The pilot pushed at the rocker switch on his fuel panel. Aardvark 101's two external fuel tanks were already empty and the wing tanks were beginning to transfer. Buzzell keyed the ICS and held the rubber oxygen mask against his face.

"Sixteen thousand, one hundred pounds of gas, Notso. We can hang out here all day. Wake me up when it's time to go home."

Bandar 'Abbās, Iran
1440

Omid and his RIO followed Ali and Nori off the 8,000-foot runway. The F-4 trailed the F-14 as it climbed above the airfield in a left-hand spiral. Ali's fighter would escort Omid in his F-4 fighter-bomber to a target in northern Oman. Those had been Reza's explicit orders. The two IRG aircraft leveled at 2,000 feet and slowed to 250 knots. On a signal from the ace, both aircraft switched their UHF radios to the Site Two ground-control frequency.

Thumrait, Oman
1450

The warm afternoon sun had driven Major Carlton into semiconsciousness. The crackling in his helmet earcup awakened him. It was a few seconds later when he recognized the voice on the other end of the radio transmission. Lieutenant Colonel Thomas was instructing him to start his Hawker Hunter. The Number 6 Squadron commanding officer had already lowered his canopy and begun the starting sequence in his fighter-bomber. Carlton snapped his oxygen mask into its bayonet fittings on either side of his helmet and waved the start-up signal to his plane captain. He ignored the feeling in his right leg. It too had fallen asleep.

Aardvark 101
1515

Buzzell heard the broken English of the Saudi aircrew as they checked in with Banger on button 10. The AWACS aircraft was overhead the aircraft carrier, awaiting two VF-231 Black Eagle escorts before driving north through the Strait of Hormuz on its first *Burning Sand* mission with the *Enterprise* air wing. Thirty minutes earlier, the E-3 AWACS had launched out of Masirah, an island airstrip off the coast of Oman and 200 miles due south of the ship. The huge early-warning aircraft carried fuel enough to fly fourteen hours—far more than it needed to transit the strait on its route back to the Ryadh air facility in Saudi Arabia. The VF-231 fighters would ride shotgun on the E-3 until it reached the northernmost tip of Oman. Then, when it turned west, skirting Iran's Qeshm Island and moving away from Bandar 'Abbās at the top of the strait, the *Enterprise* F-14s would hand over escort duties to a division of Saudi F-15s. Buzzell and Bright would guard their flanks, acting as a BARCAP, forming an airborne barrier between the *Burning Sand* mission and Jask—and the F-4 Phantoms that might launch from there.

Wrongway Harrington was flying the A-3 Whale. Occasionally, Buzzell could hear Harrington's voice over the UHF, reporting the A-3's fuel status and verifying its station positioning with the Hawkeye. Inside the Aardvark fighter, Buzzell tried to imagine what the Whale and E-2 could see as the AWACS pushed north, closing to within twenty-five nautical miles of Bandar 'Abbās, and the heaviest concentration of Iranian air power in the gulf.

With each turn on CAP station, Bright painted Iran's western shoreline on his pulse radar scope. He slewed the Tomcat's antennae until the mouth of the strait filled his DDD. There was no front cockpit repeat of the pulse display the RIO saw, but Bright was in the habit of commenting on everything he saw. That satisfied Buzzell. In the middle of his scope, three tiny radar returns showed the AWACS and the two Black Eagle F-14s approaching their turn point—the tiny island outcropping of Didamar.

"Hard to say exactly, Buzz, but it looks like the AWACS is coming left now. Got good Data-Link to a group of four further west, too . . . I got 'em on IFF . . . they're 'squawking' friendly. That's got to be the F-15s."

Buzzell followed Bright's play-by-play, verifying the Didamar turn point against the small topographic chart clipped to the top of his knee-board.

"Good," Buzzell answered. "Sounds pretty quiet up there—you see anybody farting around at Jask?" Aardvark 101's nose swung through east to north until the rocky southern coast of Iran lay sprawled before them. Visibility was better than usual near the entrance to the Persian Gulf. Buzzell stared through his windscreen at the small spit of land that marked the Jask airfield. The winds aloft were weak, and there was little sand and dust hazing the sky. He could discern the outline of the runway at Jask from his CAP just off the coast. Aardvark 101's AWG-9 radar looked through the haze. It searched, with Greg Bright directing its antennae, for airborne targets.

"Nope. Jask is 'clean.' Don't see a thing. Looks like nobody's home."

Buzzell clicked off the autopilot, then climbed and descended 2,000 or 3,000 feet. He was bored. He reversed the F-14's turn, tired of droning left for the better part of an hour. He was toying with the idea of descending even farther, down to less than one thousand feet above the water, where he saw a scalloped layer of clouds that he wanted to race through. Nothing was likely to happen this afternoon, he had decided. He and Bright deserved a little diversion.

"Black Eagle Two-oh-One and Two-Twelve, Banger. Show a possible contact your 010 at 40. Composition one."

Dirk Buzzell sat straighter in his ejection seat with the radio call. He pulled his jet back up to 23,000 feet. His mind jumped from the cloud deck below him, then up the strait to the *Burning Sand* escort. The secure-voice UHF frequency was suddenly busy with voices.

"Two-oh-One, Banger. I now show two possible targets of interest. Feet dry. Say your contacts."

Buzzell exaggerated the time between the E-2's transmissions and the response from the section of F-14s.

Why hadn't the Black Eagles seen those same targets? Or had they? Why don't they answer? How many bogies? Maybe there weren't any bogies there at all . . . the E-2 often saw things that didn't really exist. Probably nothing. Still, he steadied his fighter on a course away from Jask, pointing his jet's nose toward the center of the Gulf—in the direction of the Black Eagles. If there *was* something there, maybe Greg Bright could see it, too.

"Banger, Two-oh-One. We've got two contacts there . . . 015 at 41. Concur feet dry. Show them in an orbit." Then, almost on cue, Buzzell heard another transmission. It wasn't Dan Harrington's voice, but it was someone riding with him in the Whale.

"Banger, Deep Sea here. We have a single 'Ghost' and a single 'Kitten' at low altitude over 'Bullseye.' "

Dirk Buzzell thumbed through his knee-board cards, tearing the chart from the clipboard and tossing it on the glareshield above his VDI. He read quickly across his "Card of the Day," searching for the code words he'd just heard from the A-3 Whale. Bright was already talking to him over the ICS.

"Bullseye is Bandar 'Abbās, Ghost is an F-4, and Kitten is . . . Kitten's a *Tomcat,* Buzz." The RIO was stunned by what he read from the card.

"*Holy shit*, Notso! Party time." Buzzell jammed 101's throttles and pushed the stick forward until it nearly touched the face of his VDI display. At one negative G, dirt and a small silver screw floated from the cockpit floor, past the pilot's face, then hung on the roof of the canopy. The jet accelerated immediately to 375 knots.

"Aardvark 101, Banger. Request you reset your station immediately. How copy?"

Bright answered the call while Buzzell pulled back simultaneously on the stick and throttles, reversing his course toward station.

"Oops," he said shyly to Bright. Buzzell had reacted prematurely to the radio transmission. The Rules of Engagement were explicit in this case and he knew it. The BARCAP could not act unless Iranian fighters actually launched from Jask. They hadn't. And the bandits over Bullseye were still feet dry. That fact alone did not violate the ROE. For Aardvark 101 to drive north from its CAP station now would be deemed a provocative act.

"Damned Rules of Engagement," he stated finally to Bright.

Somewhere in the admiral's spaces aboard *Enterprise*, Buzzell imagined an aging nonaviator rolling a cup of dice or consulting with his Ouija board to determine the bizarre ROE. The two-star rear admiral—the same one Buzzell had screamed at on the LSO platform—couldn't possible understand what it was to fly a fighter aircraft against *other* fighter aircraft.

"You know, Notso . . . fighting this ROE will be far harder than fighting the Iranians."

"Yep," Bright said across the ICS.

"Jesus, Notso! An F-4 *and* an F-14. There aren't supposed to *be* any Tomcats at Bandar 'Abbās. Those *Enterprise* intel geeks piss me off." Buzzell swung the jet around. Aardvark 101 was reset on-station. But the pilot wanted his F-14's AWG-9 radiating in the right direction. He throttled back—thumbing out his maneuvering devices—slowing below 200 knots, and maximizing Bright's search time up the strait.

"I can see the two escorts and the AWACS, but I don't see any bad guys yet . . . don't really have the range, and ground clutter is all over the tube." Bright was anxious too. He wanted the whole picture but could only see part of it.

"Banger, Two-oh-One. We're steady on a course of 260 degrees . . . about ten minutes to turnover. Do you still see those two targets? Our nose is off now."

"That's affirm, Two-oh-One. Show contacts still feet dry . . . driving west now. They're angels ten bearing your 025 at 46. Understand Two-One-Two is still with you?"

"Two-Twelve's tied on, Banger . . . but be advised . . . he is currently Tango Uniform. My wingman is a *non* shooter. He's got some sort of electrical failure."

Buzzell and Bright didn't need to refer to the Card of the Day to understand the UHF call. A Tango Uniform fighter had no radar or weapons system. In such a case, the admiral's restrictive

ROE was clear. Both U.S. Tomcats on a *Burning Sand* escort mission must be fully mission capable in order to defend the AWACS or to engage an enemy. Since one of the Black Eagle F-14s had an inoperative weapons system and could not defend himself against the Iranians, then technically neither of them could. It was during a similar situation that the USS *Carl Vinson* fighter had been destroyed.

"Terrific," Buzzell half yelled to Bright through the ICS. "Talk about déjà vu. Does this scenario remind you of anything, Notso?" The secure-voice frequency began to rattle again with three-way communications. Bright was too busy listening to respond to Buzzell's comment.

Cactus 01 and 02

Ali Abdul Rajani was tiring of the mission already. He despised making circles in the sky atop Bandar 'Abbās. And he despised flying in the same piece of sky as Omid.

"Site Two," he radioed. "When *may* we proceed?"

"You may proceed now, Cactus Zero One. Initial vector to intercept is 195 degrees," the controller responded. "You may climb to 25,000 feet at this time. Expect two American fighters in the strait. The Americans are accompanied by a large radar surveillance AWACS craft. You are to *destroy* the AWACS, Cactus Zero One . . . THIS mission now takes priority over the Didamar target. It appears that one of the two Navy fighters has again malfunctioned."

Ali stroked both of his afterburners and began a shallow climb out of 2,000 feet. His fighter shuttered as it accelerated. He had already decided he would climb much higher than 25,000 feet—he had tired of following orders from the GCI site controller. The ace would destroy the Navy Tomcats with his Matra Magic missiles. He would not waste a weapon on the AWACS aircraft.

"Try to keep up with me, Omid," the ace chided over the radio.

Aardvark 101

The E-2 had warned Buzzell again. Aardvark 101 had wandered twelve miles from its assigned CAP station. The pilot reversed his course while listening to the secure-voice frequency.

"Banger, Deep Sea. Recommend *abort* the mission. I say again . . . recommend abort." This time it was Dan Harrington's voice. "I show both contacts feet wet at this time. They're committing south."

"Two-oh-One from Banger . . . did you copy? Bandits are outbound. Estimating your 019 at 39. Recommend abort."

"We copy, Banger. Two-on-One and wingman are aborting south. Keep the calls comin', Wallbanger!"

Buzzell and Bright listened impotently, too far from the escort to offer any help and directed not to give any. During one of their turns on CAP, Bright swept Jask with Aardvark 101's radar. Still no activity.

Black Eagle 201 made a series of transmissions to the Saudi AWACS. A "Scram" call came first. A foreign voice from inside the E-3 acknowledged the transmission. The AWACS pilot pushed over the nose of his huge radar platform and accelerated. The aircraft turned lazily south with its two Tomcat escorts in trail. Somewhere else in the radio chatter, the four Saudi F-15s were directed to reverse their course and return to Ryadh. Their services would not be required.

Black Eagle 201 transmitted to his wingman twice but received no reply. Buzzell inferred from the one-way communications that Black Eagle 212 was joined with its lead, but still without electrical power, and most likely unaware that two Iranian fighters were also flying in the Strait of Hormuz.

Given the deteriorating situation, even Dirk Buzzell agreed that the Black Eagle flight lead had little choice but to run. Two-Twelve—the wingman—with no radios at all, had no choice but to follow. Neither could turn to engage the fighters flying south from Bandar 'Abbās. Again, the ROE would not allow it. Two radars and two weapons systems were not considered a luxury by the author of the Rules of Engagement. They were deemed absolute requirements—even against only one bandit. In addition, engaging the IRG aircraft would leave the high value AWACS unprotected. There were too many reasons for the two VF-231 jets to keep flying south.

The U.S. fighters retired, restraining their afterburners only enough to stay in position behind the AWACS jet. The E-3's four engines smoked furiously as it dove away from the strait at a little less than .9 Mach.

"Black Eagle Two-oh-One, Banger. Your bandits 018 degrees now for 22 . . . it does not appear they will be able to overtake your flight. And I show you going feet dry at this time, Black Eagles. Are you declaring an emergency?"

After an effective pause, the Tomcat crew replied.

"That's affirmative, Banger. We are declaring an emergency."

Wallbanger 603 made the cursory UHF Guard frequency call to the Ras Al Khaimah approach controller at Sharjah International Airport in northern Oman. Overflights of Omani airspace during *Burning Sand* missions, or at any other time for that matter, were strictly forbidden.

Only in the case of an aircraft emergency would the Omanis open their airspace to the AWACS and to the Tomcats acting as her escort. That ploy allowed Black Eagle 201 and 212 a back door out of the Strait of Hormuz. Then, somehow, and miraculously, after the AWACS reached the relative security of mainland Oman—and when the Iranian fighters were no longer a threat—the emergency would become suddenly less serious. The E-3 would then return to Masirah to await another escort, and the two U.S. F-14s would fly back aboard the USS *Enterprise*.

Dirk Buzzell and Greg Bright heard the Omani controller and the E-2 Hawkeye on the Guard frequency, then heard the Black Eagle flight lead make his final radio call.

"Banger, Two-oh-One. Our flight is clear. We're canceling our emergency and returning to home plate. But be advised . . . we just flew underneath a section of aircraft heading toward those Iranian contacts to the northeast. Are you in comms with that flight? Who are they?"

The Wallbanger E-2 radar *had* displayed two tiny targets flying in a direction opposite the AWACS and the *Enterprise* F-14s, but had also been unable to contact them. The two Omani fighter-bombers were operating on another UHF radio frequency.

A section of Hawker Hunters

Lieutenant Colonel Reginald Sheffield Thomas and Major William Carlton flew in tight formation at 17,000 feet. The two Hunters maintained barely 275 knots of airspeed as they climbed. Theirs were aircraft designed for high speeds at low altitudes—their single-shaft turbojet engines found the air too thin at high altitude to generate the necessary thrust.

"Low at one o'clock, Major . . . three aircraft, including a very large one. Those are *not* our targets." The lieutenant colonel watched the AWACS and its two Tomcat escorts move under his nose toward the south. He had heard of the *Burning Sand* missions, but he had not expected to see one of them overflying Oman. "We will continue north, Major. Our bandit is also an F-14 . . . quite possibly a Phantom as well. Their markings will not be American." If the Number 6 Squadron commander was excited, Major Carlton could not detect that fact in his voice.

Cactus 01 and 02

Ali Abdul Rajani had not expected American fighter aircraft flying in the Strait of Hormuz on this mission. Neither he nor Omid had been briefed on that eventuality. Judging from his radio calls, the Site Two controller had not been so surprised.

"As predicted," the controller stated, "the large radar craft and the two Navy fighters are retreating south. You may resume your attack heading to Didamar Island, Cactus Zero One."

"Yes, I have them," Nori announced over the UHF. "A group of three accelerating and descending at twenty-five miles."

"Of course. The Americans are cowardly," Ali told his RIO across the ICS. "They dare not fight me. They desire not to die."

"Two other targets together at eighteen miles . . . 19,500 feet." It was Mottahadeh's voice from inside Omid's Phantom. "Do *you* see them, Site Two?" There was no immediate answer from the GCI site controller. The pause gave Ali in Cactus 01 the opportunity to scream at his RIO through the ICS.

"Forget the Americans, idiot! They are running. Find the *other* two."

"Yes I have them," the controller said finally. "They are likely to be Omani jets. They were not expected."

"Then they will die," Ali reported over the Site Two frequency.

"Cactus Zero One and Zero Two, this is Site . . . your mission now is the target at Didamar. It is not required that the Omani jets be engaged . . . Do *not* engage the Omanis unless they prevent you from accomplishing your mission at Didamar. Do you hear me, Cactus Zero One?"

Nori had found the Omani Hawker Hunters. Ali could see two targets on his TID repeat. The ace was pleased by what he saw there.

"We must engage the Omanis," he announced matter-of-factly. "They are between us and the target. I must destroy them while Cactus Zero Two delivers his bombs." Ali did not allow the Site Two controller to respond. He had already decided he would kill both Hunters. He keyed the UHF to explain his plan to the crew in the F-4 Phantom.

"Listen carefully, Omid. When you are precisely five miles from the Omani jets, you will begin a descending spiral to the right. The Omanis will not see me, and I will destroy them both."

Omid watched Ali pull the F-14 above and behind his Phantom. The ace had taken a high cover position—at least 10,000 feet high at his seven o'clock.

"No. No, Ali! You will stay with me . . . you *must* stay with me. You would enjoy seeing me killed, Ali!" Omid was screaming across the radio.

"That is true, Omid. But it does not serve my purpose to see you killed," Ali made the admission with his usual amount of sarcasm. "You are bait for the Omanis, yes . . . but you will not be killed. You must trust me, old man. Range to the Omani jets is now twelve miles."

Omid did not trust Ali Abdul Rajani, but he had little choice in the matter. He carried eight 500-pound bombs on his Phantom. The jet had not been loaded with missiles.

A section of Hawker Hunters

Major Carlton had been genuinely relieved to see the U.S. fighters and the Saudi AWACS flying past his jet and out of the Strait of Hormuz. It was likely, he thought, that the Iranian fighters were not headed for Oman's northern territories at all, but had simply been chasing the Americans and the large E-3. Perhaps the Iranian Tomcat and Phantom had already turned north toward their airfield in Bandar 'Abbās. The two Iranian Revolutionary Guard had already landed there, he prayed. Most likely, there would be no fight over the strait. The major was not comfortable in his new role as an air-to-air fighter pilot. His commanding officer, Lieutenant Colonel Thomas, seemed to relish it.

"I've a tally on smoke. Dead ahead and slightly high . . . do you see it, Major?"

Carlton's stomach sunk. He did see the smoke—it emanated from a black speck in his windscreen. He took his eyes away from the target, still six or seven miles from his Hunter. He and the lieutenant colonel were moving over the broken chain of islands that made up the northernmost Omani territories. The island of Didamar stood out clearly at his three o'clock position. The island was now more than 20,000 feet below him and very tiny. The major hated flying that high.

"Yes, Colonel. Tally the smoke! But I have only *one* target. Which is it . . . the F-14 or the Phantom?" Major Carlton had little difficulty displaying his excitement over the radio.

"We'll know in a moment, Major. Most likely it's the F-4. I don't recall Tomcats blowing that much exhaust. Prepare to turn on him. I will pass him close aboard on his left side."

The closure between the Phantom and the two Hawker Hunters was more than 800 knots—the jets were five miles from merging. Still, neither Thomas nor Carlton had seen any Iranian aircraft other than the Phantom. That fact seemed to worry the RAF major more than it did the lieutenant colonel. Without an air-to-air radar in his Hunter, Carlton felt incredibly vulnerable, almost naked in the slow-moving fighter-bomber.

When the range between the flight of Omani Hunters and the IRG F-4 was just outside four miles, Thomas and Carlton were both certain the Phantom was turning. And the jet was descending in altitude. The turn was toward the north—back toward mainland Iran. The Iranian F-4, traveling at more than

500 knots and loaded heavily with eight large bombs, did not turn quickly.

Thomas pushed the nose of his aircraft at the Phantom. He followed the Iranian fighter across its arcing reversal, estimating that when the F-4 was established on a northerly heading, he and Carlton would be less than one mile behind it. The Hawker Hunters accelerated downhill with their target—the airspeed of the IRG Phantom was now only 150 knots faster than theirs. There would be time for one or two missile shots. The Number 6 Squadron CO wanted to take those shots from the Phantom's rear quarter—it was the most effective firing aspect for the Firestreak heat-seekers he carried.

"Master arm is coming on, Major. This is going to be relatively simple."

"Too simple," Carlton said to himself. The Phantom had turned tail to the Hawker Hunters. The F-4 crew seemed either too eager to die or was intentionally decoying him and his commanding officer. The major preferred to believe the latter possibility. He remained in formation with his flight lead, but pulled his eyes off Thomas and the F-4 to scan the skies above and behind the two Hunters. He found the Iranian Tomcat instantly, just as a white flare of smoke appeared from under its port wing.

"Colonel . . . *break left, break left!* Bandit your high eight o'clock! *Missile in the air!*

The IR-guided Matra Magic pulled lead on Lieutenant Colonel Thomas's Hunter instantaneously. It pulled even greater lead as the Hunter rolled left and overbanked into the missile. The Magic twisted like a bottle-rocket. It snaked above and then below its target—correcting for each of the colonel's defensive maneuvers. The missile would not be easily defeated. In less than five seconds, the heat-seeker had eaten up the one-mile range between the IRG Tomcat and the Hunter.

Major Carlton looked on helplessly as the Magic's warhead detonated beneath Thomas's tail pipe. The warhead blast was surprisingly tiny, and for a moment, as he heard the lieutenant colonel utter something incomprehensible over the UHF frequency, he believed his CO's aircraft had survived the attack. It had not.

The Hunter's tail section, including both the horizontal and vertical tails, simply dropped from the fuselage. The jet began to tumble queerly, first rolling to the right, then falling over onto its back and somersaulting down toward one of the small Omani island outcroppings in the Strait of Hormuz.

Cactus 01

Ali roared inside his cockpit. Nori sat in the backseat, fighting the effects of a descending 7-G turn. He blinked his eyes into focus. His pilot was screaming again through the ICS.

"Give me a lock on the *other one*!"

Ali Abdul Rajani had one Omani kill. The second would come with even less effort. The other Hunter jet had turned away. It was diving toward the brown Omani peninsula. Cactus 01 pulled toward the south, and slid into trail of the tiny fighter-bomber. Across the GCI control frequency, Nori reported his radar lock.

"Three miles."

"He is running, but we will catch him," Ali replied.

The ace pushed at his throttles. The afterburners

staged again, and the Iranian Tomcat began closing from behind the Hawker Hunter.

"Cactus Zero One, this is Site Two. Break off your attack. The remaining Omani jet is no longer a threat. Break off and resume your escort of Zero Two. Resume your escort of the Phantom bomber! Do you understand, Zero One?" The controller heard nothing in response. "You must conserve your weapons, Cactus Zero One. They may be needed at Didamar."

Nori was surprised to see his pilot respond to the order. He felt the Tomcat decelerate as the ace pulled both engines out of afterburner.

Ali rolled the jet left and descended toward Omid and Mottahadeh in the F-4. He could see the Phantom's black jet exhaust from six miles distance. He would follow Omid to Didamar, though he did not expect to find more Omani jets there. But he had not expected any Omani jets on this particular mission, and he was satisfied enough to have destroyed one of them.

DAY TWENTY-THREE

JANUARY 27

USS *Enterprise*
Stateroom 03-93-2L
0615

Dirk Buzzell had learned to ignore most shipboard noises. Even as Tomcats and Intruders and Prowlers and Corsairs launched from the catapult just above the overhead in his stateroom, he managed to sleep. The steel lockers and bed frames in the tiny room would rattle each time the cat shuttle slapped the water brake at the end of its stroke. The sounds of cruise were annoying to him, but no longer unusual.

It was instead the rare quiet of the morning that kept him awake. There had been no early morning launches—no deafening catapult strokes above his rack and no jet engines screaming across the flight deck. Soon, he knew, reveille would be piped over the ship's 1-MC. A voice would then announce shift changes and make duty section assignment. Sometimes the captain would make a few announcements. Each morning aboard the *Enterprise* began in exactly the same way.

He grabbed the padded catapult steam return line

that ran parallel to his rack and lowered himself to the floor. A copy of the Aardvark flight schedule had been slipped under the stateroom door sometime during the night—they were always delivered that way. His name appeared at the bottom of the schedule. For the first time in a week, he would get a night trap. According to the schedule, he and Greg Bright and another VF-141 Tomcat would fly intercepts against a pair of A-7s.

Buzzell needed the sortie to remain "night current." CAG's policy had not changed. Every airwing pilot landed aboard the ship at night only once each week—just often enough to satisfy the currency requirements, but far too infrequently to allow that pilot any proficiency in doing so. The moon had been full and bright seven nights earlier. It had been the kind of moon that fighter pilots pray for—one that had allowed Buzzell to see the *Enterprise* from ten miles distance. There would be no moon tonight. And if the stars were out, they would be dull through the ever-present Indian Ocean haze. Buzzell turned from the stateroom door and stared down at Mark Caine, who was still asleep in the center rack. Caine had been flying three nights earlier, also to get current, and had very nearly killed himself in the process. Dirk Buzzell loved flying the F-14 Tomcat. He loved flying it a little less at night.

He pulled open the sliding metal drawer under his desk, and grabbed at the one pair of running shorts there. The other three he'd packed for this WestPac deployment had not survived the ship's laundry, and had been either ripped to shreds by the mammoth dryers down on the third deck, or been returned to the wrong stateroom—never to be seen by him again. Buzzell didn't really feel like working out, and he could better utilize the morning hours by wading through his mailbox. He knew it was again full of overdue Ops Department paperwork. But the *Enterprise* gym would be uncrowded just before shift change, and it had been days since he'd had any real exercise.

He wound his way forward of the 0-3 level, stepping down two ladders, through the enlisted berthing spaces and under the forecastle to the remodeled Reactor Department training classroom. It was not much of a weight room. J. T. Lester, Buzzell's wingman for the upcoming night sortie, was working out on the bench press machine with two other Aardvark officers. Buzzell didn't feel like working with heavy weights, either. Across the tiny space, two more officers rode Life-Cycles. The machine Dan Harrington straddled was minus its handle bar and most of one pedal.

"Looks like you and your bike are in pretty bad shape, old man," Buzzell teased. Harrington looked up. Sweat beads came together on his large forehead and rolled down his nose.

"Hi, Buzz . . . I was just trying out this brand-new F-14 Tomcat trainer here in the gym. Nice airplane you fly, pal," Harrington shot back. Buzzell laughed. But it was too early and already too hot in the room to begin verbal fisticuffs. He stood back and watched Harrington pedal down a hill made up of blinking LED lights. The machine had been installed after the *Enterprise* had departed the Philippines. Buzzell had been one of the first to ride it. But new equipment, especially a relatively sophisticated piece of gear with several breakable parts—like the electronic bicycle—rarely survived a month in a makeshift weight room too small to accommodate the five or six hundred men who used it daily. He scanned the rest of the room, searching for an unoccupied rowing machine. There were none.

Dirk Buzzell had already decided to talk to Dan Harrington about what he'd heard—about the things that had happened during his *Burning Sand* BARCAP mission the day before. He was somehow convinced that his friend knew more about the mission than he was saying, and more about the Iranian Revolutionary Guard fighters that had flown out of Bandar 'Abbās. But it was early, and Dirk Buzzell hadn't expected to find Harrington riding a bike in the gym. And he hadn't taken the time to think all the way through the questions he wanted answered. Harrington looked up, wiping more sweat from his eyes.

"You want to use this thing when I'm finished, Buzz? I only got another 300 miles to ride." Buzzell smiled again, watching Harrington's foot slip off the half-pedal.

"No thanks. I think I'll just hang around for a while. Maybe I'll help the corpsmen carry you down to Medical after your stroke. Besides, I don't want to be seen talking to an A-3 puke. Bad for my fighter pilot image, you know."

"Oh, is that a fact? You seemed fairly interested in what this A-3 'puke' had to say yesterday up there in the Gulf. I heard your voice a couple of times, Buzz." Harrington stopped pedaling. "Did you and Notso see anything?"

Buzzell welcomed the shift in conversation. He wondered if Dan Harrington would really admit to knowing more about the *Burning Sand* specifics.

"Didn't see a thing. We were hangin' out south of Jask," Buzzell said innocently.

"Yeah, we knew you were there. The E-2 sends

us Data Link of the jets they're talking to. We see pretty much everything those guys do, and then some. Too bad you guys weren't a little closer to Iran. Your sister squadron had to run away."

Buzzell already knew the story. He'd heard the same radio calls the Whale pilot had.

"Sounded to me like the Black Eagles had a little system problem up there. The ROE won't let them fight like that. I guess those guys didn't have much of a choice, huh?" Harrington looked at Dirk Buzzell and flashed a toothy grin.

"That's their *official* story, Buzz. But I'm here to tell you that story is bullshit." Harrington's face was red with the strain of exercise. "The Black Eagles didn't have any real problems out there. The whole mission . . . the whole thing was staged—start to finish. That's why you and Notso were told to remain on-station, even though everybody knew there would be no air activity out of Jask yesterday. Sorry, Buzz."

Dirk Buzzell stood there, staring. He was indignant and confused. The statement made him angry. Harrington started up again before Buzzell could ask the first of a dozen questions pinballing through his mind.

"Remember when the ragheads shot down that Tomcat from the *Carl Vinson*? Well, that's what yesterday's *Burning Sand* was all about."

"*What*?" Buzzell shot back, wanting to say something before Harrington continued. "So you're gonna tell me that the AWACS and two *Enterprise* Tomcats ran into Oman on purpose?"

"Yep. The Omanis didn't know anything about it, but the Saudis were in on the plan. Their F-15s were hanging out to the west because they were told to do so. Rear Admiral Curtiss knew, of course.

We knew about it in the Whale, the Wallbanger E-2 guys knew, and so did the two Black Eagles." Buzzell hung on every one of Harrington's words, knowing full well that his friend was telling him things he wasn't cleared to hear.

"Your CAP station was out of harm's way. But since there's always a BARCAP at Jask, and because everything was supposed to look normal to the Iranians, you and Notso were sent up there." Harrington wiped at his massive forehead. "The admiral's staff decided the two of you didn't have a 'need to know.'"

"A *need* to fucking *know*?" Buzzell looked around the weight room. He hadn't planned on raising his voice. "And you knew the IRG had an F-14 at Bandar 'Abbās? Intelligence told us there were a bunch of Phantoms there, but no Tomcats!"

"Yeah. We saw some TARPS imagery a few days ago. It showed two of 'em had been flown to BA . . . probably from the north . . . up near Teheran where their F-14s usually hang out. The story goes the Joint Chiefs wanted to force a reaction from the Iranian Tomcats before they left the coast. The JCS wanted to test some silly theory of theirs . . . we were directed to send the *Sand* escort into the strait to flush out the IRG Tomcats. As far as I know, only a couple of the ship's intel folks were briefed on the plan. By the way, Buzz," Harrington said in an even more hushed voice, "you never heard this from me." Buzzell nodded his head, hoping that his friend wasn't finished yet.

"Pretty risky, wasn't it," Buzzell asked, "sending the AWACS up there with two bad guys waiting to jump it?"

"The staff didn't seem to think so. Besides, the E-2 saw the two Iranian jets as soon as they got airborne. Originally, we had hoped they would launch both of their Tomcats at the escort yesterday. We got one F-14 and one F-4 instead. And the one Tomcat that did get airborne never got within range to threaten the AWACS or the Black Eagles. Still, the plan called for the *Burning Sand* to go home through Oman. And that's what they did . . . we'd already gotten the info the JCS was looking for." Harrington read the expression on Dirk Buzzell's face. "Hey, it was their theory, Buzz, not mine."

"What theory?" Buzzell was simply angry now.

"After that *Vinson* shoot-down, somebody up in COMMIDEASTFOR came up with the idea that the Iranians had compromised the U.S. fleet's KY-58 secure voice UHF radio. That system's been around for a while—I'm surprised those camel-jockeys didn't steal it a long time ago. Anyway, that's why the Whale flew aboard this tub in the first place. I imagine we're sort of taking notes for somebody back in Washington, D.C.

"But what we saw yesterday was a *very* big data point, to say the least. The Iranian GCI controllers are simply monitoring our KY-58 frequencies. If they think they can get an easy shot, they launch a couple of their Tomcats or Phantoms. That's exactly how they nailed that *Carl Vinson* F-14. Simple, huh?" Harrington peered around the corner of the weight room. The banter of officers and enlisted men filled the space. The gym was already crowded. Occasionally, barbells and other loose weights hit the deck with loud thuds. He was convinced that no one but Buzzell was listening.

"Yesterday, that section of raghead fighters got airborne about the time you and Notso reached station. The Iranians stayed low . . . they stayed feet dry until the Black Eagles and the E-3 turned the corner at Didamar. They just flew orbits over the Bandar 'Abbās airfield. We think they were talking to a GCI site farther south on the coast. The IRG jets stayed inland until the Black Eagle lead radioed Banger . . . he was still talking on the secure voice radio, by the way . . . explaining that his wingman had no radar or weapons systems. Hell, Buzz, the Iranians fly F-14s, too. They know that a Tomcat with those kinds of problems can't shoot back. And I'm sure they've figured out our ROE by now.

"That Black Eagle radio call was a big part of the plan, and it was just what their GCI controller wanted to hear. The Iranian F-14 and F-4 vectored less than *thirty* seconds later. Personally, Buzz, I think the whole plan sucked. But it did work as advertised."

Buzzell felt sick to his stomach—he felt suddenly like the victim of a huge conspiracy. *Why didn't somebody tell us? Weren't he and Notso part of the same goddamned team? Who else knew . . . did the Aardvark CO know about it? Probably not. Because if the CO had known, he and Notso wouldn't have been scheduled . . . a more senior crew would have flown the BARCAP sortie . . . that was the CO's style. He couldn't have known, either.*

"CHRIST!" Buzzell was frustrated. It was suddenly even hotter inside the gym. "The IRG fighters had obviously taken the bait, Wrongway, and there had been a clear violation of the damned ROE on their part. Launching a few missiles of our own could certainly be justified—even by the President. Why didn't the admiral take advantage of the opportunity?"

Dan Harrington shook his head sideways. He didn't have an answer.

"So the JCS and the admiral got their data point yesterday," Buzzell stated. "Now what?"

"Oh, I imagine Rear Admiral Curtiss is drafting up a message to D.C. as we speak—you know, patting himself on the back. Somebody in COMMIDEASTFOR will probably get a medal for figuring out the KY-58 connection. I don't know what'll happen. Probably nothing.

"Sorry about not letting you in on the details sooner, Buzz. But I really shouldn't be telling you any of this shit." Dirk Buzzell nodded again. He wasn't sure what to say next. "But it could have been worse. It could have been one of *our* fighters that got bagged yesterday." The comment rolled off Dan Harrington's tongue like old news.

"What happened? Who got bagged yesterday?"

"Remember yesterday when the Black Eagles reported seeing those two Omani jets? We're pretty sure those were British-built Hawker Hunter bombers—with British Royal Air Force pilots at the controls. The two RAF Hunters were trying to find the two Iranians—trying to run an intercept on them. Well . . . they found what they were looking for . . . because one of the two Omani bombers went down. Best guess is that the Iranian Revolutionary Guard Tomcat scored the kill. That second Omani jet returned undamaged to its home base . . . someplace called Thumrait." Harrington paused, seeing the infuriation in his friend's face.

"And since I'm spilling my guts, Buzz, I might as well tell you what else happened." Dirk Buzzell wasn't in the mood for more bad news, but he didn't interrupt Dan Harrington.

"The IRG Phantom apparently had a bellyful of bombs. When the Black Eagles were clear of the strait and that other RAF pilot had gone home, the Phantom dropped his load on Didamar. Luckily, the F-4 pilot wasn't too accurate. Only two of his bombs did any real damage. One small Omani fishing trawler is underwater, and part of the island's southern pier is gone.''

''So, overall . . . not a bad day for the Iranians,'' Buzzell said. He was livid. ''The IRG chases two U.S. fighters and a Saudi E-3 out of the strait, blow some Brit and his Hunter out of the sky, *and* drop bombs in Oman.'' He was shaking his head while he stared at Harrington. ''God dammit, Wrongway . . . the Black Eagles led those Iranians into Oman yesterday. They tucked their tails between their legs and ran home. In the meantime, some sucker in an old British bomber tries to finish *our* business for us. And he's probably dead for trying.''

''Feel like taking out your frustrations on this bike, Buzz?'' Harrington climbed down from the electronic bicycle. He was drenched with sweat. Buzzell didn't move. ''Hey, I'm on your side, Dirk, remember? I think we should have done something yesterday to help out those RAF guys. But that would have been a violation of the Rules of Engagement.''

''Fuck the ROE!'' Dirk Buzzell took a quick step toward the bike, then kicked at the center of its thick frame. The machine slid sideways, then fell heavily against a steel bulkhead. The lights on the bicycle's LED display went dark. Both of its pedals were now broken.

''Yeah,'' Harrington said as the Life-Cycle was suddenly surrounded by most of the officers and enlisted men in the gym. ''Fuck the ROE.''

Ready Room Six
1740

Greg Bright was going to brief the night sortie. He was making notes on the board behind the duty desk as Buzzell walked into the ready room. Two A-7 pilots from VA-49 sat in the tall chairs in front of the board. Five aircrew from the Wallbanger E-2 squadron were also seated there. The air conditioner moaned at the back of the spaces. Standing in front of it, his head pressed against the air exhaust, was Yeoman Jordan Michaels. He held an armload of papers that rustled against the cool airflow. His eyes were closed when Buzzell got close enough to see them.

"You got a second, Michaels?" Buzzell asked as he pulled open the door at the back of Ready Six. He stood against the passageway bulkhead outside, waiting for the young sailor to join him.

"I got another copy of the *Cottonwood Colt*, sir," Michaels said weakly as he slinked against the opposite wall. The yeoman was wearing a white turtleneck jersey that fit him loosely around the neck. Dirk Buzzell couldn't see any bruises.

"Not interested, Michaels." Buzzell's voice was impatient, like that of a parent preparing to scold a child. "You made me look pretty stupid with the skipper, you know. He was convinced that you and I had an agreement— Hell, I was convinced, too. I could have had you back in the States in a month or two."

"I know it, sir. I'm sorry." Jordan Michaels hung his head. Buzzell knew it was only a matter of seconds before he saw tears. "But I got to get there now. I didn't think I could wait that long, sir."

"Did you want to get there *dead*? That was a stupid thing you tried to do." Buzzell wasn't angry with Jordan Michaels anymore. He felt sorry for him.

"I couldn't even kill myself." The yeoman wiped his eyes before continuing. "I didn't know how to . . . I kept trying to hook the other side of the belt on something but I couldn't. I spent one hour in that shower and I couldn't even figure out how to do it."

Dirk Buzzell had to stifle a laugh. It was somehow pathetically humorous that Jordan Michaels had been unable to hang himself.

"So, when are you gonna try it again?"

"I'm not, sir . . . I swear it. I promise I won't." Yeoman Michaels stood up straighter against the passageway bulkhead, then stepped back slightly to allow a group of Aardvark plane captains to pass. "Even if the commanding officer makes me go to that court-martial I won't try it again."

"Tell you what, Michaels," Buzzell said sympathetically. "I'll talk to the CO again. Maybe I can fix it so you don't go to court-martial. But if you pull another stunt like this one, I'll make sure they put you away forever."

"Yes, sir," the yeoman said weakly.

The door to the ready room opened. Greg Bright stood there. Buzzell knew his brief had already begun. He stepped toward the door, but felt Jordan Michaels tugging at his flight suit sleeve.

"But I still think it's not right what they're making me do out here, sir," he said. " 'Cause sometimes the Navy is wrong in what it tells you to do." Dirk Buzzell smiled again at the statement. Maybe Yeoman Jordan Michaels was brighter than he looked. Buzzell walked past the sailor and through the open doorway into the ready room.

Aardvark 112
2100

Dirk Buzzell's mind hadn't been on the sortie. That bothered him—he had never before had difficulty compartmentalizing his thoughts. He shouldn't have been concentrating on his conversation with Dan Harrington while flying around the ship at night. He shouldn't have, but he had. He went over and over the *Burning Sand* mission in his head—remembering every detail, every radio call he'd heard the day before, and everything Harrington had told him. It was a dark night, and navigating his F-14 through the black Indian Ocean skies should have taken priority over his swelling mistrust of the one-star battle-group commander and the Rules of Engagement.

And he shouldn't be preoccupied with thoughts of Jordan Michaels. The sailor had attempted suicide. It was that simple, and it might already be too late to help the yeoman now. But Dirk Buzzell had promised he would try.

Luckily, the night Air Intercept Control mission had gone exactly as briefed, and had been uneventful. His RIO, Greg Bright, remained busy managing the intercepts—too busy now to listen to him ramble about a conversation he'd had with an A-3 pilot. But Bright would be a good listener—maybe even a sympathetic listener—Buzzell hoped. He had to tell somebody. Maybe later, he thought, after the movie in the Aardvark ready room. Dirk Buzzell still had a night trap to worry about.

J. T. Lester was flying just off his starboard wing as Buzzell led the two Tomcats toward the Marshal station thirty nautical miles behind *Enterprise*. He slipped his left forefinger around the outside of the port throttle grip and flipped the F-14's external lights master switch to the off position. His jet disappeared into the blackness. After a second or two, he repositioned the toggle to its normal position. Lester saw the signal, and detached from his flight lead. Both fighters would orbit alone, one stacked 1,000 feet above the other.

The night was clear as Buzzell flew, clearer than he had expected. Venus was bright, and he could make out a faint horizon above the haze. He clicked on the autopilot, and Aardvark 112 circled around its marshal point with a little more than three minutes to push time.

The ICLS needles appeared on his VDI display just as he nosed the fighter out of 8,000 feet. He was always relieved to see the needles. They showed him left of centerline and below glide slope. He ignored the altitude indication—it was inaccurate at this range from the carrier, but rolled his aircraft right to correct for the azimuth error. Below and in front of him, a pair of EA-6B Prowlers descended from 6,000 and 7,000 feet respectively. He could see their swirling taillights through his windscreen—they would be the first two aircraft to fly the ball on this particular recovery. Bright could see them too, on his radar DDD screen. In front of the Prowlers, the RIO could make out the huge form of the *Enterprise* itself. Its radar return nearly filled his display.

"I show us on lineup and slightly high, Buzz . . . maybe ten feet high. Comin' up on two miles," Bright said over the ICS. Buzzell cross-checked his Vertical Speed Indicator—the VSI, then rechecked the needles.

"I'll go along with that . . . a little high." The pilot rolled forward of the stick-mounted Direct Lift Control thumb-wheel. As he pushed at the DLC wheel, spoilers flit into the 160-mile-an-hour airflow on top of each wing—not enough to change the Tomcat's airspeed, but enough to increase the jet's drag and slightly increase its rate of descent. The

VSI moved down the gauge from 600 feet per minute to 700. The glide slope needle moved with it, and centered with the azimuth needle in the center of his VDI.

"I got us 'on and on' now, Buzz," Greg Bright reported.

Red drop lights hung off the fantail of the aircraft carrier. At just outside one mile, Buzzell could see them clearly. They joined a string of strobing white centerline lights at the aft-most portion of the landing area. They verified his lineup. He could see the ball, faint and blurred with its green datums across the center of the fresnel lens. Bright could make out the dim VSI gauge over his pilot's left shoulder—there was no such gauge in the backseat—and he called a steady rate of descent across the ICS. Buzzell's eyes jumped from the ICLS needles to the amber ball on the lens, then back to the needles.

At three-quarters of a mile, the RIO called the ball and an LSO answered. Buzzell was looking outside now. It was too late in the approach to look inside Aardvark 112 for clues to its airspeed or altitude. Bright called the VSI. At less than ten seconds from touchdown, Buzzell bumped the throttles forward then back, working about the null power setting that flew his fighter on-speed. The jet accelerated two knots. He felt it and the RIO called it at the same time. Again, Buzzell rolled in DLC and pulled the throttles back, but only momentarily. The ball crested above the green datum lights then recentered. The jet's lineup looked good. Inside his helmet earphones, he heard himself breathing, and occasionally there were Notso's calls from the backseat. Yellow sodium vapor floodlights surrounded the island tower and filled his peripheral vision. He dared not look away from the ball. Again, it slowly climbed out of the middle of the datums, just as the aircraft flew through the burble of air that flowed down over the *Enterprise* ramp. The ball fell across the center of the bright green lights.

Stateroom 03-93-2L
2320

It was late, but Dirk Buzzell didn't feel like sleeping. Mark Caine and Spanky Pfister were also in their racks. Pfister's snoring was even louder than usual. And it was too late, he decided, to go somewhere else to write a letter. He climbed down from the top rack and went to his desk. He was convinced that neither of his roommates would be bothered by his desk lamp. He clicked on the small light and began the obligatory *Dear Marti* atop the yellow legal pad.

We need to be together tonight, he began. *Back in that little hotel room in the Philippines. I really want to be with you right now.*

Buzzell held the pen in his hand, uncertain how to continue the letter. He wanted to tell her about Mark Caine—about the accident on the flight deck and how he had been standing on the landing signal officer platform during Coke's most recent mishap. Maybe all of it would become somehow clearer in his mind if he wrote her about it in a letter—maybe it would become suddenly obvious to him what should be done. Or better yet, maybe she could tell him what to say to Caine. But she had never met Coke, and she might not understand.

Buzzell wondered if Marti had read anything in the papers about Seed Hansen yet—about an A-7 pilot killed while flying around the *Enterprise* as the ship operated in the Indian Ocean. It bothered Dirk Buzzell that he hadn't given much thought to Hansen's mishap, or about Kurt Hansen for that matter. But not thinking about how and why a friend dies around the ship is always more important than dwelling on it. Not writing about it was just as important.

She would certainly understand about Yeoman Jordan Michaels—he was a sailor who detested living aboard an aircraft carrier, and he was someone who had illustrated that fact by attempting suicide. Marti could certainly understand those kinds of feelings—they were not unlike the feelings he had expressed to her in numerous letters. But Michaels's problems were now Dirk Buzzell's problems, and he would have to solve them alone. And she wouldn't want to read about an attempted suicide either.

What the Enterprise is doing up here in the Persian Gulf is wrong, he wrote finally. *We fly into Iranian airspace and dare those ASSHOLES to come out and play. When they do, we turn tail and run away. It's not right, Marti. The Iranian Revolutionary Guard is literally getting away with murder, and the United States Navy does nothing to stop it from happening. The way I see it, it's pretty simple*, he wrote her. *We escort the AWACS through the Strait of Hormuz and protect it from the bad guys. If the AWACS is threatened by the bad guys, then we shoot them down. Simple. The Navy isn't committed to doing the right thing up here.*

Dirk Buzzell dropped the pen again. He imagined Marti as she read the letter. She would read about his launching missiles at Iranian fighters, and she would equate that to war. He couldn't write her about war.

It's the ROE, Marti. Our hands are tied behind our backs up here. We CAN'T do what NEEDS to be done. But she couldn't possibly understand the concept of the admiral's Rules of Engagement, Buzzell decided. He wasn't sure *he* understood it.

Mostly, he wanted to tell her how much she meant to him. He felt as if he'd never been able to prove that fact to her, and he hoped it was something she wanted to hear.

I received two letters from you today, he started again. *In both of them you said the same thing. You said that you needed to know where we stood . . . what's going to happen when I get back from this cruise. I do love you, Marti, and I'm not even sure that I've admitted that to you before. If I haven't, I apologize. You deserve better. You deserve to know, babe.*

I'm scared to death, Marti. I'm scared to make the ultimate commitment to you . . . to, you know . . . to be married.

Dirk Buzzell reviewed the letter, and laughed to himself at what he read. The comparison seemed suddenly very obvious. He felt like a hypocrite.

Maybe I shouldn't be pissed off at the Navy, he wrote. *Because the Navy and me . . . we're a lot alike. The Navy knows what needs to be done here in the Persian Gulf, and it's not doing it. I know what needs to be done between you and me . . . and I'm not doing that either. Neither one of us are doing the right thing.*

Mark Caine slid out of his center rack and walked to the stateroom sink. He wet his face cloth, pressed it against his forehead, then turned toward Dirk Buzzell.

"Writin' a letter to your sweetie?" he asked.

"Nah. Not really," Buzzell said as he tore off the top sheet of the yellow legal pad, wadded the letter into a ball, then tossed it into the garbage can.

DAY TWENTY-FOUR

JANUARY 28

USS *Enterprise*
Aardvark 100—Alert Alpha
0840

Dirk Buzzell had made up his mind. He had decided to confide in Greg Bright. In the forward cockpit, he practiced his lines.

Bright was a U.S. Naval Academy graduate. And the RIO was proud of that fact. To the majority of naval aviators who gained their commissions via ROTC or, as Buzzell had, through Aviation Officer Candidate School, Academy graduates were frequent targets of Aardvark harassment. The jokes invariably revolved around the Academy's restrictive dating policies. According to the jokes, Annapolis graduates were described as frustrated celibates who became instant sex fiends following commissioning ceremonies. But attending the Naval Academy, at least for Bright, had been well worth any harassment. It had always been his dream to be educated there. It had been his father's dream as well.

Greg Bright's father had been a radioman and tail-gunner in the backseat of Navy SB-2C Helldivers during the final months of World War II. According to the story, the elder Bright had lied about his age to enter the war, and he had seen combat only once. On that occasion, the elder Bright and his pilot had been patrolling in company with three other Helldivers south of Ryukyu Island, the southernmost island in the Japanese chain.

The division of dive bombers had happened upon a lone enemy destroyer transiting north toward Okinawa. To find a single Japanese combatant was unusual. The destroyer was an easy target—it had not expected attack. The ship's captain had gambled that heavy seas, and a thick overcast of low clouds offered him protection enough as he steamed toward port. The captain undoubtedly knew the U.S. fleet was operating nearby, but felt certain their patrols would not locate his ship in the weather.

Bright's father found the destroyer through a rare hole in the overcast, and all four Helldivers spiraled over it. The ship and its captain did not die easily. The SB-2C's carried only one weapon each—and only two of the four heavy bombs dropped from the aircraft would find their mark. The first had detonated as it creased the ship's bow, and most of its explosive charge blew harmlessly into the water. There was no fire, and only minimal damage to one of the destroyer's forward gun turrets. Eventually, a half dozen more deck-mounted antiaircraft guns blazed at the SB-2Cs. Dark flak surrounded the swooping Helldivers. The second bomb—the one dropped by Bright and his pilot—had fallen amidships, just aft of the ship's island—a perfect delivery.

Bright's father saw wisps of gray smoke circle away from the destroyer from where the bomb had struck home. But there had been no explosion. The Navy aircraft rendezvoused, then dove again, this time strafing their target. It was during the four-plane's second and final strafing run that Greg Bright's father had earned his Purple Heart. A 40-millimeter Japanese antiaircraft shell had erupted outside the Helldiver canopy, ripping it from the aircraft. Small shell fragments pierced its tail section. Some tore into the gunner's shoulder and neck.

Later, while recovering from his wounds aboard a hospital ship, Bright's father learned that the Japanese ship had indeed been sunk. The second bomb had fused late, but it had fused. And it had been deep inside the enemy vessel when it detonated.

"I was lucky," Bright's father would always say to end his story. "I had an opportunity to fight the enemy and I won. That prize is worth any price." Greg Bright had heard the story many times from his father, and told it many times himself. Dirk Buzzell had heard it.

As he sat in the alert Tomcat, Buzzell knew his RIO was steeped in the traditions and ceremony intrinsic to an Annapolis education. And Bright didn't seem to mind the Academy jokes, either.

The pilot hoped Greg Bright shared his frustration with the Rules of Engagement, too. And he wondered if Bright was willing to do something about the ROE. Most of all, Dirk Buzzell needed another ally like the one he'd found in Dan Harrington. Without Bright in the backseat of his F-14 Tomcat, his plan could only fail.

Buzzell double-checked his ejection seat. When it was safed at both handles, he unsnapped his leg restraints and harness fittings. Aardvark 100 was forward of the island just aft of elevator number two. One hundred feet behind the fighter, and alongside *Enterprise* in perfect formation, steamed the USS *Clairmont*, a *Mars* class replenishment vessel fitted to ferry combat stores and groceries to the larger aircraft carrier. A spiderweb of cable lines attached the two ships. Boxes of fresh fruit and vegetables crossed the cables, while CH-46 helos lifted pallets of ordnance and bulk goods onto the carrier's flight deck. More than two dozen of the the pallets blocked the path Aardvark 100 would take to reach the catapult. If an alert launch was called away, Buzzell knew he would have plenty of time to strap in again.

The pilot propped himself against the rear cockpit where it hinged with the raised Plexiglas canopy. Bright looked up from the letter he was writing, surprised to see Buzzell out of the jet.

"What's up, Buzz. Gotta go pee?" he asked with a grin.

"Nope. Just felt like stretching my legs. If they decide to launch us, we're not going anywhere in a hurry." Buzzell gestured toward a twin-rotored helicopter as it dropped another crate of lettuce in front of the Tomcat.

"Yeah, I can see the newspaper headlines now," Bright said. "USS *Enterprise* bombed by Iranian aircraft . . . flight deck transformed into giant Caesar salad." Buzzell laughed, then paused.

"You know, Notso, I've been thinking a lot about our BARCAP sortie the other day." The pilot stated his words loud enough to be heard above the sounds that enveloped them. "And I'm a little embarrassed for the United States Navy."

Bright nodded his head and lifted the note pad from his lap.

"Yep. I was trying to write my folks about it. I can't decide whether to lie and tell them nothing happened out there or blame our sister squadron for flying airplanes with crummy systems. I probably shouldn't write about it at all . . . but what the hell, my dad will get a kick out of the story."

Dirk Buzzell flashed an encouraging grin toward the RIO. He felt like a kid with a secret to share.

"I had a little chat with the Whale driver who was flying that day. He's a pretty good friend—we went though flight school together." Buzzell hoped the statement would add credibility to his source. "Seems all was not as it appeared to be on that sortie."

Bright tossed his note pad onto the rear cockpit glareshield, listening intently to his pilot. The conversation was one-sided. Bright didn't interrupt, and Buzzell wouldn't have allowed him to try. The two were instantly oblivious to the helos that whipped overhead and to the countless flight deck forklifts moving pallets around them.

Dirk Buzzell repeated exactly the words passed to him by Harrington. He didn't embellish the facts, hoping they alone would evoke the same reaction from Bright they had from him. Opinions would only serve to confuse and slant those facts, he had decided. And if Buzzell and Bright were to act together at a later day, it couldn't happen if the RIO felt obligated to Buzzell's scheme. It would happen because the two of them, along with Dan Harrington, had built the plan together.

He recounted the events leading up to their BARCAP mission, reminding Bright first of the shootdown incident with the F-14s flying off the *Carl Vinson* and the speculation by some that the KY-58 secure voice encoder system had been compromised by the Iranians. The RIO looked down into his cockpit, and thumbed the controls to his radio while Buzzell continued. The pilot then explained why the A-3 had been ordered aboard the *Enter-*

prise—he described how the latest *Burning Sand* escort had been nothing more than a cover for an intelligence-gathering mission.

Bright swung his head back against the top of his ejection seat, as Buzzell outlined the collaboration between the Whale, the E-2, the two Black Eagle F-14s—even the Saudis—as the plan went into action in the Strait of Hormuz. The RIO learned of the one-star rear admiral's role in the giant pretense. Finally, Buzzell described the fate of the British-built Hawker Hunter flown by a mercenary for the Sultan of Oman Air Force.

And Dirk Buzzell surprised himself. Not unlike a politician shaking hands and kissing babies at a fund-raiser, he seemed to speak the words his RIO wanted to hear. Bright was an audience that needed little convincing.

Iranian Revolutionary Guard Hangar
Bandar 'Abbās, Iran

Ali Abdul Rajani was used to posing for photographers, and he stood easily in front of them in the cramped ready room. Omid had never before received such attention, and he relished the moment. Ahmed stood between them. The heir of the Ayatollah Khomeini mystique and the avowed leader of the new Iranian military machine was a slight man. His beard was white as had been his father's, but was stringy and unkempt. He was short, barely five feet tall, and more feeble than his years would normally indicate. The son of the Ayatollah had come to Bandar 'Abbās to meet the two pilots standing on either side of him. There was tremendous propaganda value in these men, he had decided. Reza stood to the side of the three, nearest Ali. He had coordinated the photo shoot.

The ace was not impressed, neither with the media event nor with this man who was the son of the Ayatollah. Reza read from a carefully scripted press release that had been sanctioned by Ahmed himself.

"Together, these two warriors have obliterated the Sultan of Oman's Air Force and totally destroyed the Didamar Island anchorage. It is men like these who will assist the Iranian Revolutionary Guard in bringing the Great Imperialist Satan to its knees. No longer does the United States Navy dare intervene against us. Islam has won yet another battle." There were cheers inside the room and the photographers snapped more pictures.

One of the state journalists there—another who knew of Ali and had followed the ace's many victories—pushed his way forward through the crowd to the group of three men standing at the front of the room.

"And what exactly was *your* role at Didamar, Ali, as Omid dropped the two bombs atop the anchorage? What did you see?"

"I saw the four other bombs he dropped off target and into the water," the ace chided. "The splashes he made were most impressive. Omid has killed many fishes for our cause." Ali laughed with his comment, and Omid took a step toward the taller bearded man. Reza grabbed Ali and pulled the two pilots apart. He ordered the newsmen there to ignore Rajani's statement.

USS *Enterprise*
Aardvark 100

Dirk Buzzell finished his monolog, and felt suddenly exhausted. Again, he was aware of the CH-

46s hovering low over the flight deck forward of the island, and the *Clairmont* bobbing in sync with the aircraft carrier. Bright's attention had shifted. He stared down, below Buzzell and toward the bottom of the Tomcat's boarding ladder. There, Aardvark 100's plane captain, an airman named Fuentes, was tugging at the pilot's G-suit. Buzzell looked down too, hoping the interruption would be brief.

"What's up?" he asked.

"Flight deck control says you're supposed to start up the jet, sir. I think they wanna launch the Alert," Fuentes answered. Buzzell would have to finish his conversation with Greg Bright later.

He straddled the port canopy rail and slid into the front cockpit, reaching first for his leg restraints and lap belts. The plane captain pulled himself up the boarding ladder behind the pilot, and snapped Buzzell's oxygen mask and G-suit to their port console connections. Even before he was able to signal for it, electrical power was supplied to the aircraft. He heard Bright through the ICS, and Buzzell answered the check with two clicks.

"Lieutenant, we just heard that someone's attacking one of our ships with missiles," Fuentes said before climbing down the ladder to the flight deck.

Iranian Revolutionary Guard Hangar
Bandar ʻAbbās, Iran

But Ahmed had come to Bandar ʻAbbās for another reason as well. The IRG's push south into Oman was being spearheaded from Iran's southern coast, and he had come to supervise the latest stage of that push. He had come to monitor the launch of a Silkworm surface-to-surface missile. A bank of electronic gear pressed against one of the ready room walls. A few of the newer Iranian RAAM shortwave sets were there, along with portable VHF radios and a few television monitors. But the technicians there concentrated their attention on a single UHF receiver. They twisted its controls and made adjustments to its volume and squelch. Twenty-five miles to the south and west of Bandar 'Abbās, on the island of Hengām, was another UHF radio of the same type. When a voice began transmitting through the radio speaker, Reza ordered silence from the men in the room.

"Jazireh-ye Hengām has a successful launch from S-1," the voice reported. "The battery is away." The state journalists yelled inside the ready room. Their yells were loud enough for Ahmed to speak unnoticed to Reza.

"Tell me again . . . how many missiles comprise a Silkworm battery?" he asked in a whisper.

"Four missiles have been launched from the S-1 site, Imam," Reza explained. "Launching four missiles improves our probability of kill."

"This is truly a day to be remembered," Ahmed stated as he stared up at Reza. "We will litter the strait with the wreckage of a thousand ships and choke the world of its precious oil. There can be no mistakes now."

Ahmed stroked the chin beneath the stringy beard, then walked to the far ready room wall. The wall was plastered with charts and maps of the entire Persian Gulf region. He stabbed a dirty finger in the center of Iran on one of the maps, then moved it slowly around the Gulf in a counterclockwise direction—through Iraq, Kuwait, Saudi Arabia, the United Arab Emirates, and finally Oman.

"I will have all of it," Ahmed told Reza. "It is

Allah's wish that I have it all. With his blessing, I cannot fail."

Ali Abdul Rajani was bored. He was the only true hero in the ready room, and he could not understand why the journalists there would rather talk about surface-to-surface missiles than about his prowess as a fighter pilot. The voice came across the UHF radio again—it reported that the Silkworms had found their target. A ship was burning somewhere south of the launch site. When the cheering and celebrating began again, Ali walked out of the room.

USS *Enterprise*
Aardvark 100
1005

Dirk Buzzell chopped both throttles to off. A path had been cleared between his fighter and catapult number two, but he had been directed to shut down. He and Bright had idled in the jet for more than one hour. They had listened in on the Strike frequency while they idled there, but had not been allowed to taxi. A vessel had been hit, but it was not an American warship. It was Dutch, the Strike frequency confirmed. And it had not been sunk. The large merchant vessel had been operating near the center of the Strait of Hormuz—about eleven miles south of Hengām Island—and had been struck by a single warhead. The ship was burning, and its crew had apparently abandoned it. The information over the Strike network originated from a U.S. frigate patrolling the strait fifty miles northwest of the *Enterprise*. The frigate was alongside the burning merchant ship. The voice on the frequency said something about a Silkworm missile.

But the decision had already been made to scrub the Alert launch. Buzzell and Bright would not fly toward the burning vessel, or anywhere else for that matter. Since it was a Dutch ship that had been taken under attack, the only assistance available from the U.S. Navy would come in the form of search-and-rescue operations—no F-14 fighters would be required.

A ship had been fired upon and hit by a missile originating from Iran. The ship had been badly damaged and some had died. But since it was not an American ship, there had been no violation of the ROE.

Buzzell stepped quickly down Aardvark 100's boarding ladder. Bright followed, and caught up to him as Buzzell entered the aircraft carrier's island at flight deck level. Inside the island, beside the entrance to Flight Deck Control, Rear Admiral Jeremiah Curtiss stood with his chief of staff, a short and grossly overweight Navy captain wearing thick trifocal eyeglasses. The admiral and his captain halted their conversation as the two VF-141 aviators walked by.

"Sorry about scrubbing your mission, gentlemen." Curtiss grinned. There was little apology in his voice. "But it's not our fight."

The pilot stopped and turned toward the battle group commander. Greg Bright didn't say anything, but he knew Dirk Buzzell was about to.

"With all due respect, sir." He paused only briefly before finishing his statement. "Maybe it fuckin' should be."

Greg Bright had closed his eyes. He fully expected to hear his pilot—his friend, a lieutenant—begin an ugly conversation with the highest-ranking naval officer within 1,000 miles. When he opened his eyes, Buzzell was already halfway down the ladder well leading to the 0-3 level. Rear Admiral Curtiss said nothing as the pilot disappeared beneath the hatchway.

DAY TWENTY-SIX

JANUARY 30

USS *Enterprise*
Ready Room Six
0740

Greg Bright stood beside the air conditioner at the back of Ready Six. The machine groaned deeply as it came to life and pushed chilled air toward the ready room chairs. The giant cooling unit was unique to the VF-141 Aardvarks. It was far larger than the machine that cooled the Aardvarks' F-14 sister squadron, VF-231, or any of the ship's eight other squadron ready rooms for that matter. The air conditioner was integral to Aardvark officer morale. It was also the sole responsibility of the squadron duty officer. If the air inside the ready room was cool, then the CO—who spent most of his day sitting there—would also be cool. If the air became sticky, warm, and stale—as it always did when the cooling unit suddenly failed—the SDO was in duty-stander's hell.

Again, Mark Caine was the duty officer. Bright watched him as he unplugged the unit, then pulled a large drip pan from beneath its condenser assembly. The pan would fill to the brim in less than an hour on humid days like this one. Caine steadied the pan and walked past Bright. He purposely ignored the RIO—*his* former RIO—then continued out the back of Ready Six toward the nearest head, where he would empty the pan. Greg Bright stood there—he didn't particularly enjoy being ignored by Caine. The door slammed shut as Bright pulled the wall phone off its hook. He was alone in the room.

Bright dialed the four-digit number scribbled on a tattered briefing card he kept in his flight suit pocket. He immediately recognized Dan Harrington's voice.

"Howdy, Wrongway. Notso here. I got your message . . . what's up?"

"Good news and bad," Harrington answered, his voice somehow more official over the phone. "A few things have changed since our little chat last night. And since this is not a secure line, I was wondering if you and Buzz were free for lunch. I hear they're offering up some *haute cuisine* at today's midday meal. I don't think we should miss it."

Bright faked a laugh into the phone.

"Sure, no problem. Our brief isn't 'til 1245 anyway." Bright covered the phone and quickly glanced around the ready room. "Please tell me there aren't any problems on your end, Wrongway."

"Hope not, Notso. I'll see you guys about noon," Harrington said. "Make sure Buzz gets the word, will ya? It's kind of important we all talk before the Spam hits the fan."

"Okay. We'll be there," Bright said, pushing the phone into its receiver. The RIO tried to interpret the tone of Harrington's voice. He decided it wasn't too early in the day to begin worrying—he was getting used to it. Behind him, Mark Caine had already reentered Ready Six and was replacing the air-conditioner drip pan.

Wardroom One
1150

Dirk Buzzell rounded the passageway bulkhead across from the wardroom scullery. He took a plastic tray and slid it along the silver metal shelf that paralleled the kitchen. A pan of chili steamed into the sweating face of the messman leaning over it. Next to the chili was rice and a pile of "sliders"—hamburgers and cheeseburgers. Buzzell pointed past the sliders to a collection of triangle-shaped fried fish patties.

"A couple of the fish," he said.

A deep bowl at the end of the shelf was empty. Buzzell could tell it had once contained tartar sauce. The enlisted man explained how there was apparently less sauce for the fish than fish patties themselves, and that he was sorry. Buzzell picked up the tray, stepped over a knee-knocker, and away from the kitchen. He filled two glasses with iced tea, then scanned the sea of flight suits in the wardroom—searching for Bright and Harrington. He found them, finally, in the smaller half of the wardroom farther forward. They were alone at the small table. Harrington looked up as Buzzell slid his plate across the table.

"Ah, I see you've selected the Fresh Catch *du jour*, Mr. Buzzell. Wise choice. It's especially greasy today," Harrington teased.

"You know, I've seen fish in squares and triangles and circles. I keep hoping one shape will taste better than the other. Unfortunately, there's no difference,'' Buzzell said while reaching for the catsup bottle. Bright interrupted what he knew would be needless banter between his pilot and Harrington.

''We might have a problem, Buzz,'' the RIO whispered across the table to his front-seater.

''Another problem . . . you mean besides all of us losing our wings and getting court-martialed for what we're trying to do? Fill me in. I can hardly wait.''

Bright leaned across his empty plate toward Buzzell. But Harrington cut him off instead.

''Listen, Buzz . . . as of 1700 yesterday, the Whale has been hard down. Right now it's unflyable. Something to do with the starboard landing gear . . . a hydraulic valve or uplock . . . I'm not exactly sure which. Anyway, our maintenance folks say it might be ready for a 1430 launch this afternoon. And since we're flying another *Burning Sand* mission, I think the mechs will fix it in time. That's the good news.''

Buzzell dropped his fork onto the plastic tray in front of him. He could not stomach the fish piece in his mouth, and spit it into his napkin. He wasn't in the mood for fish or bad news.

''My Ops department screwed me,'' Harrington said. ''I was supposed to be flying this afternoon's sortie. I write the schedule, you know, so I figured there would be no problem, right? But the only other A-3 pilot out here is senior to me . . . he's the maintenance officer . . . and the asshole is pulling rank. Since I had that *last Sand* mission, he wants *this* one. I'm still working on it, Buzz, but I may not be out there for you guys today.''

Buzzell pushed himself away from the table, sitting back in his chair. He looked at Harrington and then Greg Bright. The RIO pushed a larger-than-usual plug of tobacco into his lip. It seemed no one would say a word until Buzzell did—no one would suggest delaying or canceling the plan unless Buzzell did. And since it had originally been his, no one would suffer the consequences of a failed plan more than Buzzell. The pilot wadded his napkin, tossing it in a large arc onto his plate of uneaten fish triangles.

"So. Do we shit-can the whole plan, Notso? We've figured all along to have Wrongway out there." Dirk Buzzell reviewed the options and contingencies in his mind. "We'd be lucky to pull it off *with* the Whale. I'm not sure if you and I can do it alone."

Greg Bright didn't answer. Instead, he pulled his half-empty coffee cup from the table and spit into it. He shrugged his shoulders and slid back into his wardroom chair.

"Like I said, Buzz," Harrington interrupted, "I'm still trying to get into that flight. Or . . . I could brief my maintenance officer. I could let him in on the deal. He might even see things the way we do."

Dirk Buzzell was already shaking his head. "No. No way. It's too late to bring anybody else into this mess. We've already told too many people. It's gonna happen this afternoon or it's not gonna happen at all. If you don't get airborne, Dan, we'll call the whole thing off. Shit, Notso and I had to pull some pretty big strings to get scheduled on this afternoon's escort, too. And we're not going to have another chance. Shit! You *gotta* be out there today, Wrongway!"

Harrington and Bright nodded in agreement.

"Listen, we've been through this thing a thousand times, and I know we haven't forgotten anything. It's a simple plan, and we've got everything on our side—assuming a couple of things." Dirk Buzzell reiterated the plan more for his own benefit than that of the two officers at the table with him. "We need one good Tomcat with an even better radar . . . and we've got that already. Notso and I are flying in One-Twelve. It's probably the best Aardvark fighter on the flight deck.

"And we need at least one Iranian jet to come out and play with us. If the IRG doesn't launch, then we don't have anything to worry about, right? And nobody will even know we had a plan . . . and we'll fly the standard *Burning Sand* escort. But they'll launch, Notso. Especially if we make it worth their while to launch."

"Yeah, if they listen to our little white lie," Greg Bright interjected with a grin.

"*And,*" Buzzell added, "we need the Whale . . . and we need Wrongway driving that ugly son-of-a-bitch."

Greg Bright didn't feel the need to verbalize his agreement. He spit again into his coffee cup.

"If Dan isn't flying the Whale this afternoon, I'm not gonna have that same warm and fuzzy feeling. We may not know what kind of airplane we're shootin' at or how many of them there are, for that matter. We're probably gonna be outnumbered. And the IRG will try to shoot us first, Notso." Buzzell looked down at his plate, reluctant to finish the statement or to return the stares he could feel through the top of his head. He was asking his RIO to risk more than just a reprimand for violating the Rules of Engagement.

"So we gotta have the Whale . . . and, so . . . I

say the plan should go away if Wrongway isn't out there today,'' Dirk Buzzell decided at last.

''But you *will* be out there, won't you, Danny boy,'' Bright stated hopefully. ''And we will have a sweet radar and we *will* launch a missile and we *will* ruin the entire day for a couple of Iranians.'' Greg Bright was smiling. ''And what's the worse that could happen? So I'll be a lieutenant for the rest of my life. I didn't want a promotion, anyway.''

''I don't think that's gonna be a problem,'' Harrington said flatly. ''We'll most likely be making little rocks out of big rocks in Leavenworth for this one. My wife's gonna be pissed.''

''Thanks for the pep talk,'' Buzzell said, sliding back in his chair. ''Anybody bring a bottle of whiskey? Shouldn't we make a toast or something?''

The bushy-browed A-3 pilot smiled and leaned forward.

''Tell you what, Buzz. If I get airborne and you guys somehow make it back aboard this ship in one piece, I'll buy you a case of Jack Daniel's.''

Harrington and Bright lifted glasses of water while Buzzell grabbed at one of his iced teas. They were about to drink to their decision when they heard someone yell from the forward half of the wardroom.

''Attention on deck!''

Buzzell didn't get to his feet right away. He peered through an open hatchway toward the scullery.

''Oh shit,'' he muttered as he stood out of his chair. Harrington and Bright followed his lead.

Rear Admiral Jeremiah Curtiss walked past the wardroom ice cream machine, then turned in the direction of Buzzell and Bright and Harrington. The admiral hesitated before entering the forward portion of the space. Every officer was on his feet.

"At ease," he ordered. "Please sit down and enjoy your lunch."

Buzzell quickly reseated himself and grabbed at his tea. His back was turned toward Curtiss—exactly the way he preferred it to be. The admiral stepped toward the table, but was intercepted on his way by a group of officers from the Black Eagles of VF-231. After a brief conversation and a few handshakes, Curtiss turned and walked directly toward Dan Harrington.

"How's the food?" Curtiss asked.

"Delicious, sir. I was just about to go back for seconds." Harrington made the statement with more than a little sarcasm in his voice.

"Liar," the admiral said. Buzzell was surprised by the comment. He glanced up at the one-star standing beside his chair. "We really need to do something about the fish. That stuff tastes like dogshit . . . bad for morale."

"Well, I think I'm finished. How about you, Buzz?" Greg Bright was already standing out of his chair, smiling politely at Curtiss. "Won't you excuse us, sir?"

Dirk Buzzell stood up. His six-foot frame was a full five inches shorter than the admiral's.

"Lieutenant, I'd like to finish the conversation we began up in Flight Deck Control the other day. Do you have a few minutes?" Jeremiah Curtiss flashed a congenial smile. As far as Dirk Buzzell was concerned, that conversation was a mistake, and was over. He wanted to forget it ever happened.

"I'd like to apologize for that, sir. I was way out of line."

"Oh, I don't know. I admire your frankness. And I'd really appreciate it if you could stop by my office in, say, fifteen minutes. Do you know where it is?''

Buzzell was stunned. He had no desire to talk further with Jeremiah Curtiss—especially if the topic of conversation was Buzzell's blatant disrespect to a flag-rank officer.

And the battle group commander didn't really appreciate his frankness. The admiral simply did not want to embarrass Buzzell. Not in the wardroom—not in public.

Just let me go. Let me go fly and launch something at an Iranian fighter this afternoon, Admiral. Then you can do anything you damn-well like. Buzzell was taking too much time to think. He wasn't sure how to answer Curtiss.

''Yes, sir, I know where it is. I imagine you'd like my commanding officer to be there as well.''

''No . . . hell no. Come alone. See you at 1230.'' Rear Admiral Curtiss turned and strolled out of the wardroom. Buzzell sank in his chair. Greg Bright returned to his seat.

''I'm a dead man,'' Buzzell said. There was little humor in his voice.

''Oh, I don't know, Buzz,'' Dan Harrington offered. ''They don't make lieutenants walk the plank anymore.'' Buzzell managed a slight smile before the three aviators stood up together and walked out of Wardroom One.

Dirk Buzzell walked past the Marine guard standing in the passageway outside the flag secretary's office at exactly 1230. The guard carried a semiautomatic weapon—Buzzell knew the weapon was not loaded. Still, the Marine made no attempt to stop him. The door leading into the office was open, and Buzzell walked slowly across the blue tile floor leading to a reception desk. A lieutenant commander sat behind the desk.

"Lieutenant Buzzell. I have an appointment with Admiral Curtiss."

Rear Admiral Curtiss walked from the adjoining space. The lieutenant commander did not have the opportunity to say a word.

"C'mon in, Buzz. That is your call sign, isn't it . . . Buzz?"

"Yes, sir." Dirk Buzzell stood rigid at attention.

"Do me a favor and relax, Lieutenant," Curtiss scolded. "In here."

Buzzell followed the admiral through a wide reception area to a neatly appointed office—it alone was larger than the entire VF-141 ready room, and it too was tiled in blue. The fat captain with thick glasses was seated in one of the eight overstuffed chairs that surrounded a long table. A dark desk butted up against the forward-most bulkhead in the office.

"I think you know Captain Stanton, my chief of staff."

"Yes, sir." Buzzell was confused, but somehow flattered by the attention his disrespect had warranted.

"So, Buzz. What am I going to do with you?" The admiral lit a pipe while the pilot tried to think of the right answer. The admiral did not look the type to smoke a pipe. It looked odd in his mouth.

"I don't know, sir. That comment up in Flight Deck Control was uncalled for." When Curtiss sat at his desk, Buzzell lowered himself into the chair at the far end of the long table.

"Give me a little credit, will you, Lieutenant. This meeting is not about your goddamned comment. Hell, I probably deserved that one. It's refreshing to hear that kind of honesty every once in a while.'' The one-star glanced toward his chief of staff, who scribbled onto a note pad and pretended not to hear his boss. ''If I wanted to put you in the brig, young man, it certainly wouldn't be for that comment.''

Dirk Buzzell's stomach ached. He tried not to show it.

''Don't you have a flight to brief in a few minutes, Buzz?'' The admiral was already refilling his pipe. Buzzell was certain the battle group commander didn't regularly read the Aardvark flight schedule. There was a reason he knew.

''At 1245, sir. But I'm not gonna make that brief, am I?''

''To tell you the truth, Buzz, I haven't made up my mind yet. You might, although I imagine you'll be a few minutes late. Suppose we discuss your mission this afternoon. You were going to lead a section of Aardvark F-14s on the *Burning Sand* escort, right?''

''Yes, sir.''

''And you had something else in mind besides simply escorting the E-3 AWACS, didn't you?''

Buzzell sank deeper into the oversized chair. He reviewed the names of every officer he had talked with about his plan—Notso, Dan Harrington, his roommates Spanky Pfister and Mark Caine, and the squadron schedules officer—all of them could be trusted—he couldn't believe any of them would betray him.

''Yes I did, sir. But how did you find out I was—''

''Let's just say that this is a very small ship, Buzz. Word gets around.''

Dirk Buzzell didn't hang his head. It was a good

plan, and he wouldn't apologize for it. He was fairly certain he'd go to the brig for dreaming it up, but he had no regrets.

"Let me guess," the admiral said, sitting forward in his chair and propping his elbows onto the mahogany desk. "Once you got out there, you planned on coming up on your KY-58 radio and claiming some sort of aircraft malfunction. Then, when the Iranians scrambled a fighter or two, you planned on nailing them, right?" The admiral paced as he talked. He stared past the long table at the pilot. "Did you figure on taking your wingman in there with you, Buzz? And what makes you so sure you could shoot the Iranians before they nailed you?"

Dirk Buzzell had been found out—he was trapped. There was nothing to be gained now by denying the plan existed. "My wingman doesn't know anything about this, sir. I planned on keeping him with the escort. I was going to do it alone."

"Alone? Alone with Lieutenant Greg Bright and Lieutenant Dan Harrington who flies the A-3, I believe? Weren't those two with you at lunch a little while ago?"

"It was my idea. They don't have anything to do with this, Admiral."

"I doubt that very seriously, Buzz. And this is no time to be noble. Instead, I want you to listen to what I have to say. I don't want you to say a goddamned word until I'm finished."

Rear Admiral Jeremiah Curtiss stood up. He leaned toward the F-14 pilot, and placed his palms down onto the dark finish of the desk.

"You must think I'm a *complete* asshole, Lieutenant. You're certain that the Rules of Engagement out here are mine alone, aren't you? You think I somehow enjoy seeing innocent civilians and United

States Navy personnel killed by gangs of Iranian fanatics. And you want to makes things right. Trust me, you don't know *shit*, Lieutenant." Curtiss grabbed the pipe that burned in the crystal ashtray on his desk. He sat down.

"The Joint Chiefs of Staff are driving our actions out here. My orders have their stamp on them. But that doesn't necessarily mean I agree with their decisions, Buzz. In many ways, those assholes don't have a clue, either. In point of fact, I've been working *very* diligently to get all *Enterprise* F-14s a clearance to fire on the Iranians. And I have copies of the message traffic to prove it," he said, then paused. "I don't know why I feel it necessary to explain all this to you.

"For instance, the JCS does not believe the Iranian Revolutionary Guard intends to invade Oman. They do not believe the IRG is truly capable of such an attack. They believe that recent attacks on Omani soil are aimed entirely at discouraging Oman from allowing freighters to travel within her twelve-nautical-mile buffer zone, and nothing more.

"I am convinced that the invasion of mainland Oman is Iran's primary goal. And I believe it is going to happen very soon . . . the IRG will strike into the northern territories and secure new land-based Silkworm sites. And they can expect little opposition from the Omanis. That fact is crystal clear to them now—they have destroyed an airliner, dozens of Omani vessels—not to mention the Spanish oil tanker and that Dutch ship yesterday. They've dropped bombs on Omani soil and shot down one of the Sultan's air defense fighter-bombers . . . they've killed women and children. There has been *no* response from Oman.

"Unless the U.S. Navy steps in, the Iranians will

succeed in securing a stranglehold on the Strait of Hormuz, and thus the gateway into the Persian Gulf. Shit, the IRG will roll across Oman like Iraq rolled across Kuwait. Unfortunately, the U.S. doesn't enjoy diplomatic ties with Oman. If we did, and if the Sultan had requested official assistance, this entire mess would be a simpler matter. In his folly, the Sultan actually believes his RAF mercenary pilots are capable of handling any such Iranian attacks. The Brits have proven him dead wrong once already. The IRG will be knocking on the Sultan's door in downtown Musat before he admits he needs a little help.

"Here's the bottom line, Buzz. The President and his JCS will *not* permit us to squelch an IRG invasion of Oman—we have been directed *not* to intervene in the dispute. That is one of the reasons why the Black Eagles were not allowed to return fire during the last *Burning Sand* escort. That fake mission wasn't my idea, either. I opposed the whole idea—it put our people at risk and it only served to prove what I've been telling the JCS all along. Even after that mission, I tried to convince those idiots in D.C. of the Iranian Revolutionary Guard's invasion plans, and that this air wing should launch a retaliatory strike into Iran. Bandar 'Abbās should be blasted from the face of the earth. I still feel that way.

"However, I was unable to convince them. They listen to their C.I.A. and their State Department intelligence advisers instead of the people who know—the people who do what *we* do for a living. The intel people don't have a damned clue about the Iranians.

"During the last *Burning Sand* mission, the IRG purposely waited for our escorts to round the corner at Didamar in the strait. They knew we would turn and run when their jets got close to the AWACS, and that gave them the perfect opportunity to continue south and bomb that island in Oman—that was their original intent. Unfortunately, an RAF aircraft was shot down in the process. Those Iranian bastards also know that we're unable to 'officially' assist the Royal Air Force pilots who defend Oman. They're playing us like a deck of cards. I'm sick of it, Lieutenant. That's why I'm telling you this."

Rear Admiral Curtiss checked his watch. It was nearly 1300, and Dirk Buzzell was late for his brief.

"Here's the deal, Buzz. Take it or leave it. If you leave it, you walk out of here and we both forget about your plan. I can't have a Navy lieutenant take on the entire Iranian Revolutionary Guard, regardless of his good intentions. If you take it, however you may still have the opportunity to fire a few missiles." Curtiss looked toward Stanton. The captain had spilled coffee on his khaki trousers.

"I want to kick some Iranian ass, Buzz. But I need your help. You see . . . I've got a plan, too. The President and his JCS will absolutely shit when they get wind of it.

"You would launch on this afternoon's *Burning Sand* escort as scheduled. When the Iranians take off out of Bandar 'Abbās—and you'll have to trust me when I say they will—you and your wingman will take the AWACS and fly into Oman exactly like the Black Eagles did last time. I've got to have your word on this one, Buzz. If you go, you've got to give me your word that you'll do it my way."

Dirk Buzzell was fascinated. He didn't have to think long before he answered. "You've got my word, sir."

"Good. When you are convinced that the

AWACS is headed safely back toward Masirah, I want your two Aardvark F-14s to land at the Thumrait air facility in Oman. Don't come back here. Not today, anyway. Do the best you can to get into Thumrait quietly. Don't use your radios any more than absolutely necessary. Turn off your IFF transponders and fly as low as you're able. Thumrait is expecting you. I know for a fact that the Brits are praying they'll see U.S. fighters over their airfield this afternoon. I'll take care of the details personally. I'll convince the *Enterprise* CO and the CAG that this plan comes straight from the top. They'll have no reason to doubt my word. I am the senior man around here, after all."

Dirk Buzzell fully expected to hear someone yell "Candid Camera" from a hidden corner of the large office. He still could not believe what he was hearing.

"A message will go out tonight. It'll say that VF-141 lost two F-14s to a midair collision as the jets returned to the USS *Enterprise* from their escort mission. The JCS will be the addressee, but we're going to do our best to 'accidentally' leak that message to the Iranians as well. Those two jets will be you and your wingman.

"Nobody will fly off this ship tomorrow. It will appear that the entire *Enterprise* air wing is conducting another one of those safety stand-downs. That way, the IRG won't expect to see American fighters airborne anywhere near the Persian Gulf. Everything this ship does tomorrow is designed to convince the Iranians that you and your wingman dropped into the water. That will arm your two aircraft with the element of surprise. You'll need that tomorrow.

"Listen, Buzz." The admiral glanced over to his

chief of staff. "Very few people know about this, and most of them are in this room. But since you were bold or crazy enough to take the risk in the first place, you're my first choice to lead those fighters into Thumrait."

Dirk Buzzell looked toward the fat captain then back at Jeremiah Curtiss. He wasn't certain whether he'd been complimented or was being sacrificed. Either way, if he was expected to make a statement, he had no idea what to say. Curtiss stood again before Buzzell had to fumble for words.

"Actually, to be completely frank with you, Buzz, you're my *only* choice. What do you think?"

"Admiral, what am I supposed to do after I land at Thumrait?"

Curtiss curled open his hand and pointed toward Captain Stanton. The captain stood clumsily out of his large chair and read from the legal pad.

"At approximately 1100 hours on 31 January—that's tomorrow—two divisions of Omani Hawker Hunters—eight airplanes—will launch on a retaliatory strike into Iran from the air base at Thumrait. The attack aircraft will be loaded with various air-to-surface weapons ranging in size from 500 to 1,000 pounds. Their target will be the Silkworm missile site on Hengām Island. A secondary strike target is these piers located on the southeast side of the island." Curtiss's chief of staff waddled toward Buzzell. He carried two large black-and-white reconnaissance photos of the island. "Twelve IRG Boghammer patrol craft are moored at the piers. The two U.S. F-14 Tomcats will act as fighter cover for the strike—that's you and your wingman, Lieutenant Buzzell. IRG opposition can be expected in the form of F-4 Phantoms and, quite possibly, Iranian F-14s. As far as we know, both types of fighters are still positioned at Bandar 'Abbās."

Buzzell studied the photos. He was a fighter pilot, and ground targets meant little to him. He returned the photos to the captain.

"We have been told the Hunter strike will go as scheduled, even without the benefit of U.S. Navy cover," the chief of staff said. "A few of the RAF pilots will carry air-to-air missiles . . . for self-defense purposes."

"The Brits will get slaughtered without an escort," Buzzell said matter-of-factly.

"Then you'll go?" Curtiss stated more than asked. "And you'll do it within the framework of the plan I've just described?"

"Yes, sir, Admiral. It's . . . it's better than my plan. But am I allowed to make a few recommendations, at least as far as the aircrew who fly with me on the *Burning Sand* this afternoon and on the strike tomorrow?" Admiral Curtiss was overwhelmed. He would have field-promoted Dirk Buzzell to commander if the pilot had requested it.

"It's your show, Buzz," he announced.

"I'll fly with Kyle Herrin. I've logged more time with him than anybody else this cruise. And he'll be up for it." Buzzell paused. There had been no contingency for another Aardvark F-14 in his original plan. He and Notso had been prepared to engage the Iranians alone. But if Notso Bright couldn't be in his backseat, he wanted him there as his wingman's RIO.

"Lieutenant Greg Bright will fly in the backseat of the other jet. He's real good with the system." The admiral sat on the corner of his desk while Dirk Buzzell finished. The chief of staff made more notes on his pad.

"Bright usually flies with Mark Caine. Caine's

been grounded for the past couple of days, Admiral. Can you get him back into the air?''

''I know who you mean—he's the pilot with a couple of mishaps, I believe. Are you sure he's your first choice as a wingman?''

''I'm sure,'' Buzzell said confidently. Curtiss looked toward the overhead.

''Then I feel I should point out that Lieutenant Caine was the source of my information, Buzz. He's the one who told me about your plan. Now . . . do you still want him with you on this mission?''

Dirk Buzzell hesitated only a moment before answering. It suddenly didn't matter that Coke had betrayed him. ''Caine's got the most to prove by going, sir . . . and nothing much to lose. I'd still like him on my wing.''

''Then I'll make it happen.'' Rear Admiral Curtiss picked up a folder from his desk top and walked toward Dirk Buzzell.

''This is everything I've got on Thumrait. There are some longitudes and latitudes in here, as well as some data on the mission itself. It's not much, but you'll be briefed in detail when you get there. Your point of contact in Oman is a Brit by the name of Hill. He's the gent who requested our help in the first place. That request, I know for a fact, has *not* been endorsed by his superiors in England. And I'd bet a year's pay that the Sultan of Oman hasn't been consulted, either. This man Hill is taking a great risk, Buzz. But I do like his style.

''Find Hill when you get there. Talk to the RAF Hunter pilots too. Look at how they want to use your fighters. If it doesn't make sense to you, change it. You're the fighter expert—they're not. If they're smart fellows, they'll listen to you. And remember, Buzz . . . the RAF is accustomed to being shot at by Tomcats, not being escorted by them.

"And since we're kind of making up the rules as we go along, I expect you're wondering about the ROE."

"It had crossed my mind, Admiral."

"Red and Free on anything airborne out of Iran. But do me a favor. If it looks like an airliner, don't shoot a missile at it. And if you can arrange it . . . don't get killed out there. When it's all over, get your asses back aboard *Enterprise*. This ship will be ready for you and your wingman anytime after noon tomorrow. We'll probably both be out of a job by then, but what the hell. We're doing the right thing."

"Yes sir, we are."

Ready Room Six
1315

Dirk Buzzell stepped into Ready Six through the open door at the rear of the space. He wasn't sure what to expect when he arrived there. Kyle Herrin stood behind a high-backed chair near the refrigerator and popcorn machine. He was eavesdropping from the back of the room. The VF-141 Aardvark commanding officer stood against the white board beside the SDO's desk. His arms were folded tightly. He held the telephone to his ear with his right shoulder.

"Yes, Admiral," Buzzell and Herrin heard him say. "Of course I'm curious. And I have no doubt about your intentions, sir. I'm sure they are the same as mine. My only suggestion would be that you allow me to send more senior aircrews."

The CO stopped talking into the phone. He was listening.

"Get your shit together, Bird," Buzzell said. "We're on the *Sand* escort today . . . unless you'd rather not fly?" The young RIO looked up at Buzzell with a predictable look on his face. There was no hesitation in his voice.

"You kiddin' me," Herrin said eagerly. "I'm ready. Let's do it."

The squadron commanding officer hung up the phone. He stared angrily at Dirk Buzzell from the front of the ready room, then turned his attention to the officer in khakis sitting behind the duty desk.

"Get your flight suit on, Coke," he ordered. "Seems you're going flying." Mark Caine did not try to guess why he had suddenly been added to the schedule, or why the CO was again peering at Buzzell.

"Seems you have some friends in high places, Lieutenant," the commanding officer said as the pilot sat down in the high-backed chair next to Greg Bright. "That was Admiral Curtiss on the phone."

"Yes, sir."

"I don't suppose you'd care to fill me in on the details? Specifically I'd like to know why *four* lieutenants are flying this escort—all very junior lieutenants of your choosing, I might add."

"Don't really know the details, Skipper. But thanks for sticking up for us on the phone." Buzzell turned toward Bright, handing him the folder he'd received from Rear Admiral Curtiss's chief of staff. He acted as if the CO had already walked away. He hadn't.

"My hands are tied. But you'd be grounded right now if I had things my way. Your butt is mine when you get back."

"Thank you, sir," Buzzell said with all the respect he could muster.

A section of VF-141 Tomcats
1640

The E-3 AWACS climbed steadily through 5,000 feet then turned south and east toward the island of Masirah. As the huge jet reached the Omani coastline near Musat, Buzzell lost sight of it in the haze. He keyed his UHF radio thumb switch while turning the flight of two toward west.

"Let's switch button 21," he said. Two mike clicks indicated that Caine and Bright, in the airplane flying less than 100 yards off his starboard wing, had heard and understood the call. There was no button 21. Only 20 preset frequencies could be selected in the Tomcat's UHF radio. Both fighters switched their radios to the Thumrait Tower frequency instead.

In the front seat of the lead fighter, Dirk Buzzell manually swept Aardvark 112's wings aft to 68 degrees. Mark Caine did the same in Aardvark 114. Both Tomcats accelerated to a little more than 500 knots as they dove into the break over Thumrait's main north–south runway.

Dirk Buzzell slowed Aardvark 112 to taxi speed and exited the long runway at its end. A yellow Chevrolet pickup truck with flashing lights appeared at the taxiway throat and made a U-turn in front of his Tomcat. The pilot had heard no radio transmission, nor made any, since detaching his section of F-14s from the AWACS eighty nautical miles to the east. He keyed the ICS.

"Looks like we have an escort of our own, Bird."

Kyle Herrin looked around Buzzell's ejection seat, through the canopy's Plexiglas side panel and down at the truck. He looked behind the jet too, where Mark Caine was also clearing the runway.

"Coke's right behind us, Buzz," he said.

The two aircraft taxied in formation, their wings all the way back into oversweep. The "follow-me" truck guided the section of U.S. fighters through a maze of off-duty runways and dirty asphalt access roads until Buzzell found himself rolling onto the sun-bleached tarmac beside the Number 6 Squadron hangar. His stomach was queasy, and he left his mask dangling from his helmet at the left bayonet fitting. The oxygen that blew from it cooled his face. By now, his flight would be overdue to the *Enterprise*. The admiral would have briefed the ship's captain, and every officer in Ready Room Six would know about the plan. By now, his CO would be livid. That thought brought a smile to his face.

Two dark-haired directors guided the F-14s into their parking spaces abeam the long line of Hawker Hunters. To Dirk Buzzell, the attack jets seemed very small. He could not imagine their being able to carry much ordnance. RAF enlisted personnel stood on top of the Hunters nearest to the fighter's parking spots. They dropped their tools and climbed to the tarmac as Buzzell and Caine shut down their engines and unstrapped.

At the bottom of the boarding ladder, Buzzell removed his helmet and unzipped his SV-2 flotation vest. Already, more than a dozen RAF personnel had scrambled underneath his aircraft. They seemed far more impressed with the Tomcat's weapons load-out of four Sparrow and four Sidewinder missiles than with the pilot who flew the machine.

A tall and wide man in a flight suit approached Buzzell first. Two men in suits and ties followed.

"Name's Carlton, Major William Carlton of her majesty's Royal Air Force. Damn nice you could join us."

"Dirk Buzzell, United States Navy. Damn glad to be here," he said while accepting the handshake.

Carlton walked past Buzzell and grabbed at Kyle Herrin's extended hand. The taller of the two men in suits and ties waited for the pilot to step out of his flight gear and walk away from the Tomcat.

"Would one of you be Hill?" Buzzell asked.

"Indeed. Terry Hill, and this is my secretary, Malcolm Jennings." Buzzell and Hill sized each other up during the cursory introduction. To Hill, Dirk Buzzell looked far too young to be a fighter pilot. To Buzzell, Terry Hill looked nothing like a man who could organize a strike into Iran. His secretary looked gay.

"I understand you are a volunteer to this project, Lieutenant Buzzell. Thank you for that. Admiral Curtiss has high praise for you."

"I wouldn't miss this for the world, Mr. Hill."

Hill nodded his head and smiled. "If you and your fellow naval aviators are ready, Lieutenant, I'd like to offer you the hospitality of dinner at the Officers Club. There is much we need to discuss."

Thumrait Officers' Club
1835

Dirk Buzzell nursed his second tin of British ale. He was surprised by its quick effect on him. He replaced the tin on the table, and promised himself he would drink no more of it. He wasn't in the mood to get drunk. Greg Bright was still working at his meal of mutton and potatoes. Mark Caine and Kyle Herrin sat across the table. Terrance Hill, the envoy's secretary, and two RAF officers—Major Carlton and an RAF captain whose name Buzzell had already forgotten—carried on four separate conversations. Terrance Hill decided it was time to talk directly about the mission.

"Lieutenant Buzzell," the envoy began. "I am by no means an expert in the area of air-to-air warfare, but I was under the impression that your Tomcats would be carrying the Phoenix missile system."

Buzzell considered himself lucky that he could at least answer the first question. "The AIM-54 is a very fine missile, Mr. Hill. Unfortunately, it's also a very heavy missile, and designed primarily as a stand-off weapon—a long-range weapon. I didn't ask that it be loaded on our jets. I don't think we'll have the opportunity for long-range shots tomorrow."

"Its weight is also a major consideration," Greg Bright said, jumping into the conversation. "If we have to turn hard with the Iranians, we don't want a 1,000-pound Phoenix slowing us down."

"That makes good sense," Major Carlton agreed. "I imagine the Phoenix would also slow you blokes down at low altitude as well. Our ingress will be very low tomorrow. Can your Tomcats maintain 500 knots at 200 feet above the water for our journey across the strait?" Greg Bright didn't wait for Dirk Buzzell to answer the question first.

"I think we could keep up, Major. But we don't want to be down in the weeds with your Hunters."

The major had a perplexed look on his face, but he preferred not to express his ignorance of the F-14 and its operational capabilities.

"Naturally, Lieutenant, we assumed your fighters could best avoid the IRG air-search radars by flying low with our eight aircraft." Greg Bright looked toward Buzzell before continuing.

"By all means, fly as low as you can during ingress to the Silkworm sites, Major. I hear your squadron pilots are famous for flying low, and I'm bettin' the Iranians won't see you down there," Bright said. "Our F-14s, on the other hand, need to be higher—at least 25,000 feet higher." Suddenly, the RAF captain across the table was feeling the effects of his fourth ale.

"How in God's name can your American Tomcats protect us from 25,000 feet? I predict they will be unable to do so."

"We have certain system advantages at that altitude, Captain," Dirk Buzzell explained. "First of all, the Iranians will not be expecting our Tomcats. The two of us will fly in a welded-wing formation—very close together. On radar, we will appear as one aircraft. We'll fly the high altitude profile normally reserved for airliners transitting between Muscat and Bandar 'Abbās. To the IRG, we will appear to be just that—an airliner. We're counting on them not detecting your strike package until it's too late. If your Hunters are 'tapped' by the IRG, we'll be in position to counter their air-to-air threat. It would be helpful if your Hawker Hunters could fly directly under the high-altitude jet route . . . directly beneath us."

The captain stared toward Terrance Hill. His expression was obvious.

"We had planned another route," he responded.

"Is fuel a problem, Captain?" Hill stated more than asked. "Couldn't your fliers adjust their ingress route?"

Major Carlton would be the senior RAF pilot in the flight; the route of flight would be his to determine.

"Fuel will be no problem, Mr. Hill," he stated. "We can adjust. Actually, I like the idea, Lieutenant. And if there is no opposition from the IRG tomorrow, I imagine your Tomcats will simply reverse course after our bombs are on target?"

"Exactly," Buzzell said while finishing his second ale. He had decided it would be impolite not to drink. There were two unopened tins still positioned in front of him. "Still, I think we should work out a time line for the strike. We may not be able to keep your Hunters in sight. We'll need to know exactly where you are on the route."

"I'll work on the time line myself, Lieutenant," Carlton said confidently. He lifted his glass and began a toast. "But first, to our American friends and to the memory of the Number 6 Squadron commander, Lieutenant Colonel Reginald Sheffield Thomas. Let us drink to success on the 'morrow."

Buzzell toasted with his third can. He did not want to fly on the strike suffering from a hangover, but he insisted on keeping pace with the British pilots in the consumption of ale.

When Terrance Hill left the table and walked toward the Officers Club bar, Dirk Buzzell stood up and followed him.

"I'm a little tired of the ale, Mr. Buzzell. Could I interest you in a gin?" Hill said cordially.

"No thank you, sir. Actually, I was wondering if I might be able to make a phone call. It's a personal matter. Would that be possible?"

"Of course. I don't believe the Iranians have tapped our phones yet. You'll find a telephone in the foyer of the club. Pick up the receiver and give the operator my name. He'll connect you."

The phone connection was good when Marti finally answered the call.

"Hello?"

"Hi, babe, it's Dirk. I miss you."

"Dirk? Oh my God! Where are you? Please tell me you're at the airport and want me to pick you up."

"I wish. I'm in Oman . . . in the middle of nowhere. We're gonna do a little flying with the Omanis. I wanted to call you. I haven't seen a real telephone in a long time. How are you? What time is it there?"

"I don't know . . . early, I just got up. I want you to know that I'm not making the bed these days, Dirk. And the house is a mess. I've become kind of lazy lately." Marti was rambling. Dirk Buzzell had never heard her talk so quickly. "So you miss me?"

"You don't want to know how much, babe."

"Dirk, I want you to know that I really hate the Navy. I hope you don't mind that I say that."

"Nope. I don't blame you." Dirk Buzzell paused, turning away from the crowd of RAF pilots who had filtered out of the club. "Listen, I just called to, uh, to tell you I love you, Marti. I wanted you to know that . . . I just wanted you to know." Buzzell listened to the silence at the other end of the phone call. "Marti, you still there?"

"Yes." Dirk Buzzell knew that Marti was crying. "I want to know what's going on out there. I don't like the sound of your last few letters, Dirk. What's going on with those Iranians? It's on the news every day."

"Nothin' much is happening, Marti. We really haven't been flying much." Dirk Buzzell had always been a terrible liar—especially with Marti. More than anyone else in the world, he wanted to tell her what was going on. But nothing could be gained by explaining the admiral's plan to Marti now. It was going to happen regardless of whether she knew. And it would terrify her.

"Good, 'cause I have some news, Dirk. I wanted to tell you about it when I was in the Philippines. But you had to go back to the ship and I didn't know how to say it. It's just like you to hit the road when I have something important on my mind."

"Shoot, babe. You can tell me if all my plants are dead."

"Well . . . the plants aren't dead, Dirk. But the rabbit is . . . I'm pregnant."

Marti had expected the sudden silence from him. She tried to imagine the expression on his face.

"I know exactly which night it was, Dirk," she said into the phone. "It was Thanksgiving night. Your mom and dad were in town. They were in the guest room. Remember? Dirk?"

"Yeah . . . I remember. I remember being hung over the next day, too. Shit." Buzzell was considering the timing of Marti's announcement. "I don't know what to say, Marti. I need to be there with you right now."

"No shit, mister. You knock me up, then go on cruise for six months. I'm running out of clothes to wear." Marti paused this time. "I've been thinking of taking care of it, you know? I know I wasn't supposed to get pregnant, Dirk."

"What do you mean, taking care of it?"

"You know, take care of it. There are things you can do to take care of it, Dirk." Marti had rehearsed the words a hundred times in her head. She had trouble saying them without her voice cracking over the phone. "If that's what you want, Dirk. I don't want to mess things up. Or I could have it and then give it up. I wanted to talk to you about it first."

Dirk Buzzell could barely hear Marti speaking. And there was nothing wrong with the phone connection.

"*No!* No way, Marti! Don't do a goddamned thing. Have it and keep it. We'll keep it, Marti. I'll be there . . . soon. Trust me, babe. This doesn't change a thing. I love you." He sounded frantic, almost unreasonable.

"Are you sure, Dirk? I've never heard you talk like this. What's going on there?"

"Nothing. Really, nothing. I'll be back aboard the ship tomorrow. I gotta go. I'll send you a telegram when I get back. Okay?"

"Okay." Her voice trailed away from his ear weakly.

Dirk Buzzell hung up quickly. He leaned against the phone as it lay in its receiver. Greg Bright tapped his shoulder from behind. The RIO held two fresh tins of lukewarm stout.

"Everything going well on the home front, Buzzer?" Bright asked. His speech was slightly slurred.

"Perfect, Notso. Couldn't be better. And Marti's great . . . she says hi."

DAY TWENTY-SEVEN

JANUARY 31

Visiting Officers Quarters,
Sultan of Oman Air Force Base
Thumrait, Oman
0705

Dirk Buzzell hadn't slept. But he couldn't blame the king-sized bed for that fact. His accommodations were incredible—the VOQ room was equipped with central heat and air-conditioning, three ceiling fans, a thirty-plus-inch television monitor and four speakers. The bedroom and kitchen were furnished completely in teak. The refrigerator made a few noises, but was stocked with meats, fruits, cheeses, and several bottles of cold gin. There was champagne in there, too, imported and expensive. He thought immediately of Marti.

He went to the kitchen table—it was large enough to accommodate six—and reviewed his knee-board cards. He would carry the cards with him during the mission. He stared at his wristwatch, comparing its time with the digital clock on his nightstand—his brief would begin in the Number 6 Squadron spaces in less than one hour. His stomach was tied in knots—he could feel his heart pounding in his temples. In a few hours, he was going to war. If the opportunity presented itself, he was going to launch live air-to-air missiles at live Iranians flying real IRG fighter aircraft. He stood the chance of killing or being killed in the process. That fact alone tied up his stomach. But mostly, his mind was on Marti.

Pregnant. The word had taken on a new meaning to him. He picked a pen out of his flight suit pocket and made lazy black circles on the card that contained the Hawker Hunter strike time line. He tried to concentrate on it. But each time he stared at the numbers, his mind drifted back to San Diego and to Marti. She was eight weeks' pregnant. She would have the kid sometime in midsummer.

Cruise would be over by then. For him, it would most likely be over by the end of the day. At best, he'd be out of a job. Greg Bright and Kyle Herrin and Mark Caine and the admiral back aboard the *Enterprise*—they'd all be out of jobs. He imagined how he might support Marti and a child. Flying the Tomcat was the only job he'd known.

"Shit!" he said aloud at the kitchen table. What if he didn't survive the goddamned strike? "What the *hell* are you trying to prove, Dirk?" He tried again to concentrate on the time line. He unfolded a large TPC chart. The northern peninsula of Oman began at the bottom of the chart. Iran filled the top of it. The Persian Gulf and the Strait of Hormuz filled in its middle. He reviewed the strike route and copied it onto the chart. Marti's pregnancy was the only time line that made sense to him.

The knock at his VOQ room door wasn't an interruption—he wasn't getting anything accomplished.

"Good morning, Lieutenant. Thought I'd drop by to answer any questions you might have about today's sortie." Major William Carlton invited himself into the room.

"Call me Dirk, will ya? Have a seat."

"Good enough, Dirk. How do you find the facilities here?"

"I find them incredible. You ought to see my stateroom aboard the *Enterprise*. I could get used to this kind of living."

"The very least we could do. We expect you and your F-14s will repay us in spades. Any comments on the time line I've worked up?"

"Nope. Looks pretty straightforward, Major. Your bomber's ingress airspeed is a little less than I expected—but we can adjust our Indicated Mach Number at 26,000 feet to make it work out. No big deal . . . the two of us will be a little slower than your average airliner. I think it's more important that all of us are overhead the target at the same time. Hopefully, our airspeed difference will be too subtle to be noticed by the IRG. The Aardvarks will be exactly five miles above the strike package. You're leading the eight-plane, aren't you, Major?"

"Yes. And I hope to do so in a representative fashion. Our colonel would have been the perfect man for the job, but . . ."

"Yeah, sorry to hear about that. Any success with the search—did you find any wreckage, or . . . anything?" Buzzell assumed the subject was a sensitive one.

"Nothing. I watched his aircraft go down just south of Didamar. I believe he had the opportunity for ejection, but I saw no parachute. The search-and-rescue operation discovered nothing. Nothing at all."

"Sorry. I had no idea you were flying the other Hunter that day." Buzzell felt like changing the subject.

"Indeed. It was a day I'll not soon forget. I fully expected to go the same way as the lieutenant colonel. The Iranian Tomcat either didn't see my aircraft or chose to ignore me altogether. I believe the latter was the case. When I turned toward the south, he had the perfect opportunity for a shot. But he did not take one. And I did everything wrong. I watched my flight leader struck by a missile, then turned away. I do not understand why I was spared, Dirk—unless perhaps it was destined that I lead today's retaliatory strike to Hengām Island."

"Your Hunters carry Firestreak missiles, right?" Buzzell asked.

"Yes, that is correct."

"Not much of a match for the ordnance the Iranian was carrying, Major. I don't see that you had much choice but to 'bug out.' Sometimes, in a dogfight, the decision to leave is more critical to survival than the decision to stay." Buzzell didn't know the details of Carlton's engagement, but he attempted to help him justify his actions.

"Still. I should have remained. Perhaps I'd have gotten a shot. Perhaps I'd have gone down in flames. Either of those two options is preferable to the course of action I chose." Dirk Buzzell said nothing.

"I would enjoy it very much if you or your wingman could 'splash' that same IRG Tomcat today, Dirk. Or, for that matter, any other Iranian aircraft you happen to see." The RAF officer managed a smirk with his statement.

"Trust me. I'd enjoy that too, Major. But I wouldn't mind your jets getting all their bombs on target and haulin' ass home before the IRG has a chance to get airborne."

"That too would be totally acceptable." The major opened the door, then paused before walking out. "But if the Iranians do not get airborne today, they will most certainly do so tomorrow or the next day . . . in response to our strike into Iran today. I imagine you and your Navy fighters will be unable to assist us then."

Buzzell shrugged his shoulders—he was more worried about today than about tomorrow or the next day.

The major pulled a set of keys from one of his flight suit pockets.

"I have an auto, Dirk. Can I offer you a lift to the hangar?"

Dirk Buzzell collected his knee-board cards and piled them into his green helmet bag, then followed Major Carlton out the door.

Iranian Revolutionary Guard Hangar
Bandar 'Abbās, Iran
0940

Ali Abdul Rajani opened the door of his apartment. It was far cooler outside the room than inside it. He was convinced that the air conditioner he'd been promised would never be delivered. A steady stream of Iranian women moved past his door—walking with their jars to and from the well. He considered taking another one of the women from the street—but he was already dressed in his flight suit, and it would be inconvenient for him to dress again after taking one of them.

The two red Cadillacs were also just outside the door. He stared, almost lovingly, at the newer of the two convertibles, then jumped into the older car. He reached into one of his flight suit chest pocket, the same pocket that held the silver .45 caliber. Also in the pocket was a small switchblade knife. Ali pressed the side of the knife, and its blade snapped into position. He stabbed the blade into the passenger side of the front seat. The white leather split easily, revealing beneath it a combination of padding and metal springs. He adjusted the knife in his fingers, then slid its blade up the seatback toward the passenger-side headrest. When the front seat and two door panels had been shredded, he began on the massive backseat.

The switchblade was beginning to dull as he finished slashing the white convertible top. He stabbed the knife into the dashboard beneath the rearview mirror, then started the car. Reza had ordered Ali Abdul Rajani to keep only one of his two red American-made automobiles. He was to deliver the other one to Omid. Ali had decided that Omid would receive the older Cadillac.

The Number 6 Squadron Briefing Spaces
Thumrait, Oman
1015

Carlton had led the brief. It had been detailed and excruciatingly long. There were a total of ten Hawker Hunter pilots in the large briefing room inside the Number 6 Squadron hangar. Two of the Hunter aircrew would man spare bombers. In the event one of the eight primary aircraft could not fly, the spares would launch in their place. Buzzell and Herrin and Caine and Bright were grouped together near the room's side entrance. Terrance Hill and his effeminate secretary sat in the back of the spaces during the major's presentation.

Surprisingly, very little time was dedicated to the actual strike on Hengām Island. There was no mention of the targets themselves nor the manner in which the eight Hunters would coordinate their ordnance drops. Most of Carlton's monolog centered on the subject of Iranian Revolutionary Guard fighter opposition. The major repeatedly warned his pilots—dared them in many instances—to keep their wits about them in the target area. He told and retold of his engagement with the IRG Tomcat, and how he had seen the Iranian fighter only after it had launched its weapon at his flight leader. He spent far too much time on the subject of bogey aircraft, Buzzell thought, and not nearly enough on the actual mission. If the nine other Hunter aircrew were not terrified of the IRG before the brief, they certainly were by its conclusion.

"The Aardvarks will be up your strike frequency all day long," Greg Bright had interjected once during the brief. "We'll tell you what we see." Carlton had all but ignored the RIO's comment, passing it off with a cursory "Thank you, Lieutenant." Bright sucked at the Skoal in his mouth.

The time line was discussed near the conclusion of the two-hour briefing, and checkpoints were assigned to latitudes and longitudes along the 166-nautical-mile strike route. The major traced the route on a large wall chart at the front of the room.

The flight of eight bombers would transit north, along the eastern coastline of Oman. They would fly low—as low as they were able, Carlton said, and hug the eastern side of the shallow mountain range that ran parallel to their course. The Aardvarks would fly a high-altitude airway over the same route. The Hunters would fly in two groups of four, and one division would trail the other by three miles. Their ground speed would remain a constant 480 knots throughout the ingress, thereby enabling the U.S. fighters to judge the bombers' progress toward the targets at exactly eight nautical miles per minute. The Hawker Hunters would be heavy with ordnance. At extremely low altitude, flying at eight miles per minute was very fast indeed.

The terminal checkpoint on the strike route was the island of Didamar. At Didamar, the Hunters would turn northwest toward Hengām, and leave Omani airspace. The final leg of the strike route was 18.1 nautical miles in length, Carlton had figured, and would consume two minutes and sixteen seconds of the time line. During that final leg, the eight Hunters would face their greatest risk of detection by Iranian air and surface search radars. The major challenged his wingmen to fly even lower as they approached Hengām over the watery surface of the Strait of Hormuz. Carlton did ask finally that Dirk Buzzell explain the fighter cover's route of flight to the target.

"Our fighters will launch exactly nine minutes before your two divisions. We will climb and accelerate to the east, toward Musat, then turn north and level off at 26,000 feet. We will decelerate slightly to conform with standard commercial airway navigation and drive toward Didamar at .8 Mach. By the time your aircraft reach Point A on the route, we should be directly overhead." Buzzell acknowledged Terrance Hill at the back of the room before completing his short presentation.

"Mr. Hill has been so kind as to file a flight plan for our two Tomcats. We will be simulating a 727 en route to London, England, via Ankara, Turkey.

That precise route was Mr. Hill's idea as well. Our IFF transponder codes will be those of an airliner on that flight plan. Without going into minute detail on how we operate the F-14's radar system in situations like this, we will deviate from our flight plan only if it appears the Iranians are countering your strike. If no opposition is encountered, we'll reverse our course and cover your egress back to Thumrait."

None of the Hawker Hunter pilots had questions for Dirk Buzzell. He sat down while the major reiterated his concern for the Iranian F-4s and F-14s.

Bandar 'Abbās, Iran
1030

If he had driven directly, Ali's apartment was less than ten minutes from the Iranian Revolutionary Guard hangar at the aerodrome. But he had not driven directly, and the route he had chosen was frequented more by camels than by luxury automobiles. He aimed the Cadillac at the deepest holes in the roadway, bouncing in and out of them. He wore a sadistic grin on his face as he accelerated and decelerated not by using his brakes, but by alternating the convertible's transmission between Drive and Reverse.

There were no street signs on the roadway, only rock and mortar pillars that indicated the intersection of dusty trails. Ali slalomed through the pillars, grazing first the left, then right, side of the car until both sideview mirrors had been removed. Three of the four stainless-steel wheel covers had also popped from the wheels.

Ali paralleled the uneven coastline south of the Bandar 'Abbās airfield, choosing the uneven surface of the train tracks over the smoother roadway. He bounced off the tracks, then turned north toward the gate leading to the IRG hangar. The sentry at the gate heard Ali Abdul Rajani before he saw him—the Cadillac's muffler had long since broken free of its brackets. As the convertible approached him, the sentry expected it to accelerate. Instead, Ali stopped and climbed out of the long car, then walked once around it to survey his work. The sentry stared at the convertible and its driver in disbelief.

"I require your weapon," Ali stated to the sentry. "Just for a moment."

The young man clutched at an AK-47, bringing its short metal stock to his side. Its barrel was pointed at the ace.

"No, I cannot. I know you, but I cannot. It is not allowed."

Ali ignored the direction in which the automatic was aimed, and reached for the silver .45 in his flight suit pocket. He carefully cocked the gun, then raised it slowly. He squinted past the sight into the horrified face of the sentry—less than three feet separated the two Iranians.

"Please," Ali said.

Omid stood outside the tall Iranian Revolutionary Guard hangar. Ali was late, as usual. The red Cadillac powered slowly across the tarmac, then slid to a stop beside the hangar. The ace jumped out of the car and tossed the keys to the older pilot, whose mouth hung open with what he saw. Across the driver's side of the automobile, spelled out with more than 100 bullet holes, was the name *OMID*.

"Now all will know this is *your* Cadillac," Ali

said before walking up the stairway toward the IRG ready room.

Thumrait, Oman
1045

Kyle Herrin was already standing on top of Aardvark 112 when Buzzell had made his way around to where he had begun his preflight inspection—at the aircraft boarding ladder. He slipped an orange-and-black helmet liner over his head. It was damp and in desperate need of laundering. Halfway up the ladder, he tested the Mark-61 cannon EMI filter connection beneath the steps. A few of the gun's 400 20-millimeter rounds were visible in the gun belt. He snapped his helmet chin strap and finished his preflight on top of the fighter.

1055

Herrin ran through his weapon system BIT checks while Buzzell waited for the INS to reach a fine alignment. When it did, he signaled to the RAF plane captain with a thumbs-up. The enlisted man returned the signal, though he was not certain what it meant.

"How's it look, Bird?" Buzzell asked across the ICS. The RIO was nearing the end of his weapon and radar checks.

"Some degrades in 'Track-While-Scan,' and 'Pulse' is a little shaky. But we can shoot somebody if we need to," he said optimistically.

Buzzell reviewed the location of his fighter's eight air-to-air missiles. Two AIM-7 Sparrows filled his belly stations between the Tomcat's twin Pratt and Whitney engines. Two more AIM-7s were attached to the F-14s inboard shoulder stations. Stations 1a, 1b, 8a, and 8b held AIM-9 Sidewinders—two each on the outboard pylons. Mark Caine and Greg Bright were armed in exactly the same way.

The plane captain was familiar with Buzzell's signal to remove the chocks from in front of and behind his main landing gear. When Aardvark 114's chocks had also been pulled, Buzzell added power to his Tomcat and began a slow taxi toward runway 18.

Iranian Revolutionary Guard Hangar
Bandar 'Abbās, Iran
1110

Reza stood outside the IRG hangar. He pressed his fingers into his ears against the sound of the screaming jet engines. Omid and his RIO, Mottahadeh, sat in the idling Phantom. Ali and Nori finished their checks in the Tomcat. Reza had heard Omid promise to kill Ali for what the ace had done to the Cadillac. He had heard Ali laugh aloud at the threat. As a result, he stood there—in front of the Phantom and the Tomcat—to ensure that this particular launch went smoothly.

Reza reentered the hangar as the two fighters began their taxi toward the runway. When he pushed open the door into the ready room, he saw more than thirty Iranian Revolutionary Guard pilots and RIOs standing there.

"Why is it that only Ali and Omid are allowed to fly?" one of the pilots asked him. "The rest of us are equally capable."

"We have received information that two or more military jet aircraft are airborne in Oman. The possibility exists that those aircraft are flying in a northerly direction,'' Reza stated plainly. ''In such a situation, I am under specific orders from Ahmed. It is *his* wish that Ali and Omid should fly. If the rest of you *were* equally capable, you would not be standing here now.'' Some of the men left the room after the statement. The rest mumbled among themselves, then filtered to a corner of the ready room where a UHF radio set had been switched on. A frequency number appeared in the LED readout on the radio. The men, if they stayed, could at least listen as Ali and Omid flew the two fighters.

Aardvark 112
1130

''Buzz, I still can't believe we're doing this.'' Kyle Herrin wasn't any more amazed than his pilot. But Dirk Buzzell didn't answer his RIO. He was preoccupied with the position of Mark Caine's F-14. He couldn't afford to make a radio call to his wingman. Instead, he used hand signals through the Plexiglas canopy. At .82 of Indicated Mach, both Tomcats' CADC computers had already begun to sweep the fighters' wings aft. Buzzell decided there was too much room between his and Coke's airplane—enough room, potentially, for a ground controller to see two radar returns where there should be only one. His thumbs-up to Caine came when the wings of the two seventy-two-foot-long fighters overlapped.

Dirk Buzzell wasn't used to making lazy turns through the sky. But airliners turned slowly, so he too slowly rolled his Aardvark fighter overhead Musat. Both aircraft steadied on a heading of 340 degrees. He couldn't see it through the haze, but the island of Didamar lay dead ahead at 112 nautical miles.

"At this speed, Buzz, sixteen-and-a-half minutes to Didamar," Bird Herrin reported. Dirk Buzzell nodded to himself in the front cockpit.

Desert Dog 1
1133

Major William Carlton knew the geography of Oman nearly as well as had Colonel Thomas. Every mountain peak was familiar to him. Each empty riverbed and valley floor reminded him of the hundreds of sorties he'd flown as the colonel's wingman.

He would have to risk radar identification as he led his flight of eight Hunters up and over the high valley separating the Al Gharbi and Al Jabal al Akhdar mountain ranges just west of the Omani township of Rostak. There was little risk, he decided. The Iranians would not be expecting them. And it was doubtful their sensors could locate the bombers—at least not this far south and this low over mainland Oman. Carlton's altitude was 1485 feet, about thirty feet over the ascending desert floor. The valley rose above and in front of him, up to nearly 2000 feet. The shallow climb—if it was to continue at exactly 480 knots—would require more power. His three wingmen brought their noses up precisely as he did, until all four fighter-bombers in the lead division matched the incline. The trail division of Hunters followed the same path over the ground.

Carlton added power cautiously as his indicated airspeed dropped off in the ascent. It climbed slowly again toward 480 knots. The control stick felt sloppy in his hands. The drag of his bomb load was more than he had anticipated. His jet waffled through the air. Eventually, as he crested the top of the valley, his throttle was all the way forward—at 100 percent power—to maintain the scheduled airspeed. He pulled back on the lever as his division descended over the top of the crease between the mountain ranges, then down toward the alluvial plain on the other side. The major decided it was time to offer some encouraging words across the discreet radio frequency—something to motivate his seven wingmen.

"We're Point Bravo and on time" was all he could manage to say.

Dirk Buzzell heard Carlton's transmission. He checked his knee-board card. According to the time line, the two Aardvarks were supposed to be exactly thirty-six nautical miles northwest of the Musat way point. The Tomcat's INS reported 36.7 miles. He pulled back slightly on his two throttles, then peered over his left shoulder toward the gray-brown plain under his port wing. From 26,000 feet, he had hoped to visually acquire the flight of eight Hawker Hunters below him.

"They're down there, Bird," Buzzell said over the ICS. "Somewhere at our eight o'clock position. Do you see anything up ahead?"

"I got one target. He's on our nose but he's up at 35,000 feet. He's headed 040 and drifting east."

"Probably an airliner. Probably no factor, but keep an eye on him," the pilot said nervously, wondering if Greg Bright, in Aardvark 114, saw anything else. The absence of radio communications made him think not.

Major Carlton became suddenly dissatisfied with the formation of his division as it crossed over the abandoned airfield of Suhar New on Oman's eastern coastline. His wingmen were strung out, and one of them was at least 100 feet higher in altitude than his own. He had wished to keep his radio calls to a minimum.

"The Desert Dogs are point Charlie," the major radioed. "Tighten it up, number three."

"The 'Varks copy. We're clean," is what he heard in response. "Clean" meant that his American fighter escorts saw no airborne Iranian fighters.

Cactus 01 and 02
1141

On this particular mission, Ali and Nori in the IRG F-14 had the lead. Omid carried no bombs on his F-4—only two Matra Magic heat-seekers—and was Ali's wingman. Ali carried four Magics.

Omid had lifted off the runway at Bandar 'Abbās behind Ali, and was still behind him as the two Iranian aircraft flew west. They had flown low, and paralleled the coast away from BA, toward Qeshm Island. Those had been their orders. At the designated geographic point, the two fighters turned south and climbed, then switched to the Site Two frequency. It was the same frequency being monitored by Reza and the Iranian Revolutionary Guard aviators in Bandar 'Abbās.

"Follow me, Omid, and today I will teach you to be a fighter pilot," Ali said across the UHF. In the IRG ready room, a few of the pilots and RIOs were laughing at the remark. Reza did not laugh.

"I will kill you one day, Ali," Omid countered.

"Cactus One and Two, this is Site Two . . . say again?" Neither of the two fighter RIOs answered the GCI controller. Ali and Omid would have to wait to continue their war of words.

"Cactus One is on your frequency," Ali stated finally. "What do you have for us?"

"Possible multiple targets south at forty miles. Your vector 160 degrees. The targets are probable Omani attack jets," the controller said.

"Then this will be simple," Ali stated coolly.

Aardvark 112
1144

Buzzell could see the island of Didamar disappearing beneath the bottom of his windscreen. His flight would be overhead the turn-point in less than two minutes. He could also see a target materializing in the middle of his front-seat repeat of the TID display.

"Whatcha got, Bird?" he asked.

"Single contact, 344 at twenty miles. He's low." The report didn't emanate from Buzzell's backseat. He recognized Greg Bright's voice from the F-14 still tucked under his left wing.

"I've got the same contact," Herrin reported. "It's overhead Bandar 'Abbās."

"Desert Dogs copy. Approaching point Delta." Carlton and his two divisions of bombers were just south of Didamar, almost directly below the Aardvark fighters. The major's voice had a more severe pitch to it.

"Don't turn to mush on us now, Carlton," Buzzell commented to his RIO across the ICS.

"Aardvarks . . . Deep Sea here. Show a single contact orbiting Bullseye. Could be military . . . could be commercial air. Can't tell yet. How copy?"

Dan Harrington's voice came across the discreet UHF frequency. The Whale was airborne and Harrington was flying it.

"*Loud* and *clear*, Wrongway," Buzzell called. "Glad you could make it."

"You can thank the admiral for that," was Harrington's response.

"Lieutenant Buzzell from Carlton." The major was confused—it was obvious from his call. "Who is Deep Sea, and why is operating on this frequency?"

"Just a friend of ours from *Enterprise*, Major. Say your position."

"Over point Echo turning to the target now. Am I to understand there is a fighter airborne at Bandar 'Abbās? Do you recommend a retirement?" Major Carlton was frantic over the radio. The anxiety in his voice was disturbing.

"Negative, Dogs. Continue." Dirk Buzzell studied the radar return on his TID. The airborne target there was in a turn. "That contact is in an orbit at least twenty miles northeast of your target. We're not even sure it's a IRG fighter. Recommend you continue." The major was saturating the frequency. He began babbling incoherently to the other Hawker Hunters. The frequency was not being protected by KY-58 secure-voice radios—every transmission was being broadcast in the clear. Anyone with a UHF receiver dialed to the correct frequency could be listening.

But that fact had been carefully figured into Admiral Curtiss's plan. The Iranian Revolutionary Guard GCI sites had been successful in eavesdropping on the KY-58s. But only the U.S. Navy transmitted across such secure-voice networks, and the U.S. Navy wasn't supposed to be flying today. If, somehow, the Iranians were able to determine that the RAF was conducting a strike into Hengām, and if they were also able to determine that the RAF were being assisted by Navy fighters, the GCI controllers would begin monitoring the KY-58s. When they heard nothing there, they would attempt to monitor clear frequency UHF transmissions. There were thousands of such frequencies to choose from. By the time the IRG figured it out, the admiral planned, the strike into Iran would be over. Buzzell keyed his ICS between Major Carlton's communications.

"Sparrow selected, Bird. Let's set up the tanks."

A SP appeared on Buzzell's HUD, VDI, and TID repeat displays. Superimposed over the top of the missile acronym was an *X*. The *X* would disappear when the pilot raised his master arm toggle switch.

Aardvark 112's external drop tanks were expendable. They hung on stations 3 and 6, and limited the fighter considerably—in turn performance, in G-available, and, most important, in achieving high speed. The Hawker Hunter's strike into Iran, and the Aardvark's role in it, was totally dependent on the element of surprise. If the plan failed, and if the Tomcats were required to engage IRG fighters or run away from them, the tanks could be blown clear of the jet. At $100,000 apiece, the tanks were not usually considered jettisonable. And if Dirk Buzzell returned the jet to the ship without them, he would be asked a lot of hard questions. But considering his mission and his covert partnership with the RAF and with Rear Admiral Curtiss, hard questions about fuel tanks were the least of his worries. Buzzell rechecked his fuel gauges. Aardvark 112's externals read empty. Twelve thousand pounds of gas remained in his fuselage cells. Another two thousand pounds of fuel was indicated in the wings.

"Tank jettison all set up back here, Buzz... stations 3 and 6. Let me know and we'll get rid of 'em."

Aardvark 112's second radio came alive with a different voice. Buzzell listened as his RIO began and ended a short conversation with an air traffic controller from the Ras Al Khamah facility near Sharjah International Airport in Oman. The British envoy, Terrance Hill, had apparently made all the right phone calls. The controller's call was cursory—exactly the type of routine transmission a 727 should receive. The airliner ruse was working.

Dirk Buzzell resisted the temptation to switch off his autopilot and descend toward the eight attack jets five miles below him. It was not yet necessary—and the descent would certainly catch the eye of an Iranian GCI controller, and every other controller within 150 nautical miles of his position. If the aircraft over Bandar 'Abbās was a fighter, it was not a threat. At least not yet. It was still possible for Carlton and his Hunters to complete their mission.

"Ninety seconds to target," the major reported. "Desert Dog Two, say your posit." Carlton could not see the second division of Hawker Hunters. He knew they were behind him, but he could not be certain how far.

"Still three miles in trail, Major," a voice reported. "Two minutes to the target."

"Hell, Bird... this is easy. The Brits aren't gonna need our help. Nobody knows they're down there." Dirk Buzzell regretted making the ICS call as soon as he completed the statement.

"Buzz, Wrongway. Check your 290 for 19. Two

targets airborne west of the target. Show them hot for your strikers. Do you copy?''

Buzzell checked his heading. It was 300 degrees. He could see the outline of Hengām Island in his windscreen. A bearing of 290 degrees was *left* of his nose. If the IRG launched, they would launch from the airstrip at Bandar 'Abbās, which was nearly 40 degrees *right* of his Tomcat's nose.

''Copy, Wrongway. We're looking. But how can there be anything from that sector? Where did they—'' Time would not allow Kyle Herrin to let his pilot finish the sentence.

''Contact, Deep Sea. Range is 18 miles, bearing 291. I see one, Notso. He's low.'' Herrin hoped Greg Bright saw the other contact on his radar.

''One fourteen's breaking out two. Two at 16 miles now. Showin' 6,000 feet, Wrongway.'' Bright's voice wasn't totally controlled, either. Dirk Buzzell knew Major Carlton was listening.

''We see only two . . . they're together.'' Dan Harrington was giving the Aardvarks all the information he had. ''Don't have a clue how they got that far west. At least one of them is a Tomcat, Buzz.''

Buzzell cursed from 112's front cockpit. Suddenly, the plan had turned to shit. Carlton's lead division was one minute from ''bombs away.'' The second group of Hawker Hunters would be over the target thirty seconds later. He saw neither division of Omani jets from his 26,000-foot perch. Something was orbiting over Bandar 'Abbās—it could be another IRG fighter—maybe it was some kind of decoy. He suddenly wasn't sure about the strike into Iran. He wasn't sure about Major Carlton's ability to get his wingmen there. He wasn't sure of anything anymore. But he did know that two Iranian

Revolutionary Guard aircraft had somehow appeared between the Hunters and the Silkworm site on Hengām Island. Dirk Buzzell decided to worry about that fact first.

"The ragheads aren't supposed to be this smart," he said to his RIO.

"Lieutenant Buzzell, this is Carlton. I am retiring my two divisions to Thumrait. Do you hear me? I understand there are an unknown quantity of aircraft . . . quite possibly Iranian fighters . . . I believe we have been found out . . ."

Dirk Buzzell pounded his fist against the side of his canopy. Major William Carlton was beginning to piss him off. The RAF officer had diarrhea of the mouth.

"Listen, Major, I want you and your flight to *pump*!" Dirk Buzzell had expected the RAF aviator to understand his terminology. He didn't.

"Say again, Lieutenant. Understand pump? I am not famili—"

"Shut up, Carlton. The bogies are twelve miles on your nose. We're 26,000 feet above you. Pump south . . . give me a 360 degree turn in your present position. We need time to get down there and check these guys out. Do you understand?"

"Understand. There is no cause for—"

"Coke, let's go." Buzzell's radio command served two purposes. It gave his wingman the opportunity to break away from his welded-wing position and into a more tactical formation. It also kept Major Carlton off the radio.

Buzzell shoved both of Aardvark 112's throttles past the military power detent into mid-afterburner—just shy of zone three. From five miles high, the two Tomcats descended and accelerated quickly past Mach One. At 690 knots, the F-14's wings were swept fully aft. He overbanked and pulled the nose of his jet toward Qeshm Island and the two bandits there. The next radio call he heard was reassuring.

"The aircraft orbiting over Bandar 'Abbās was an F-4. But we show him on deck now . . . he's landed." It was Dan Harrington's voice. "The only bandits airborne are your 293 for 10. Confirmed group of two . . . a single Tomcat and one F-4 Phantom. A two versus two, Buzz. Looks like a fair fight," Wrongway commented.

"Contact." Kyle Herrin had them. "A trail formation. Breaking out two now." Greg Bright had the same radar picture, and he made the announcement across the UHF frequency.

"They're still low, Buzz. Forty-five hundred feet and descending . . . but I can't see the Hunters on my scope." Greg Bright was thinking the same thing as Dirk Buzzell.

"Dogs, confirm you are heading south and below 500 feet."

Carlton's voice answered Buzzell's: "Confirmed. Headed 170 at 100 feet. Why? Isn't that what you wanted us—"

"Yes, Major. Maintain that heading for now. The two bandits are heading south too. Stay low. We don't want to mistake your flight for the bad guys. We don't see you yet. Stand by to resume your attack heading!"

An air traffic controller somewhere had seen the two U.S. Tomcats descending from their assigned altitude. He was busying the second radio with his chatter.

"Turn that shit off, Bird. Range!"

"Eight miles. Twelve hundred knots of closure. Good lock on the lead bandit." Dirk Buzzell raised the guard on his master arm panel. As the lever came up, his hot trigger light blazed red. He rechecked his HUD diamond. Even at less than seven miles, there was nothing but haze inside it. Underneath the diamond, he verified the SP in his windscreen.

"What the hell," he said over the UHF strike frequency. "Fox-One." Mark Caine and Greg Bright were a little more than one nautical mile abeam him. A missile plume erupted off their fighter at the same time.

"Fox-One." It was Caine's voice. Buzzell's Sparrow appeared from under his radome. It flew in perfect formation with his wingman's down into the haze.

"Don't think the Iranians know you guys are up there," Harrington's voice guessed.

"They're about to figure it out," Bright said.

Cactus 01 and 02

"The group of Omani attack jets in front of you have begun a turn to the south," the GCI controller observed.

"Yes," Nori confirmed the fact to Ali. "Left-hand turn at six miles. There is another group doing the same thing at ten miles. They are very low."

"They are retreating, but we will overtake the cowards," Ali called over the radio. "The skies are full of targets, Omid. Perhaps even you will get a kill today." In the hangar ready room in Bandar 'Abbās, some of the IRG aviators began cheering with Ali's comment.

"Look high!" came blaring across the radio from the GCI controller. Ali looked high, and found the two missiles. The pair raced downhill together at

his Tomcat. He lost sight of them as he jerked back on the control stick. Nori sunk in the backseat under the weight of eight-and-a-half instantaneous Gs. Omid was still behind Ali and followed him through the maneuver, though his Phantom did not climb as quickly. It didn't need to.

Both Sparrows had been guiding on Ali's F-14. Both had been defeated by his missile defense maneuver—they passed together beneath his fighter, then fell one after the other into the Strait of Hormuz. The ace knew that Omani Hawker Hunters did not possess the capability of firing forward quarter weapons. He didn't wait for the GCI controller to verify his suspicions.

"Our American friends have returned," he yelled into the radio.

Aardvark 112 and 114

"Throttle back, Coke." Dirk Buzzell saw 5,000 feet on his altimeter. He saw Mach 1.6 on his airspeed indicator. The range between his section and the lead bandit was three and a half miles. The altitude readout from Bird's radar lock reported 2,450 feet.

"They're still below us. Let's level off at a thousand feet." Buzzell couldn't believe he was still unable to see anything. No Iranian fighters—not even the one that was supposed to be inside his HUD diamond. The two missiles should have reached the bandits by now.

When Aardvark 112 and its wingman were still descending toward the water but momentarily co-altitude with their targets, Buzzell's diamond suddenly swung away from the center of his windscreen.

"Lost our lock," Herrin reported with a squeal. Dirk Buzzell could only assume the same thing had happened to Mark Caine and Greg Bright in Aardvark 114. There were no fireballs in the air in front of him.

"*Good lock*! Two miles, ten high." Bright's call was more of a scream over the UHF. He had reacquired at least one of the two Iranian fighters.

"Atta boy, Notso," Buzzell said to himself, then keyed the ICS. "Let's find the other guy, Bird!"

"Tally smoke. No ID yet . . . but I got 'im." Mark Caine saw something. Dirk Buzzell followed the nose of his wingman, trying to find the same thing.

Nothing in the world smokes like the engines of an old F-4 Phantom. The Iranian Revolutionary Guard flew F-4s just like those Buzzell and Caine had seen during workups off the coast of San Diego. The jet's twin General Electric J-79 power plants each generated 18,000 pounds of thrust. It was the black funnel of J-79 smoke that Caine saw in his HUD diamond, and that Buzzell found high at his eleven o'clock position. The smoke curled off, high and behind the tiny speck that was its source.

At something less than one-and-a-half miles from the smoke, Buzzell pulled his nose to it, too.

"Tally your Phantom, Coke. Shoot!" Buzzell had expected to see another Sparrow jump free of his wingman's fighter.

"He's too close now. Switchin' heat." Caine had no choice.

Dirk Buzzell did the same thing, thumbing from SP to SW, and brought to life the first of his four Sidewinder missiles. He swung his nose through the Phantom, hoping to hear the familiar growl of a Sidewinder seeker-head. But there would be no opportunity for a forward quarter shot against the F-4—neither from Buzzell nor Caine. The closure between the jets was too great and the track crossing angle too excessive.

"Comin' port, Coke. He's still high at our ten o'clo—" Buzzell's words disappeared in a G-induced grunt from the front cockpit of Aardvark 112. Both American Tomcats pulled in phase to the left in a nose high turn. Buzzell's jet slid into trail of his wingman in the pull. The Phantom was also in a left-hand turn—the F-4's nose was low and across the huge circle formed by the geometry of the intercept.

"Buzz, Deep Sea. Threat sector now your two o'clock at less than one mile." Buzzell didn't second-guess Harrington's call. He reversed his turn and held the G on his jet in a tight S-turn toward the call.

Even before he had seen the aircraft that launched it, Buzzell saw the stark white plume of a missile at his 0230 position. It was slightly high and pulling for his fighter.

"Chaff, chaff!" the pilot yelled. Buzzell had intended on making the call to his RIO over the ICS. Instead, the order came across the UHF strike frequency. The call was one his wingman needed to hear, anyway.

But Kyle Herrin heard it. He also heard other voices over the UHF—probably Mark Caine or Major Carlton—something about the Phantom or the Hawker Hunters. Whatever it was, it didn't register to him. Above the handhold bolted to his DDD, he thumbed at a coolie hat switch. The switch sent electrical impulses to the ALE-39 chaff and flare dispenser under the aft-most boattail of Aardvark 112. He pushed at the switch like a man possessed—

the way he knew his pilot was punching a similar control in the front seat.

Small charges deep in the ALE-39 dispenser chaff buckets blew in rapid succession. A cloud of aluminized metal ribbons filled the hazy sky below and behind the Tomcat. Each time the pilot depressed his DLC button, a bright flare also dropped from the jet. Buzzell didn't know if the missile coming at him and Herrin was a radar-guided or a heat-seeker—but he did know it was coming at them. Mark Caine and Greg Bright were somewhere to the south with an F-4. It wasn't necessary that he advise them of his predicament now—both Aardvark Tomcats were on their own.

Through the turn, Dirk Buzzell fought the force of gravity—magnified nine times. The accompanying tunnel-vision stole most of his peripheral sight—like peering through a straw at a zigzagging bottle rocket. In front of the plume, he knew he would eventually find a missile, though it was still invisible to him at less than a half mile.

If it guided like every other air-to-air missile in the world was supposed to guide—radar-guided or otherwise—it would pull lead on a course to intercept Aardvark 112. It didn't. Finally, Buzzell saw the faint, dark silhouette of missile planform move farther aft, back toward his five o'clock position. Behind the missile and slightly above it, still on its original bearing from Dan Harrington's call, he found an F-14 Tomcat painted in brown camouflage.

The Iranian's missile had found the chaff cloud or the decoy flares and been suckered. Buzzell was sure of it as he saw the white plume disappear behind his wing then under it.

"Wrongway . . . this is Buzz. We're engaged

with an Iranian Tomcat south of the target. Coke is tied up with the Phantom. Any other bandits?'' Buzzell didn't really have the time to wait for a response. One came immediately.

''Negative, Buzz. There's nothin' else out there.''

Aardvark 112 turned easily at six-and-a-half G-s—not as quickly as it had during the missile defense, but with more controlled determination. It met the IRG Tomcat head-on in a right-to-right pass. The bandit had followed its missile from high to low, diving straight down at Buzzell and Herrin. He guessed the nose-low F-14's airspeed was nearly 500 knots as it blurred past his starboard side less than fifty feet away. Buzzell's Tomcat was too slow. His airspeed indicator read only 330 knots.

''Major, Aardvarks here.'' Buzzell paused a few seconds before finishing the transmission. ''Get your Hunters to that island. The bad guys are busy with us. How copy, Major?''

''Already headed north, Lieutenant. Fifty seconds to bombs on target.'' At least Carlton's voice was less strained.

Aardvark 114

For the first time since the Phantom emerged from the haze, Mark Caine saw his bandit maneuver. The ailerons jumped on its lower wing as the F-4 tore left, still trailing its familiar black engine exhaust. The fight should have progressed into a classic one-versus-one—a two-circle fight—with each fighter turning across the other's tail. It was the fight the Phantom pilot had chosen. It was a game plan that Coke and Notso could have chosen as well. The Tomcat would win a two-circle fight—it owned a turn rate and turn radius advantage over the older F-4, especially an F-4 moving through the air as fast as this one. But a two-circle fight took time, and even if Caine and Bright could come nose-on first before their opponent, the small distance between them might jam even a minimum-range Sidewinder opportunity. That would mean another two-circle turn, and even more time.

Cactus 02

Omid was alone with a U.S. Navy Tomcat. He had not expected such a situation. He was terrified, and his jet was outclassed. He no longer cared about being an ace like Ali—he no longer wanted to feel the pride that an ace would feel. He wanted Ali's help.

"Cactus One . . . Ali. I'm . . . I am fighting a Tomcat. I do not see you. Will you shoot him?"

Ali Abdul Rajani was typically cool in his response. "I too am engaged, Omid. But I will kill mine quickly and save you, since it appears you cannot save yourself."

The ready room in Bandar 'Abbās was filled with IRG pilots, RIOs, and thick cigarette smoke. Reza and the men there listened. None of them said a word. Equally quiet was the GCI controller at Site Two. He had not seen the two American fighters until after they had launched missiles at Ali. He had only seen the Omani attack jets. Nothing he could say would help.

Aardvark 114

If there was going to be a kill, it had to come quickly. There was an Iranian F-14 Tomcat somewhere to the north, and Dirk Buzzell—Caine's flight lead—was engaged with it. Buzzell's fight would be more difficult. Mark Caine decided to reverse his turn.

"Head fake, Notso," he said to his RIO over the ICS. Coke continued his left turn until he saw only the orange afterburners behind his bandit as it crossed his tail. A one-circle fight was his choice. The same turn rate and radius advantage would work for him there. He prayed that the Phantom would stay fast.

"Comin' right," he advised Bright across the ICS.

Cactus 02

Omid was not prepared for a long fight with an American Tomcat this day—he and Mottahadeh hadn't expected to see any fighters. Omid's mission had been very simple: Attack a relatively defenseless group of Omani Hawker Hunters as they approached Hengām Island, shoot one or two of them, then fly back to Bandar 'Abbās to accept the cheers and adulation of Reza and the entire Islam nation. It was a simple mission. He and his RIO could not expect to die from the impotent load-out of Hawker Hunters—the GCI controller had told him as much. So he stayed fast in his F-4 Phantom. He could not afford to wait for Ali. Omid decided he would run.

Aardvark 114

Greg Bright fumbled with the dogfight radar modes in the backseat. The diamond flashed on Coke's HUD, then disappeared.

"Shit! Broke lock again. Stand by!" the RIO shouted.

Even in Zone 5 afterburner, Caine could hold barely enough airspeed to maintain a steady bearing line on the Phantom through its arching left turn. Aardvark 114's turn to engage the Iranian F-4 had cost it valuable knots—knots it could not regain in a climb to follow the faster bandit. When the radar diamond reappeared, the target inside it grew smaller.

"One-point-two miles, Coke . . . and some opening," Bright added. "One-point-three. He's haulin' ass."

The Sidewinder missile on station 1a liked what it saw in its seeker-head field of view. The Phantom's twin afterburners were an attractive heat source. The missile growled in Caine's headset, but the pilot wanted a sweeter shot—a shot with a higher probability of kill. He verified the position of his two throttles. Both were full forward—still in maximum afterburner. But he pushed at them, trying to extract even one more knot of airspeed from the Pratt and Whitneys. The growls strengthened and weakened as the heat-seeker looked at the Phantom—Caine could tell by the sound in his headset that the missile was also looking at the bright haze surrounding the Iranian fighter. The growl was raspy and unclear—the 'Winder was being distracted. The range between the two aircraft was too great.

The F-4 Phantom continued its sweeping arc through 270 degrees of turn with Aardvark 114 still in trail. In another four or five seconds, Caine knew the Persian Gulf sun would become a further annoyance. If the missile was being distracted by the haze, it would almost certainly be decoyed completely by the brighter orb 45 degrees above the horizon. Again, time to kill would not allow him to wait for another 90 or 120 degrees of turn, or until he could finally close to more lethal Sidewinder missile range. He wondered suddenly if Harrington was still tracking Dirk Buzzell's airplane and the Iranian F-14 it was fighting. He was amazed that he could think at all.

"Sparrow selected, Notso. Sidewinder's not gonna hack it." An SP appeared in his HUD windscreen. "What's the range now?"

"One-point-six, Coke. It's a good lock."

Mark Caine unconsciously scanned his armament panel. The hot-trigger light glared bright red in his face. The master-arm guard and toggle were up. There was no X over the HUD Sparrow acronym. Even after he had squeezed the stick-mounted trigger, while he waited an eternity for the missile's short launch-to-eject cycle, he was dazed. The moment became mechanical and unemotional. He was relieved to feel no anger, no feeling of remorse or sympathy for the two F-4 crew members in his sights. The AIM-7 dove off its launcher on the belly of his jet, then descended farther below it until its rocket motor came to life. The missile rose from under Aardvark 114's radome and filled Caine's HUD diamond before jerking violently left, pulling lead on its target. The F-14 bucked slightly as it flew through the exhaust gases of the weapon it had just released, then steadied.

The Phantom never moved or tried to move, neither from its place in Caine's windscreen, nor from its position relative to the closing missile. The sun was directly above the F-4. The radar-guided Sparrow wasn't bothered by the sun.

At just inside two miles, the Sparrow's detonation was over in an instant. The fragmenting warhead mixed with the Phantom's gray-black jet exhaust, and the F-4 emerged from the aerial burst, still turning and still flying. The left engine emitted the same dark rope of smoke behind its orange afterburner plume. The right burner was out, snuffed by missile impact. Lighter-colored smoke came from the motor—Caine had time to recognize it as burning hydraulic fluid or oil, or both. A small chunk of motor or engine nacelle separated from the Phantom and tumbled toward the water.

"He's hit but not down, Notso. Let's try the Fox-two again."

Caine followed the F-4 through east to north. The bandit leveled his wings and descended through 1,500 feet with Bandar 'Abbās airfield 16 nautical miles on its nose. The black smoke of his operative engine mixed violently with the streaming stuff from the inoperative one. Caine bunted his nose, chasing the crippled Phantom downhill—using his new-found airspeed advantage to eat up range. Lower, at only 200 feet off the water, the Sidewinder was bothered neither by the haze above it nor the sun now more than 90 degrees left of its seeker-head. The missile chirped with a solid IR lock at one mile.

Cactus 02

"We have a fire light . . . we are hit! *I have lost a motor. ALI!*" Omid fought the control stick in his hands, countering the F-4's yaw with full left rudder against his single functioning J-79 engine. The right engine was dead, but continued to burn inside the Phantom's fuselage. Mottahadeh turned in the rear seat, searching for indications that the fire was marching forward. The ejection seat beneath his butt was hotter than before, and a tiny river of smoke began entering the cockpit.

Omid's left leg was already cramping. He pulled the port engine slowly out of afterburner, back to military power, and let up slightly on the rudder pedal. The F-4 immediately decelerated below 200 knots and descended toward the strait now less than 100 feet beneath him. He reselected burner—he could not remain airborne without it. But even with the afterburner, the Phantom did not climb. Only when his crippled fighter was in ground-effect—when its altitude above the water was equal to its wingspan—did Omid finally level off. His altimeter read 38 feet. His jet was barely flying.

"The Navy Tomcat is *still* behind us," Mottahadeh said to his pilot with complete resignation in his voice.

"*Ali. ALI! Where are you? We are hit badly,*" Omid screamed, then suddenly changed the tone of his radio call. "I am unable to defend myself, Ali. If you do not help us, we will be killed."

"Then you will be killed," Ali's voice came across the frequency. "And I will be forced to destroy *both* of the American fighters."

Reza stopped his pacing in the IRG hangar ready room. He stood beside the UHF receiver, listening. There was no way to transmit to Omid or Ali across the radio. The pilots and RIOs in the room sucked at their cigarettes.

"I wish Ali would be killed instead," one of them said.

Aardvark 114

Mark Caine stared at the Phantom. It flew awkwardly. It was cocked up and yawed to the right, barely maintaining flying airspeed. The F-4's wings then began to rock back and forth. They rocked that way for only one of two reasons, Caine had decided—either because the wing rock was indicative of a flight control malfunction, or because the Phantom's pilot was acknowledging Aardvark 114's offensive position.

In mock ACM, Caine had seen aircraft rock their wings in the same way. He'd seen it over the waters off the coast of San Diego while training against F-5s and A-4s when they too had been defensive. He'd seen it when fighting Air Force F-15s during Red Flag exercises over the Nevada desert. He'd rocked *his* wings when fighting F-16s. Universally, the wing rock signaled a "knock-it-off." It was the honorable way for a bogey or fighter to disengage from a dogfight—to graciously admit defeat or to recognize he was inside a lethal envelope. Caine hoped the Phantom pilot was experiencing difficulty with his flight controls, but he was somehow certain that was not the case. This shot would be too easy, and both pilots knew it.

Caine pulled back on his throttles when 114's range to the F-4 was less than half a mile. The Tomcat pilot could see salt spray splash out of the Strait of Hormuz just behind and below his target.

" 'Vark One-one-four . . . Coke, this is Deep Sea. Buzz is eleven miles south of your position now. What's going on? Will somebody tell me what's going on out there?"

Mark Caine looked down through his HUD combining glass at the pitiful F-4 Phantom now only 3,000 feet in front of his jet. The Phantom would be lucky to survive its trek back to Bandar 'Abbās. There was no chance it could turn to engage him, let alone defeat a heart-of-the-envelope Sidewinder shot from its dead six o'clock position.

"One-fourteen's coming south, Wrongway. The IRG F-4 is headed for home. I need a vector to Buzz!"

Aardvark 112

Kyle Herrin had no need to refer to his radar displays in the backseat. The camouflaged Iranian F-14 Tomcat was just outside his canopy, less than one wingspan away, and traveling in exactly the opposite direction. It was a Tomcat that carried no external tanks.

"Tallyho, Buzz. I got 'im," the RIO yelled through the intercom system. "He's nose high now, going uphill!"

Up was Dirk Buzzell's only option as well. Water lay beneath him less than 500 feet away, and Herrin's airspeed call told him he had enough potential energy for a vertical move. More like two lawns dart than fighter aircraft, the Tomcats flew straight up through the haze. The distance between them grew to one-half mile.

The Iranian fighter was "clean." It carried no drop tanks, no heavy Pheonix missiles and only two launcher rails. Two or three missiles remained on the launchers—Dirk Buzzell couldn't be certain of the number. Those missiles might be Sidewinders or French-made Magics or Soviet-built Atoll heat-seeking air-to-air missiles. It didn't really matter—all three were lethal. And the IRG fighter was still flying at 400-plus knots as it climbed.

Aardvark 112 was heavy. It too carried no Phoenix. But two Phoenix launch rails hung beneath his airframe—he wished they too had been removed. Each of the rails weighed as much as the weapon they were designed to carry—1,000 pounds. He cursed into his oxygen mask

He had fired only one missile—an AIM-7 Sparrow. He was hauling around seven others—three more of the Sparrows and four Sidewinders. Both external fuel tanks still clung to the Aardvark fighter. And Buzzell had fewer knots than his opponent. It was not the optimum way to begin a fight.

"Blow the tanks, Bird. My master arm is on!"

Dirk Buzzell had rolled his jet left. He adjusted his position relative to the horizon and found the brown F-14 through the canopy's side panel. Working stick and rudders together, he fought to keep his jet completely vertical. He could afford neither to lose sight of the Tomcat nor to arc from exactly 90 degrees nose up as he climbed. He could not afford to waste a single knot of airspeed, either.

This part of the fight belonged to his pilot alone, and Herrin worked at his jettison toggle switches in the backseat. The pilot and RIO both felt a dull thud beneath their seats as the two external fuel tanks broke free.

The fight had already been defined. It would be vertical. Against another F-14 Tomcat, it was the best fight. Buzzell understood that fact. The Iranian Revolutionary Guard pilot seemed to understand it as well.

A vertical fight meant a looping fight between two equally matched aircraft. Pilot skill and aircraft energy packages were the only two variables now. Aardvark 112's airspeed—the whole of its kinetic energy as it rose—was less than that of the brown Tomcat's package. The U.S. fighter was now 200 knots slower than the Iranian Revolutionary Guard jet.

Buzzell could only guess about the man at the

controls of the IRG jet—a man whose country had been at war with Iraq for more than a decade, a man who might have ten years experience dueling with other fighters. Buzzell hoped the Iranian had never before fought a Tomcat one-versus-one. He was certain this man had never fought one whose tail markings were Aardvark orange.

He also doubted that the missiles strapped to the Iranian jet were as capable as his Sidewinder. The *Enterprise* spies had said they were not. But the spies had also told him there were no F-14s at Bandar 'Abbās. Buzzell decided against speculation. He couldn't simply hope to defeat the Iranian's heat-seekers. He had to defeat his aircraft—he had to defeat the man.

It was all too obvious that the camouflaged fighter would outzoom Aardvark 112 in the beginning of this looping dogfight. A looping fight would eventually go to the Tomcat whose loops bottomed out above his opponents. After two or three or four climbing and descending loops, separation would be established between the fighters. The IRG pilot was working for separation equal to the minimum range of his air-to-air missile. When he had that range, he would pull the nose of his Tomcat to Aardvark 112, and fire.

Since the Iranian F-14 would top out above Buzzell, and assuming each pilot flew an identical airplane in exactly the same way, Buzzell and Herrin might only be able to maintain their disadvantaged position. If they were lucky—and Buzzell could never remember winning a fight by luck—he and his RIO might slowly nibble away at the separation they had already given their opponent. Time favored neither fighter. Either he or the pilot of the brown F-14 would win this engagement long before Mark

Caine and Greg Bright could fly south to lend a hand. And this was not a fight whose winner would be determined in a ready room debrief. The winner of this fight would be the Tomcat pilot that remained flying.

Buzzell flew straight up, decelerating as he climbed. He weighed other factors in his mind, and took the time to read his fuel gauge. He saw 7,500 pounds in the gauge window—barely enough to reach the *Enterprise* from his present position. He rechecked his engine afterburner nozzle indicators. Both read Zone 5. He was burning 2,000 pounds of fuel per minute. The Iranian jet had not been airborne as long as his had, and therefore, Buzzell assumed, had not burned as much fuel. He was not in the mood to see which airplane was first to run out of gas.

Cactus 01

Ali Abdul Rajani justified his arrogance in the way he piloted the Tomcat. In all things outside the cockpit he was impatient and boorish and full of conceit. And though he carried some of those traits into the cockpit as well, he became somehow transformed when he strapped on the F-14, and became a more perfect form of himself. He did not simply fly the aircraft, but made it do his bidding as few others could. Ali did not understand the aerodynamic formulas and physics that ultimately controlled how he flew and fought another airplane—he had no desire or need to understand such things. He was a fighter pilot, and he knew what to do. And he would not be distracted in doing it.

Omid had been a distraction. But now Omid was gone—he was limping home to Bandar ‘Abbās.

Thus, Ali's plan of attack had been simplified. He would outmaneuver this Navy F-14, kill it, then find the second American fighter and do the same a second time. He had fought many fights and won each of them. It did not occur to him that this fight would be any different from the others. And he had plenty of Magics for the job. Only when both of the U.S. Navy Tomcats had been blasted from the air would he fly home to Iran. He was not concerned with the whereabouts of the Hawker Hunters or the damage they might cause with their bombs.

His first missile shot against the American Tomcat had failed. But he was winning this fight. He was faster and would fly above this opponent. He would be patient, because patience was the quickest route to a kill in this case.

"We will not have him quickly," Ali spoke calmly across the ICS to Nori, "but we *will* have him."

Aardvark 112

At 200 knots, the controls became sloppy in Buzzell's hands. Now less than a half-mile away, the Iranian pilot and his backseater were beginning their move over the top of their first loop. Buzzell saw 14,100 feet on his slowly winding altimeter—he guessed the other pilot was looking at 18,000 or 19000 feet. Buzzell could climb no more than another 500 or 600 feet before committing his nose back down toward the horizon. Bird Herrin relayed Aardvark 112's decreasing airspeed in 10-knot increments across the ICS.

"This sucks, Bird. We got to do something else," he commented to the RIO.

At 140 knots, Buzzell opted for another game

plan. Instead of rolling farther toward the brown aircraft above him and programming his nose to take out the vertical and lateral separation between them as they descended together, he ruddered his huge fighter the opposite direction. The Aardvark's belly now faced the Iranian. Buzzell pushed the landing flap handle to its down position.

The Instantaneous Lead Computing Optical Gunsight display flashed on the HUD a fraction of a second after he thumbed his weapon switch from Sidewinder to Gun.

"Gimme range if you can, Bird. Hang on and pray."

Cactus 01

Ali's Tomcat moved easily across the top of its loop at 200 knots. He knew exactly where the Navy fighter would be, but he rolled left slightly as he descended to make sure. The F-14 with the orange tails was slow. It hung in space, still nose high. It should have started down by now, Ali thought. This was a looping fight, and just like him, the American had to descend in order to gain airspeed to loop again.

"This American is stupid. He will die all the faster." Ali made the comment over his UHF radio. Nori heard it, as did the Site Two controller and the Iranian Revolutionary Guard aviators in the ready room. It was not too early for a few of the pilots and RIOs there to begin laughing and cheering. If the Navy fighter was not willing to fly down in altitude as he should, then Ali would do so alone. When he and Nori began their second loop from the bottom, the American would still be high and slow. Separation for the missile shot would come quickly and automatically, and Ali would use one of the Magics. The nose of Ali Abdul Rajani's Tomcat was coming down. In less than thirty seconds, he figured, he would record yet another kill.

"Cactus 01, this is Site Two. The second Navy F-14 is your 020 at ten miles."

"Ten miles. Too bad. He will arrive just in time to see his wingman in flames," the ace commented.

Aardvark 112

Kyle Herrin hated negative G. It was unnatural and uncomfortable. And given the option, he'd choose an hour of seven-and-a-half Gs over even ten seconds of negative one or two. He knew that the negative G would lift him out of his seat. Everything that wasn't tied down in the cockpit would suddenly rise to the canopy top. He couldn't work that way. If he had a stick in the backseat, he'd never allow negative Gs.

The gunsight responded as Buzzell pushed forward on the control column. The ILCOS pipper was pegged at the top of his windscreen HUD. Well below the pipper, nearly obscured by 112's radome, was the camouflaged Tomcat. The Iranian fighter was on its back and already through 90 degrees of turn at the apogee of its loop. Soon, its airspeed would begin to increase.

"We're a hundred knots, Buzz. I don't like this!" Negative G also made Bird Herrin sick to his stomach. "He's at point-three."

The twin afterburning Pratt and Whitneys could barely move the Aardvark fighter through the air. They worked against nature in the negative G pushaway. When the airspeed indicator read less than 90 knots, Buzzell moved the stick to the center of his instrument panel and steadied the rudder pedals against his rocking wings. The airplane mushed, becoming something less than a pure flying machine.

"Point-two on the range, now. Seventy knots, Buzz!"

Buzzell kept the stick neutral—any left or right stick inputs would cause the jet to depart controlled flight. He could only lose the fight if that happened. But he pushed the stick full forward, against the front cockpit TID display repeat. The jet sliced right and Buzzell again countered with opposite rudder—the nose fell from above to just below the Iranian fighter. But the pipper hung persistently at the edge of its HUD scale, breaking free only with minor transients in the negative G, then returning to its useless position at the top of the windscreen.

The distance between the two Tomcats would grow no closer. Aardvark 112 was neither climbing nor descending—it had no forward velocity—Buzzell and Herrin seemed frozen in the haze. The Iranian accelerated downhill. Dirk Buzzell held the stick, verifying it was full forward against its stops. He could do nothing else. And his fighter would descend when it was ready—when it decided to stop waffling at 50 knots and seek the surface of the earth. Dirk Buzzell and Kyle Herrin were along for the ride. Only the fact that the brown F-14 was now belly up to 112 offered Buzzell any consolation. In a few seconds, the Iranian Revolutionary Guard pilot would dive below him and take away any opportunity for a gun-tracking solution.

"Still point-two. We're 85 knots." Herrin was reading his gauges dutifully, but his tone was reassuring. At least their jet was building airspeed—it was trying to fly.

The negative G broke as suddenly as it had begun. Buzzell used both hands to push himself off the forward canopy bow. His feet slammed down against the steel deck underneath the rudder pedals. The ILCOS pipper dropped from the top of his HUD, fell to the bottom of it, then recentered just above the ADL in the middle of the windscreen. Even the master caution light went out—it no longer sensed the low engine oil pressure that accompanied negative G flight. Well inside minimum range for a missile shot, Buzzell had gambled away any chance of fighting a prolonged one versus one for a quick gunshot.

With greater airspeed came larger air loads across Aardvark 112's spoilers and huge tail stabilizers. Most of Dirk Buzzell's stick feel had returned as well. He pulled aft, then centered the HUD Armament Data Line below the nose of the falling bandit. The gunsight pipper followed and Buzzell moved his eyes to it. At 900 feet of range, the brown Tomcat's wingspan was wider than the edges of the ILCOS pipper. The camouflage paint scheme was clear in his HUD. Buzzell squeezed the trigger and the pipper swung up and then aft through the fuselage in his sights. He released the trigger then squeezed again. He felt the Mark-61 cannon spooling up.

Every tenth round was a tracer. The tracers rose like shooting stars, then fell through the center of his pipper. They looked too high, Buzzell thought. Only the flashing pinpoints of white on the underside of the Iranian fighter eased his concern about the accuracy of the gunsight.

He had gotten off two gun bursts. Most of the 20-millimeter rounds had fallen aft of the gunsight aimpoint. Some of the rounds had sped above or below his target. But Buzzell could easily see where the explosive rounds had struck the brown Tomcat. Worst damaged was the fuselage and tail section aft of its wide sweeping wings. The HEI rounds had torn through the F-14's aluminum and metal composite frame, slicing nearly in half its port stabilator tail and freeing a chunk of its rudder surface on the same side.

Cactus 01

"No. No No!" Ali's scream came loudly across the UHF. He could not hear Nori's scream. The Radar Intercept Officer's ICS amplifier had taken one of the 20-millimeter rounds. It was the same round that had shredded Nori's left shoulder before exiting the brown Tomcat through the top of its canopy.

The Iranian pilot fought his flight controls. His jet rolled sluggishly with little more than half a tail, but it rolled. Ali watched the Aardvark jet rise from behind his starboard wing, a wing that streamed tiny rivers of fuel through a half-dozen holes. He had not expected the American fighter pilot to use his gun.

His brown Tomcat had already accelerated to 330 knots in its dive. Ali had enough airspeed to begin the loop.

"Not bad . . . not bad," the ace said over the radio as if Dirk Buzzell might hear the compliment. As he made the transmission, Ali pulled aft on his control stick. The remaining horizontal stabilizer did not move. Cactus 01 continued to accelerate toward the Strait of Hormuz.

Aardvark 112

Buzzell and Herrin hung back, high and behind the Iranian Revolutionary Guard fighter, anticipating the full effects of their attack—waiting for the brown Tomcat to pull out of its 90 degree dive toward the waters northeast of Didamar.

"Bombs away, *bombs away!*" Major Carlton's voice sang out across the strike frequency.

Herrin's radar held its lock. The IRG jet gained airspeed below them.

"One mile and opening," the RIO commented. "He's getting low."

Buzzell throttled back, pulling his nose to the horizon and breaking Bird's lock. He cycled his weapon select switch up to Phoenix/Sparrow, then down to Sidewinder, through Guns and finally to the off detent. He safed his master-arm toggle, and the red Hot Trigger light went out. He raised the flap handle slowly.

Bird Herrin waited for the Iranian bandit to scoop out at the bottom of its dive. Buzzell was somehow certain it wouldn't.

The camouflaged Tomcat porpoised its nose, her pilot pushing forward and pulling aft on its control stick. The horizontal tail, or what was left of it, could no longer direct the big fighter away from the surface of the water. Instead, against every attempt by the IRG pilot to arrest its sink rate, the brown F-14 flew faster toward a gap between two small islands in the strait. Its wings swept aft automatically as it dove.

Cactus 01

Nori could not pull his ejection seat handle, and Ali wouldn't pull his. He had been beaten. To the ace, the price of being beaten included riding his defeated aircraft into the water. He and Nori were already supersonic as their jet passed through 9,000 feet.

"Omid, are you still alive?" Ali asked over the UHF as he stared into the wave tops below him.

Omid and Mottahadeh were not only alive, but had managed to climb their F-4 Phantom to 200 feet of altitude as they limped toward Bandar 'Abbās.

"Yes, Ali. But I will be unable to 'assist' you against the Americans. And it appears that you are in *need* of assistance." Omid's statement burned with sarcasm.

"You will live as a coward, Omid. I die as an ace. But you may drive the new Cadillac," he said. "It will at least give you the appearances of a fighter pilot." Ali would not live to hear a reply from Omid. His Tomcat shuddered as it continued to accelerate downhill. The control stick in his right hand was useless, but both throttles still responded to his left. He selected Zone 5 afterburner and flew into the Strait of Hormuz at 810 knots.

The *Khasaab*
1510

Shail Bakhash steered the *Khasaab* north toward Didamar. He hugged the eastern edge of the Omani peninsula, keeping his dhow within 300 meters of its rocky shores. The waters were rougher there, and the going slow. The shoreline to his left was pitted with dozens of small inlets and coves—each offered quick sanctuary. He could not see Iran across the waves and through the haze, but he knew the Boghammers would come from there, if they came.

The *Khasaab* would be forced into less protected waters during its final four miles to Didamar. The larger inlets and coves disappeared behind him—only a few rocky outcroppings rose in front of the dhow. He pushed his diesel's throttle to maximum and motored to the east side of the tiny island chain. The course change would add more time to his transit, of course, but the islands would offer him protection from the Boghammers. He traveled alone in the dhow, although a few of the older sailors from Bukha had insisted on accompanying him. Sailing a large load of cotton and tobacco was too much for one man, the sailors had told him.

The sun had long ago crested the Strait of Hormuz and was descending to the west. The *Khasaab* would anchor overnight at Didamar, then start for Bukha at dawn, Bakhash had decided. The sun, as it fell, cast orange and red lines on the islands beside his dhow. On a smaller island, where there should have been no red lines from the sun, Shail Bakhash saw it. The red color seemed to move on this island, as though it had some purpose in moving. The island was not inhabited, so Bakhash looked away and ahead toward Didamar. When he looked back one final time toward the outcropping, the thing that had been red was now on fire. Black smoke rose from a red blaze.

He pulled his old rifle from under one of the burlap bags near the *Khasaab*'s engine. He had never before carried the weapon. Again, the Boghammers. If there were Iranians on the island, Shail Bakhash would surely kill them with the rifle.

He reversed his course slowly, cutting his dhow's throttle toward idle speed as he approached the blazing red thing. The portion of it that wasn't burning billowed and flapped in a light breeze. Someone, perhaps more than one person, sat beside the fire. He or they were waving their arms. The old Omani squinted his eyes to focus them. It was only one man, and he wore a uniform. The Iranians on the

Boghammer had worn uniforms, too. Bakhash checked that a round was inside the chamber of his rifle.

The man did not run to the beach to greet the *Khasaab* as it rode onto a sandy spit near the fire. The man remained seated, as though he could not stand or run. It was a uniform the man was wearing, but it was not an Iranian uniform—the man was not Iranian. His skin was fair and his hair was white. Shail Bakhash stepped from the dhow and tied it to a part of the rock island. He saw no reason to carry the rifle with him as he stepped onto the gravel beach.

"Good God, man. Damn glad to see you! I was becoming desperate."

Shail Bakhash stopped and stared. He did not recognize the language.

"I'd get up and shake your bloody hand, sir. But as you can plainly see, I've come up lame. I'm with the RAF out of Thumrait . . . name's Thomas! I'd begun to think one of you chaps would never spot my parachute." Thomas pointed toward the fire. Most of the red chute had been consumed by it. "The damned Iranian Revolutionary Guard did this to me," the lieutenant colonel said while rubbing at the bloodsoaked flight suit covering his left leg.

Bakhash did not understand the strange words of the fair-skinned man. But he pulled the man up onto his good leg, and helped him aboard the *Khasaab*.

"You've no idea what I've been through, my good man," Thomas said wearily as he slumped onto a bale of cotton. "But it is just as well you cannot understand a word I'm saying. You've probably never heard of the IRG."

DAY FORTY-ONE

FEBRUARY 14

The Number 6 Squadron
Sultan of Oman Air Force Base
Thumrait, Oman
1800

Inside the Omani RAF ready room, the chairs had been pushed back. Three bartenders—one of them Major William Carlton—sipped at tins of ale throughout the entire ceremony.

British envoy Terrance Hill had made all the necessary arrangements. There had been some legal obstacles, of course—the endless paperwork required by the U.S. Navy, the Department of State and a few other U.S. agencies. As a rule, ceremonies of this kind were not "officially" recognized back in the states. Hill stood beside Vice Admiral Jeremiah Curtiss, who had been asked by Dirk Buzzell to officiate at the proceedings. Hill's secretary, Malcolm Jennings, had not been invited. Neither had the VF-141 CO and XO.

Mark Caine and Kyle Herrin stood together near the middle of the room with Dan Harrington. And every Number 6 Squadron pilot was there. Lieutenant Colonel Reginald Sheffield Thomas sat throughout the ceremony. He had insisted on wearing his green RAF dress uniform, but had been forced to cut the thick wool trousers to accommodate the plaster cast on his broken leg.

Seventeen Aardvark junior officers filled the remainder of the seats. Except for Dirk Buzzell and Greg Bright—his best man—the Aardvark pilots and RIOs wore black T-shirts under their bright orange flight suits. Buzzell had requested that too.

Dirk Buzzell's choker white uniform was brilliant white. Marti's dress was the same color. The vice admiral turned toward the aviators gathered in the ready room and introduced the couple as "Lieutenant and Mrs. Dirk Buzzell." Dirk turned, offering his arm to Marti, and his medals clinked together like chimes. Above the medals, his gold wings gleamed brightly.

They turned together after a long kiss, and walked toward the bar at the back of the ready room. The Aardvarks and the Brits immediately began competing in the volume of their cheers. The Aardvarks won. Dirk and Marti toasted each other. He held a tall glass filled with ice and Jack Daniel's—there was a case of the stuff there, compliments of Dan Harrington. Marti allowed herself only one glass of champagne.

Major Carlton was having difficulty standing behind the bar. But he managed to look less drunk as Dirk Buzzell and Marti approached him.

"Mrs. Buzzell," the major started. "It is truly unfortunate that your husband is still gainfully employed with the United States Navy."

Marti looked at her husband and then at the RAF officer.

"Why is it unfortunate, sir?" she asked.

"We had hoped he might consider flying with us here in Thumrait. I know he would have enjoyed the opportunity to pilot the Hawker Hunter. It is the *finnist* aircraft ever built." The major was smiling. "Did I mention, Mrs. Buzzell, that its motor is manufactured by Rolls-Royce?"

"Thanks for the offer, Major, but I think I'll stick with the Tomcat awhile longer," Buzzell answered, then offered a small toast of his own to Carlton. "And congratulations again on the strike. You and your Hunters put so many holes in Hengām Island that I'm surprised it's still floating in the Strait of Hormuz. I think the Iranian Revolutionary Guard will think twice before messin' with the RAF."

"That is very kind, Dirk. It is also gratifying to read that the Iranians are otherwise engaged with Iraq at this time—their truce is not going well, I'm afraid. In the interim, the Iranians have apparently lost interest in Didamar." The RAF officer snapped himself to attention and saluted with his tin of ale. In the process, he managed to spill most of the can's contents onto his uniform. "But the Number 6 will be ready if those heathens dare change their minds."

"To the Hawker Hunter and the F-14 Tomcat," Buzzell said to make the toast official. He finished his whiskey, and Carlton finished the remainder of the stout.

Marti grabbed Dirk by the sleeve of his choker whites before he could say or drink anything more.

"Dirk, when did you say you have to be back aboard the ship?"

"We have three glorious days, babe. The *Enterprise* is leaving the Indian Ocean after that."

"Then we *also* have three nights . . . right?" Marti said while she stared at him with those pale blue eyes.

"Right. And time's a wastin', ma'am." Dirk Buzzell's John Wayne imitation was no better now than it had been in the Philippines more than one month earlier. Dirk took her arm and they walked together out of the Number 6 Squadron ready room. He pulled a key from his pocket as they turned out of the hangar and headed across the wide flight line toward the Thumrait VOQ. "It ain't exactly Baguio City," he said to her as they watched the sun settle toward a flat and brown Omani horizon. "But I think you'll be impressed with the room."

GLOSSARY OF TERMS (AND NAVY JARGON)

A-3—The Skywarrior. Sometimes called "The Whale." U.S. electronic surveillance and countermeasures platform

A-6—The Intruder. A medium-attack U.S. bomber

A-7—The Corsair. A light-attack U.S. bomber

ACM—Air Combat Maneuvering

ADB—Aircraft Maintenance Discrepancy Book

ADL—Armament Data Line

AIC—Air Intercept Control

Aileron—Movable surface attached to the trailing edge of a wing

Air Boss—Carrier Air Department Officer

Air Wing—Commanded by the CAG, and composed of all carrier aircraft

Angels—Altitude expressed in thousands of feet

AOCS—Aviation Officer Candidate School

AOM—All Officer Meeting

Apex—Soviet-built air-to-air missile

ASW—Anti-Submarine Warfare

Atoll—Soviet-built heat-seeking air-to-air missile

AWACS—The E-3. The Sentry. U.S.-built Airborne Warning and Control System aircraft
AWG-9—Radar system unique to the F-14 Tomcat
Ayatollah Ruholla Khomeini—Former religious leader of Iran

Badger—Soviet reconnaissance/bomber aircraft
Bandit—Confirmed hostile aircraft
BARCAP—Barrier CAP
Battle Group—The carrier and her escort ships
Bear—Soviet reconnaissance/bomber aircraft
"Big E"—Nickname for the USS *Enterprise*
Bits—Built-in tests
Blind—Term used by a pilot when he does not see his wingman
Bogey—Unknown but potentially hostile aircraft
Boghammer—High-speed patrol boat, built by the Swedes, and utilized by the Iranian Revolutionary Guard in the Persian Gulf and Strait of Hormuz
Bullseye—A geographic reference point

CAG—Air Group (Air Wing) Commander
CAP—Combat Air Patrol
USS *Carl Vinson*—CVN-71. Nimitz-class nuclear-powered aircraft carrier
Cat—Short for Catapult. Carrier aircraft launching equipment
Chaff—Radar reflective material dispensed from aircraft
CO—Commanding Officer
CVIC—Carrier Intelligence Center

DACT—Dissimilar Air Combat Training
DDD—Digital Data Display in the F-14 Tomcat

Dhow—Small Arab cargo vessel

Diamond—Radar designator displayed on the Tomcat's Heads-Up Display

DLC—Direct Lift Control. Utilized by the F-14 Tomcat during carrier approaches

DME—Distance Measuring Equipment (expressed in nautical miles)

EA-6B—The Prowler. U.S.-built carrier-based electronic countermeasures aircraft

E-2C—The Hawkeye. U.S.-built land-based early warning aircraft

E-3—The Sentry. U.S.-built land-based AWACS aircraft

Eagle—The F-15

ECS—Environmental Control System

ELINT—Intelligence gathered via electronic sources

USS Enterprise—CVN-65. America's first nuclear-powered aircraft carrier

5-MC—Flight deck loudspeaker system usually operated by the air boss

F-1—The Mirage. Widely exported French-built aircraft

F-4—The Phantom. U.S.-built fighter-bomber exported to Iran

F-14—The Tomcat. U.S.-built fighter exported to Iran

F-15—The Eagle. U.S.-built fighter

F-16—The Falcon. U.S.-built fighter

Flares—Infrared decoys dispensed from aircraft against heat-seeking missiles

Flogger—The MiG-23. Soviet-built fighter aircraft

Fox-1—A Sparrow missile shot

Fox-2—A Sidewinder missile shot
Fox-3—A Phoenix missile shot
Fresnel lens—Optical landing system utilized by carrier pilots

GCI—Ground Controlled Intercept
Gimbals—Edge of a radar-scan volume
Goo—Aviator term for thick clouds and/or associated weather
Guard—A UHF/VHF radio frequency normally associated with distress calls

Hawker Hunter—British-built attack aircraft
HEI—High explosive incendiaries
Helo—Helicopter
HUD—Heads-up Display
HUMINT—Intelligence gathered via human sources

ICLS—Instrument Carrier Landing System
ICS—Inter-cockpit Communication System
IFF—Identification Friend or Foe electronic interrogation equipment
ILCOS—Instantaneous Lead Computing Optical Gun Sight in the F-14
IO—The Indian Ocean
IR—Infrared. Usually associated with heat-seeking missile systems
IRG—The Iranian Revolutionary Guard. An extremist Iranian military organization

JBD—Jet Blast Deflector
JCS—Joint Chiefs of Staff
JP-5—Aviation jet fuel

Knots—Measurement of speed slightly faster than miles per hour

KY-58—Secure voice radio equipment. Utilized in hostile environments

Ladder—Navy term for stairs
LED—Light-emitting diodes
LOX—Liquid Oxygen
LSO—Landing Signal Officer

MACH number—Airspeed of an aircraft in relation to the speed of sound
Maneuvering devices—Leading edge and trailing edge wing flaps on the F-14 Tomcat. Utilized to optimize the Tomcat's turning ability and slow speed handling characteristics
Merships—Merchant ships
Military power—Maximum power, but excluding afterburner
Mikes—Minutes
Miramar—Fightertown, USA. The Pacific Fleet master jet fighter base

NATOPS—Naval Air Training and Operating Procedures Standardization Program
NFO—Naval Flight Officer
No Joy—Pilot term used when he does not see a bogey or bandit
Nordo—An aircraft unable to transmit or receive radio transmissions

OBC—On-Board Checks
OLS—Optical Landing System. Sometimes referred to as "The Ball"
1-MC—Ship's loudspeaker
Ops O—Operations Officer
Oversweep—For the F-14, when its wings are swept to 72 degrees aft

Phoenix—The AIM-54. Long-range air-to-air missile
P_k—Probability of kill. Expressed in percentages
Plane Captains—Enlisted men responsible for the care of aircraft
PIM—Point of Intended Movement. Associated with the carrier's location
Pipper—Part of the ILCOS gunsight. Used by the pilot to direct the Tomcat's gun
Pesos—Filipino money
PLAT—Pilot Landing Aid Television
Port—Left

RAF—Royal Air Force
RIO—Radar Intercept Officer
ROE—Rules of Engagement
ROTC—Reserve Officer Training Corps
RTB—Return to Base/return to the carrier

S-3—The Viking. An ASW platform sometimes referred to as the "Hoover"
SAM—Surface-to-Air Missile
SAR—Search and Rescue
SAS—Stability Augmentation System associated with the F-14 Tomcat
Scram—Term used to clear aircraft from a geographic area
SDO—Squadron Duty Officer
SH-3—The Sea King. Carrier-based helicopter utilized for SAR efforts
Sidewinder—The AIM-9. Heat-seeking air-to-air missile
Silkworm—Chinese-built surface-to-surface missile system
SINS—Ship's Inertial Navigation System
Slider—Ship's hamburger

SOP—Standard Operating Procedure

Sparrow—The AIM-7. Medium-range air-to-air missile

Starboard—Right

Tagalog—Native language of the Philippine Islands

Tallyho—Term used by a pilot announcing he has sight of a bogey/bandit

TARCAP—Target Combat Air Patrol

TCS—Television Camera Set on the F-14 Tomcat

Thumrait—A remote military airstrip in Oman. Home to the Number 6 Squadron and to the Sultan of Oman Air Force

TID—Tactical Information Display

Trap—An arrested landing

UHF—Ultrahigh Frequency. Associated with aircraft radio equipment

VDI—Vertical Display Indicator. In the F-14, the aircraft's attitude display

Vertigo—A condition affecting the middle ear in which an aircrew senses flight conditions that differ from reality. Usually associated with operations in poor weather or extreme darkness, or both.

Visual—Term used to announce that a pilot has sight of his wingman

WestPac—Western Pacific Ocean

XO—Executive Officer

Zone 1—Minimum afterburner

Zone 5—Maximum afterburner

Zulu time—Greenwich Mean Time

ABOUT THE AUTHOR

MICHAEL LAWRENCE DUNN is a United States Navy Lieutenant and F-14 Tomcat pilot. Formerly with the Fighting Aardvarks of VF-114, he has accumulated more than 2,000 hours and 300 carrier landings in the cockpit of Navy fighters. He has also completed two overseas deployments to the Mediterranean Sea, the Pacific, the Atlantic, and the Indian Oceans. Dunn is a graduate of Pepperdine University, the Navy Fighter Weapons School (TOP GUN), and served as a landing signal officer while deployed aboard the USS *Enterprise* between 1985 and 1988. He is currently assigned to the Bandits of VF-126 as an adversary instructor pilot where he flies the F-16 Falcon and the A-4 Skyhawk from Miramar Naval Air Station in San Diego, California. He resides in Escondido, California, with his wife Linda and their son, Hunter.